THE SHADOW

NOVEMBER 15th, 1937

10 CENTS

TWICE A MONTH

REG. U.S. PAT. OFF.

ANOTHER
SHERIDAN
DOOME
STORY

CASH PRIZES
FOR CODES

TEETH OF
THE DRAGON

The Mystery of the East and
the Action of the West in a
Complete Novel

The Crime Oracle

AND

The Teeth of the Dragon

TWO ADVENTURES OF THE SHADOW

---

by Maxwell Grant
(Walter B. Gibson)

With New Introductory Essays by
WALTER B. GIBSON and JOHN L. NANOVIC

DOVER PUBLICATIONS, INC., NEW YORK

This Dover edition, first published in 1975, is an
unabridged republication of the text and illustra-
tions of two stories from *The Shadow Magazine*,
as originally published by Street & Smith Publications, Inc., N.Y.: "The Crime Oracle" from the
June 1, 1936 issue, and "The Teeth of the Dragon"
from the November 15, 1937 issue. Typographical
errors have been tacitly corrected in the present
edition.

Two new essays, "My Years with The Shadow"
by Walter B. Gibson and "I Never Called Him Bill"
by John L. Nanovic, have been written specially for
the present edition, which is published by special
arrangement with Conde Nast Publications, Inc.,
N.Y.

International Standard Book Number: 0-486-23116-X
Library of Congress Catalog Card Number: 74-15002

Manufactured in the United States of America
Dover Publications, Inc.
180 Varick Street
New York, N. Y. 10014

Contents

My Years with The Shadow

by WALTER B. GIBSON

The saying that "Coming events cast their shadow before" applied quite definitely where The Shadow was concerned. Sheer chance was forging a chain of irrevocable circumstance that afternoon early in 1931 when I stopped at the editorial offices of Street & Smith, the one place where I had no good reason to be that day or for some time to come.

For nearly ten years, I had been a full-time professional writer, supplying daily features to the Ledger Syndicate in my home town of Philadelphia. These included simple "After Dinner Tricks," "Brain Tests," "Crossword Puzzles" and other items that ran into the hundreds and were sold to newspapers everywhere. For three years, I had done a "Puzzle a Day" for the Newspaper Enterprise Association in Cleveland, along with various articles for other syndicates.

Particularly successful were two quarter-page weekly series, of fifty articles each, which I did for the Ledger. One, "Miracles—Ancient and Modern," explained such mysteries as the Hindu Rope Trick, the methods of fake spirit mediums and such stunts as walking upside down under the dome of a theater with the aid of secret suction cups. The other, "Bunco Games to Beware Of," revealed the methods of carnival "grif-

ters," who were rampant during that period. Much of this material was published in the form of books which are still available after fifty years.

Both Howard Thurston and Harry Houdini, the leading magicians of the 1920s, had me do articles or booklets for them under their names and I actually "ghosted" some Thurston articles for *Ghost Story Magazine,* which was a rather whimsical achievement. I placed Thurston articles with *The Saturday Evening Post* and lesser publications, fictionizing some of his adventures so effectively that most readers accepted them as fact. I did two Thurston books that were later combined under the title of *400 Tricks You Can Do,* which has been in print ever since.

During most of the summer of 1928, I stayed at Thurston's home on Long Island, helping him shape his autobiography, which I personally sold to *Collier's* on the strength of a first reading. They ran it in five articles, leaving out the final chapters which included material from previously published articles; but the entire story appeared in book form as *My Life of Magic,* which I also placed for Thurston. During the next year, I wrote fictionized fact articles for Macfadden's *True Strange Stories,* while it lasted, and I did a book on *Secrets of Magic* for Harry Blackstone, who since Houdini's death had begun to rival Thurston; and in 1930, the Houdini Estate gave me access to all of his unpublished notes, enabling me to prepare a book on *Houdini's Escapes,* the first definitive and only authorized recording of the master mystifier's actual methods.

The Houdini book did so well that Harcourt, Brace and Company, the publishers, wanted a companion volume, *Houdini's Magic,* if I could supply enough usable material from the remaining notes. So I had come to New York with a table of contents, which promptly clinched the project. I then stopped to see George Sully, the publisher of *Secrets of Magic,* and found that he wanted another Blackstone book, which we decided to title *Blackstone's Modern Card Tricks.*

Those two contracts for new books were like stepping stones to my big ambition, which was to crack the mystery field with a hard-cover, full-fledged novel. For that, I needed an outstanding character and I had been thinking of one who would be a mystery in himself, moving into the affairs of lesser folk much to their amazement. By combining Houdini's penchant for escapes with the hypnotic power of Tibetan mystics, plus the knowledge shared by Thurston and Blackstone in the creation of illusions, such a character would have unlimited scope when confronted by surprise situations, yet all could be brought within the range of credibility.

As an opening, I had pictured a cloaked figure emerging from a night fog to prevent a despondent young man from taking a suicidal leap from a high bridge. The mysterious stranger would supply the rescued man with a hotel room, money and orders to obey whatever command he might receive. By so doing, the rescued man would become involved in dangerous adventures along with other persons who had been aided by the same benefactor. United in a common cause, all would be mutually swayed by the dominating power of their unknown master, who would always be on hand when further rescues were required.

That was as far as I had gone, but now, while working on the two new magic books, I could begin mapping out my mystery novel. I was thinking in such terms when I started toward Penn Station, only to remember that there was time for a stop-off at Street & Smith's, on Seventh Avenue above Fourteenth Street. From there, I could continue down to the Liberty Street ferry and go back to Philadelphia on one of the Jersey Central flyers, which would be less crowded than the Pennsylvania. I had recently sold a short fiction story to Street & Smith for one of their detective magazines and Frank Blackwell, the editor-in-chief, had expressed a possible interest in a series of shorts on factual crimes. Such an assignment would serve as an added carry-over along with my two books, so I entered the staid old portals at 79 Seventh Avenue, went up to the sixth floor in the antique elevator and asked to see Mr. Blackwell.

I was ushered in quite promptly, but when I mentioned the proposed factual articles, Blackwell dismissed the subject completely. He had something quite different to discuss and came right to the point. Street & Smith were testing new magazines to meet increasing competition and they had decided to revive the "character" field. It would be a flashback to the days of Frank Merriwell and the original Nick Carter, or even Buffalo Bill, but with a modern slant. Specifically, they wanted a character to be called "The Shadow," as a tie-in with an announcer's voice that was being used to introduce *The Detective Story Hour,* a weekly radio program that dramatized a short story from each new issue of *Detective Story Magazine.*

Blackwell wanted a novel-length story very fast and he regarded my chance arrival as timely indeed. As a factual writer with a flare for fiction, I could be the very man to turn out a streamlined job with a nostalgic touch to meet a prompt deadline. I learned, long afterward, that Blackwell had been a feature writer with the New York *Sun* before he had come to Street & Smith, so he had personally geared over from fact to fiction without diffiiculty. Possibly he felt that the rule would apply in my case as well, but it was a far cry from the old dime-novel days, when the Buffalo Bill stories had been based on a living personage and Frank Merriwell was such a typical All-American boy that his exploits were equally believable. With The Shadow, it would mean bringing a so far nebulous and utterly incredible concept into the realm of reality.

Yet that intrigued me, for it fitted with the very type of character that I already had in mind. When Blackwell asked if I had any ideas, I went right into a verbal description of the night scene on the fog-shrouded bridge and the incidents that followed, saying that was as far as I had gone. It was far enough for Blackwell. He told me to use my character as The Shadow and pick it up from there, putting The Shadow and his agents on the track of a mystery involving murder and robbery with whatever cross-purposes or false trails I needed. I was to come back with a few opening chapters and a general outline within a week. The word rate would be low, but that didn't worry me, as Street & Smith paid on acceptance, whereas many publishers in the field paid on publication, and some, never.

On the train trip back to Philadelphia, I began roughing out my chapters, and the next morning I went to work from my notes. I named my would-be suicide Harry Vincent and titled my first chapter "Out of the Mist," describing his rescue and detailing the instructions that he was given. That led into the next chapter, which covered "The First Message" that Harry received at his hotel. It told him to watch "The Man in the Next Room," the title for Chapter Three. His vigil was brief, for the man's life was snuffed out in Chapter Four by "A Bold Murder," committed by fellow crooks who discussed it openly in Chapter Five, titled "The Shadow on the Wall." This denoted the presence of an unseen listener, and resulted in Harry Vincent receiving "The Second Message" in Chapter Six, which put him on a further trail.

I banged those out in a few days, keeping notes toward further chapters, with suggested headings leading to the solution of a big-time robbery that gathered up all the loose characters from the story. Whenever The Shadow emerged from darkness, he blended back into it in the same weird fashion. Occasionally, he appeared openly in suitable disguises, even baffling crooks by doubling as members of their own crew. That all led to a final solution of the riddle.

Within the week, I took all that to Street & Smith, where the early chapters were okayed after an immediate reading, but with one proviso. Among the early pages, I was to introduce a Chinese angle, to carry the story into Manhattan's Chinatown, where The Shadow would play an active part. For purposes of economy, the firm had decided to use an old cover painting for the new magazine and the only one that tied in with The Shadow was a man in Chinese costume, clutching an upraised hand that cast a huge shadow on the wall behind him.

Instead of causing complications, this proved helpful. It introduced an intriguing setting that gave The Shadow opportunity for a new disguise. After an intervening chapter, I titled the next "The Tea Shop of Wang Foo" and took the reader to Chinatown, along with Harry Vincent, who ran into trouble in Chapter Nine, styled "The Room of Doom," only to be rescued by a Chinese gentleman who spoke such perfect English that Harry knew he was The Shadow. From then on, the story rolled faster and faster. Ideas sprang to mind quicker than the typewriter keys could keep up with them. I was using an Underwood portable set in the lid of its carrying case, on a smooth-topped table. At my left was a ream of paper and finished pages of manuscript; on my right, a large copper bowl, serving as an ash tray for the innumerable cigarettes that I smoked in those days.

Whenever I pulled the return lever, bringing the carriage over to the right, it jogged the typewriter a fraction of an inch in that direction. In the course of a few chapters, this worked the copper bowl to the table edge, something that I never realized until it toppled to the floor with a resounding *bong!* that reverberated like the stroke of a brass gong in the lair of Wang Foo.

I finished the manuscript and titled it *The Living Shadow* because of the way The Shadow moved in and out without revealing his real identity. I delivered it a week ahead of deadline. Since four issues were to be printed, to establish the magazine as a quarterly, I was given an order for a sequel, with the promise of two more in due course. That brought up the point of using a pen name instead of my own, as it was considered wise policy to publish a series under a *nom de plume* in case the original author should fall by the wayside or move on to more lucrative fields.

As an added factor, it was customary for a writer to use two different names if he had two stories in the same issue

of a magazine. It applied here, for "The Green Light," the short story that I had already placed with Street & Smith, had been scheduled to appear in the first issue of the new magazine under my own name. *The Living Shadow* would have to be under another name, unless the two could be switched about. But as a final point, the editorial staff had decided to treat The Shadow as the living character that the story title implied, in order to impress juvenile readers. So they wanted to play up the author as a raconteur who alone had access to The Shadow's annals and was too deeply engrossed in them to be concerned with anything else.

That produced a paradox. Under my own name, I was already working from actual notes left by Houdini, the greatest mystifier of all time. Now I was to fictionize the imaginary exploits of The Shadow, a mythical master of mystery, yet vouch for them as real. So I naturally decided that, having committed myself to the factual field under my own name, I should stay with it. Quite as naturally, in entering the fictional field, I should use a fictional pen name. However, for the record, I wanted one that I could somehow link with myself, as a proof of authorship.

As a sideline I had taken on the editorship of a magic magazine and I had made up a list of magic dealers with whom I was personally acquainted, to contact them regarding advertisements. I now lined up their first and last names in two separate columns and began interchanging them to form catchy combinations. One of the best was formed from Maxwell Holden, who had a shop on Forty-second Street in New York, and U. F. Grant, popularly known as "Gen" Grant, who operated from Pittsfield, Massachusetts. So I established "Maxwell Grant" as my pseudonym for the Shadow novels.

Since *The Living Shadow* was going

to press shortly, I arranged to start the next novel right away. It was titled *Eyes of The Shadow* and had another makeshift cover showing three big goggling eyes surrounded by a question mark. I started with another young man in a jam. His name was Bruce Duncan and it required The Shadow and a team of agents to pull him out. In this story, The Shadow was to establish himself as an actual personality, rather than merely a master of many disguises, but I had no trouble whatever on that score.

In order to wage a continually successful war against crime, The Shadow had to have a millionaire's bankroll. That enabled him to keep his agents well supplied with funds and to maintain a well-staffed mansion conveniently located in New Jersey, some twenty miles from New York City. He had his own plane handy at a private airport and in due course he was to acquire an autogiro, a prototype of the present-day helicopter, enabling him to land beside the penthouse of a Manhattan apartment building and take off after settling whatever business had brought him there. The Jersey manse had a tower room outfitted as a wireless station, which was operated by both its owner and a quiet young man named Burbank, who took over duty whenever required. Adding other appliances was simplicity itself, but my problem as a writer was to supply a suitable name for The Shadow when he appeared in his guise of a millionaire.

The name had to convey affluence and distinction; it had to sound strikingly familiar, yet actually be uncommon. Names were a specialty of mine, for I had done books as well as syndicated articles on the subject, but that didn't seem to help. On the back cover of *The Shadow Magazine,* they were running the query, "Who Is The Shadow?" and I was ready to echo,

"Only The Shadow Knows!" Actually, I had to find out and I'd have to hit the right one to realize that I had it, a name that once people heard, they would remember, because it fitted the person it represented—like Houdini.

That reminded me that I had to finalize the contents of the forthcoming Houdini book, so back home I took a breather from The Shadow long enough to complete that stint. One batch of notes dealt with anecdotes that Houdini had gained from other magicians, so I decided to include a few. The one that was by far the best concerned a Scottish theater owner named Baillie Cranston. This name carried something of the swing I wanted, but the "Baillie" wouldn't do, though the "Cranston" might. Two names, of two syllables each, both family names: that would do it.

So I began thinking back to last names that I had heard used as first names, or that sounded as though they could be. It was a rapid process, because I rejected any that didn't have a distinctive touch—which applied to most. I did it alphabetically, a trick that I had used in devising crossword puzzles, when I needed an important key word. On this occasion, when I reached the letter L, about the third name that came to my mind was Lamont, and that was it: Lamont Cranston.

From then on, *Eyes of The Shadow* was a breeze. I delivered it early and was told to do a third story that could be advertised, with suitable blurbs, in the second issue. So I went ahead with *The Shadow Laughs,* in which I developed Lamont Cranston as a world traveler who might take off for Tasmania or Timbuctoo tomorrow, but return the next week, if the mood seized him. But instead of his absences accounting for the activities of The Shadow, it was often the other way about. When one

Cranston departed, another took over, and the two were so much alike that nobody, with the possible exception of Burbank, realized that there had been a switch.

So by merely doubling as Lamont Cranston, The Shadow still kept his real identity shrouded in mystery, which left him free to adopt other personalities, any of which might really be his own. But that of Cranston was the most convenient, as with it went membership in Manhattan's exclusive Cobalt Club, where The Shadow could stroll in and out in the casual manner of a man about town, between his forays as the cloaked phantom who brought terror to the underworld.

When I delivered the third story, I was so far ahead of schedule that I was sure there would be a lapse of several months before the fourth, and perhaps last, story would be needed. That would give me time to finish the two magic books, and still better, I could start turning out short stories, which would probably come easily and have a ready sale, now that I had geared myself to fiction writing. I had a story in mind, to be called *The Purple Girasol,* involving a rare fire opal that exerted a hypnotic effect upon anyone who viewed it steadily. But I didn't have a chance to mention it at Street & Smith.

To my amazement, I learned that the first issue of *The Shadow,* which had been on the stands a month or more, had practically sold out. Magazines weren't supposed to do that in those hard times and when anyone asked how it had happened, the stock reply was, "Only The Shadow knows!" But such a showing meant that the magazine would definitely be continued as a quarterly and might eventually go monthly. I was to go right ahead with Number Four. I did.

In an early chapter, I placed The Shadow in his sanctum, a black-walled room hidden deep in Manhattan. There, his long-fingered hands were working above a polished table, beneath the glow of a bluish light, sorting papers that one of his agents had dropped through the mail chute of an unused office in a dingy building on Twenty-third Street, to which only The Shadow had access. From a finger of the left hand gleamed a large strange gem that shone with a deep crimson hue, an unmatched fire opal that seemed like a living coal reflecting the glow of its owner's hypnotic eyes. As Maxwell Grant, I had presented the purple girasol to The Shadow, confident that he would find better use for it than I could.

I can't recall adhering to a fixed writing schedule during the formative period of the Shadow stories. Once I had the elements of a plot in mind, I would start typing and after a few chapters, my output of words would become rapid indeed. All my work was first draft, the way I had turned out copy as a reporter on the Philadelphia *North American* and later the *Evening Ledger,* prior to my entry into the syndicate field. If a chapter needed to be rewritten, I could do that afterward, but it seldom happened with the early novels, as they ran to 75,000 words or more and didn't have to be tightened.

But I was forced to take breaks between, to keep up my syndicate work, which was declining because of the depression, and to handle other loose ends. Through attending to the Shadow novels ahead of schedule, I suddenly was confronted by a deadline on the Blackstone book, which I hadn't even started; but I knocked out most of it over a weekend, by including card tricks that I had already done for my magic magazine. Beginning with the sixth Shadow novel, the length was cut to 60,000 words to allow for more short stories in the magazine, which would be a help if it should change over to a monthly basis.

By then, the second issue was on the newsstands, with a print run twice the size of the first. That, plus the fact that magazine sales lagged during the summer months, indicated that the supply would be more than ample; perhaps too much more. The first number had been dated April–June; the second was July–September; and the third would be October–December, which would tell the tale where The Shadow's future was concerned. Since I was about four issues ahead, there was no rush to deliver more while editors were away on vacations. I had been working at intervals on the Houdini book; now I gave it my full time until it was nearly completed. Then a long-distance call came from Street & Smith, saying to rush the next Shadow novel. The second issue had sold out like the first, so the magazine was to go monthly with the October number.

From there, The Shadow practically took over in person. I began turning out his 60,000-word adventures on a three-week basis, introducing new factors in nearly every issue. I spent more time on the plots, but often I was thinking one or two stories ahead, so the details fell in line when I came to them. During breaks, I checked on guns, gems, cults, wills, spies, ghosts, morgues and all sorts of deadly devices that The Shadow might encounter. I briefed myself on unusual localities and strange legends that would intrigue readers.

Instead of being cramped for time, I found that the stepped-up schedule increased my rate of output. The first two thousand words of my daily quota were just a warm-up, and frequently I hit my peak around the five-thousand mark. This was at variance with the opinions of many writers who felt that anywhere from a thousand to fifteen hundred words was a good day's stint. In due deference, I might have shared their view, if I hadn't been forced into a more exacting schedule; and again, the continuity of The Shadow stories was conducive to speedy writing. As the tempo of a story increased, I found that I could carry it over to the next day and in some instances into the next novel, all of which increased my enthusiasm for my work.

I began pitting The Shadow against adversaries who were worthy of his mettle, such as The Silent Seven, The Black Master, Double Z, The Blackmail Ring, The Ghost Makers, The Five Chameleons and Kings of Crime. All made good titles in their own right and to thwart their vicious designs, I provided The Shadow with new agents, who teamed with Harry Vincent, whenever and however required. The Shadow himself appeared openly in various guises as well as disguises, but for his convenience and my continuity, he adopted the personality of Lamont Cranston as his principal *alter ego*. As an habitué of the Cobalt Club, Cranston established a close friendship with Police Commissioner Ralph Weston, who was a fellow member; and Cranston was often present when the commissioner received confidential reports from Inspector Joe Cardona, who had begun as a headquarters detective in *The Living Shadow* and had gone up the ladder ever since.

One agent whom The Shadow constantly contacted while in the guise of Cranston was Clyde Burke, a reporter on the New York *Classic*. Later, The Shadow was to enlist another recruit in the person of Moe Shrevnitz, popularly known as "Shrevvy," a cab driver who was constantly at his chief's service. Going in or out of the Cobalt Club, The Shadow frequently changed to Lamont Cranston or vice versa in the commodious confines of his own limousine, which was piloted by a chauffeur named Stanley, who never fully realized what was taking place; but when The Shadow was really on the rove, Shrevvy's cab was far preferable for his quick changes.

When The Shadow required gadgets, I took pains to make them valid. I patterned his escapes from traps on those found in Houdini's own notes. The Shadow was skilled in climbing cliffs or buildings in the fashion of a human fly; but when he encountered a wall too sheer and smooth to allow finger grips or toeholds, I supplied him with a set of suction cups, like those used in "Walking Upside Down" beneath the dome of a theater, as described in my old syndicate article. He could cast a hawkish silhouette on a wall, making crooks think he was still around, only to find that he was gone when they surged to the attack.

Often I applied the techniques of stage illusions to some of The Shadow's disappearances. Gangsters once spotted his cloaked figure bulging from a curtained alcove and riddled it with bullets. But when they snatched off the cloak from the fallen form, it proved to be a skeleton that The Shadow had brought from a handy medical lab and left in place of himself. That scene was turned into the cover picture for an issue that became another sellout. In another story, I stationed The Shadow in a stack of huge truck tires outside of a garage. By thrusting his automatic muzzles between the tires, he drove off a horde of gunmen whose own shots failed to penetrate his improvised pillbox. When finally sure that he was out of ammunition, the gunners charged *en masse* and snatched away the tires from the top of the stack to the bottom, only to find that The Shadow again was gone.

I sent that story on to Blackstone the magician, along with some appropriate suggestions. Before the season was over, Blackstone was presenting a stage illusion in which a girl crawled into a rack of tires, only to vanish when the tires were rolled away and formed into an upright stack, from which she reappeared. Blackstone continued to perform the tire illusion as an outstanding feature of his show throughout his career as America's foremost magician.

When The Shadow was trapped under the looming gun muzzles of gloating, trigger-happy crooks, he managed to stay his execution momentarily by raising his ungloved hands with palms wide open. A thrust of his right hand, with a snap of its thumb and fingers— and a loud blast, accompanied by a vivid flash and a puff of smoke, wiped the leers from their evil faces. Blinded, the staggered would-be assassins recoiled, with their puny guns popping harmlessly upward, while The Shadow, whipping a brace of .45 automatics from beneath his cloak, slugged his way through his stupefied foemen, turning himself from victim into victor.

Whenever The Shadow staged that caper, I would supply a footnote (signed by Maxwell Grant) stating that The Shadow used two highly potent chemical substances to produce the blast—so potent, in fact, that to reveal their composition might prove disastrous. Today there are Shadow "buffs" who hark back to those days before they were born and wonder why such an impossibility was thrust upon them under the head of scientific fact. It may surprise them to learn that this startling effect was listed by magic dealers under the title of the "Devil's Whisper" and was guaranteed to wake up any audience when a magician walked on stage and snapped his fingers to prove that he was there.

It went off the market after a Chicago magic dealer demonstrated it for a customer, using several times the recommended amount. He lost his hand in the blast, which knocked both men unconscious. People arriving on the scene found the office so badly damaged that they thought a time bomb had exploded there. So the description in the Shadow novels was by no means fanciful and the warning footnote, with its refusal to divulge the secret formula, was significant indeed.

The introduction of new characters and specialized devices was not a hurry-up job. Instead, it extended over many months and eventually ran into a dozen years. The stories themselves underwent gradual stages of development, all for the better, if judged in terms of circulation, which eventually topped 300,000 per issue. The Shadow Club, composed of 50,000 constant readers, demanded new surprises and stunning climaxes; and as time went on, polls were taken, listing the novels that the club members liked best. Even the villains were to have their share at outvying one another in popularity. To appreciate this fully, we must look back to those early days when The Shadow went monthly and see what happened from there on.

When I delivered the very first Shadow story, it was assigned to John L. Nanovic, one of the newer editors at Street & Smith. Since John and I were both fresh in the field, our literary tastes were untrammeled by the stereotyped conventions that made so many pulp magazine stories read like warm-overs. Naturally, we recognized the basic formula that the market demanded: the stories had to be direct, exciting and strong on action as well as surprises. But to inject one element at the expense of another was not only injurious to both, it could detract from the validity of the story as well as its overall impact.

As a character, The Shadow was different; and so were his novels. They invited situations that violated some of the outworn pulp taboos and gave them a distinctive touch. John recognized this and went along with it to a marked degree, introducing editorial changes largely to keep a story within bounds, without disturbing its continuity. As a result, the changes, though often pointed, were seldom drastic and served as excellent guide lines for future stories. In my opinion, John Nanovic was unequaled as a fiction editor in one important respect. As he went over a story, he would mentally file every trifling mention or bit of dialogue that might have a bearing on the plot and link it up when the right time arrived. Consequently, instead of blue-penciling an important item in a lagging paragraph, he would stress it to impress it on the reader. If he had questions, they were equally vital, which proved a tremendous help to authors where novel-length stories were concerned.

To keep up production, I did all the Shadow novels on a first-draft basis, red-hot out of the typewriter, with no rewrites if I could help it. I had gone beyond the chapter-by-chapter system and had each story fully, though roughly, outlined before I began it, though there were some rather sketchy stretches between the high spots. With 60,000 words as a quota, the stories had to be tighter and with The Shadow strongly developed as the lead character, the plots and devices had to be more elaborate or ingenious, to keep ahead of the regular readers who expected The Shadow's next exploit to top all that had preceded it.

If a story lagged or became too complex, John was prompt to notice it and call for revisions, but his criticisms were always constructive and served as reminders of what to avoid in future stories. As a case in point, to maintain writing speed, I was apt to clutter a story with too many characters, bringing them in and dropping them whenever it seemed expedient. That hadn't mattered with the earlier stories, where characters were expendable on side issues and false trails; but in the newer, streamlined jobs, each segment had a bearing on the next, often in overlapping fashion.

Hence, minor characters stayed long enough to loom as suspects and then fade out when no longer needed, which could leave an astute reader wondering why they had been introduced at all. John Nanovic frequently called for the elimination of such human impedimenta, which was usually a simple task of rewriting a few pages and blue-penciling some others, running into several chapters. In redoing these passages, I turned two characters into one, so instead of two weak suspects, the story gained a single strong one.

That proved a valuable pattern for future outlines. If a night club figured in a story, instead of introducing the manager in one chapter and the owner two chapters later, I gave the place an owner-manager. I would also check in two characters at the same hotel, instead of having them go from one hotel to another in order to make their plans. The fewer loose facts the reader had to remember, the better, as it also meant fewer rewrites for me to do.

By the end of the first year, I was several months ahead of schedule and had bought a new Smith-Corona typewriter, one of the first portables to come out with a single shift. I carried it everywhere, so I could keep writing in a hotel room when I stayed in New York overnight, or in offices where I happened to be during the day. So far, this bonanza had exceeded all my expectations, past, present and even future—or so I thought, until one day an appointment was set up for a meeting with Henry W. Ralston, General Manager of Street & Smith, who had been with the company nearly thirty-five years.

The "W" stood for William and he was known as "Bill" to others who had been there during much of that same period, but to all the rest, he was Mr. Ralston. One meeting with him told you why he had gained his key position with a publishing house as famous and as long-established as Street & Smitth. He was direct, fair-minded and the epitome of integrity. After a few more such meetings, you not only felt that you had a friend for life; you did have.

Ralston had come up through the circulation and promotion departments, which with a concern like Street & Smith were much closer to the public than the editorial department, for it was circulation's job not only to gauge but to foresee the coming trends of the mass-magazine market and thus set the patterns that editors and writers were to follow. It was Ralston who had called the turn and decided to launch The Shadow as a streamlined successor to the old dime-novel heroes; now that the magazine was paying off, he had hopes of pushing it still further.

I had been doing the stories on a freelance basis, delivering them as called for, but with no guarantee as to how long the demand would last. Now that question was to be settled. I was to receive a contract to deliver twenty-four full-length Shadow novels in a single year, from March 1, 1932 to March 1, 1933, with the promise of an automatic renewal for the year to follow. That meant that if the magazine continued as *The Shadow Detective Monthly*, which was then its actual title, I would be doing four years' work in two and would be that far ahead of the game.

That was attractive indeed, but it offered still brighter prospects, which Ralston outlined in his forthright way. Surveys showed that an increasing number of eager readers were buying up copies of each new issue soon after it hit the newsstands, so some were practically sold out within two weeks, while others showed a marked decline after that period. Should this trend continue, the magazine would be stepped-up to twice a month; Ralston, thinking well ahead, wanted to put the story production on that basis.

The contract stipulated that Street & Smith could call for stories other than Shadow novels and also that they would buy whatever additional output I was willing to supply beyond the mark of 1,440,000 words that represented twenty-four novels of 60,000 words each. That clause seemed a bit humorous, since nobody had ever turned out that amount of wordage on a single mystery character within a year. But there was more to it than that. From the start, Ralston had felt that The Shadow was good for at least five years, so the contract would take care of the remaining four, even if the magazine stayed as a monthly, or was forced to drop back to that schedule after a twice-a-month trial.

Whatever the case, since The Shadow had started a character trend, Street & Smith intended to follow through with others of a similar type. So if I happened to be many months ahead, with The Shadow still on a mere monthly schedule, I might be called upon to come up with a new character for another magazine that would run concurrently with *The Shadow*. Either way, far-sighted Mr. Ralston was prepared for what might come, and more. With a new writer, a new editor, and a new magazine, all he needed, in effect, was a new department, so that was soon established, with John Nanovic as its editor, working directly under the auspices of H. W. Ralston.

To meet the twice-a-month schedule, I began working up plots that were timely, purposeful, and above all, a challenge to The Shadow, who had emerged so far from the nebulous stage that many such prospects were feasible. It was no longer merely a case of The Shadow coming to the rescue of some lesser hero, or heroine, or both, either personally or through his trusted agents. Nor did he simply rove the underworld, looking for wrongs to right. Even the lure of an unsolved mystery that all the established forces of law and order had failed to crack was not enough to divert the Master of Darkness from some more pressing aim where major issues were at stake.

Those themes were still good, but needed strong situations or unusual angles; otherwise, steady readers would feel that The Shadow had relapsed into his earlier routine either through his own indifference or because crime's menace had been fully met and conquered. The Shadow himself had become a menace where gangdom was concerned, and that provided a nucleus for surefire novels in which master crooks not only arose to meet The Shadow's challenge, but even took up The Shadow's elusive trail themselves, so that he, the hunter, would become the hunted. Other criminals concocted ingenious devices to conceal not only their schemes, but their identities, and these had to be cracked before The Shadow could get at the core of crime itself.

All such angles called for fuller and more comprehensive outlines, which in turn demanded detailed situations. I was able to supplant false trails with cross-purposes, which strengthened the stories further. To delve into the intricacies of The Shadow's evolution during that first year of doubled production would require a book in itself, if all the facets were to be fully covered. All those, however, were more grist for my mill and really aided the rapid production.

I found that I could turn out a Shadow novel in seven or eight days of writing time. That allowed for a couple of days for rest, diversion or travel, with three or four more to complete a working outline or synopsis. Occasionally, I took off time for special research, but I made up for it by knocking out a goodly number of stories in six days and some in even less. For a while, when I was making frequent trips to New York, I did the stories on a five-day schedule and actually banged out a few in four days in order to get to the city, deliver a story and get back before a weekend. On the average, I did a story every two weeks, so when sales of the magazine stayed up in the summer and it was put on a twice-a-month schedule with the issue dated October 1, 1932, I was more than six months ahead of schedule. By the end of the year, I had done my twenty-four and when I asked how I should fill my spare writing time, I was told to keep right on with The Shadow. While so doing, I saw an exhibit of some books that had been written on Smith-Corona portables, so I told John Nanovic about it and he sent a memo to the Street & Smith promotion department. They made up a life-size cutout figure which showed me drawing an elongated sheet from a giant Corona typewriter, announcing that Maxwell Grant had set a world's record of 1,440,000 words in ten months in the creation of The Shadow. This was displayed in the Smith-Corona window and, meanwhile, I did four more stories in the next two months, for a full year's total of 1,680,000 words on The Shadow.

By then, at Street & Smith, we had developed this procedure: I would come to town and go over plot ideas with John Nanovic. Armed with notes, we would invade Ralston's commodious paneled office, and in a setting that Lamont Cranston personally would have relished, we would go over all the details of one, two, or occasionally even more Shadow plots and settle upon their merits. The thirty-year-old brick building had been sturdily built, but when the high-speed printing presses were going full tilt, you could feel a steady vibration, which I always found intriguing, because it could mean that one Shadow magazine was coming into actuality while another was just entering the projective stage.

These discussions with Ralston tied in with company policies, circulation opportunities and other factors that were foreign to the editorial needs of more general magazines. Even with the magazine running twice a month, I had still gone so far ahead that I could get the okay on three stories with a special setting—say in England—and write them in succession, using the same basic research for all three; but John could later schedule them three or four issues apart. Stories with a Chinese background also were scheduled at regular intervals; those dated back to the first story, *The Living Shadow,* with its makeshift cover. Readers had liked the Chinatown chapters that I had to include to justify the cover, so necessity had indeed stimulated invention.

My big bugaboo during that first contract year was that of getting hung up in the middle of a story, for I knew that it would be hard to make up for lost time if I ever fell behind with such an exacting schedule. Rewrites also offered the same hazard, as I had learned from earlier experience, so I gave meticulous care to the preparation of a detailed list of characters and a chapter-by-chapter synopsis, before starting on a story. This could prove rather grueling at times, but minor questions were sure to iron themselves out during the actual writing. To handle real difficulties, I could always drop that story for the time being and go on with an alternate plot that had also been approved. As a result, I was never hung up at all in the middle of a story, nor did I ever have to do any more rewrites or extensive revisions in any of two hundred and eighty-three Shadow novels that I authored over a period of more than fifteen years.

No longer were chapter headings the tabs on which a flimsy synopsis hinged. They simply reflected or identified the status or progress of the story at that particular point. With twenty or more chapter titles to a novel, averaging close to three words each, we have a rough estimate of more than 15,000 words of chapter headings that I wrote for the Shadow stories, which is about the length of an average novelette.

Our three-way accord continued for nearly a dozen years, until after the magazine reverted to a monthly schedule in May 1943, because of limitations on paper in World War II. The next few years marked a decline in that type of publication and *The Shadow* was combined with *Mystery Magazine,* which appeared every other month. In 1948, *The Shadow* was revived as a quarterly under its own title and I wrote the last five stories, still using the pen name of Maxwell Grant. The final issue, dated Summer 1949, was titled *The Whispering Eyes.* In 1963, fourteen years later, I wrote a paperback novel, *Return of The Shadow,* under my own name, Walter B. Gibson, bringing back the Cloaked Avenger, with his entire crew of agents.

Along with the Corona display in which I was depicted as Maxwell Grant setting a year's record of 1,440,000 words in 1932, there were other milestones to establish proof of output. In May 1937, a feature writer from the New York *World-Telegram* interviewed me as Maxwell Grant in the Street & Smith office, where John Nanovic estimated that my Shadow wordage had by then passed the 7,000,000 mark. Four years later, my own identity had become so well known in the magazine trade that Street & Smith arranged for me to do an article on The Shadow for *Writer's*

Digest, which appeared in the issue of March 1941, under the title, "A Million Words a Year for Ten Straight Years, by Walter (The Shadow) Gibson." When *The Shadow* ceased publication, some eight years later, my total was around the 15,000,000 mark, so there it stands.

In those later years, Street & Smith also published *The Shadow Comics,* which introduced the character to a whole new set of readers. From the start, I wrote the comic-book scripts, adapting them from the magazine stories, some of which were admirably suited to pictorial treatment.

Soon after The Shadow had zoomed to fame in the guise of Lamont Cranston, efforts were made to place a radio program that would promote the magazine. In 1936, after more than one hundred of the Shadow novels had appeared in the publication, The Shadow went on the air. The scripts were adapted from the printed novels; Lamont Cranston was aided and abetted by his girl friend, Margo Lane, who also appeared in some of the magazine stories, chiefly those in which Cranston posed as a debonair man-about-town. Police Commissioner Weston, Inspector Cardona and Shrevvy, the cab driver, all familiar figures in the novels, were also featured regularly in the radio programs, which continued a few years after the magazine suspended publication.

I Never Called Him Bill

by JOHN L. NANOVIC

I worked for him—and with him—for some thirteen years. On the friendliest, closest, most enjoyable terms; not as boss and editor, but just as two guys. Yet I never called him Bill, as all the writers did. I always called him Mister Ralston.

I was working in the editorial department of Street & Smith, the famous pulp house, back in 1931. Fresh out of college, and probably on the basis of a cover story, "Notre Dame, College of the Masses," which I sold them for *Sport Story Magazine,* I was asked if I wanted to be editor of *College Stories,* a new magazine.

If they'd given me a choice between a million dollars and the title of Editor of *College Stories*—well, even though I was just out of college, I'm sure I wouldn't have refused the million dollars. But they didn't offer me a choice.

And, probably because nobody else was interested, I was told to work with Walter Gibson, a writer, on a novel he was doing, and which was to be printed in a new magazine, to be called *The Shadow Magazine.*

So one Friday afternoon, Frank Blackwell, editorial director of Street & Smith, who was my boss, stuck his head in the door and said: "I'm going home now and almost forgot to tell you that beginning Monday you're going to work for Bill Ralston, not for me. Bill's a good guy. You'll like him."

I don't know whether I had even heard the name Ralston in the few months I'd been working there. Us editors worked on the fifth floor, along the windows. The center of the huge floor was filled with large rolls of newsprint—the pulp paper from which the pulp magazines got their name. Upstairs, on the sixth floor, were the Smiths and other big shots. On the seventh floor was the composing room, and sometimes you got the impression that the seventh floor was the most important floor in the house.

As soon as Blackwell went to the elevator, I picked up the phone and asked for Mister Ralston. His secretary answered; I told her who I was and what Blackwell had just told me; and what should I do? She said Mister Ralston was at a meeting (at the American News Company) and would not be back until Monday morning, but that she would ask him to call me Monday morning.

I didn't wait for his call. I called first thing Monday, and every morning. His secretary always said he would get to me, but not to worry, just keep working as I had been.

It wasn't until that Friday that a large, well-built man (reminded one of Doc Savage, who was soon to be created) stepped into my office and said, "I'm Bill Ralston, John. We're supposed to get together, but there were so many other things that had to be done I couldn't get around to it, and you're doing all right, so I don't have to worry about you. We'll get together some day next week. We'll work out all right."

We did get together. The following Tuesday. The phone rang; it was Mister Ralston. If I could come up now it would be fine; but if I had something else I wanted to do, I could just come up any time I was ready.

I couldn't be any readier! I didn't even wait for the elevator; I ran up the stairs and into Mister Ralston's office.

Mister Ralston was waiting for me. He had the largest office—next to O. G. and G. C. Smith—as was befitting the General Manager. He sort of indicated a chair while he "fired up" his cigar And I mean fired up. When Mister Ralston lit his cigar, it flared out like a rocket before it finally settled down to good puffing. And with those initial puffs, great clouds of smoke.

That "firing up" grew to be a ritual which all the writers got to know well.

He began to extend the cigar box toward me, but then figured I wasn't a cigar smoker and left it on the desk. (I wasn't; not even cigarettes.)

Then Mister Ralston told me what he had in mind. He said that though he wasn't an editor, he had lots of ideas about magazines and stories. (Wow! I thought to myself: here's another one of those who's going to try to tell a "professional" editor like me how to do his job. After all, though I was young, I had had lots of experience. I was practically born in a printing shop; worked on the local paper and was editor in my high-school senior year; worked as the "short

pants" reporter on the Allentown *Morning Call,* and even had Sunday feature stories; at Notre Dame, I was on the staff of just about every publication, and edited *The Juggler* in my senior year. Wow! And he's going to tell *me* how to edit?)

He said we'd work out these ideas together. (I didn't think he meant it; but he did, and we did work out thousands of ideas together.)

While I concurred with that, I pointed out that those writer fellows had plot ideas of their own, and they might not like to have us force our ideas on them.

"The way we'll tell 'em," Mister Ralston said, "they'll practically think they are their own."

And that's how he told the writers, and that's how I learned to tell them. No, the writers never really thought these plot ideas were their own. They knew a good plot when they saw one, whether their own or ours. Further, they knew that the plot idea was one thing, but finishing it into a story was something else, and that was their job. But most of all, they saw that this was a sincere effort to help them, and I don't think anybody else ever did that for writers.

We worked with Walter Gibson first, since he was our only "contract" writer at the time. Later we worked the same way with all the others.

Now, *The Shadow* was really an outgrowth of the character called The Shadow on the air. At that time, The Shadow was only an announcer on the *Detective Story* radio program. But Mister Ralston saw the value of this character when newsdealers began to report that people were asking for "that Shadow magazine" when they meant *Detective Story.*

So Mister Ralston gave the editorial department instructions to get a writer to write some sort of novel about The Shadow. Maybe rewrite an old Nick Carter novel. The idea was to get the magazine into print and into interstate commerce to protect the name. Also, the story should have a Chinese scene, because there was a set of cover plates on hand showing some Chinese action, and by using these, a few hundred dollars would be saved, both for artwork and plates.

The Shadow Magazine was a tremendous success from the start. From a "quarterly," which usually means "we'll see if it works," to a monthly, then to twice a month, in a little over a year.

Then one day Mister Ralston said to me, "Let's go out to lunch, and take a little time." At that lunch, he said he had an idea, maybe just half-baked, and that I would probably have to do a lot of work on it.

The idea was another magazine, *Doc Savage*. Like *The Shadow*, it would feature a full-length novel, but the hero would be more in the adventure line, with some science thrown in.

The idea wasn't half-baked. At the first sitting, Mister Ralston had all of the characters well defined, even to their names. He had most of their background, most of their characteristics.

It took a few more sessions in Mister Ralston's office, with the big cigar, before we were sure we had the Doc Savage idea solid. Lester Dent was called in to write it. When he saw what we were talking about, he thought it was the best thing ever, and his efforts made it become so.

I gave Lester a seventy-page "plan" for *Doc Savage Magazine*. The characters, the basic concept, the background, etc., were all there, and most of these were to remain the same all through the Doc Savage years.

This does not mean that Les Dent did no creative work on Doc Savage. What we gave him was the bones. He put on the flesh, the life, the excitement. Like Walter Gibson with The Shadow, and all the others, the real work was done by the writers, not by us. Whether it was

contributing something toward a plot, giving characters a new angle, or whatever, we might have thrown out a germ, but the writers did the job.

These discussions were more or less "brainstorming" sessions, though that word was unknown at the time—at least to me. By the time we got through, it would be pretty hard to say who had contributed what to the discussion. The idea was to get something good. It was a perfect blending mechanism of editorial and writing which Mister Ralston introduced into the pulp field.

After *Doc,* other magazines followed: *The Avenger, Pete Rice, The Whisperer, The Skipper, The New Nick Carter,* and others. On all of these, we worked the same way with the authors. All of them were given the "plan" for the character. Then they developed it according to their own talent and ability.

This was far from an "assembly-line" procedure. The writers appreciated the help and interest, and the individual attention. The fact that most of these magazines were more than normally successful was proof of the effectiveness of the system.

Yet, though everyone in magazine publishing knew what we were doing, I don't think anyone else really followed our system. Most fiction stories were then—and still are, I suppose—written on "speculation": no guarantee of purchase. In our method, once the plot was agreed upon, the writer came back to me with a fairly complete outline, and after that was approved, his sale was assured. By doing all the revisions and changes in outline form, the writers were sure that the resulting story would be just what we needed.

Nor was our "plot factory" a routine thing, holding a writer to a strict pattern. Early in my career I learned that the best editing was the least editing. Once there was agreement on the story line, each writer had his own way of doing it.

Trying to make him conform to any other style would just result in a stilted product.

Just for comparison, let's look at our two stars, Les Dent and Walter Gibson.

Lester Dent was a careful writer, a very strong plotter. His basic plot belief was "The Triple O," which he later explained to all writers in one of the writing magazines. The Triple O was simple: Object — Obstacles — Outcome. Very simple. But only Les Dent knew how to make the best of it; how to put the zing right in the first paragraph, to make you want to read more.

Les also had a way with his writing. One of the things I have never lived down in my family is the time one of my sons asked everybody in the house to listen while he read something from Doc Savage. What he read was: "Doc's arm drifted outward with lightning speed." If you were a reader of Doc Savage, there was nothing wrong with that. If anybody could drift his arm outward with lightning speed, Doc could do it. Nobody else could. And the way Les wrote this, you believed it. It was just right.

Walter Gibson's writing was different. Of course, a detective-mystery theme should have different treatment from an adventure-mystery theme. But the big difference in writing was that Gibson was a newspaperman, having worked on the Philadelphia papers, and that he was an accomplished professional magician as well. He had the newspaperman's knack of giving you enough facts so that you wanted to read on to the next paragraph, and enough of the magician's flare to flash things before you long enough to intrigue you, but not give his point away.

Les Dent had adventure and excitement in his writing; Walter Gibson had mystery and magic.

And both had action! That was the secret to pulp success, as it is in any fiction, I believe. Many of the pulp fans today analyze the Shadow and Doc novels for psychology and what have you. All we were giving the reader then is what he wanted—action. If there were other things in them, I never knew about it!

Incidentally, many people have asked how these writers could turn out 60,000 words at such a rapid pace. The plotting helped, of course. But they had to work. They couldn't wait for "inspiration." Gibson had a trick that I have never heard from any one else. Most writers, when they break away from the typewriter, finish a page, or at least the paragraph. Gibson learned that the best way to get back to the thought trend he left was to break in the middle of a sentence. When he got back to the script, he knew the finish of the sentence, and went on from there.

This is how I edited *The Shadow, Doc Savage,* and the other character magazines in the Street & Smith line. The success of these trail-blazing magazines kept the pulp magazines alive at least an extra decade. And for this success, I invariably was given most of the credit, since I was the editor.

We never kept our editorial method a secret. I explained it in detail at meetings, dinners, and other occasions when writers gathered. Gibson, Dent, and the others also spoke often about how this was done—and the part Mister Ralston played in it.

These meetings with Mister Ralston were frequent, because he wanted to help in every single plot. And these sessions with the writers became a "thing," a tradition, a ritual. They were the most enjoyable meetings any of us ever had.

Mister Ralston's big cigar; passing the box around; some small talk; a little bit of philosophical comment on current situations from Mister Ralston, and then into the plot!

But, as friendly as these meetings were; as often as we had them, as well as many other meetings I had with Mister Ralston without writers; with every one calling him Bill a couple of minutes after their first meeting, I never called him Bill.

Not at meetings with writers; not at meetings alone; not at any time. It wasn't that he was stuffy, or pompous, or overbearing. In fact, in all those years he treated me with fatherly interest, like the kid next door, or something. Anything I wanted, I could get. (Except raises; they were a bit tougher!) And everybody at Street & Smith knew that Mister Ralston would back me up no matter what I wanted.

Mister Ralston always called me "John," rarely using my last name. Even when I was ushered into the august presence of the two Smiths, O. G. and G. C., Mister Ralston simply said: "This is John." I suppose the Smiths knew my last name from the payroll. Anyway, that didn't matter; just being permitted to enter their office was a supreme honor.

But I knew that Mister Ralston liked me, and enjoyed working with me, teaching me the things he knew about editing —and they were plenty. Though I was a straight "John" at meetings with writers, many times when we had our own sessions, about stories, the magazines, or other things, it was almost always, "Sit down, Johnny my boy," while he lit his cigar. Or, "What would you suggest about that, Johnny me lad?" on other questions.

Maybe that's why he made it a point to stay in the background when it came to credit for the editorial success of these books. I was the one to get the bows, the bouquets, from the trade; even from Les, and Walt, and the other writers, even though they knew better.

Or, on more personal occasions, like when I was getting married (to a lovely Street & Smith *Love Story Magazine* cover girl), he sat me down and told me what I should do; like putting down roots, buying a house, and so on. He often gave me what you might call fatherly advice. I guess I didn't take as much as I should have; but my own kids don't take too much of mine, either, so I guess that's natural.

But, during all those years, at all times, I always called him Mister Ralston. Not because he was the kind of guy you'd be afraid of calling by his first name; but because, somehow, to me Mister Ralston always felt and sounded better.

Even in the years after I left Street & Smith, and after *The Shadow* had died its natural death, I continued to call him Mister Ralston. Even when he died—at a time when you talk of "good old Jim" or "good old Bob"—I could only think of "So long, Mister Ralston."

That was the only way I could show my respect, admiration and love for a most unusual editor, and a very special sort of man.

I could never call him Bill.

The Crime Oracle

The CRIME ORACLE

**A Complete Book-length Novel from the Private
Annals of The Shadow, as told to**

Maxwell Grant

CHAPTER I.
CRIME AFTER DARK.

THE northbound elevated train rattled to a screechy stop. The gate of the last car swung open. A sallow, squint-eyed passenger stepped to the rough planking of the old station platform. Start-ing toward the exit, he paused to light a cigarette, while the train jolted away on its journey.

The squint-eyed man turned about. His gaze steadied after he had blinked. His lips formed a satisfied smile, as he looked toward the south end of the deserted platform. It was early eve-

Out of thin air came this bodiless specter — a gruesome, leering head that talked! Murder was done at this monster's bidding! But from the mind of The Shadow came knowledge that counterbalanced the twisted brain that was The Head!

ning; the platform was dimly lighted, for it was above the level of the avenue lights. The squint-eyed man was barely able to discern a huddled figure by the rail of the platform's lower end.

The squint-eyed man approached. As he neared the huddled figure, he noted that the fellow was half crouched across the rail, looking down toward the street.

Calmly, he clapped a hand upon the hunched shoulders. The huddled man snapped about with a snarl.

The mellow glow of a platform light revealed a pasty, tight-lipped face. Cunning eyes gleamed; then dried lips twisted in a grin. The huddled man had recognized the arrival. He whispered a hoarse greeting:

"H'lo, Squint!"

"Hello, Chip!" The squint-eyed man puffed at his cigarette. Then: "You've spotted Koker's crew?"

"Yeah." "Chip" retained his grin. "Lamp 'em yourself, Squint. They're parked in a sedan down in front of that eatin' joint——"

"Casey's?"

"Yeah. That's what the sign says."

"All right, then. Let's hop along, before another train shows up. Koker and his outfit can stay where they are."

"Squint" led the way, with Chip following like an obedient dog. They walked to the exit and descended the steps. This course brought them to the side street, a dozen yards from the corner. But instead of turning back toward the avenue, Squint moved along the side street. Chip followed, puzzled. Squint explained.

"Koker don't know the lay," informed Squint. "He's not in on it at all. I just told him to be on the avenue, in case I wanted him."

"Was that on the dope sheet, Squint?"

"No. Just an idea of my own."

"But if The Head didn't tell you to——"

"I'm following the orders that came from The Head. Listen again, Chip; Koker isn't wise to the racket. So what does it matter, him being here?"

They had reached the depressed entrance to a side-street tea room. Shuttered windows told that the place was no longer in business. A weather-beaten sign proclaimed the name: "THE YELLOW PARROT," with a picture of the bird in question. Squint drew Chip down to the closed doorway. He began to work at the lock with a skeleton key.

OF the many characters in Manhattan's underworld, Squint Proddock and Chip Mulley were unique. Each was a specialist in his own direction; each was wise enough to admit his own limitations.

Squint Proddock was an ex-racketeer who had feigned retirement in order to turn to other crime. His shifty, blinking eyes had given him his nickname; they also rendered him easy to identify, which was the chief reason for Squint's carefulness when he crossed the path of the law.

Chip Mulley also carried a descriptive title. Originally, his pals had dubbed him "Chipmunk," a title that befitted his dryish, small-lipped face. His nickname had been shortened to Chip; and he was known as a competent subordinate who served various big-shots. Chip Mulley was an able hand at gaining needed information. He was a competent go-between, who kept what he knew to himself. It was not surprising that Squint had found Chip useful.

The door of the Yellow Parrot had opened under Squint's manipulation with the skeleton key. The two men edged into the tea room and closed the door behind them. Squint clicked a flashlight and passed it to Chip to hold. Under the glare, Squint produced an envelope. From it, he took a typewritten sheet and studied a list that looked like a schedule.

" 'Enter Yellow Parrot,' " read Squint. " 'Time: 7:15.' Right to the dot, Chip!"

Squint had brought a watch into the light. Chip whispered a comment, wisely:

"That's the ticket, Squint! The Head knows his stuff. This ain't the first dope sheet I've lamped. I'm tellin' you, it's a set-up when you follow one of them time-tables!"

"Come along, then." Holding the paper in his left hand, Squint took the flashlight with his right. "The next stop is the second closet on the left, in the back hallway."

They reached their objective. Squint focused the light upon the door and ordered Chip to open it. The squirrel-faced hoodlum obeyed. Squint raised the schedule into the light, then growled:

"Unscrew the coat hooks on that cross-board. Then yank the board away. Make it snappy!"

Chip complied. After he had removed the hooks, the strip of wood came away. Chip issued an exclamation when he saw the top edge of a low door. The other edges were obscured by a baseboard and upright corner strips.

"Shove it upward."

Again Chip followed Squint's order. The barrier slid easily. Squint's flashlight showed a narrow, darkened passage. Squint added an order:

"Move ahead. We're going through."

The passage ran a dozen feet; then turned to the right. The two crooks followed it until they reached a stairway. There, they ascended. They came to another barrier, which was held in place by screws. Squint brought out a screw driver and handed it to Chip.

"Get busy," he ordered. "This is to be off by 7:25. You've got six minutes, Chip."

Four minutes were all that Chip required. Squint helped his aid to shift the blockade aside. They advanced into a musty, windowless storeroom. Squint's flashlight showed heavy crates and packing cases, with cobwebs everywhere. There was a door beyond.

"It won't be locked," informed Squint. He blinked the flashlight for a final consultation of the dope sheet. "We'll listen there, until we hear the buzzer. That comes next. I'll do the rest—but stick with me, in case of trouble."

They moved to the door and waited there in darkness. Squint's hand was on the knob. They were ahead of schedule; so the wait became prolonged. Then came the sound that the pair expected: a sharp, repeated buzz from the other side of the storeroom door.

Squint waited five full seconds; then turned the knob and pressed the door inward.

CHIP saw a small, lighted office; at the right, a desk placed in front of a window that opened into an airshaft. There was a door at the left of the room; straight across, a paneled wall that had a ledge and window like a bank teller's wicket. There were no bars, however; the wicket was a solid wooden panel, which prevented view beyond.

There was a man at the desk, a stoop-shouldered, gray-haired fellow who had been going over an account book. He was wearing a green eyeshade, with rimless spectacles beneath. He had heard the summons of the buzzer. Looking past Squint's shoulder, Chip saw the gray-haired man reach out and press a switch that was attached to the desk.

That done, the gray-haired man arose. He turned toward the wicket. Hence his direction was away from the two crooks who were watching him. It was obvious that the gray-haired man had admitted a visitor from a front door on the avenue. He was going to open the wicket and meet the arrival. But he never accomplished that mission.

The gray-haired man had stopped long enough to stoop and turn the combination of a small safe directly beneath the wicket ledge. Chip had not noticed the safe until that moment, for it was obscured in the blackness beneath the ledge. As the door of the safe swung open, Squint stalked forward. Chip saw a blackjack wriggling in the hands of his companion.

The gray-haired man heard Squint's approach. He started upward, too late. Squint snapped his wrist in artful fashion. The blackjack thudded the gray-haired man behind the ear. Chip, bounding forward, saw the victim succumb. Squint snarled a warning for quiet.

"The white box," he whispered. "A tin one—in the safe! Snag it, Chip! No noise!"

Chip found the box. He turned around to see Squint bending over the motionless body of the gray-haired man.

Withered fingers of the victim's left hand were clutching a small key that the man had drawn from his pocket. Squint tugged the key from the victim's clutch. It came easily, for the hand had relaxed.

"Out again," whispered Squint, nodding as he saw the white tin box that Chip exhibited. "Speedy—but no noise!"

THEY sneaked to the door of the storeroom. As they reached it, they heard a pounding at the wicket. Some visitor had entered from the front. He was wondering why the wicket was not open.

Squint closed the door from the storeroom side. He polished the knob with a handkerchief. He and Chip reached the stairway. Together, they shoved the barrier in place. Chip made quick work of replacing the screws. They hurried down the stairs to the Yellow Parrot.

There, while Squint whispered hoarsely for speed, Chip put back the strip of wood and screwed in the coat hooks. They made for the outer door.

"Wait!" Squint's whisper stopped Chip. The flashlight glimmered downward. Again, Squint nudged it into Chip's hand; then used the key to open the white tin box.

A gasp from Chip; a pleased chuckle from Squint. The interior of the tin box was filled with packets of crisp bank notes.

"Fifty grand!" chortled Squint. "Easy pickings, eh, Chip? Come along. Let's scram. But take it easy when we get outside."

They made their exit to the street. Squint polished the doorknobs on both sides; but did not bother to lock the barrier. Tucking the tin box under his coat, he urged Chip toward the nearest street lamp.

"We won't need Koker," whispered Squint. "The Head was right, Chip. It worked just like he expected it."

"What're you stoppin' here for, Squint?"

Chip's rejoinder was an uneasy one. They were just within the range of the street lamp.

"Instructions," responded Squint. "The last on the list. A signal. It means all jake."

He made a sidewise gesture with his left hand. Then, nudging Chip, Squint started eastward at a swift walk. Chip kept close beside him. They neared the next corner. Squint chuckled.

"A few blocks up," he said to Chip. "We'll take the crosstown subway. This was a pipe, Chip!"

Chip nodded, as he looked back over his left shoulder. He saw a car which had been parked in darkness. It was moving forward slowly, going back along the route which they had come, for this was a westward street.

"The Head! He had that bus posted there!"

Such was Chip's whispered comment. He had guessed the reason for Squint's signal. Koker's crew, on the avenue, had been Squint's own idea. But a superman of crime, the hidden master of this night's doing, had also taken due precaution. Some watcher from the dark had spotted Squint's tip.

Crime after dark had been accomplished with ease and precision. The perpetrators were departing with their swag—fifty thousand dollars. All through the prearranged plan of an evil chief whom Chip Mulley had dubbed "The Head."

Even Squint Proddock, though he termed himself a big-shot, had been no more than an instrument in the machinations of a master schemer!

CHAPTER II.
TRAPS REVERSED.

JUST after Squint and Chip had made their departure by the side street, a stir took place upon the front avenue near

Casey's beanery. It began when an excited man came out from a doorway near the corner. Tall, heavy of build, this man was attired in gray hat and overcoat. He was carrying a suitcase—an empty one, from the ease with which he handled it.

The man in gray spied a patrolman near the corner. He hurried up and spoke to the officer.

"Something—something has happened!" stammered the man. "I'm afraid that there has been foul play——"

"Whereabouts?" demanded the patrolman.

"In there." The man pointed to the doorway from which he had come. "That's where the trouble may be."

The patrolman eyed the sign above the door. It bore the name:

J. G. SAUTELLE
WHOLESALE CLOTHING AGENCY

"You're Mr. Sautelle?"

The gray-clad man shook his head in response to the officer's query.

"No," he stated. "My name is Jennings. Luber Jennings, from Cleveland. Mr. Sautelle was to be in his office. When I rang, he pressed the switch to let me enter. But when I reached the office, I couldn't rouse him."

"We'll take a look."

They went to the door. It was latched. Jennings explained, nervously:

"It swung shut when I came out. I tried to stop it but I was too late."

The patrolman looked dubious. But as he eyed Jennings more closely, he saw that the man's attire and bearing marked him as respectable. The panels of the door were thin. The officer considered smashing one to reach the knob from the inside. Jennings urged him to follow such a course.

FROM down the street, men were watching. They were stationed in a parked sedan; the car that Chip had spotted from the "L" platform. Beside the driver was a pasty-faced man who showed an ugly scowl. He was Koker Hosch.

"Lamp the harness bull, Koker——"

"I'm watching him," growled Koker, interrupting the man at the wheel. "But it ain't the copper that counts most. It's that mug in the gray coat. He came out of that clothing joint."

Two men in back leaned forward to hear their chief's comments.

"I'm covering for a pal to-night," commented Koker. He referred to Squint Proddock, although he did not

Landing upon the moving car, the rescuer was just in time.

mention the racketeer by name. "He's staging something hereabouts and I've got a hunch that it was in that joint."

"Maybe the bird in the gray coat butted in——"

"That's just what it looks like. Get that typewriter ready."

"You're going to rub him out?"

"Yeah!" Koker's tone was savage. "Him and the harness bull, too! He may have spilled the works to that dumb copper. Come on—shove ahead, Pete!"

The chauffeur started the sedan forward. From the back seat, the barrel of a machine gun nudged into the light. Murder was in the making. Neither Jennings nor the patrolman saw the death car that was looming toward them.

Across the avenue, a taxicab was rolling southward. Its driver had spied the sedan. So had a passenger in the cab. A hissed whisper reached the driver's ears. It was a command. The taxi slowed, almost to a stop.

A door opened. A blackish shape sprang from the rear of the cab and landed beside an "L" pillar. The door slammed shut. The taxi sped forward as if impelled by the jar. The driver was following instructions to get clear of the neighborhood.

The black being from the cab had timed his drop to a break in traffic. He sprang across the car tracks that ran beneath the elevated pillars. He reached the opposite posts. His figure seemed to vanish as it stopped there. Only a keen observer could have caught a passing glimpse of that cloaked shape.

The sedan was abreast the pillar where the cloaked form had halted. Twenty feet more would bring it to the doorway where the patrolman had begun to bang at the panel, while Jennings stood beside him. Blue uniform and gray coat—both were conspicuous in the glow of street lamps.

"Give it!"

The growl came from Koker. In the

back seat, the man on the right was guiding the machine gun, while the one on the left was pressing a ready finger to the trigger. Another instant would mean double death.

Something thudded the running board, on the left of the sedan. A blackened figure had swooped from the darkness beneath the elevated. Landing upon the moving car, the rescuer was just in time. A black-gloved hand sledged through the opened window. The muzzle of a .45 automatic drove down upon the machine gunner's head.

Koker Hosch heard the crack. With a snarl, he twisted about. A revolver glittered in his fist. His lips mouthed an oath; then spat a startled cry of recognition:

"The Shadow!"

LIGHTS from across the street formed a background against which Koker saw his silhouetted foe. A cloaked shape of blackness, with eyes that burned from beneath the brim of a slouch hat. The Shadow—master fighter whom all gangdom feared! He was the unexpected adversary who had knocked off Koker's machine gunner.

Viciously, Koker fired. Though the range was but a few feet, his shot went wide—for the simple reason Koker had aimed for the top half of the window, just behind the driver's head. That was where he had seen The Shadow's eyes. But The Shadow had rolled backward, outward. Only his left hand clutched the lower edge of the rear window.

"Get him, Skibo!"

Koker howled the command as Pete, the driver, jammed the brakes. The order was to the man in the rear seat—the one beside the stunned machine gunner. Skibo lurched to the window at the left. He swung a vicious blow for the hand upon the window edge.

The hand came up as Skibo's arm descended. Like a mechanical clamp, it caught the ruffian's wrist. Skibo's head and shoulders shot through the window. The rowdy jammed there. Shifting his hold to the crook's neck, The Shadow jabbed his right hand in through the window, to take aim at Koker.

With the move came a sinister laugh. It was a burst of fierce hilarity that spoke of doom for crooks. The laugh of The Shadow, dreaded by all who belonged to the underworld!

Pete heard it. Wildly, the driver jolted the sedan forward. Skibo, though helpless, gave a frantic twist. The Shadow's gun spoke; his bullet sizzed above Koker's ear, thanks to Skibo's disturbance of the aim. The Shadow shifted outward; then suddenly dropped his hold and went rolling to the street.

In his haste, Pete had let the sedan swing from the curb. He was yanking the wheel to the right, to avoid an elevated pillar. Pete had not designed the maneuver; purely through accident, it balked The Shadow. The left running board was about to graze the pillar. The Shadow had dropped away just in time to save himself from a smash against the steel post.

THE patrolman had heard the shots. He had yanked a revolver; from the doorway, he was opening fire at the departing car. Skibo had rolled back into the rear seat. Koker, seeing no sign of The Shadow, had swung about to exchange bullets with the bluecoat.

The officer ducked into the doorway; but Jennings, out to the middle of the sidewalk, was rooted where he stood. The sedan was making a left turn at the corner; Koker, leaning across, had gained a bead on Jennings. But before Koker could press the trigger, a black shape hurtled up from the curb.

It was The Shadow. Gripping Jennings, he sent the man staggering against the patrolman in the doorway. Falling away as Koker fired, the cloaked battler stabbed quick shots toward the escaping sedan.

An elevated pillar stopped a bullet that was designed for the sedan's gas tank. The Shadow dispatched a second slug, this time with sure result. It pinged a rear tire just as the car was making its get-away, westward on the side street. The sedan lurched, but kept on.

Then began an amazing sequence. Traffic had deployed along the avenue, automobiles and trolleys stopping in alarm at the gunfire. Halted near The Shadow was a taxi. It was not the cab in which he had come here; but it was one that would suit his purpose, for it was pointed northward and nothing blocked its path.

The taxi was of the convertible type; its top was down, for the weather was mild. That was another advantage for The Shadow. Leaping from the sidewalk, he whipped open the door and boarded the cab. The staring driver saw his unexpected passenger; then shivered as he heard the commanding voice:

"Start ahead! Swing left at the corner!"

Mechanically, the taxi man obeyed. As the cab moved forward, another car crossed its path. This was a roadster, that shot in from the right and turned left on the avenue. It was the same car that Chip had seen when he and Squint had ducked eastward on the side street.

As the taxi hurtled forward up the avenue, the roadster passed it, going down the other side of the broad thoroughfare. There were many intervening pillars; and The Shadow, settling in the cab, had not spied the roadster at the moment of its crossing. But those in the roadster saw The Shadow.

He was rising upon the rear seat of the taxi, ready when the driver swung left. From high above, he would be able to deliver bullets above the driver's head, once he might spy the crippled sedan upon the side street.

Instantly, the roadster changed its course. Its driver yanked the wheel. The trim car made a turn in the middle of the street, skidding between elevated pillars. It was a complete U turn, before the roadster reached the blockade of stalled cars on the avenue. The roadster was on the trail of The Shadow!

FIRST tokens of this new entrant came just before the taxi made the left turn at the corner. Shots rang out from behind. The Shadow was a black shape towering up from the topless cab. He darted a quick glance down the avenue. Two guns were belching from the very front of the pursuing roadster. Its windshield was down; the man beside the driver was handling two weapons. The Shadow was the target!

The cab was negotiating the left turn, directly under the elevated station. For the moment, The Shadow was protected from the fire in back. But a hoarse cry from the scared driver told that danger lay ahead.

"They're waiting for us!"

It was true. From the crossing, the taxi man could see the sedan. It had halted on the side street, fifty yards west of the corner. Halted, the car had swung across the street to block the thoroughfare. The side street was a trap.

It was too late to avoid the turn. The cab, moreover, needed distance, to get away from the pursuing roadster. The Shadow was trapped between two fires. With a competent driver, he could have counted upon mobility in battle. But his chance hackie was frantic. Fear alone impelled the driver to follow a last command:

"Straight down the side street!"

The hissed order came as the cab was directly in the center of the crossing. The driver stepped on the gas. The cab leaped forward. Then a ma-

chine gun began to rattle from the blockading sedan.

At the same instant, the pursuing roadster whizzed into view from the pillars at the avenue. The taxi driver saw the spurts of the machine gun. He glimpsed the lights of the roadster in his mirror. Wildly, he swung the cab to the curb and dived for the sidewalk.

The Shadow was no longer in view. Apparently, he had dropped to the floor of the cab. Koker, Pete and Skibo came piling forward, relying upon revolvers instead of the machine gun. They let the cab driver scurry away. They were out to get The Shadow.

They reached the cab and leaped upon the running board just as the roadster arrived and swung up beside the taxi. Glaring eyes looked from the roadster, as fists brandished guns. But the pursuing marksman and his chauffeur were treated to the same astonishing sight as Koker Hosch and the latter's pals.

The rear of the taxicab was empty!

Weirdly, The Shadow had eluded the trap. Somehow, he had made a complete evanishment. He had rescued Jennings and the patrolman from their dilemma; then had been forced into one of his own. But he was out of it; and those who had sought him independently were baffled!

SIRENS whined from the avenue. A snarl came from Koker. A fierce growl was given in the roadster by the marksman who sat beside the driver. Police cars were arriving. Crooks had failed to get The Shadow; it was their turn to be trapped.

The roadster hurtled forward. Its occupants had opportunity for a getaway and they took it. The speedy car careened to the sidewalk and squeezed past the deserted sedan. The motor roared as the two-man car sped westward. It had a chance to reach the next avenue before police arrived there.

Koker and his pals were left in a

jam. A patrol car came whining from the blocked avenue behind them. They turned to fight it out. Pete and Skibo opened fire. The police car halted; they sprang toward it, only to be felled by prompt bullets. Koker saw a chance for flight. He leaped to the wheel of the abandoned taxi.

Copying the example of the roadster, Koker jolted the cab past his abandoned sedan; then whizzed away to the west. The police car took up the chase. Pete and Skibo lay sprawled upon the street for others to pick up. More police arrived. Excitement followed, for nearly half an hour.

IT was after the street had cleared that a singular happening occurred at the crossing where the side street ran beneath the elevated station. The superstructure there was low; a traffic light hung from the heavy girders that supported a foot passage beneath the elevated tracks.

A taxi happened to cross the avenue. Like the one that The Shadow had commandeered, this cab was open-topped. It had no passengers; nevertheless, the driver was careful enough to slacken speed as he hit the jolty car tracks of the avenue.

To the hackie's surprise, the rear springs gave a sudden thump. It worried him; but he kept on slowly and decided that the cab was all right. Two blocks further on, he received another surprise. He was about to turn left from the westbound street when a quiet voice spoke from the back of the cab. "Take me to Times Square."

Looking about, the taxi driver saw that he had a passenger. They were near bright lights; in their glow he could see a tall, calm-faced personage riding in the car. The passenger was attired in evening clothes; he was smoking a thin cigar. His countenance was hawklike; his eyes carried a gleam.

When and how this stranger had boarded the cab, the hackie could not guess. He removed his hat and scratched his head; then reached over and pulled the metal flag to start the meter ticking.

A soft laugh came from the fixed lips of the mysterious passenger. The driver had not noticed folded garments of black that lay upon the seat beside the hawk-faced rider.

Only The Shadow knew the mystery of his own disappearance. Half an hour ago, he had ridden into a trap. He had seen it while his commandeered cab was making that left swing beneath the low structure of the elevated platform. The Shadow had given an order to his former taxi driver. Then he had sprung up from his standing position in the rear seat. He had caught the nearest girder beneath the elevated. He had swung to safety, a blackened, unseen shape, just before the roadster had whizzed leftward beneath him.

Thus had The Shadow changed the trap. He had known that the taxi driver would duck for safety. He had left criminals to the law. The police themselves were to blame for the escape of the roadster and the taxi flight of Koker.

Safely ensconced above the crossing, The Shadow had retained his perch until after excitement had died. Then he had waited for another open-topped cab. One had come along. He had taken it. He was riding serenely toward Times Square. To his credit he could charge the rescue of two doomed men: Luber Jennings and the patrolman who covered the beat along the avenue.

Yet The Shadow's laugh lacked mirth, and with good reason. Men of crime had escaped him to-night. Because of that, The Shadow could foresee new trouble. Not from Koker Hosch; The Shadow knew him to be nothing more than the leader of the cover-up crew.

The Shadow's concern involved the marksman who had ridden in the speedy roadster. That enemy, arrived so timely, was one who impressed him. The Shadow could see the menace of a superfoe—one who had been behind to-night's doings. More must be learned; for, later, there would be new and bitter conflict.

The Shadow was right. To-night's adventure had been but the preface to events that were due. Chance had brought The Shadow into a game that would become the strangest epoch in all his warfare against crime.

CHAPTER III.
CRIME'S NEW TRAIL.

It was dusk the next day. Two men were seated on opposite sides of an office desk. One was bald-headed, bespectacled Wainwright Barth. Barth was acting police commissioner in the absence from New York of Commissioner Ralph Weston. The other man was stocky, swarthy-faced.

He was Joe Cardona, crack ace detective of the New York force. Joe, at present, was an acting police inspector.

The air in the room held that electric quality that comes when two strong-willed men hold forth in argument. Barth had been raking Joe over the coals about the stick-up of Sautelle's wholesale clothing firm; and the street fight that followed. Cardona was restraining himself while the acting commissioner was pounding his fist and enumerating the crimes that had preceded the wholesale clothier's.

Barth roared out, "Two weeks ago a gold shipment, consigned to a bank, was landed from the steamship *Arabia*, and robbed from under the very noses of the guards on the dock! And not a clue to the theft!

"Three nights ago another crime was perpetrated! Securities valued at one hundred thousand dollars were stolen from the offices of Mullat & Co. by a man who posed as the Chicago partner of the firm—Herbert Threed! There hasn't been even a suspect arrested!

"And now this Sautelle stick-up, and the gun fray following! What have you found out, Cardona?"

Joe was uneasy. He wished Commissioner Weston were back, for Cardona understood Weston better than he did Barth. But he looked at Barth and said:

"We found out that Koker Hosch and a crew of gorillas were the ones who were in the sedan. Koker escaped, but one of his men, dying in the street, blabbed that Koker was to cover the stick-up at Sautelle's."

Barth leaned forward on his desk, his chin perched upon his hands.

"About the gun fray," he remarked. "Who began it? Who prevented the murder of Jennings and the patrolman?"

Cardona hesitated; then replied:

"The Shadow."

A glower from Barth. He drove a fist to the desk top.

"The Shadow!" he snorted. "More folderol, Cardona! Always The Shadow! When no other explanation seems plausible, you invariably resort to that one! Fiddlesticks! I can no longer tolerate such absurd conclusions!

"I've made up my mind that these crimes are linked," he decided, "and I still insist they cannot be termed as perfect ones. One link must be located; it may carry us along the chain. Find Koker Hosch, Cardona. Use your own measures. Spare no effort! A round-up of all criminals, if necessary. For the next forty-eight hours, you shall have *carte blanche*."

"You mean full leeway?"

"That expresses it quite aptly."

Joe Cardona wore a pleased smile when he left the acting commissioner's office. For once, he had arrived somewhere with Wainwright Barth. There was still a slim chance that Koker Hosch was in Manhattan. If not, other clues might come within the stipulated time limit. A round-up, however, was not in Cardona's plan. He preferred to utilize stool pigeons rather than the dragnet. Tipsters with information usually proved more efficient than a mass movement of the law. The latter gave crooks a chance to take to cover.

Koker Hosch! That name would be whispered in the bad lands; and soon listeners would be on hand to hear it. Stoolies might gain other tips as well. Cardona was inclined to Barth's theory, that these crimes were not perfect. The fact that they were linked was a discovery that Joe put to his own credit.

THERE was one place on the East Side that Joe Cardona would have liked to visit in person. That was the Hotel Spartan, a dingy-fronted hangout where crooks of known repute were wont to congregate. A visit there would have been a give-away, however. As bad a move for stoolies as for Cardona himself.

The windows of the Spartan's lobby opened upon a sidewalk beneath an elevated railway. Boastful rowdies—those who had covered themselves too well for the law to pluck—were among the strollers who went in and out of the Hotel Spartan. Frequently, their conversation continued after they had reached the sidewalk.

This evening, two such men were speaking. Their words were plain as they sauntered to the street. A wizened-faced man was lounging outside the doorway. He caught a snatch of the conversation.

"Well—if Koker Hosch is on the lam——"

"It makes Hunk Lomus likely, don't it?"

"An' you say Hunk's goin' out somewhere?"

"That's what was piped to me——"

The speakers had passed. The wizened-faced man waited a few minutes; then lighted a cigarette and shuffled across beneath the elevated. His wise lips showed a grin. This unnoticed listener was a well-known figure in the bad lands. Thugs called him "Hawkeye," for he had the peculiar ability of seeing much that went on about him.

Last night, Hawkeye had learned that Koker Hosch was going on a cover-up job. He had gained that information as last minute news; and Hawkeye had passed the word along to a hidden chief: The Shadow. To-night, Hawkeye had been hoping for another hit. He had gained one.

There were dozens of characters like Koker Hosch, still in Manhattan—small-time leaders who could summon a crew if needed. The question was which one to trail. Hawkeye had heard mention of "Hunk" Lomus. That was all Hawkeye needed. He was on his way to report.

Long before Joe Cardona's stoolies would be about their tasks, this chance tip would be known to The Shadow!

CHAPTER IV.
DESPITE THE SHADOW.

A BLUISH light was glowing upon the polished surface of a table. Beneath the glare, two hands were sliding earphones toward the wall. Upon one finger of the left hand glimmered a resplendent fire opal. This jewel was The Shadow's girasol.

The bluish light clicked off. Solid darkness pervaded the room. A cloak swished; lips formed a quivering laugh. Then silence held within the blackened sanctum. The Shadow had received final reports from his agents. He was leaving his secret abode.

Instructions had gone across the private wire from the sanctum. Word to Burbank, The Shadow's contact man. Detailed orders to be passed to roving aids. Crime was due to-night. Again, The Shadow had learned of a cover-up squad. This time, he had been able to form broader plans.

NEAR Seventy-second Street, a huddled watcher was looking toward a lighted corner. It was Hawkeye, covering an appointed spot. A taxi was cruising about the block. It was the same vehicle that The Shadow had used at last night's outset. It was manned by another aid: Moe Shrevnitz.

Parked elsewhere was a trim coupe, wherein a man sat low behind the wheel. This was Harry Vincent, most capable of The Shadow's agents. He was in readiness for any signal. Harry was watching Hawkeye. He strained, as he saw a blot of blackness pause by the doorway where the wizened-faced spotter crouched.

At the same instant, Hawkeye heard a whisper. Tensely, he listened. He knew that The Shadow had arrived.

"Instructions!" intoned the low voice. "Wait for Marsland. He will come by subway. Board the cab. Instructions to be given Shrevnitz: Follow the coupe and obey signals."

Hawkeye nodded, as blackness moved away. A blurred form took the momentary shape of a cloaked figure; then faded into new darkness.

In his coupe, Harry Vincent heard the door open. A blackened form settled beside him. The door closed. Harry caught the gleam of burning eyes. The Shadow had joined him.

Many details had been learned regarding Hunk Lomus, even though that rowdy had not been spied. Hawkeye had spotted members of Hunk's crew and had heard mention of two meeting places: first, a rendezvous at a Tenth Avenue garage; later, a coming contact with a second car at this corner near Seventy-second Street.

Time had not been mentioned. The Shadow had ordered Cliff Marsland, another aid, to cover the garage. Cliff had reported the arrival of four hoodlums; and their plans for prompt departure. The Shadow had calculated that nine o'clock would be the meeting hour of the two cars. Hunk Lomus would have two crews upon the job. The Shadow, to combat him, would be present with a quartet of agents.

To-night, The Shadow was banking upon Hunk Lomus to lead him unwittingly to a scene of coming crime. Koker Hosch had served that turn last night; but belated news had cost The Shadow opportunity. He had gained no time for a preliminary survey of the neighborhood. This time, matters would be different. The Shadow would reach the goal as soon as Hunk's double crew.

Yet, at this very moment, events were brewing elsewhere. Chance was destined to play The Shadow false.

TEN blocks distant from the corner where The Shadow waited, two men were crouched in the gloom of a passageway behind an old brownstone house.

One of the pair was Chip Mulley. Hoarsely, the round-shouldered crook was arguing matters with a bulky companion who was almost twice his size.

"Listen, Moose," Chip was saying. "It ain't my business to tell you how to work this lay. But you've got the dope sheet, an' it don't say nothin' about no stall."

"I'm waiting," growled "Moose." "Hunk Lomus is showing up to cover. He's taking the front—like Koker did for Squint."

"Yeah? An' look at the jam that Koker got himself in."

"What of it? Squint didn't lose nothing, did he?"

"He might 've. Koker wasn't needed. Havin' him there was Squint's idea. The Head didn't say to have Koker on the job. It ain't good business, this waitin' for Hunk an' his mob."

"Gimme a reason why not."

"That's easy. Supposin' Hunk Lomus spills somethin'—like sayin' he's a pal of Moose Sudling——"

"Hunk won't squawk on me."

"Well, supposin' then that The Shadow has got a lead on Hunk——"

"Lay off that stuff about The Shadow!"

"Gripes you, huh?"

Moose Sudling grunted an affirmative. A pause. Then a flashlight shone, guarded, upon a sheet of paper in Moose's hand.

"Goin' to start?" queried Chip.

"Yeah," decided Moose. "Sounds like you had the right idea, Chip. We'll let Hunk cover afterward. First thing on the list is this guy Percy Rydler, who lives in the old house. You saw him leave?"

"Yeah. An hour ago. They had to load him in a taxi, out of a wheel chair. Sick-looking gazebo."

"Then we're ready. Come along."

The two moved through the passage, Moose lumbering in advance. They came to a basement door. Moose's flashlight shone upon a formidable lock.

The big man produced a long key. He opened the heavy door with ease.

"A cinch!" whispered Moose. "The Head said it would work sure! How he got the key, I don't know. Ease the door shut, Chip."

Chip obeyed. Moose led the way to a flight of stairs. They ascended and stopped by a closed door. He ran the flashlight along the right edge; then jabbed a knife blade into the crack. A spring clicked. Moose reached farther down and repeated the operation. He moved to the left of the door and found two other springs.

"What's that for?" queried Chip.

"Some goofy automatic bolts," chuckled Moose. "They close from the other side. The Head gave me the dope on how to fix them. We don't need a key, now that's done."

Moose opened the door. He and Chip stepped into a darkened kitchen. Moose found a flight of stairs. The two ascended. They reached a hallway where a single light was burning. Moose whispered: "The rear room! That's where we'll find the old caretaker!"

Moose moved forward and entered. Chip was a few paces behind. As he crossed the sill, he heard a sharp cry from the other side. Then a hoarse snarl; followed by the noise of a sudden scuffle.

In the center of the rear room, two

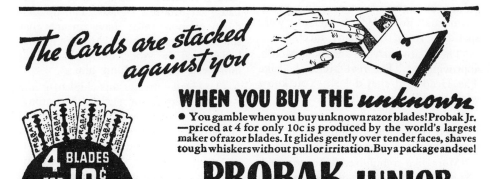

men were struggling. One was Moose Sudling, big and brawny, almost as large as the doorway through which he had entered from the hall. The other fighter was a wiry, white-haired man who clutched a gun. Frantically, he was striking at Moose's head; while the huge ruffian, bobbing, was clutching the old man's throat.

The struggle ended before Chip could join. The old man gurgled helplessly as his last wild stroke missed his adversary's skull. Moose drove the victim up against the wall. With one vicious heave, he battered the white head against the solid surface.

The old man sagged. Moose twisted the scrawny neck and gave another bashing stroke. He released his clutch and let the victim sprawl. Methodically, he pulled a paper from his pocket and consulted new instructions.

"Into the next room."

Moose led the way into the middle room. The flashlight shone upon a portrait that adorned the wall. Moose raised his left hand and pressed the gilt frame upward. A *click* sounded; the picture swung out upon a hinge. Behind it was a wall safe.

"Wait'll I read the combination."

Another glance at the dope sheet. Then Moose manipulated the knob. He opened the safe, found a long jewel box and brought it beneath his light. The top of the box popped open. Chip gulped at sight of glimmering gems. Diamonds, imbedded in velvet, were sparkling from their many facets.

"There's ice for you!" croaked Moose, approvingly. "The real McCoy! Like The Head said they'd be! You know what these'll bring, Chip?"

"Fifty grand?"

Awed, Chip was thinking about last night's haul. Moose laughed gruffly.

"More like a hundred," he affirmed. "And you can leave it to The Head to get rid of them."

MOOSE closed the safe and turned the dial. Clumsily, he wiped away finger prints. He swung the picture shut and mopped the lower frame. Followed by Chip, the big man moved back to the rear room. There he stopped to look at the white-haired figure on the floor.

"Looks like you croaked him, Moose," Chip said.

"Yeah." Again Moose mumbled. He fished out the paper from his pocket. "That means we gotta scram."

"The Head says so?"

"Yeah—here in the dope sheet. The Head didn't want me to croak this mug."

With disregard for silence, the pair made their way to the back stairs. They descended to the kitchen; then down to the basement. Moose made final consultation of the dope sheet; then extinguished his light altogether.

"Leave the door open," he whispered, as they moved out into the rear passage. "Take it slow after we get to the next street."

Passing between silent buildings, they gained the rear thoroughfare. Like Squint the night before, Moose led Chip toward a street lamp. There the big thug stopped and moved one hand up and down. That done, he urged Chip toward the next corner.

Looking over his shoulder as they turned, Chip spied the outline of a parked roadster. Some one in that car had seen Moose's signal. The up-and-down motion must have meant that something was wrong. Moose Sudling had gained the swag; but he had left a murdered victim behind him.

The Head—mysterious chief of crime —had prepared for such a happening. That was why the waiting roadster stood on duty. Measures would be taken to make up for Moose Sudling's blunder.

Again, burglary had been accomplished; this time it had produced murder. Moose Sudling's early action had

don't want to stop over, Jerry? It's a long ride up to Boston."

"I'll have to travel on, Hal," returned the driver. "Business appointments tomorrow. But I'm wondering if you'll find any one home

offset The Shadow's measures to be present before crime began.

Double crime had been completed despite The Shadow's knowledge that evil had been due to-night.

CHAPTER V.

FIGURES IN THE GLOOM.

AT the time when Moose Sudling and Chip Mulley were making their departure by the rear street, an automobile was halting in front of the brownstone house that they had left. The car bore a Massachusetts license. It had two young men as occupants.

"This is the house," remarked the man beside the driver. "Are you sure you

The old man gurgled helplessly as his last wild stroke missed his adversary's skull.

here. The house is dark. Maybe you'd better let me drive you to a hotel."

"Don't worry about me," laughed Hal. "I have a key to the place. My brother is always glad to have me stop off at the house. Percy is probably asleep. That's why the house is dark."

"But it's only nine o'clock——"

"And Percy sometimes goes to bed as early as eight. He's been sick, you know."

Hal Rydler stepped from the car. A street light showed his face to be a friendly one, smiling and well-featured. A crop of light-brown hair projected from beneath his side-tilted hat. Hal shook hands with Jerry. The Massachusetts car drew away.

Humming to himself, Hal ascended the brownstone steps. This visit was not an unusual one. Often before, Hal had dropped in to see his brother Percy. In fact, it was the frequency of his visits and the odd hours of arrival that had caused Percy to give him a duplicate pass-key.

To-day, in Baltimore, Hal had run into a friend, Jerry Lester, who was driving up to Boston. Hal had agreed to accompany Jerry as far as New York. Another chance to see how Percy was; for Hal was concerned about his sickly elder brother. Hal had left Baltimore before the afternoon mail delivery. Hence he had failed to receive a letter sent by Percy, stating that he was leaving for a steamship cruise.

Using his key, Hal unlocked the front door and stepped into the lower hallway. All was silent in the old house. Hal closed the front door quietly. He decided that Percy must be asleep; it would be unwise to awaken him. The best plan would be a silent ascent to the guest room on the third floor.

Hal started up by the front stairway. He reached a landing; there he paused. A flashlight was blinking from beyond a door that stood ajar. It was the door to the middle room on this floor. Hal noted a light from another doorway, which opened into the rear room. That glow was steady.

Something was wrong in the house. Hal's first worry concerned Percy. His brother occupied the front room. A semi-invalid, he would be unable to protect himself against thugs or burglars. As the flashlight blinked out, Hal decided to investigate.

Just as he was about to enter the middle room, he heard a sound that stopped him. The noise was a peculiar thump; it was repeated. Hal realized that he was listening to clumping footsteps. Some one had gone from the middle room to the back; that person was returning. Tensely, Hal waited.

Clump—clump—clump——

A figure suddenly blocked the opposite doorway; then shouldered into the middle room and paused. Against the light from the rear room, Hal could see the prowler. An instinctive dread seized him. He was staring at a distorted, evil shape that seemed hardly human.

The man in the middle room was short and chunky. His form was almost like a square. Thick, bulky arms and legs; a body that bulged like a barrel; hands encased in large, big-fingered gloves; and above the wide, straight shoulders a face that was hideous.

Sight of that visage made Hal Rydler remain where he was. One look had the same effect as if the young man had heard a rattlesnake's warning. The venom that showed in the prowler's glare seemed beyond human expression. Hal was watching the face of a living fiend.

The face was large, long-jowled and darkish. The nose was wide, with nostrils that spread with every breath. The eyes were glaring balls that bulged from their sockets. They were topped with bushy brows; above them loomed a high, broad forehead that was furrowed with V-like wrinkles. Jet-black hair, shaggy and unkempt, completed the living picture.

Clump—clump——

The monster was advancing, firm despite his clumsiness. Hal could hear fierce breathing that came from lips which formed a twisted leer. He saw the lips move as if mumbling. As they grinned grotesquely, white teeth shone like fangs. Horror held the watcher. Hal felt his knees quake, despite his efforts to fight down fear.

HAD this monstrous prowler kept on to the front doorway, Hal Rydler would have been paralyzed, unable to offer battle. However, the chunky figure changed its course. Away from the outlined light, the glaring man became no more than a square, wide shape that clumped with mechanical tread. He had turned toward the wall.

A flashlight glimmered from one gloved hand. Staring ·toward the focused glow, Hal saw the hinged picture on the wall. He watched the man's other hand press the panel. The picture swung out. The same hand turned the dial of the wall safe. Thanks to the light, Hal could see every subsequent move.

The gloating creature took nothing from the safe. He simply used his free hand to polish the interior, using his gloved fingers as a mop. The hand closed the safe, but did not lock it. The fingers simply swabbed the dial. Then the hand closed the picture and carefully wiped the frame.

The monstrous figure stamped toward the rear room. Hal noted that the man did not turn sharply. Instead, he clumped in circling fashion and thus arrived at the doorway. Again, the light was partially blocked. Gauging, Hal observed that the shoulders were almost as wide as the doorway itself.

A full three feet; yet the clumping man was less than five in height. Allowing for his large head, the rest of his shape—arms, body and legs—were almost an actual square, that fitted Hal's first impression. That was something to remember.

For Hal was sure that his brother's safe had been robbed; not by this monster, but by some one who had preceded him. The square-built fiend might furnish a clue, if captured. But Hal doubted his own ability to overpower so formidable a foe.

That bulky body had given an impression of superstrength. Hal feared, moreover, that the fiend was armed. It was not until the creature had marched mechanically from view that Hal gained the nerve needed for action. Despite the fact that he could not forget the venomous glare of the inhuman face, Hal steeled himself and started across the middle room.

The clumsy footsteps had faded when Hal reached the lighted door. The man had gone through the back room to the hall. The thumping tread told that he was descending the back stairs. Hal gave a leap, intending to overtake the monster. He knew that the fiend had not guessed that he was in the house. He saw opportunity in pursuit and a surprise attack. But as he reached the center of the rear room, Hal stopped short, quivering.

A body was lying upon the floor, face downward. White hair was clotted with blood.

"Jemley!" gasped Hal. "Jemley—dead!"

Hal knew old Jemley, the caretaker whom Percy hired to look after the house whenever he was absent. Jemley here was proof that Percy was away. But relief over his brother's safety was lost with Hal's discovery that Jemley had been slain.

"Jemley—murdered!"

WHAT to do?

The question gripped Hal as he let Jemley's head and shoulders settle to the floor. Justice was what Hal wanted —against that fiend and all who might have served him. The house was stilled; yet it seemed charged with the evil menace of the bestial figure that had just departed. Perhaps lurkers had remained here!

From downstairs, a clock was chiming nine. It was after that hour, Hal realized; for the old grandfather's clock was always a few minutes slow. Much had happened in the short while that Hal had been here. Much might happen yet, if he invoked the law. There was still a chance that the police could capture that square-shaped fiend, particularly since the monster had not known of Hal's presence and might, therefore, fear no pursuers.

The telephone was in the front room; but Hal's worry about possible lurkers restrained him from using it. He wanted to get out of the house at once; to take the front street to a lighted avenue. There he could find a patrolman and spread the news of Jemley's death.

THE HEAD

Rising, Hal crept from the death room and descended the front stairs. He opened the front door cautiously, closed it behind him and sprang down the brownstone steps. Excitedly, he started for the nearest corner, making long strides to increase his pace. Hal feared no danger; for he was sure that the clumpy fiend had gone out by the back door. Hence he did not try to render himself inconspicuous.

A touring car was rolling slowly from the avenue. Hal saw its dimmed headlights approaching; but gave no thought to them until the car suddenly shifted its direction. The lights brightened. Hal Rydler was caught in the brilliant glare. The flood of illumination awoke his thoughts of danger. With a sharp cry, the young man dived toward a wall, seeking the dark cover of some house steps.

Guns barked. Spurts of flame stabbed from the interior of the car. Bullets ricocheted from sidewalk and steps. The car lurched forward, to drive down upon its diving victim. New death was in the making. Hunk Lomus had arrived with part of his cover-up squad. Thugs were leaping from opened doors. Their plan was to blot out a helpless man in rapid style.

Then came another roar. A second car wheeled into view—a coupe with a searchlight that clicked on as the new machine approached. A fierce, weird laugh resounded with the echoes of the wild barrage that thugs had delivered. The boom of automatics followed.

Another combatant had arrived. One who had come to deal with men of crime. Again The Shadow was prepared to save a helpless man from doom!

CHAPTER VI.
THE LONE CLUE.

THE SHADOW had delivered a timely stroke. He had chosen the right moment to open fire. Had he started battle with the sound of the first barrage, Hunk Lomus and his men would have stayed within the shelter of their car. As it was, all of them had leaped to the street, with the exception of Hunk himself. Those on the street were targets. Hunk had the touring car to handle.

The Shadow had swung from the opened door of the coupe. His first cannonade began while he was riding closer. But as he neared the snarling thugs, he dropped to the sidewalk. Directly beneath a glowing lamp, he formed a silhouetted figure after the coupe rolled onward.

The Shadow had clipped the killer

who was nearest to Hal Rydler. The other three had wheeled. Their revolvers spoke as they saw The Shadow. Already, he was weaving from the light; for his purpose was accomplished. He had drawn the fire from the intended victim. As The Shadow faded, his big guns blasted anew. He, too, had located targets. His were standing ones.

Rooted thugs went sprawling, as they fired vainly. The Shadow's bullets found their marks. The slugs that came in his direction were spattering all about. Only Hunk Lomus had a chance to fire unmolested. He was past the steps where Hal Rydler crouched. Leaning back, Hunk loosed two shots.

Both were wide, for they were hurried and the touring car was moving. The bullets flattened against a brownstone wall. Hunk might have found his target with a third shot; but he was interrupted. Harry Vincent was on the job to take care of that.

Cutting sharply, Harry jammed the coupe against the touring car. Hunk yanked the wheel to avoid a smash. The front of the touring car jolted upward. The car tilted; then regained its balance on the sidewalk and rammed to a stop against a house wall. Harry had forced Hunk off the street.

Hunk still gripped his revolver, though he had grabbed the wheel with both hands. Savagely, he swung to aim for the driver of the coupe. Harry's car was at the left of Hunk's; and Harry had not drawn his own gun. But he was set for what was coming.

As Hunk aimed, Harry kicked the left door open and rolled out to the street. He hit the asphalt with his shoulder, came up with his left hand on the running board and drew an automatic with his right.

Hunk had started fire. His bullets were high. Harry thrust his gun upward and returned the shots. Entrenched below the step of his own car, he had the advantage. Though he fired

blindly, he scored a hit. A howl came from Hunk. Harry bobbed up beside the wheel of the coupe.

These events came as The Shadow finished fire. With them, a new glare bathed the street. Another car was roaring from the corner. Revolver muzzles were bristling from its sides. Hunk's second crew was charging into battle. Hoodlums began a long-range fire.

FORGETTING Hunk Lomus, Harry Vincent turned. There, in the glare, he saw The Shadow, squarely in the middle of the street. About the cloaked fighter lay the thugs whom he had downed. Crippled crooks were crawling toward the curb. But The Shadow was faced with new enemies; and he had no time to head for shelter.

Harry aimed, to join The Shadow in what seemed hopeless resistance. The Shadow's automatics were already booming. Harry aimed squarely for the lights ahead, just as The Shadow performed a sudden shift to the right. Then the oncoming car skidded. Its right wheels jounced the curb. The car careened; then swung half about as it came to a stop.

The Shadow had aimed for the side of the windshield. He had guessed that the car would be equipped with shatterproof glass, so he had picked the edge of the opened front window. He had winged the driver. The fellow had lost control; but had managed to apply the foot-brake. The Shadow's hope had been to wreck the car; though he had not accomplished it, he had broken the attack.

The jouncing thugs had lost all chance at aim. One crook, unlimbering a machine gun, had half fallen from an open door. Others were grabbing him; but they acted too late. The Shadow delivered a final shot. The machine gunner took a headlong dive to the gutter and his weapon clattered with him.

New brakes screeched. A taxi had wheeled up behind the thug-manned car. Two fighters sprang from it: Cliff and Hawkeye. They fired from the darkness of the street. Crooks leaped out to battle when they found themselves trapped. The Shadow and his agents had the edge. Hoodlums withered.

A man sprang suddenly from a spot across the street. It was Hal Rydler. He had seen Harry beside the coupe. He knew that this fighter must be a friend. Harry beckoned Hal forward. He saw the rescued man stop short; then give a cry. The reason dawned instantly. Harry spun about.

He had forgotten Hunk Lomus. Though wounded, the rogue was still capable of action. He had crawled from the wheel of his own car. He had shifted into Harry's coupe. Gun in hand, Hunk had seen Hal coming. He was aiming to down the victim before Harry knew it.

Harry made a grab for Hunk's right arm. As he nailed the wrist above the aiming hand, a shot roared from the center of the street. Hunk's arm sagged in Harry's grip. The trigger finger pulled; the muzzle, dropping, blasted a useless bullet to the asphalt. Hunk rolled out of the coupe.

The Shadow, like Harry, had heard Hal's cry. Swinging about, the cloaked fighter had picked off Hunk while Harry was trying to stop the mob-leader's shot.

Hal stumbled up to where Harry stood. A moment later, a machine wheeled forward. Moe Shrevnitz had swung up with his cab.

SIRENS were sounding, as a sequel to the cessation of gunfire. Shrill whistles could be heard from the avenue. Police were converging. It was time to leave the field to the law.

Harry heard The Shadow's voice hiss an order. The cloaked chief had arrived beside him. Nodding, Harry shoved Hal Rydler into the taxi. Moe had opened the door in readiness. As Harry slammed it, the cab rocketed forward.

Cliff and Hawkeye arrived. They heard The Shadow's next order. They sprang aboard with Harry. The coupe followed the path that Moe had taken. The cab had already turned the corner when the coupe started. The Shadow, silent, remained by Hunk's touring car and watched the coupe whizz from sight.

Sirens were closer. Their location was elusive; for they were coming from various directions. Listening, The Shadow stepped close to the dark side of the touring car. He had spied a man rising from a spot across the street. It was one of Hunk's wounded underlings.

This hoodlum was still capable of battle; but The Shadow could easily have dropped him, for the man had not seen the waiting figure in the darkness beside the car. Instead, The Shadow stood silent. He watched the thug come to the spot where Hunk Lomus lay, a dozen feet away.

"Hunk!" The thug exclaimed the name hoarsely. He crouched beside Lomus. "Did De Shadow get you? Like he did de odders?"

The Shadow heard a snarl from Hunk's lips.

"Dis is Louie," persisted the stooping thug. "You can hear me, can't you, Hunk? Listen: de bulls is comin'; I gotta scram! Anyt'ing you want me to do?"

Hunk's head had raised feebly. He uttered a name that Louie repeated; but The Shadow did not hear it. A police car had entered the street. The wail of a siren had drowned the spoken words. Then came Louie's hurried question.

"But if dere ain't no way to find him, Hunk?"

Again Hunk spoke, gasping. His

head dropped. The Shadow saw Louis nod.

"I get it, Hunk. Sure—I'll get aholt of Chip Mulley. I'll tell him you wanted me to pipe de word to——"

Louie stopped before he again spoke the name that Hunk had previously uttered. The police car was bearing down upon him. For the first time, he realized its closeness. Louie snarled and came to his feet. His left arm, wounded, was hanging limp; but he raised his right and aimed with a revolver.

The police car had veered, to avoid a sprawled body. Its light had swung away from The Shadow. The cloaked watcher raised an automatic, ready to drop Louie before the thug could fire. The Shadow's action proved unnecessary. Revolvers tongued flame from the patrol car. Louie sprawled across Hunk's body.

Hunk Lomus had given his last gasp. Louie was coughing out his life as two officers sprang to the street.

The Shadow edged past the touring car. Rounding the back, he quickly gained a passage between two darkened houses. He had reserved that outlet for a last-minute exit. It was time for prompt departure. Running bluecoats were coming down the street. Other police were arriving in a second patrol car.

Though The Shadow had lingered, he had experienced less trouble in departure than had his agents. Moe's cab and Harry's coupe had been forced to run the gantlet of arriving police cars. Moe had swung into a side street, to continue slowly; while Harry had sped along an avenue, to finally draw away from the police zone.

Moe had chosen canny flight because of his passenger. As he wheeled along the side street, he kept looking in the mirror. He saw Hal Rydler deep in the rear seat, relaxing after the excitement. Moe grinned. He knew that his passen-

ger thought this cab was a chance one. Soon, Moe would circuit to the corner back near Seventy-second Street. The Shadow would be there.

But as Moe swung out to an avenue, he saw an approaching patrol car. He knew at once that he would be questioned, if he stopped. Moe stepped on the gas and roared down another street. He heard shots behind him; but they were no more annoying than a flock of mosquitoes. Moe was a smart driver. He expected to leave the police car far behind.

Zipping through another side street, Moe suddenly jammed the brakes. Straight ahead, he saw a blockade. The street was under construction. Moe turned about. Regardless of the curb, he backed the cab clear up on the sidewalk and thumped a house wall. Then he jolted forward, reached a corner and whirled right, just as the patrol car's headlights gleamed from a block away.

More twists and turns. Moe paid no attention to the mirror. He was dodging out of the region where too many questions might be asked. He grinned, as he arrived close to the corner where he expected The Shadow to be. Moe applied the brakes. He looked in the mirror and his grin ended.

His passenger had left the cab.

Recalling circumstances, Moe remembered how and where the man must have departed: at the blockade, when Moe had backed the car upon the sidewalk. That was where the rescued man had decided to decamp.

A voice spoke from beside the cab: "Report!"

Moe winced as he heard The Shadow's fierce whisper. Disgruntled, he told his story. He had not even talked to the rescued man. He did not know the fellow's name; nor where he wanted to go.

When Moe had concluded, The Shadow spoke again from the darkness: "Off duty!"

Moe drove away, sluggish and de-jected. The Shadow remained, his tall form barely discernible in the dull light of the street. A mirthless whisper came from his hidden lips. The Shadow had wanted to talk with Hal Rydler; to learn the man's name and all that he could furnish in the way of clues. That chance was gone. Again, The Shadow had lost an opportunity to gain a lead to the actual crime which an outside crew had covered.

Yet The Shadow had found one lone clue; and he was banking on it. He had heard the mention of a name: Chip Mulley. Before long, The Shadow would find the owner of that name. Then would his trail begin.

CHAPTER VII.
CHIP MEETS A PAL.

TWENTY-FOUR hours had passed. The bad lands were agog. Late news of crime had created a huge stir in the un-derworld. The grapevine was alive with rumors. So many tales had passed along the invisible telegraph that crooks were leery of every new one.

Boiled down, the facts were simple. A job had been done at the home of Percy Rydler. Diamonds, valued at one hundred thousand dollars, were missing. Burglars had found a way in; they had opened a safe to take the gems; they had left a dead man on the premises— a caretaker named Jemley.

It was murder. More serious than other recent robberies. Yet the law was as baffled as before. Percy Rydler had gone on a cruise ship. Contacted by radio, he had sent back word that dou-bled the bewilderment. He could not imagine how the crooks had learned of the gems, or had gained the combina-tion.

There had been a battle after the burglary. That news, particularly, con-cerned the underworld. Hunk Lomus,

like Koker Hosch, had found trouble. But Hunk had not escaped in Koker's fashion. Hunk had taken the bump. The underworld knew who had spelled Hunk's finish.

The Shadow!

The dreaded name was whispered everywhere. Gangland feared the menace of its greatest scourge. Some smooth supercrook was staging cunning crimes; The Shadow had as yet been unable to forestall that mastermind of evil. But in the meantime, The Shadow was roving wide, picking off lesser rogues in an endeavor to reach the big-shot.

That was why the small-fry worried. Any of them might be next.

Who was The Shadow's adversary?

That was the question that puzzled scumland. It produced vague theories throughout the underworld. Four ma-jor crimes had been accomplished by a hidden perpetrator: the gold snatched from the steamship *Arabia;* the secur-ities stolen from Mullat & Co.; the money grabbed from Sautelle's secluded office, and, finally, last night's theft of Percy Rydler's diamonds.

A crime master had amassed a har-vest, without leaving a single clue. Un-questionably, he had gained his spoils through the aid of competent workers. Every crime bore the earmarks of an underworld job. But who were the men that this supercrook had employed?

None could give the answer. Koker Hosch and Hunk Lomus were classed as mere outside workers. One had fled; the other was dead. But neither had been in the know.

Nevertheless, rumor mongers of the underworld could foresee a shift in tac-tics on the part of the unknown big shot. The Shadow had entered the game with a vengeance. No supercrook, no matter how confident, could afford to disregard the menace of the cloaked fighter who could bob up from nowhere.

AMONG the gathering places in the bad lands, "Red Mike's" formed a most notorious hangout. Red Mike's was located close to the Hudson River, in the district known as "Hell's Kitchen." The dive was on a second floor, above a dirty restaurant; it was named after the proprietor, a rowdy called "Red Mike."

The police had their eye on Red Mike's; thus no recognized underworld members hung out there.

On this particular night, the dive was filled with small fry only. Red Mike, himself, was on the job, keeping an eye upon all who entered. If stoolies were present, they were welcome. Rumors —and unlikely ones—were all that they would hear at Red Mike's.

Off from the main part of the dive was a smaller room that formed a passage to the side exit. This room was reserved for the select few whom Red Mike trusted. A solitary rowdy was in the room to-night. He was crouched at a table, nursing a bottle of grog and keeping wary watch toward the half-opened door that led into the main room. The lone hoodlum was Chip Mulley.

No rumors had involved Chip. He had chosen the side room on the pretext that there were too many bums in the main joint. Red Mike had accepted the explanation. Chip, nervous at first, had become quite at home in the little room. He could hear the buzz from beyond the door. Pushing aside a bottle and glass, he arose from the table and strolled toward the main room.

Just as he reached the threshold, Chip heard a sound behind him. He wheeled about. His face showed startlement; then regained its half grin. Chip recognized the tall, stoop-shouldered arrival who had entered from the side passage. He waved a greeting and came back to the table.

"H'lo, Beak!" expressed Chip. "Squat an' help yourself to a slug outta the bottle!"

The arrival nodded. He sat down, poured himself a drink and raised the glass. He stopped to look at Chip; then clamped down the glass without drinking. Chip's face showed puzzlement.

"The drink can wait," decided Beak, gruffly. "There's something I want to talk about, Chip. That's why I came up here."

Chip eyed Beak warily. The pair had been pals long ago; they had remained friends when they split. Chip Mulley and Beak Thungle had found different lines of crime.

Like Chip, Beak had an appropriate nickname. His face, otherwise flat, was distinguished by an overlarge nose. His eyes were deep-set; he kept them half closed as he looked toward Chip. The latter remembered that habit of Beak's.

"What's it about?"

Chip's query was hoarse. Beak gestured with his right hand, up and down, to quiet his old pal's nerves.

"Just something that was spilled to me," he informed. "By a bimbo that we both used to know."

"When, Beak?"

"A coupla days ago."

Chip remembered something.

"Say, Beak," he remarked, "I t'ought you was laid up. Heard you was crip-

pled in that fight with the bulls, down at the Black Ship——"

"I was," interposed Beak, harshly. "I was flat on my back in my room at the Hotel Spartan when this bird came to see me."

"Who was it?"

Beak eyed Chip carefully. Then he spoke:

"Hunk Lomus."

Chip's pursed lips twitched at mention of the dead mob leader. Beak gave a hoarse guffaw; then leaned forward and whispered hoarsely.

"Don't let it give you the jitters," he confided. "I ain't been piping what Hunk told me. Keep your shirt on, Chip."

Chip quelled his nervousness.

"What Hunk said was this," resumed Beak. "He was going out on a cover-up job; but he wouldn't tell me who for. I didn't want to ask him, anyway, because I knowed it was confidential. Hunk figured there was other jobs coming, savvy?

"That's why he wanted me to be ready. The last thing he says—all of a sudden like—was that if I heard from you, it would be O. K. Said you was working with the same guy that he was. Then Hunk goes and gets croaked."

Beak guffawed sourly, in remembrance of Hunk. Chip watched his old pal finger the glass. Beak became silent, as if expecting Chip to speak. Chip's nervousness returned during the pause. Suddenly, he began to pour out words.

"You're a pal, Beak," piped Chip. "That's why I can talk to you, seein' as how Hunk told you some of it. I ain't had nobody to talk to, since last night. It's made me jittery, Hunk being croaked!"

Beak Thungle nodded, in rough sympathy.

"It's screwy!" continued Chip. "The whole thing—right from the beginning.

Hunk didn't know the real lay; he was just on the outside. There ain't many guys that would believe this goofy business, Beak. That's why it's got me talkin' to myself. But you know I ain't off my nut—you'll listen——"

Beak nodded again, as Chip paused. Chip licked his lips, picked up the glass that Beak had discarded. He gulped a drink; then resumed.

"It began with Pinky Garson," he whispered. "You know Pinky. Him an' me was pals. Pinky's took it on the lam; he's got his outta the racket. So it don't matter if I mention him. Anyway, first Pinky comes to me. Says he wants me to take a trip with him."

"Where to?"

"I don't know. I went with Pinky; but it was night an' he drove all over the map. Anyway, we come into the cellar of some house, outside of New York, an' Pinky takes me upstairs. We go into a room; an' that's where I sees The Head."

"The Head?"

Chip nodded.

"Whatta ya mean?" queried Beak. "Is that some fancy moniker they tacked on a guy? Calling him The Head because he's a big-shot?"

Chip shook his head. He tightened his grip on the glass.

"It wasn't no guy we saw. It was a head, Beak! A livin' head, sittin' in a square box, with the front open! On top of a table——"

Beak's eyes narrowed. Chip paused; then continued:

"It's straight, Beak! It sounds screwy; but it's real! It was a head that I saw. Only I wasn't there to see it. The Head wanted to see me. That's why Pinky took me."

Beak's eyes turned toward the half-emptied bottle. He was gauging how much Chip had drunk.

"I ain't been hittin' the bottle, Beak," protested Chip. "I ain't had the rams. I ain't cracked, neither. Listen; Pinky

Garson was takin' on a job an' The Head had told him what to do. He needed a guy to help him——"

"Yeah?" Beak laughed, gruffly. "So The Head talked, did it?"

Chip nodded.

"That's what it did," he expressed in an awed tone. "It tells Pinky all about a bird named Herbert Threed, that was to have some stocks passed to him, in an office. Pinky brings me back to New York. We go to the buildin' an' we grab the elevator man. It was night —only one guy on the job.

"I run the elevator, while Pinky passes himself as Threed. We gets the swag an' beats it. Pinky was headin' out of New York anyway. So he kept on goin'. Tells me I'll hear from The Head—through somebody else."

"Who was that?"

"It was Squint Proddock."

"What job did he pull? That one at Sautelle's?"

Chip nodded. He was feeling steadier through this chat with an old pal. He explained further.

"Squint had Koker Hosch there," sad Chip. "To cover up, see? Because Squint was goin' to send Koker along to see The Head. But Koker gets in a jam; he takes it on the lam. So Squint had to pick another guy."

"Who'd he pick?"

"Moose Sudling. An' Moose uses me, like Pinky an' Squint had done. Moose an' me stages the job last night at Rydler's. It was Moose who croaked the old guy."

"And Moose had Hunk Lomus on the outside?"

"Yeah. The same as Squint had Koker. Hunk was supposed to be the next in line. But he got bumped. There ain't no tellin' who'll be next. Squint will have to name another guy."

"Why Squint? It ought to be Moose's turn."

"Moose is out. He's on the lam be- cause he croaked that caretaker at Rydler's. It goes back to Squint. He's still in town. Where, I don't know. But, listen, Beak. Any job that The Head stages is a pip. It's his brain runs it, all the way through."

"He needs somebody to swing the job, though. Like Pinky, or Squint——"

"Or Moose. Sure. But they don't have to use the bean. The Head gives 'em all the dope. They put it down on paper. Where to be an' when. What to do. It runs like a clock! Every job is a set-up——"

Beak Thungle was looking past Chip Mulley, toward the half-opened door to the main dive. Beak could see men seated at tables beyond the doorway. Buzzing chatter and raucous guffaws were coming from the smoke-filled hang- out. Beak gripped Chip's arm in inter- ruption.

"Listen, Chip," said Beak, in a low tone. "This ain't no spot to do too much talking. This is great stuff you've spilled! I want to hear more of it. Somewhere else, though."

"Sure. That's a good idea."

"I'm going out by the side way. You stay here. Finish a couple of drinks; then go out through the main room. I'll be in there, but don't say nothing to me. Maybe a hello, if I holler to you—but go on out, right after. Head over toward the Black Ship. I'll come along later."

CHIP nodded. Beak arose and strolled out by the side door. Chip gulped the remainder of his drink. He made an- other reach for the bottle. Just then, the door from the main room swung wide. A tall, stoop-shouldered rowdy came stumbling inward. He guffawed a greeting:

"Hello, Chip! How're you, pal? Red Mike says you were in here——"

Chip Mulley gazed, rigid. The man who had entered from the main room was the very one who had left, only a minute before, by the side door! He was staring at the face of Beak Thungle!

"Whassa matter, Chip?" Beak plopped at the table. Chip saw that he had been drinking heavily. "Say— you look like you was seein' things! Whatta ya been doin'—talkin' to The Shadow?"

Beak guffawed as if his remark had been an apt jest. He reached for Chip's bottle, raised it and took a long swig. He sprawled half across the table and chortled again, in maudlin manner.

"Thassa good one!" croaked Beak. "Chip Mulley been talking to The Shadow! Thass another good one for the grapevine! Like the rest of the hokum they've been piping!"

Chip heard no more. He had risen; he was stumbling toward the door to the main room. He reached his objective; quivering, he faltered to a table, amid groups of riotous hoodlums. Terror had seized the chipmunk-faced crook. He had encountered two Beak Thungles: one false, the other actual.

He knew why the first had gone so suddenly, with suggestion for a later conference. The first Beak had been looking out into the main room. He had seen the second Beak enter. The first Beak Thungle was the pretender; and he was the one whom Chip had spilled the secret news.

But the second Beak Thungle had unwittingly supplied the answer. His drunken jest had hit the truth. His face distorted with fear, Chip Mulley realized the true identity of the person who had played Beak's role.

Chip Mulley knew that he had talked with The Shadow!

CHAPTER VIII.

TWO APPOINTMENTS.

THE underworld was not the only portion of New York that buzzed with news of crime. At the very hour when Chip Mulley had guessed his own mis-take, persons elsewhere were discussing the robbery of last night. Two, in particular, were finding such conversation important.

One was Hal Rydler. His companion was a woman a few years older than himself, although her artful make-up gave her a younger appearance. The woman was Adele Rayhew; until a few months ago, she had been engaged to Hal's brother Percy. This evening, Hal had called Adele and invited her to dinner.

They were finishing their meal, in the roof garden of a swanky New York hotel. Their corner table was a secluded one; near-by diners had departed. Adele decided that she could speak in confidence to Hal.

"Nice of you to take me to dinner, Hal," remarked the girl. "I was afraid you would be prejudiced because I broke my engagement to your brother. Percy was very much upset about it. But, really, Hal, it could not be helped——"

Hal made no comment. He had a reason for his silence; and his meeting with Adele Rayhew was part of it.

"I could help Percy," the girl was saying. "Really, Hal, I could. But I'm sailing for Europe day after to-morrow, and all the packing that must be done to-morrow——"

"Wait a moment." Hal had found the opportunity he wanted. "You say that you could help Percy. I suppose you mean that you might find a way to recover the stolen diamonds. Am I right?"

Adele nodded, slowly.

"I know why you say that," continued Hal. "About six months ago, some jewels of your own were stolen. You regained them, didn't you?"

Again a nod. Adele's face was troubled.

"As I recall it," persisted Hal, "you hired a private detective. He visited a servant who had once been in your employ. The ex-servant had the gems. He handed them over."

Adele made no reply. Her silence indicated, however, that Hal's account was a correct one.

"That was an inside job," remarked Hal. "This robbery was not. Why do you still think that Percy's diamonds might be reclaimed?"

Adele started to speak; then bit her lips. She looked across the table and saw a steady expression in Hal's eyes. Alede's gaze dropped. When she spoke, her voice trembled.

"It—it was a very odd circumstance," she said—"the one that enabled me to recover my gems. Months ago, I heard of something spooky—something so ridiculous that I laughed at it. I couldn't bring myself to believe in spirits. But when I heard that this was something

scientific, I went to it. A friend took me there."

"A spirit seance?"

"No. An oracle."

"An oracle? What do you mean?"

"An old professor owns the Oracle, Hal. His name is Professor Caglio. He lives near the town of Littenden, in New Jersey. In the strangest sort of a house."

"Littenden," mused Hal. "I know where it is. Only twenty miles from Newark. Yet it is wild country thereabouts."

"Professor Caglio has a house with no windows," explained Adele. "In it is a weird room, with many strange mechanical figures. One of them is the Oracle. It is a head that talks."

"A living head?"

"It seems to be alive. But the pro-

fessor says it is purely a mechanical creation, endowed with human wisdom. He calls The Head by an odd name that begins with Z. I think I can remember it—yes, the name of The Head is Zovex."

Hal laughed.

"What does The Head do?" he queried. "Sing songs and tell fortunes? You can't cross its palm with silver. What do you do—hand money to Professor Caglio?"

"You must be serious, Hal," implored Adele.

"Of course! Tell me more about Zovex."

"I asked questions of the Oracle. It answered them, very wisely. The Oracle told me where my stolen jewels could be found. My gems were worth almost four thousand dollars, Hal. The detective that I hired did just as I told him. He went to Logan's home—Logan was the servant whom I had discharged—and threatened him with arrest. Logan gave back the jewels."

"And how much did you have to pay Zovex? Or the owner of the Oracle, Professor Caglio?"

"Not a cent. Professor Caglio does not need money, Hal. He is a scientist. He has invented a great many worthwhile things——"

"Including the talking head." Hal chuckled. "Well, Adele, the next step is to visit Professor Caglio and see what Zovex has to say about Percy's diamonds. Maybe The Head will make another lucky stab."

"It is not luck, Hal. Really, the Oracle is uncanny! But I am afraid that it will speak no longer."

"Why not?"

"I was the last person to consult it. All the others—my friends—had left New York. The Oracle advised all of them. It told me that my trip to Europe would be wise. In fact, I should have left two weeks ago, according to the Oracle's statement."

"I see. If you went out to Caglio's to-morrow, he might not like it? That is, The Head might be angry?"

Adele nodded.

"Zovex gives no new advice to those who do not follow the old," she said, as though repeating words that The Head itself had once uttered. "So I can not very well visit the Oracle until after I return from Europe."

"But you can send some one to see Zovex?"

"I believe so. I was taken there by friends. I suppose I would have the privilege of recommending another visitor."

"That settles it. When we go down to the hotel lobby, Adele, you can write a letter of introduction. One that I can take out to Professor Caglio."

"But the note will show that I remained in New York——

"Not at all. You can date it more than two weeks ago."

"Then Caglio will wonder why you did not come earlier——"

"Why should he? I shall tell him that I live in Baltimore, and that this was my first trip to New York since I received the letter. Moreover, I shall explain that it is the first time that I have needed advice from Zovex."

ONE hour later, Hal Rydler arrived at his hotel, after taking Adele Rayhew to her apartment. In his pocket, he carried a note that the girl had written. That note would serve as his passport to visit Professor Caglio. It was too late to make the trip to-night. Hal planned it for the morrow.

Incredible though the girl's story had been, Hal had been impressed. He had remembered the mystery of the gems which Adele had recovered. This was the first time that he had ever heard the explanation. Adele had added some further details regarding Professor Caglio's strange abode. Her statements had whetted his interests more than before.

It would be a long-shot gamble, perhaps; but the visit seemed worth-while. It appealed to Hall's love of adventure; and this curious talk of an Oracle seemed to fit with strange circumstances that Hal had already experienced. He had not forgotten that heavy, clumping prowler whom he had observed at the scene of the murder in his brother's house.

Not long after Hal Rydler had strolled to his hotel, another man began a journey along a New York street. This was Chip Mulley, departing from Red Mike's. The crouchy crook had lingered long at the dive. He had made one trip into the side room, in an effort to talk with Beak Thungle. He had found his old pal in a drunken stupor; failing to rouse Beak, Chip had decided to depart alone.

Every corner made Chip shudder. Furtively, the scared crook kept staring at spots of blackness, expecting one to come to life. He had talked with The Shadow! He could picture that dread avenger no longer posing as Beak Thungle. The Shadow—a figure of blackness!

Past one corner, Chip faltered. He saw thick gloom that looked almost like a living shape. Hurriedly, he staggered onward and dived from view beyond a corner. A moment later, the blackness moved. Chip's fear had at last been justified. It was The Shadow!

Chip's affrighted gait had been a giveaway. The Shadow knew that the furtive crook had seen the real Beak Thungle too soon. The Shadow had a remedy. He moved to a spot where a cab was parked. He whispered instructions from the darkness beside the taxi. The cab rolled away. It took the corner that Chip had turned.

The cab passed the hurrying crook and turned another corner. There, a man dropped out. As Chip neared the corner, the man came into view. Chip saw him and stopped. Sight of a square, well-chiseled face gave him a feeling of assurance.

"Cliff Marsland!"

The square-jawed man heard Chip's greeting. He recognized the nervous crook. That was not surprising. Both were known in the underworld.

"Hello, Chip!" returned Cliff. "Where are you heading? Over toward the Black Ship?"

"Yeah." Chip stopped suddenly. "No—I'm only goin' part way there, Cliff. Say—if you're goin' along——"

"What's the matter, Chip? You look jittery. Guess you're like a lot of others I've run into to-night. Been hearing too much chatter about The Shadow."

Chip quivered as he sidled along the street at Cliff's side.

"He's one mug I'd like to meet!" continued Cliff harshly. "The Shadow! I'm gunning for that phony!"

Chip's eyes widened. He remembered that Cliff Marsland had formerly bragged of being on The Shadow's trail. Others had boasted of such a mission; they had not long survived. When Chip came to consider it, he realized that Cliff was the only man who had frequently repeated such a claim.

"You think I'm kidding?" queried Cliff, as he looked at the shuffler beside him. "If you do, take another think. It isn't healthy to kid about The Shadow. Plenty of wise guys have found that out when they stopped bullets from those smoke-wagons that The Shadow handles.

"But I've got the Indian sign on The Shadow. I clipped him a couple of times, in fight. I'm one bimbo that he doesn't like to tackle. I'm ready to take a shot at him any time! But how can anybody find him? I'm likely to croak of old age before he shows up again where I am.

"I've tried to find guys that The

HAL RYDLER
who seeks advice
from Zovex, the
talking head.

Shadow is after. I've found them—yes—but The Shadow has always met up with them ahead of me. They've been lying cold, full of lead when I've come across them. The trouble is, most guys are afraid to talk when they think The Shadow is tailing them. I don't blame them; but if they'd talk to the right guy, they might live longer. And I'm the right guy!"

THEY had reached a street that led to the Black Ship. Cliff turned to head in that direction. Chip clutched him by the arm.

"Stick with me, Cliff!" he pleaded, hoarsely. "I got somethin' to spill to you—about The Shadow!"

"You have?" queried Cliff, eagerly. "Spill it!"

"I can't pipe it here, Cliff. Listen; I've got a hide-out down the line. Let's slide in there."

They followed a side street and reached an alley. Chip darted a worried glance behind him; then took to the alley, with Cliff beside him. Chip unlocked the battered door of a dingy-fronted building. He and Cliff entered. The door closed.

A soft laugh whispered from darkness near the corner. A cloaked form moved away. The Shadow had followed. He had seen results. His role of Beak Thungle was through. He had deputed Cliff Marsland to keep further contact with Chip Mulley.

Through that move, The Shadow could hope to find a trail. Soon, perhaps, he would reach that mysterious adversary whom Chip had termed "The Head." The Shadow was seeking to solve the riddle of the master brain that guided evil.

In his present course, however, The Shadow had dropped Hal Rydler as a factor. He believed that the rescued man was by this time far from danger. The Shadow had missed a possibility. He did not know that Hal had already gained the vital news and was planning a visit to The Head.

The future held a menace that The Shadow had not foreseen.

IT was one night later.

Cliff Marsland, solid and noncommittal, was slouched in a battered, broken-down chair. Chip Mulley, pale and nervous, was perched upon a stool across the room.

The two had been in Chip's hide-out for nearly twenty-four hours.

"Nine o'clock," growled Cliff, suddenly. "What's the idea? You tell me you're gonna hear from Squint Proddock, and we ain't heard a word all day. I think you're stallin'!"

"It ain't no stall, Cliff," protested Chip, with a whine. "Honest it ain't! I'm due to hear from Squint any time. That's what I got the phone here for."

Cliff eyed the telephone, resting on a soap box in a corner. It looked out of place in this dirty, ratty hide-out of Chip's.

Cliff was anxious for Squint's phone call for another reason other than Chip's. Chip wanted to tell Squint of the masquerade of The Shadow as Beak Thungle. Cliff wanted to make contact with Squint and get a line on The Head's hide-out. He had talked Chip into putting in a good word for him with Squint; and hoped to get in his gang.

Using the pretext of getting cigarettes, Cliff had slipped out of the room a few times in the twenty-four hours he had been there and contacted The Shadow and informed him of progress.

THERE came the dull ringing of the telephone bell. Chip jumped to the soap box.

"Hello. . . ." Chip had raised the receiver. "Hello, Squint. This is Chip. . . . Yeah. Been here since last night. Cliff Marsland is with me. . . . He's a right guy and I put him in the know. . . ."

"Let me talk to Squint."

Cliff took the telephone from Chip's hands.

"Hello, Squint! This is Cliff Marsland. . . . I pulled Chip out of a jam last night. Chip met the Shadow. He thought The Shadow was Beak Thungle. Chip talked too much. Told him about The Head."

An oath reached Cliff's ears.

"Now I got an idea, Squint. I'm one guy that can handle The Shadow. But I can't find him. Chip says The Head knows everything. Maybe he'll have a way to spot him. Chip says you'll fix it for me to meet The Head. What about it?"

There was a pause. Squint knew Cliff's reputation as a guy who wanted to get The Shadow and wasn't afraid. Then Squint spoke.

"It sounds jake, Cliff," was the word. "I'm in Jersey City now. You beat it right away and meet me at Duke's Tavern, outside of Newark. Tell Chip to scram."

"O. K., Squint. I'll get goin' right away!"

Cliff hung up the receiver, told Chip what Squint had said. The Shadow's agent picked up his hat, waved a farewell to Chip and left the hide-out.

A few moments after Cliff's departure, the barrier to the room opened. There was a figure on the threshold. Flickering gaslight revealed a cloaked form. The glow of the jet was reflected by burning eyes that stared from beneath the brim of a slouch hat.

Chip swung around.

"The—The Shadow!"

Through Chip's bewildered brain ran sudden thought, suspicion. Marsland must be working with The Shadow! The Shadow's entry immediately following Marsland's departure, plus Cliff's desire to meet up with The Head, could leave no other conjecture!

Quivering, Chip backed toward a corner, gaze hard on an automatic that had slipped from under The Shadow's cloak. Chip's eyes showed a plea for mercy that would have befitted a trapped rat.

A sinister laugh came mirthless. Echoes repeated The Shadow's whispered mockery. Backing to the door, the cloaked visitant thrust his automatic beneath his blackened garb. Like a living shroud, he blended with the gloom of the hall.

Chip stared. The Shadow had gone!

A SUDDEN gleam showed on Chip's face. He was free. He had learned facts. Cliff Marsland was working for The Shadow! That news could be piped to those who would pay for it!

Not in New York; but elsewhere. By contacting the right crooks, Chip could start a man hunt for The Shadow. Cliff Marsland would be the one through whom The Shadow could be traced. Shakily, but with nerve returning, Chip began to pack his few belongings. He stopped suddenly as he heard footsteps at the opened door.

Chip snarled as he wheeled about. His hand halted on the way to the pocket of his tattered jacket. Two men were at the doorway. Both were holding leveled guns. Coat lapels went back. Chip saw the gleam of badges.

"G-men!"

Chip raised his hands as he gasped the recognition. The Federal agents stepped across the threshold. One was tall and long-faced; the other, stockier, was dark and mustached.

"Is this the fellow, Vic?" questioned the long-faced G-man.

His companion nodded.

"It's Chip Mulley," he affirmed. "I know that face of his, Terry. It's lucky I was here in New York when that tip came in to-night."

"Vic Marquette!" gulped Chip. "I heard of you——"

"But didn't know I spotted you, eh? I nearly nabbed you once, Mulley, when you were passing phony money for the counterfeiting gang in St. Louis."

"I wasn't shovin' the queer!"

"Come along. We're taking you West. That's where they want you—in St. Louis. Frisk him, Terry. Then clamp the bracelets. We're taking the next train."

Ten minutes later, Chip Mulley was riding in a taxi, sulkily seated between the Federal men. He had reason to be morose. Chip knew that St. Louis would be but the stopping point on the way to a Federal penitentiary.

Another thought rankled him, also. His opportunity to make trouble for The Shadow was finished. Chip would have no chance to pass his news to big-shots. And from these conclusions Chip Mulley gained another.

Chip knew who had dispatched the tip-off to the G-men, that they might trap him in his hide-out. The word had come from one who seemingly knew everything—including the fact that Chip had been wanted for his connection with a counterfeiting band.

The tip-off had been given by The Shadow.

CHAPTER IX.

THE SPEAKING HEAD.

WHILE Chip Mulley was taking a ride that made him picture prison walls, another man was finishing a journey in New Jersey. Singularly, this chap was viewing a building that looked very much like a prison. Hal Rydler had reached the abode of Professor Caglio, near the town of Littenden.

It was a moonlight night. Hal had borrowed a coupe that belonged to his brother Percy—a car that was always at his disposal. Thanks to the brightness of the night, he had easily found the road to Littenden. He had located Caglio's residence; and again the moonlight was serving him. He could see the house quite plainly.

Adele Rayhew had described the house as a strange one. Hal saw good reason for the definition. Seen from the driveway which Hal had entered, the house appeared as a two-story structure, built of wide stone walls that formed a perfect square. It loomed like a vast gray mausoleum, and the formation of the walls held Hal bewildered.

There was not one window or doorway in the building!

Hal had come from a side road, following a driveway that curved through a wood. Thus he had gained a changing view of Caglio's house. He had seen both sides, as well as the front. Convinced that none of these three walls held an entrance, he decided that the back must be the only mode of access.

A driveway continued around the house. As Hal followed this route, he looked upward, to note that the flat roof was topped by a parapet that followed all along. The drive sloped downward as it neared the back of the house. Taking the final turn, Hal came to the rear and viewed the fourth wall. Like the others, it was blank stone.

The slope, however, had produced a space that showed a portion of the cellar wall. This was of concrete, an extension of the building's foundation. The drive turned sharply toward the house. As he reached the terminus, Hal saw a sliding door, large enough for a car to enter. The door was set in the foundation. It was made of steel, almost

There was a figure on the threshold. The flickering gaslight revealed a cloaked form . . . burning eyes stared from beneath the brim of a slouch hat.

matching the grayish-white of the concrete.

Some one must have observed the coupe's arrival, for the sliding door opened sidewise. Hal saw the interior of a large garage. He drove boldly through the doorway and brought his car to a stop upon a lighted space that was set with stone posts. He peered from the window in time to see the sliding door close behind him.

There was only one other car in the basement garage. It was a long, powerful roadster that stood in a corner. There was space enough, however, for a dozen automobiles.

A man stepped from behind a pillar and approached the coupe. Hal noted that he was slender, but of wiry appearance. The man was poker-faced. His eyes peered sharply from beneath the visor of a chauffeur's cap.

"Whom do you want to see?"

The demand was rasped. Apparently, the man had expected some other visitor and was puzzled when he spied Hal's face.

"I want to talk to Professor Caglio," replied Hal, quietly. "I am a friend of Miss Rayhew. I have a letter of introduction that she gave me."

"Wait where you are."

The chauffeur went to the inner wall and picked up a telephone. Hal watched him as he held brief conversation. The chauffeur turned and beckoned. Hal stepped from the coupe and advanced.

"I'll take care of your car," the chauffeur told him. "The prof says that you can come upstairs."

HE opened a door and showed an automatic elevator. Hal entered. The chauffeur followed. They rode up to the main floor and stepped out into a hallway. Hal noted a mellow, indirect light—a contrast to the glare of the downstairs garage.

They were at the very front of the house. The elevator had brought them up to the spot where a front entry should have been. The hall was long and wide. It ran the full depth of the building. On the right, Hal saw an opened door that led into a large, comfortably furnished living room, with a huge fireplace. At the left he saw another doorway, that revealed a dining room of similar proportions.

The walls of the living room were solid. It had no windows; nor did it have a connecting door to any other room. The fireplace was at the front; at the back of the room was a large, broad mirror, set in a huge gilt frame.

The dining room was likewise windowless; but it had a door in the back wall. One that obviously led into a

pantry, and probably on through to a kitchen beyond.

Hal had time for these observations while the chauffeur was closing the door of the elevator. Then the man joined him. They walked along the hall.

Just past the living room, Hal made new observations. There were two more doors upon the right, both to smaller rooms. There was one on the left; probably a way into the kitchen. The hallway turned left when it reached the back of the house. Hal decided that it must lead to a stairway at the rear of the kitchen.

But he had no opportunity to learn further details. The chauffeur had stopped at the middle door on the right. He had removed his cap, displayed a half-bald head. He was rapping at the door.

The portal opened. Hal stared into a small study. Then he eyed the man who had opened the door. He knew that it must be Professor Caglio. The man himself was as curious as the house.

Hal saw a tall, gawky figure, with long, disjointed arms that hung from bent shoulders. He eyed a withered, tight-skinned face, small-featured and with eyes that peered like sharp beads of light. Above, a crop of wild, shaggy white hair. Tight lips spread to show stumpy teeth.

"Good evening!" Caglio's voice was a cackle. "I give you welcome! May I ask your name, my friend?"

Caglio was jabbing a withered hand toward Hal. The visitor clasped the professor's claw. The chauffeur had stepped aside.

"Your name?"

"Rydler. Hal Rydler."

Hal saw the professor give a sudden start. Then lips croaked a pleased chuckle. Hal had already classed the professor as eccentric. He saw no significance in the white-haired man's odd action.

"Ah, yes," nodded Caglio. "A friend

of Miss Rayhew. Step right in, Mr. Rydler."

Hal complied. Caglio, moving aside, spoke to the chauffeur:

"You may go, Havelock."

The chauffeur went toward the front of the house. Professor Caglio closed the door. He motioned Hal to a chair beside a large desk. Hal handed him Adele's note. Caglio seated himself and began to read the message.

This allowed Hal time to look about him. The study was a small room; but it resembled the others that Hal had seen. Like the hall, all had one dominant feature of decoration: The walls were of paneled oak. One wide panel; then a narrow one. The same order was repeated. The panels went half way up the wall; above was a row of shorter panels; but they corresponded in width to those beneath.

The light was pleasant throughout the study. The air, too, was fresh, which surprised Hal, since the house was windowless. He noted that the professor used a desk lamp in order to read the letter. That was natural, since the room itself was not overbright.

Professor Caglio looked up suddenly, to cackle a question.

"You have come to consult the Oracle?"

"Yes," replied Hal. "I wanted to ask Zovex about——"

Caglio raised a withered hand.

"You must speak to Zovex," he croaked. "Not to me. Come!"

He led the way from the study. They went toward the rear of the house and stopped at the last door on the right. The professor turned the knob. They entered another lighted room, paneled like the study, and of corresponding size.

HAL blinked in utter amazement, when he saw the contents of the room. Professor Caglio indulged in a stump-

toothed smile, pleased at the visitor's surprise.

The room was like a miniature museum; every exhibit was an oddity. To his left, Hal saw a waxwork figure that was seated upon a large, oblong chest. The figure was almost life size. It was attired like a Turk. In front of the figure was a chessboard, with the pieces set in position for a game.

To Hal's right was a smaller figure that looked like an oversize doll. It was seated upon a four-legged bench. Its dress was adorned with ruffles. The figure's lap supported a small writing board, to which its left hand was clamped. Its right hand held a pen, and the head was tilted forward so that its lifeless eyes looked straight toward the board.

Cages were hanging from the ceiling. These contained imitation birds of varied plumage. Near the far end of the room was a square-topped mahogany table, supported by a blocky pedestal that served as a leg. Beyond the table, Hal saw a small safe in the wall; above it, a shelf with a row of cubical boxes.

Some of the boxes had open fronts. Inside them, Hall saw waxwork heads. Two had the faces of women; a third held the visage of a wise-faced Hindu. Hal wondered if this could be Zovex.

"One moment, Mr. Rydler!" Professor Caglio cackled the exclamation. "Before we proceed with the consultation, let me explain the purpose of this room. It is my laboratory; where I experiment with various forms of automata."

"Automata?" queried Hal. "You mean mechanical figures?"

Professor Caglio nodded.

"Yes." He pointed to the doll-like figure at the right. "Here we have a replica of the Jacquet-Droz automaton. It was invented in the eighteenth century. I shall have it operate."

He opened the back of the doll. Hal saw that the figure was filled with clockwork. The professor adjusted several levers, wound the clockwork and set it in motion. A slight ticking sounded, even after he had closed the back of the doll.

There was a pad of paper on the square table at the back of the room. Caglio tore away a sheet and brought it to the doll. He placed the paper beneath the figure's right hand. He opened the top of a small inkwell that was set in the board. Hal watched, while the ticking continued.

The figure's tiny hand began to move. It advanced, jerkily dipped the pen into the inkstand. The hand quivered with an eccentric motion, shaking off drops of ink that spattered into the inkstand. Approaching the paper, the hand began to write, forming quaint letters in slow, painful fashion.

Hal blinked. The figure was inscribing his own name: "Rydler." With the finish of the sixth letter, the hand raised. With a slight *click,* the doll's face looked upward, like that of a child, expecting approval.

"Remarkable!" exclaimed Hal.

PROFESSOR CAGLIO smiled. He turned to the chess player and opened a door that was cut in the cloth front of the figure's chest. He showed a mass of mechanism. Closing the door, Caglio opened another that was set in the right side of the oblong box. He revealed another display of clockwork.

Closing that door, he opened the left side of the oblong box and pointed to another collection of machinery. He wound the clockwork, closed the last door and pointed to a chair.

"Seat yourself," said Caglio to Hal. "Test your skill against that of the Turk. I presume that you play chess?"

Hal nodded. He took the chair opposite the chess player. Hal had the white pieces. He began with the Ruy Lopez opening. He made one move. The automaton swung its right hand forward. Its fingers plucked up a pawn and moved the piece.

The game progressed swiftly; for Hal was more interested in seeing the figure operate than he was in the game itself. When the chess player captured pieces, it dropped them beside the board. Suddenly, Professor Caglio clucked triumphantly.

"Check!" he exclaimed. "Check and mate! The automaton has won!"

Hal rose from his chair. He shook his head.

"Incredible!" he remarked. "How can a mechanical device be arranged to counter all the possible moves of a chess game?"

"You saw the intricate machinery," explained the professor. "Thousands of tiny levers are necessary. That is why the large chest is needed to house the elaborate mechanism. Von Kempelen invented this automaton. It is superior to the writing figure devised by Jacquet-Droz."

Caglio looked toward the bird cages, with their mechanical occupants. He decided to pass them for the present. He motioned Hal toward the back of the room. He pointed to the row of cubical boxes.

"The theraphim!"

Caglio's whisper was awed. His eyes showed a wild glare.

"Theraphim?" queried Hal. "What does that mean?"

"A name given to heads that speak," returned Caglio. His tone was hushed. "These are mechanical, yes. But sometimes they possess a human wisdom. That is why I have named each head."

"Is that one Zovex?"

Hal pointed to the waxen Hindu.

"No," replied Caglio. "That is Ganara. A head that displays no more than mechanical attributes. This box" —he picked a closed cube from the shelf —"is the one that contains the head of Zovex."

Carrying the box in careful fashion,

Caglio started to the center of the room. Hal moved along with him. The professor stopped suddenly beside the square-topped table. He pushed a stack of books away; then held the box by a handle at the top. The box was swaying in his right hand, a foot above the table. Eagerly, Caglio drew back a catch, to release the front of the box.

"Observe!" he cackled. "See! For the first time! The face of Zovex— The Head that will live forever! Zovex, the undying Oracle!"

The front of the box swung downward on a hinge. Hal Rydler saw the head within the box. He spied a face of waxwork, that gleamed in the reflected light. Spontaneously, a startled, instinctive cry gulped from Hal's throat.

The head within the box had livid lips. Its nose was wide. Its eyes were rounded orbs that bulged from beneath thick brows. Its waxen forehead was a mass of V-shaped wrinkles. Its hair was black and shaggy.

The face of Zovex was identical with the visage of that fearful, bulky prowler whom Hal had seen within his brother's house!

CHAPTER X.

THE GUEST REMAINS.

PROFESSOR CAGLIO placed the box upon the center of the table. He turned to eye Hal Rydler sharply. The visitor's exclamation had reached the old man's ears.

"What troubles you?" queried Caglio, his cackle harsh. "Others have not quailed at sight of Zovex."

"Nothing," replied Hal, abruptly. "It —Zovex—well, the face reminded me of some one——"

"You have seen a face that resembles that of Zovex?"

"No, no! It was just a fleeting thought that gripped me. I found it hard to realize that the head is not alive."

Professor Caglio laughed in cackly

fashion. His eyes took on their wildish stare.

"There are those," he chortled, "who believe that Zovex lives. Some who are wise believe it. Perhaps they are right."

"That would be impossible."

"I disagree. Remember, I am a scientist. Yet I have learned of phenomena which science cannot explain. From antiquity, there have been reports of Oracles. Some of them—the wisest— were speaking heads. Like the one that you see before you."

Caglio pointed a bony finger toward the evil face of Zovex. Hal, staring, found sight of the head more distasteful than before. The glare upon the waxen visage was hideous.

"The head of Mirme was an Oracle;" affirmed Caglio. "It was brought from Asia, into Scandinavia. The Oracle at Lesbos was a speaking head. It was the head of Orpheus; and it predicted the death of Cyrus, the Persian king.

"There was the head of the physician Dalban, that lived long after death. A legend, perhaps, of the Arabian Nights; but such stories often hold foundation, particularly when later discoveries support their possibility."

Professor Caglio paused. His cackle had become shrill. Hal wondered if this could be the old man's mania.

"The ancients called such heads 'androides,' " resumed Caglio, wisely. His tone had suddenly calmed. "The art of constructing speaking heads came down through the Middle Ages. Just prior to the French Revolution, Mical presented a collection of speaking heads to the French Academy of Sciences.

"Mechanical devices, yes. But there lies a difference between the androides and the theraphim. The androides are constructed. The theraphim are the embalmed heads of the dead. This head—the head of Zovex—is of the theraphim!"

"It once lived?" queried Hal. "Upon the shoulders of a living man?"

Caglio nodded wisely. Hal was staring at the head.

"But it is waxwork!" Hal exclaimed. "Wax—or some other composition. Yet it looks real." He stared at the fixed eyes. "It seems monstrous——"

"Zovex belongs to the theraphim," croaked Caglio in interruption. "Zovex will speak when he has heard your story."

Caglio waited, silent. Hal addressed the head.

"My name is Hal Rydler," he declared. "I have come to learn regarding stolen diamonds, that were taken from my brother's house two nights ago."

Hal paused. He watched The Head. Professor Caglio was close beside the table. The old man's claws were gripping the edge.

The lips of Zovex moved. Their motion was mechanical. A voice grated from the lips:

"Zovex has heard."

Hal stood silent as the lips ceased moving. Caglio leaned forward and put a question of his own:

"Can Zovex answer?"

Again lips moved mechanically. The voice grated:

"Zovex will answer."

Eyelids dropped like shutters. The glare was gone from the waxen face. Hal turned toward the professor. Caglio held a finger to his lips.

"Zovex sleeps!" whispered the old man. "Come! We must be gone until the head awakens. Then the Oracle will answer. Within that head"—Caglio's forefinger was wagging—"lies a living brain!"

They went from the strange room. Hal, in the hallway, caught a last sight of the waxwork head in its box upon the table. Then Caglio shut the door. With a slight smile, the professor conducted Hal forward to the living room.

"We shall wait here," declared the professor. "The Oracle must be given time to decide upon an answer."

"I had no opportunity to give the details of the robbery," remarked Hal.

"Zovex needs no details," responded Caglio. "His brain will picture every circumstance."

THEY sat down in comfortable chairs before the fireplace. Hal heard the crackle of logs. A fire was burning; as he looked about, he could see the reflection of the blaze in the wide gilt-edged mirror on the opposite wall of the room. He turned toward the fireplace and watched the sparkle of the logs.

"An idea of mine," chuckled Professor Caglio. "This house is windowless. I keep it entirely air-conditioned. The temperature varies in different rooms. An open fire is cheerful; so the living room is kept cooler than other apartments. A log fire is therefore quite in order."

The door opened as Caglio was speaking. Hal looked about; then arose as a girl stepped into the room. She was a charming brunette, whose eyes showed friendliness. Caglio introduced Hal.

"This is my niece," he told the visitor.

Then, to the girl: "Martha, meet Mr. Rydler. Remain here, Martha, while I summon Selfridge. I want him to meet Mr. Rydler."

The girl took a chair. Hal sat down as Caglio departed. As soon as the old man was gone, the girl spoke to Hal.

"You came here to see Zovex?" she queried.

"Yes," replied Hal, frankly.

"You have already seen him?" asked the girl.

Hal nodded.

"Did The Head tell you to remain?"

"Not exactly," answered Hal. "I am to talk to Zovex again, Miss Caglio."

"My name is not Caglio," smiled the girl. "I am Martha Keswick. Caglio is my uncle's name; but not his real one."

"Not his real name?"

"No. I do not know his actual name. Perhaps I should not tell you this, Mr. Rydler; but I am worried about my uncle and his eccentric notions. I promised myself that I would tell the truth to the next visitor who came here. That is, the next one like yourself. There have been others here, others whom I could not trust——"

The girl stopped abruptly. Caglio had returned, bringing a tall cadaverous man with him. He introduced his companion to Hal. The cadaverous man's clasp felt like the grip of a skeleton.

"This is Mr. Selfridge," stated Professor Caglio. "He is my technician. He attends to the detail work of the mechanical figures. Selfridge is highly competent."

The cadaverous man bowed when he heard the compliment. He remained in the room while Professor Caglio went out again. Selfridge made no effort to begin a conversation; nor did Martha Keswick resume the discussion that she had started.

Hal, silent, gained a sudden suspicion. Caglio had deliberately introduced Selfridge in order to keep his visitor under observation. This meant that the professor might have suspected something because of Hal's first startlement at viewing the head of Zovex.

Where had Caglio gone? Back to the room where he kept the automata?

While Hal was pondering on the subject, Caglio reappeared. He bowed from the doorway and invited Hal to accompany him. When he arose, Hal caught a warning gaze from Martha, who was seated near the fire. He smiled and gave a slight nod; then joined Caglio. The professor led him directly to the rear room on the right.

"Sufficient time has elapsed," remarked Caglio, in his crackly tone. "I believe that the Oracle will speak."

THE cubical box was on the table,

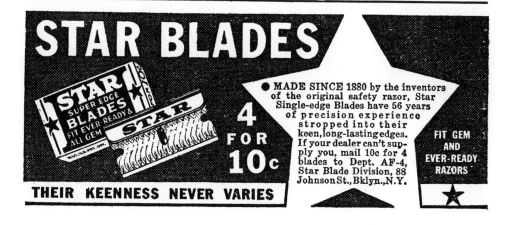

where Caglio had left it. The head was staring from within. The bulging eyes had opened. Caglio nodded approvingly, as he closed the door.

"Question the Oracle again," he suggested. "Tell The Head that you wish to know about the stolen diamonds."

Hal faced The Head.

"Tell me about the diamonds," he said. "Where are they?"

Glaring eyes remained fixed. Lips alone moved. The speaking head rasped its answer.

"All can be seen by the eyes of Zovex," it announced. "I have viewed the place where the diamonds lie. They are where they cannot be regained."

Hal gaped. His first observation had given him two theories regarding the Oracle. One, that Professor Caglio was a ventriloquist. That idea was shattered. Hal was standing closer to The Head than was Caglio. The professor could not have simulated the voice. Not on this occasion, at least. Ventriloquism was impossible, under present conditions.

Hal's second theory was that of a mechanical head. The previous statements had sounded like set remarks. The present utterance was too prolonged, too sustained to be that of a mere machine. Hal tried another question.

"When can the diamonds be regained?"

"To-morrow," responded Zovex, "I shall speak again."

"You will know the answer at that time?"

"Yes. I shall speak when the moment arrives."

"And you will know about the diamonds? Where they are?"

"All will be known to Zovex."

Hal was convinced that The Head lived. Professor Caglio was plucking at the visitor's sleeve. Persistently, the young man put another question to the Oracle.

"Since you know the future," queried Hal, "why is it necessary to wait?"

"Zovex has spoken," grated The Head. Eyes glared; their gleam lifelike. "When fools hear words of wisdom, they should not expect added explanation!"

The tone was a harsh rebuke.

Caglio was tugging Hal away.

"Come!" cautioned the professor. "Do not offend the Oracle! Zovex will speak again to-morrow. Come! We can talk together in my study."

Hal followed the professor from the room. Hal's head was in a whirl. His second theory was flattened. His chance questions, particularly the last, were ones that could not have been accurately anticipated. No phonographic records could have accounted for those sharp responses. The Head was alive!

WHEN they reached the study, Hal slumped in a chair. He was totally bewildered. He was positive that he had viewed the same head that he had seen upon the clumpy man in New York. Yet this head had rested in a box upon a table; and the pedestal leg of the table was less than two feet square.

Professor Caglio must have noted his guest's bewilderment. He clamped a friendly hand upon Hal's shoulders.

"Wait here," he remarked. "I shall bring the models of some new inventions that will interest you. We shall have time to discuss them, since you will remain overnight."

"No!" Hal was on his feet before Caglio reached the door. "I must go into New York. Positively! I can come out to-morrow."

"Very well." Caglio had opened the door. His sharp eyes saw the determination on Hal's face. "Nevertheless, I shall bring the models. It will not take long to examine them."

He stepped out into the hall and closed the door. Hal went back to the desk.

He sat down and stared at the paneled walls. His ears caught a hissing sound. Hal looked about.

He could not locate the direction from which the noise came. He walked about the room; then nervously approached the door. He tried the knob. It did not budge. Hal realized that he was locked in the study.

Clutching his hands, he looked toward the panels. They were all alike, and the walls were thick. Hal had guessed that last fact from the sizes of the rooms. Every apartment, the living room included, seemed smaller than it should have been when gauged by the length of the hall.

Hal started toward the door again. On the way, he faltered. He was becoming dizzy. The hissing was a terror to his ears. He clutched the doorknob. His hand slipped from it. His head began to swim. He sagged to the floor. He was gasping, for the air had become difficult to breathe.

Half crawling, Hal dragged himself to a chair and rolled into it. He tilted his head backward and panted as he stared toward the ceiling. The hissing ended. Hal heard the *click* of the doorknob; but he was too weak to respond. Turning his head slightly, he saw Professor Caglio.

THE old man's eyes expressed pretended surprise. Caglio called to some one outside the door. Selfridge entered. Hal heard the professor speak to him.

"Bring Marley," ordered the professor. "Mr. Rydler is not feeling well. We must help him to his room."

Selfridge returned with a smug-faced man who looked like a servant. Hal had lost his dizziness; but he was too weak either to aid or resist when Selfridge and Marley dragged him to his feet. Professor Caglio stood nodding while the pair helped Hal from the room. They moved along the hall to the back; there they turned left. Hal

PROFESSOR CAGLIO

mad inventor of various mechanical toys.

saw a stairway at the end of the side passage.

He managed one last look toward the front of the hall. Professor Caglio was standing by the open doorway of the study. Martha had come from the living room and was speaking to her uncle. Hal could see anxiety on the girl's face. He caught Caglio's cackled words of explanation:

"Mr. Rydler is slightly ill. He will feel better after he has rested."

The turn of the passage interrupted further hearing. His knees sagging, Hal moved along with Selfridge and Marley supporting him. He did not care where they were taking him. He was feeling strange after-effects of that recent dizziness.

Hal was dopy. His eyelids were drooping. He was mumbling when they reached the top of the stairs. When Selfridge and Marley had dragged him into a little room, Hal Rydler had become an inert burden. His body floundered when the two men rolled him on a cot.

The door clicked when the pair departed. Hal lay in solitary quarters, beneath a ceiling of frosted skylight through which the moonlight beamed. Deep sleep had overpowered him.

Hal Rydler was a helpless prisoner within this house where Zovex ruled!

CHAPTER XI.
THE FINAL VISITOR.

THE moon was shining from directly overhead at the time the glow had first shown Hal Rydler sprawled upon his cot. It had advanced but little farther when its mellow light revealed another sight, outside of the windowless building.

A second automobile was coming to the gray-walled house. This car was a sedan. Its driver knew the route; for he followed the curving driveway without hesitation. Yet his course, though steady, was slow. The driver was speaking to a man beside him.

"Keep watching back of us, Cliff. I'm uneasy!"

"There's nobody tailing us, Squint."

"I spotted glimmers in the rear-view mirror——"

"That was a couple of miles back. Before we hit the side road."

"We can't chance nothing, though. Keep an eye out, Cliff."

"I'm watching, Squint."

Leaning half around, Cliff gazed steadily back along the drive. He saw nothing; yet he knew that there was reason for Squint's conjecture. A car had actually been on the sedan's trail. Cliff had spied it at odd intervals. He had not mentioned that fact to Squint.

"Guess we're O. K.," decided Squint, as they took the final turn. "Lamp the house, Cliff. Screwy joint, ain't it?"

"How do you get in the place?" queried Cliff. "Seems like there's no door to it."

"Here's one. Opening for us."

They had reached the entrance to the garage. The sliding door was on the move. Squint Proddock drove the car into the space beneath the house. The door slid shut; Havelock came over to meet the visitors.

The chauffeur recognized Squint. He asked no questions concerning the crook's companion. He simply led the way to the automatic elevator and conducted the arrivals to the main floor. He took them to Caglio's study. Squint knocked at the door; when it opened, he shouldered in with Cliff.

"Hello, prof," greeted Squint, meet-ing Caglio inside the room. "Meet Cliff Marsland. A pal of mine. Come to talk to The Head."

"Ah!" Caglio's eyes gleamed wisely. "He is to be the next?"

"Maybe. Maybe not. Wait until we've talked to The Head. Cliff has some dope to spill."

"But he has never yet spoken with Zovex——"

"I know that. I'll start the speech—with Cliff here adding the details. There's been trouble, prof."

A STRAINED expression showed upon Caglio's face. Without another word, the white-haired man led the way to the room at the back of the hall. The trio entered. Cliff stared, while Squint grinned.

"Looks goofy, don't it?" queried the crook. "Wait'll you see things working, Cliff. You'll think different. Say —there's The Head on the table! Been consulting it, prof?"

"Yes." Caglio nodded. "There was a visitor earlier this evening. One whom I did not expect. His name was Rydler."

"Rydler?" Squint spun about. "Say —that's the guy who owned the fancy ice! The diamonds that Moose Sudling snatched——"

"This was not Percy Rydler," cackled Caglio, interrupting. "It was his brother, Hal. Mere chance brought him here."

"What did you do with him?"

"He is remaining overnight."

There was a significant croak to Caglio's final statement. Squint grinned again; then became serious.

"All right if I talk to The Head?"

Professor Caglio nodded an affirmative response.

"Lamp this," remarked Squint, in an undertone to Cliff. "And keep your ears open, bozo."

He approached the table and faced the open front of the cubical box. Cliff looked past Squint to view the ugly face of Zovex. He was gripped by an immediate dislike for that glaring visage. But Cliff was too experienced to give the slightest indication of his actual impressions.

"Bad news, Zovex," informed Squint. "I guess you know about Moose croaking that guy Jemley; and having Hunk Lomus around, like I had Koker Hosch. That was tough enough; but this is worse.

"The Shadow got hold of Chip Mulley. Passed himself as a bird named Beak Thungle; and Chip fell for it. He blabbed, Chip did. Told The Shadow how a lot of us come out here, to get hot tips. But he didn't tell The Shadow where this joint is. Chip didn't know.

"Might have been a bad proposition, if Cliff Marsland hadn't stepped into it. Cliff, here, is one guy that don't worry about The Shadow. Cliff stuck in the hide-out, along with Chip, and joined up with me to-night. Chip has beat it from town."

SQUINT paused, as though expecting a reply. The Head remained motionless. Professor Caglio approached the table; then turned toward Cliff.

"Zovex expects you to speak," clucked Caglio.

"Not much for me to say." Cliff looked straight toward The Head. "I'm out to get The Shadow. I'll bump him any time I get the chance. What I want to know is, how can I get at him? Squint says you can tell me."

Cliff waited. The head retained its wax-faced impression. Cliff was beginning to consider the game a hoax, when the lips of Zovex suddenly began to move. A voice grated:

"Zovex has heard."

Professor Caglio leaned forward. He questioned:

"Can Zovex answer?"

"Zovex will answer."

Caglio watched the Oracle; then added a question:

"When will the answer be given?"

The lips moved mechanically. They phrased a single word:

"To-morrow."

An interval; then eyelids dropped. Caglio turned to Cliff and Squint. He added his own statement:

"You have heard the words of Zovex. Your duty is to remain."

Squint nodded. He turned to Cliff. "That just means The Head will think it over," stated Squint. "He don't always hand out info in a hurry. There's a brain inside that bean. This is a scientific racket, Cliff."

Cliff was nodding. Caglio noted his poker-faced expression. The old professor went to the table. Deliberately, he tilted back the top of the cubical box and lifted the head from its resting place.

"I shall show you," croaked Caglio. He lifted the back of the head. It swung upward, hinged beneath the shaggy wig. "See this intricate machinery? It is a thinking device. Those wheels act under thought impulses, directed by those who speak to Zovex.

"Note the steel ribbons coiled below. They are phonographic records. They produce the voice that you heard. Here are coils that are made to shift, to change the word combinations."

He closed the head and replaced it in the box. He shut the box and put it on the shelf above the safe. Lifting the top of the square table, Caglio showed coils and batteries wedged in the upper portion of the pedestal.

"Electromagnetism operates The Head," he affirmed, seriously. "Once the mechanism is charged, it continues its operation. We might liken it to an adding machine; one devised to complete intricate calculations.

"Overnight"—Caglio paused and pointed to the shelf—"the wheels will click into new positions. One day will suffice. Then Zovex will speak again. His lips will utter wise advice. Important problems will be solved."

"That's the lowdown, Cliff," affirmed Squint. "I've listened to The Head pipe the dope I wanted. Me, sitting here, taking down the tips as fast as Zovex spilled them. Making out a list of it. That's how I swung that job the other night.

"Say—it was a cinch, the way The Head had it! A set-up! And it'll be the same when The Head gives us the dope on The Shadow. But it's different to-night than it was before. I didn't come here to tell The Head something; I came to hear what The Head has to tell me.

"This time, we've brought some ideas of our own. Zovex has got to have time to work them out. That's why he answered us the way he did. The prof has explained it."

CLIFF nodded. He doubted Caglio; and he believed that Squint had fallen for the professor's stall. The Oracle had impressed Cliff as being a simple mechanical device, set to deliver a limited number of statements. That fitted with Caglio's first explanation. It was the rest that Cliff doubted.

Cliff was sure that The Head could not think. He was positive that it could not deliver elaborate statements, unless some subterfuge should be employed. He knew that he would have to wait until the next night to learn what trick Caglio intended to use. Cliff was willing to wait. That was his purpose here.

Cliff's nod was intended to indicate belief in Caglio's statements. The professor was bluffed, along with Squint. Caglio's next action was designed purely to add new conviction. He conducted Cliff to the automatic chess player.

"I doubt that you are familiar with chess, Marsland——"

Cliff began to shake his head in the middle of the professor's statement.

Actually, Cliff was a competent chess player; but knowledge of the moves of pawns and rooks did not fit his role of a rowdy from the bad lands.

"Perhaps you have played checkers?"

Cliff nodded in response to this question. Professor Caglio produced a quantity of pawns and arranged them as checkers on the board. He also stacked a heap of flat metal rings.

"The automaton can play a checker game," declared Caglio. "When kings are made, simply drop a ring over the knob of the pawn. Use the pawns as checkers. But not until I have arranged the mechanism."

He opened the doors, one by one, closing each before he opened the next. With each action, Caglio made an adjustment of the machinery—both inside the figure and in the oblong box upon which the automaton was seated.

Cliff began his game. It was a brief one.

The automaton, playing with slow precision, outguessed its human opponent. Cliff had as bad luck at checkers as Hal Rydler had experienced at chess. Caglio smiled triumphantly when the game was over.

"This demonstration proves my point," declared the professor. "You have seen the skill of the chess player. It outmatches human intelligence. It is trivial, however, with the processes produced within the head of Zovex. I tell you once again: The Oracle possesses an actual brain!

"Come. We shall return to the study. I shall summon Marley to conduct you to your rooms. You may forget The Shadow while you are within these walls. This house is a fortress. No human being may enter it without my will. Havelock has been instructed to admit no other visitor."

CLIFF was pondering when they reached the study. The performance of the chess player had baffled him. It seemed to support Caglio's statements regarding Zovex, incredible though the claims might be.

Marley arrived and led the visitors upstairs. They entered a hallway that led into a central passage like the one downstairs; except that there were fully a dozen doors, some reached by short side passages that led off from the main one. Marley ushered Squint into one small bedroom; then conducted Cliff to another, on the opposite side of the hall.

The room was lighted; but its ceiling added a silvery tinge. Looking up, Cliff saw that it was paneled with skylights. The silver hue was moonlight. All the skylights were fixed in position by heavy frames. These appeared to be removable.

Cliff did not attempt to open a skylight. Instead, he performed a simpler action. He brought an envelope from his pocket and carefully unfolded it. The edges retained dried mucilage. Cliff moistened the borders of the envelope; then stepped upon a chair and pressed the flattened paper against the lower surface of a skylight. The envelope remained in position.

OUTSIDE the square-walled building, all was silent. Gray walls loomed forbidding, save for the sparkle of granules in the stones. Set in its lonely clearing, this house of mystery formed a forgotten structure lost amid the Jersey woods.

No watchers were on duty. There seemed no need for them; and there were no windows from which lookouts could have peered. Hence no one saw the strange phenomenon that occurred beneath the moonlight.

A shape emerged from the blackness of the tree that fronted the house. A stalking form, it moved with uncanny glide. Moonbeams revealed it as a shrouded figure cloaked in a habit of black. It was The Shadow.

The sable-hued arrival reached the front wall of the house. His form merged with the shaded stretch beneath. The moon had risen beyond the square house. Here, at the front, the lunar glow was blocked. The Shadow had found a vantage pont.

Looking upward, he could see the bulges of the wall. Protuberances showed against the silvered sky. Slight though they were, those projections offered footholds to The Shadow. When he essayed smooth surface, The Shadow used rubber suction cups; those devices would be useless upon irregular stone. The roughened wall, however, was even more to The Shadow's liking.

His ungloved fingers found cemented spaces. His toes, encased in soft-tipped canvas shoes, were equally adroit. Invisible against the single darkened wall, The Shadow began his upward course. Like a mammoth beetle, he scaled the wall at slow but constant rate.

Moonlight, bathing the top parapet, produced a sudden sparkle as The Shadow's hands arrived upon the ledge. The rays had caught the girasol; the gem was glinting from The Shadow's finger. Then the cloaked form swung to the ledge itself. Hands donned their black gloves.

Crouched upon the broad-topped rail that girded the roof of the strange house, The Shadow formed a ghostly figure against the pale sky. No one could spy him from within the house. There were none outside who might discern that shape upon the parapet.

The Shadow was a ghostly visitant— a specter that seemed conjured from another realm. His presence added to the sepulchral tenor of this outlandish abode that stood within the woods. The house itself was like a mammoth tomb; The Shadow, a spirit that had chosen a resting place upon its summit.

The final visitor had arrived. Unseen, unsuspected, The Shadow stood ready to plan a foray into the strange recesses of the house below.

CHAPTER XII.

A CRY FROM THE GLOOM.

THE roof presented an odd appearance when viewed from the parapet. It formed a floor plan of the second story. The reason was that the rooms alone had skylights. The passages of the second floor were topped by solid roof.

The Shadow studied this arrangement, viewing it clearly by the moonlight. A long, wide stretch ran from the front of the roof to the back; there it turned to cover the passage to the stairway. All along the central path were blocky projections. These indicated the short side passages that led to rooms on the second floor.

There were other wide streaks also. The Shadow noted that they were nearly as broad as the paths that represented hallways. These indicated the walls between the rooms on the second floor.

As for the rooms themselves, they were easily located by the skylights. They formed blocks, placed regularly about the roof. Each square of skylights was divided into smaller sections, like a portion of a checkerboard.

The roof offered easy access, for it was a level floor only three feet below the gray granite ledge whereon The Shadow rested. Yet the cloaked figure made no immediate attempt to reach the roof. Keen eyes were studying its surface. Concealed lips whispered a soft laugh.

The roof was striped with burnished copper, that shone like old gold in the pale moonlight. The solid pathways had close-set streaks, each a few inches in width, to form a corduroy surface. Thus each solid sector gave a ribbed appearance.

The square ends of the skylights had ten-inch frames between them. These were also of a corduroy formation. This arrangement, coupled with the choice of metal, told The Shadow why the roof had been so devised.

The entire surface was a barrier that would stop entrance from above; and would also prevent exit from the rooms on the second floor. Those copper strips were charged with electricity. To tread upon them, unaware, would bring instant death!

THE SHADOW had been favored by the presence of moonlight. The fact that the copper was new and untarnished had also aided him to spot the snare. It was a long stretch to the nearest block of skylights; even if he used the glass panes as stepping stones, The Shadow would be handicapped. Each pane was but little larger than a man's girth. To pry at one, contact would be necessary with the copper strips that fringed it.

There was a way to navigate the roof, however; and The Shadow had the means with which to accomplish the task. From beneath his cloak he produced a flat stack of rubber disks, that made a compact bundle. These were his suction cups, each six inches wide and concave on the bottom surface. The Shadow girded his cloak about his body. He attached the disks to his hands and feet.

Deliberately, he dropped inward from the parapet and stalked across the roof, keeping to the solid portions. Only the rubber disks contacted the burnished copper. They acted as insulators. No current could pass through them. Nor did the disks deter The Shadow's progress.

His tread was squdgy; but the twisting pressure of his feet enabled him to lift the disks with every step. The copper strips were slippery; moreover, there were ridges on the roof. The spaces between prevented the suction cups from taking a firm grip.

Peering toward the various blocks of skylights, The Shadow observed that some were brighter than the others. Each cluster of illuminated glass meant a lighted room beneath. The Shadow counted four such sectors. One, in particular, caught his gaze.

It had sixteen small panels, each a scant two feet in width. One of the skylights showed a peculiarity. There was a black patch in its very center. Some object had been plastered against the lower side of the glass.

A whispered laugh told that The Shadow had divined the purpose. He had found the room that Cliff Marsland occupied. The blot that cut off the lower light was caused by the envelope that Cliff had pressed against the glass.

STEPPING from the solid portion of the roof, The Shadow shifted to the frames between the skylights. He stooped; his right hand rested upon a framework. The disk upon The Shadow's hand acted like those upon his feet, serving as a protective insulation. His left hand came free from its disk; his fingers tapped the glass of the skylight.

Inside the room, Cliff had noted the blackness above the glass. His answering taps came promptly. With quick raps, The Shadow and his agent communicated. Their messages were dots and dashes in a special code.

The Shadow was ready to effect entrance to the room below. He wanted to know if the interior was guarded by bare wires. Cliff replied in the negative. The Shadow questioned, to learn if Cliff could work at the skylight from the inside. Cliff responded that the prospects looked good.

The Shadow gave the order to proceed. He waited while the sounds of a working screw driver came from beneath. Cliff had brought along a few odd tools. Such equipment was natural, since he was supposed to be an active worker in the realm of crookdom.

The task was slow and laborious; for Cliff was cautious in his operations. At last the skylight moved downward. Peering through the opening where the pane had been, The Shadow saw Cliff stepping from a chair, carrying the glass in his hands.

A hissed whisper from above. Cliff placed the thick pane upon the cot. He turned out the light. The Shadow's form swished downward through the darkness. The master sleuth had gained his goal.

"Report!"

The whisper was barely audible in the darkened room. Cliff gave detailed response. He described his arrival with Squint Proddock. He told of his first visit to The Head. He expressed his belief that the Oracle was mechanical.

After describing Zovex, Cliff mentioned the matter of Hal Rydler.

"He's in this house," whispered Cliff. "Somewhere on this second floor."

"Report received!"

The Shadow's tone ended Cliff's story. Sibilant instructions followed. Cliff was to wait until The Shadow had departed from the room. Then he was to replace the skylight and affix its supporting inner frame.

Cliff saw the door open as The Shadow tried it. He caught a glimpse of his cloaked chief. The Shadow was pausing, with the door ajar. Something about the barrier had attracted his attention.

The inner knob had yielded slightly when The Shadow had turned it. He was studying that factor. The Shadow pressed the knob inward. It acted like a plunger. Oddly, the knob still operated the latch. The Shadow tried the outer knob. It failed to turn.

He pressed the outer knob in plunger fashion. The inside knob refused to turn. The Shadow lengthened both plungers. Each knob turned with ease. Cliff had drawn close to note the process. He saw the value of the discovery that The Shadow had made.

Cliff had wondered why no doors had

locks. He understood at last. Professor Caglio had invented an ingenious arrangement. Pressure upon either doorknob would act upon the other side. This was a device that would work two ways. It was possible for any occupant to lock the door of his room. Conversely, any one on the outside could make the occupant a prisoner.

The door was closing. The Shadow had moved out into the hall. Cliff turned on the light and began a careful replacement of the skylight, in conformity to his chief's instructions.

Soft light illuminated the solid-roofed hallway of the second floor. Beneath the indirect glow, The Shadow formed a phantom figure. He was stalking silently along, eying each doorway that he passed. He stopped at a portal near the stairs.

This door bore a slight difference from the rest. Its knob was jammed farther inward. In light of The Shadow's recent discovery, this door became important. The condition of the knob indicated that the room contained a prisoner. This door alone had been locked from the outside. The Shadow knew that this must be Hal Rydler's room.

The Shadow placed his hand upon the knob. He was about to draw it outward when a slight *click* came from along the hall. With a quick turn, The Shadow swung from the doorway. He wheeled across the hall and gained a

Peering from his hiding place, The Shadow saw a girl's figure come into the light.

short passage that led to another room.

The *click* that The Shadow had heard was the opening of a door. It had come from another side passage. Soft footsteps sounded. Peering from his hiding place, The Shadow saw a girl's figure come into the light. It was Martha Keswick.

Cliff had not met Caglio's niece. Hence he had known nothing of the girl's presence in the house. Martha was attired in a dressing gown. She was going toward the stairs at the back of the hall. The Shadow saw that she was carrying a book beneath her arm. He waited for the girl to pass.

A muffled groan sounded from across the hall. The girl stopped short. She looked toward the door of Hal's room. The Shadow watched her while she listened. The groan was repeated, less distinctly than before. Martha placed her hand upon the doorknob. The Shadow saw worriment on the girl's face.

Slowly, The Shadow moved from the alcove, his tall form casting a long silhouette upon the floor beneath. Martha was facing the door of the prisoner's room. She was listening intently for new sounds from the man within. She did not suspect the presence of the tall personage who stood almost beside her.

The Shadow, too, had advanced to listen.

Those stifled groans had told him of some menace. He could foresee danger for the prisoner. He was prepared to meet the emergency, even though his deed might reveal his presence to the girl outside the door.

Then, as answer to The Shadow's expectations, came another sound from beyond the locked door. It was a token that allowed no further doubt. It was the sudden cry of a man unnerved by terror.

A scream that ended in a gurgled wail. A shriek that only quivering lips could have uttered. Though muffled by the thickness of the door, it told of anguish. The call was a plea for rescue from some inhuman torture.

Hal Rydler had delivered that cry from the gloom. The Shadow had heard the call for aid.

CHAPTER XIII.
THROUGH INNER WALLS.

HAL RYDLER had awakened from a hideous nightmare. He had opened his eyes, to stare at moonlight flooding through the skylight of the room. His brain had been in a dazed whirl, its thoughts uncollected. Then had come the happening which had produced his instinctive cry.

Dopy, Hal had lain motionless. His groans had ended. Passing seconds seemed like years. Then into the focus of his vision had come a dreaded apparition. It had loomed suddenly, terribly, from the wall beside the prisoner's cot.

The head of Zovex!

Livid, with gloating lips, the hideous countenance had thrust itself toward him. Bulging evil eyes had met Hal's own. In an instant, the awakened prisoner had realized that this was no hallucination. He was face to face with the living head itself!

As venomous breath exhaled upon him, Hal had phrased his frantic, hopeless cry. Then had come hands from nowhere. Fingers that Hal could not see; for his whole gaze was centered on the leering visage above him. Claws had gripped Hal's throat. Their tension had produced that gurgled finish to his shriek.

Hal's own eyes bulged. His lips gasped. He saw murder in the leer above him. The face of Zovex was fiendish—as it had been on that first night when Hal had seen this very head upon the bulky shoulders of the clumpy prowler who had invaded Percy Rydler's home.

Death !

That was the sentence that The Head's expression spelled; and Hal could find no strength to struggle. Brief moments were like stretches of eternal agony. Then came the interruption that ended the terrible strain: two sounds that to Hal seemed hours apart; although actually they were almost simultaneous.

Both were *clicks*. The first, when some one drew back the outside knob of the door. The second, when the same hand turned the knob.

Zovex heard the *clicks*. Two actions followed. Though simultaneous, they seemed like the distinct deeds of separate creatures. Hands left Hal Rydler's neck. The distorted face of Zovex bobbed from view.

Hal heard a muffled *click* from the wall. Then came a stream of light from the door. With an effort, Hal rolled outward on the cot. Dazed, stroking at his throat, he sat up. He saw Martha Keswick standing in the doorway.

HAL managed a weak smile. He tried to gain his feet; but failed. He slumped back on the cot; then steadied and looked toward the wall. He saw nothing but the blankness of the panel. He stared toward Martha and noticed a blackness that hovered thick beyond the girl. Hal blinked; as he did, the background faded.

"What was the matter?" queried Martha, in a tense whisper. "I—I heard your scream——"

"A nightmare!" gulped Hal. "But it was a vivid one. It seemed real! I saw a face that I remembered."

"You saw Zovex?"

The girl's query was awed. Hal nodded.

"I saw The Head," he admitted. "It was here, in this room. There were hands, too, that clawed my throat. But I didn't see them."

Hal finally managed to stand up. He smoothed his rumpled coat.

"I must have been woozy," he affirmed. "Never even took my coat off after those two chaps lugged me up here. All I remember was that my feet must have lead weights tagged to them. I was in the study when I went groggy.

"It was odd, too." Hal looked toward Martha, as though seeking an explanation. "The air became stifling down in the study. First I was dizzy; then dopy. Does that happen to every one who stops in to see your uncle?"

Martha stood silent, troubled. At last she spoke.

"It has occurred before," admitted the girl. "It—it has worried me, Mr. Rydler. Perhaps it would not be wise for you to go back to sleep. A cup of hot coffee might be helpful."

"It would be great!" Hal was finding enthusiasm. "Where's the coffee?"

"Downstairs," smiled Martha. "I could not sleep because the moonlight disturbed me. I was going down to the living room to read a book until dawn. If you will come there, I can stop at the kitchen and make the coffee."

"Swell! Thanks a lot, Miss Keswick."

Steadying himself, Hal stepped from the room. He closed the door behind him; then followed Martha along the hall. The two turned toward the passage that led to the stairway.

As soon as they had gone, a figure issued from the passage opposite Hal's room.

The Shadow had edged back into his hiding place; from that point he had heard the conversation. His path was again clear; but he had found a mission to keep him on the second floor. No occupants of second-story rooms had heard Hal Rydler's stifled cry. There was chance to investigate without disturbance.

Hal had closed the door of the room. Martha had paused to push the knob inward. From this action, The Shadow knew that the girl understood the locking device. Her knowledge of it was not quite perfect, however; for she had first tugged at the knob, then turned it at the time when she had opened the door. Only the latter action had been necessary.

How would the girl explain matters to her uncle?

Doubtless, Professor Caglio would call her to task when he learned that she had released the prisoner. Martha's last pressure of the doorknob was proof that she wished to postpone the time when she would be called to account. Caglio would not know that Hal Rydler had left the prison room—unless the old man should come downstairs from his own quarters. Hal's closed door would give Caglio no clue to the young man's absence.

But Caglio would learn eventually; and from that conjecture, .The Shadow drew a conclusion. The girl whom he had seen was probably a privileged person. She had no part in crime, although she probably knew that evil brewed within this house. Caglio would not risk a quarrel with the girl.

Because of his conclusions, The Shadow showed no hesitation when he approached the door of the vacated room. He drew out the knob; then turned it. He entered the room and closed the door. The reason for his double action with the outer knob was that he might have an exit. The Shadow

In an instant, the awakened prisoner had realized that this was no hallucination. He was face to face with the Living Head itself!

did not care to lock himself automatically within the room.

MOONLIGHT showed paneled walls, as The Shadow pressed the inner knob to prevent the entry of chance intruders. Keen eyes looked everywhere. The Shadow had heard Hal Rydler's statements. He believed that the prisoner had actually seen The Head. Hal had spoken, too, of hands. Whence had they come?

Noting the pillowed end of the cot, The Shadow saw a narrow panel of less than eight-inch width. Next, a slight space; then a panel nearly three feet broad. Space—narrow panel—space—broad panel; the arrangement continued all along the wall. The Shadow concentrated upon the wide panel that was nearest the head of the bed.

Gloved fingers tapped, but their strokes were amazingly light. It was almost as if The Shadow felt the thickness of the woodwork; as though his testing fingers could sense space beyond. His hands were moving, groping for the secret of the panel. Each hand found a vital spot. With one thumb at each side of the panel, The Shadow pressed. The woodwork gave; the panel moved inward several inches then slid toward the foot of the bed.

Dank air pervaded blackness. The space beyond the panel was not conditioned like the atmosphere of the room. The Shadow placed one knee upon the cot; then edged across and stooped through the low doorway that the opened panel had produced. He found the panel, slid it back into place. There was a muffled *click* from the wall.

A flashlight glimmered. The Shadow was in a narrow corridor. The thick wall was hollow, but it was lined with brick, except for the opening that afforded access to Hal's room. The Shadow followed the passage; he came to another opening in the opposite wall. This led to the panel of another bedroom.

A spiral staircase appeared at the end of the passage. This was in the house wall itself. The Shadow descended. At the bottom, he discovered a lengthwise passage in the house wall. He followed it, to discover other metal stairways. The passage reached the front wall of the house. It turned. The Shadow continued his progress.

He had noted openings in the bricks of the inner wall. Calculating from Cliff's description of the ground floor, The Shadow knew that these must open into the study, the living room, and finally the hall. It was at this last opening that the passage ended. The Shadow knew why.

The elevator shaft blocked it.

Probably, there was a similar passage starting on the other side of the shaft. One that could be entered from hall, dining room or kitchen; with spiral staircases to the second floor. Thus a hidden prowler, starting from downstairs, could gain secret entry to any room on the second floor.

THE SHADOW returned along the passage. He found the opening to the study. He pressed the panel. It slid aside. The Shadow stepped into Professor Caglio's headquarters. He found a light switch and pressed it.

Illuminated, the study looked quite ordinary. The Shadow had closed the panel; the walls seemed all alike. There were points, however, that concerned The Shadow. First: the passage had ended with the side opening into the study. Why had it not continued farther? There was still space.

Did another passage begin past some blockade? It was possible; for The Shadow had found no opening that indicated the mysterious corner room that housed the professor's automata, including Zovex.

The Shadow tried the wall. He found a panel near the corner, that gave beneath capable pressure. The oak moved sidewise. The Shadow saw a cavity that housed a tall, bulky safe. This was Professor Caglio's vault. Here, perhaps, was where he kept blue prints and models of his various inventions.

The Shadow closed the panel. There was no indication of a passage beginning from beside the safe. The cavity was thoroughly bricked. If there should be a passage to the Oracle room, it would be found in the wall directly between the study and the room itself.

Deliberately, The Shadow probed wide panels. Not one broad space of the side wall gave results. The panels conformed to the usual procedure, alternately narrow and wide. There were five of the broad ones. The Shadow tested them all.

Starting back toward the rear panel, The Shadow paused. He looked toward the wall that lay between the study and the living room. He decided to test it also. He came to the middle panel. He found that it yielded under proper pressure. His hands urged the barrier inward.

Instantly, the study light went out.

To any but The Shadow, the sudden sweep of blackness would have been startling. It might have signified a sudden danger. But The Shadow remained at ease. Dark was his habitat. He linked two facts immediately.

This panel had a special purpose. For some reason, no one was supposed to open it while the study was lighted. To insure that procedure, the panel was fitted with a switch that automatically cut off the lights.

To test his prompt theory, The

Shadow released the panel so that it pushed toward him, impelled by an inner spring, like the previous panels that he had opened. The movable woodwork came flush with the wall. The lights in the study glowed promptly, again revealing The Shadow's cloaked form by the wall.

The Shadow stepped over and pressed the regular light switch. In total darkness, he returned to the side wall panel. He pressed it inward and slid it to the left. Light greeted him—from a broad, windowlike space a few feet away. The Shadow stepped forward.

ONLY glass lay between The Shadow and the scene that he viewed. He was looking into the living room, through the big mirror that adorned the wall opposite the fireplace. Hal Rydler and Martha Keswick were seated by the fire, sipping coffee.

The sheet of glass was an Argus mirror.

This was a contraption with which The Shadow had long been familiar. The glass, silvered by a special process, made a perfect reflector, so long as all light struck the front of it.

To any one in the living room, the glass would appear as a framed mirror. That situation would exist always, since lights would have to be on in the living room for any one to study the glass from that side.

Conversely, any one in the wall cavity would always be able to see through the Argus mirror and watch the occupants of the living room. The cavity was a perfect spy room, so long as one precaution was steadfastly observed.

All light must be kept from the space behind the mirror. Even the flicker of a match might be a give-away.

The Argus mirror explained the cutoff to the light switch, that ended illumination in the study whenever any one pressed the panel. That was Professor Caglio's arrangement to prevent a chance betrayal of the secret.

Sound was cut off by the glass. The Shadow saw no reason for silence in motion. He probed about in the darkness of the narrow spy room. He discovered a folding beach chair at one end. This was for the benefit of any one who might be posted on a long vigil.

The Shadow stepped back through the opening into the study. He closed the panel. He sought the passage that led through the main walls of the house. He came to the blockade caused by the elevator shaft. Carefully, he opened the panel that led into the hall.

He could hear voices from the living room; but he was out of sight as he glided past the door of the elevator shaft. Reaching the panel just beyond, The Shadow opened it and stepped into

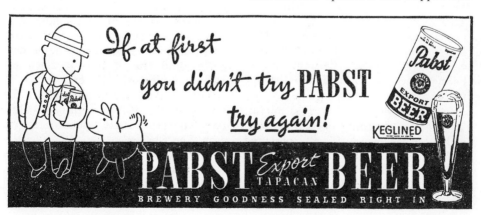

the passage which he had guessed was on the other side. He closed the opening.

THE room that Cliff Marsland occupied was above the dining room. Cliff, awake on his couch, was suddenly swung to alertness when he heard a hiss from the opposite wall. Staring, he saw The Shadow in the moonlight.

The Shadow had found Cliff's room. In this case—unlike Hal's—the opening was across from the cot. Propped on an elbow, Cliff heard The Shadow's whisper. He stared, astounded by the facts he heard. He listened to brief instructions; then repeated his understanding in a low, cautious tone.

Cliff saw The Shadow move toward the door; then glide out into the hall. Soon the cloaked master returned. He had gone to set the outer knob of Hal Rydler's door. The Shadow's figure faded. Cliff heard a slight *click* as the panel closed.

Below, The Shadow appeared again when he came out from the far passage and passed the elevator shaft. Then he was gone, into the secret corridor that skirted living room and study. This time, The Shadow took the spiral stairway that gave access to Hal Rydler's room.

He had one detail that needed attention: to unlock the inner knob of the room where the prisoner had been. That accomplished, The Shadow returned below. Again, he entered Professor Caglio's study. He did not turn on the light. Instead, he went directly to the panel that opened into the spy room.

Stepping beside the Argus mirror, The Shadow closed the opening through which he had come. Totally obscured by blackness, he indulged in a whispered laugh—a prophetic quiver of mirth that was stifled within these narrow walls. The Shadow had another view of Hal and Martha, as they chatted above their coffee cups. He watched the motions of their lips.

Finally, The Shadow stretched out in the beach chair. His whisper came like an echo of his former thoughts. Here, in the midst of Professor Caglio's abode, The Shadow had found a headquarters of his own. From here he could issue forth to new forays; and try again to find a secret entry into the room where Zovex might be found.

No space could have been better suited to The Shadow's needs than was this spy room. It extended past the end frames of the glass; hence either extremity of the space would serve a hidden lurker, should Caglio or any other enter.

Moreover, the presence of the Argus mirror meant that no light would be introduced into the spy room. With no thought of a bold intruder hiding here; with no illumination to reveal a silent, watching form, the old professor would never chance to learn of The Shadow's presence.

Through keen ability, The Shadow had penetrated to a spot where he would dwell secure. He could watch the living room; he had access to Caglio's study. Entrenched in a strategic position, The Shadow could remain.

Unseen, unheard, his very presence unsuspected, this master sleuth would await the time for action. Hal Rydler was safe for the present, under The Shadow's own surveillance. At present, The Shadow was willing to defer new moves until after Cliff had gained another interview with Zovex.

The Shadow was willing to let the Oracle speak. To hear, through Cliff, how The Head itself intended to deal with The Shadow.

Then would The Shadow plan his countermove. He, master of justice, would deal with Zovex, the living head of crime!

CHAPTER XIV.

CLIFF GIVES WORD.

It was the next afternoon.

Cliff Marsland and Squint Proddock were seated by the fireplace in the living room. Opposite them was Hal Rydler. Cliff and Squint had just finished a trivial conversation. Hal was reading a book; he had scarcely noticed the words that passed between the others.

With the lull in conversation, Cliff reviewed the events of to-day. He had risen early; he had come downstairs to find Hal and Martha talking in the living room. Having met neither one before, Cliff introduced himself. Hal had accepted him as another guest.

Professor Caglio had arrived next. He had been surprised to see Hal; but had quickly recovered from his puzzlement. Hal had mentioned that he had slept poorly; and Martha had added an explanation.

"It was the moonlight, uncle," the girl had said. "Mr. Rydler was troubled by bad dreams. I was passing his room when he awoke. I invited him to come downstairs."

Professor Caglio had pressed no further query. Cliff guessed that the old man knew that the girl had released the prisoner.

Squint Proddock had joined them for breakfast in the dining room. An uneventful morning had followed. Then lunch; now, afternoon. They had been in the living room constantly, except for the intervals at meal times. Cliff and ·Squint had refrained from any mention of Zovex.

With the day dwindling, Cliff knew that The Shadow had kept watch all the while. From his cloaked chief, Cliff had heard the secret of the Argus mirror. Cliff could almost sense keen eyes, peering from a perfect watching place. Yet Cliff found it difficult to curb impatience. He had the urge for action.

G-MAN
one of the Federal operatives who pick up Chip Mulley.

A clock was chiming six when Professor Caglio and Martha entered the living room. They were followed by Marley. The glum-faced servant was carrying wood to build a new fire, for the old one had gone out, hours before. Martha sat down and began to chat with Hal. Caglio spoke to Squint.

"I have the model prepared," declared the professor, wisely. "Selfridge is ready to give us a demonstration. Would you care to come to the study, Mr. Proddock."

"Huh?" queried Squint. "Say— what——"

"I was the one who wished to see the model," put in Cliff, quickly. "You say it is ready, professor?"

"Yes."

Caglio showed a pleased smile at Cliff's quickness to fill the stop-gap. Cliff arose, made a sign to Squint, then said:

"Wait here, Proddock. I'll be back in a few minutes."

Cliff followed Caglio through the hall, where the permanent, mellow light pervaded. They entered the study. As soon as the door was closed, the professor clamped an approving claw upon Cliff's shoulder.

"Timely work, Marsland!" clucked Caglio. "I thought that Proddock would catch the idea I gave him. That I wanted to talk about matters—but could not mention them in front of Rydler."

"Squint's slow, sometimes," he rejoined. "He ought to have got the drift of it; but he didn't. That's his way."

"You were alert, however."

"Sure. You needed a pinch-hit and I delivered."

"But you were doubly alert. You saw that I wanted only one of you to come with me."

"Why not? You only asked Squint, didn't you?"

Caglio nodded.

"Well observed!" he chortled. "Can you guess my reason?"

"You didn't want your niece to talk to Rydler."

"Right. I could not count on Marley stayin' there indefinitely. I wanted either you or Proddock to remain."

"I got it, prof. Well, it's O. K. with Squint there."

CAGLIO sat down behind his desk.

"Marsland," he stated, "young Rydler is of no use to us. I intend to be rid of him. Unfortunately, my niece has befriended him. Therefore, I cannot harm him at present, unless some emergency should render it necessary.

"Martha was here for a purpose, though she did not realize it. Originally, Zovex acted only as an Oracle, to tell the fortunes of society folk who came here. Martha entertained the visitors."

"I get it," grunted Cliff. "The moll was the front for a spook racket. How was the take, prof?"

Caglio smiled at Cliff's slang. He was convinced that The Shadow's agent was a product of the bad lands.

"The take?" queried Caglio. "You mean the revenue? The income?"

Cliff nodded.

"It was quite large," declared the professor. "But since Zovex has changed his policy, the receipts have increased immensely. Of course, you know his present terms?"

"Squint told me," answered Cliff. "Fifty-fifty. Zovex is the brain. He uses fellows like Squint and me to stage the jobs. We deliver the swag. It stays here so Zovex can figure a way to fence it. We get our cut later."

"Yes. When it is safe. Very well. There is always the chance that we may be investigated."

"Through some cluck muffing a job?"

"Yes. As was the case with Moose Sudling."

"Did Moose muff?"

"Yes." Caglio smiled, sourly. "Zovex, however, had prepared for such an occurrence. Every worker is covered during his act of crime. Nevertheless, some one might visit this house—some one not wanted——"

"Like some smart dick——"

"Yes. A sleuth expecting to find a supercriminal. But what would he find? I shall tell you. Nothing but a talking head! An automaton that can be examined. A device once used for telling fortunes."

"They can pinch you on that charge, prof."

"Never! Because I asked no fee for Zovex's services. Wealthy persons sent anonymous contributions. But no requests were made for money."

"I get it. The moll—your niece—she'll back that story. That'll crimp any wise district attorney who wants to make trouble for you."

"Exactly! Any trouble must be quickly squashed. I shall tell you why, Marsland. The mechanical brain of Zovex received much of its stimulation from information that was given by my former clients."

"You mean the society folks blabbed too much?"

"They talked a great deal to Zovex. He learned of many private subjects, that concerned money and its handling. Names were mentioned, also."

"Names like Threed? And Sautelle?"

"Yes. Also that of Percy Rydler. You are beginning to see the situation, Marsland. While we are faced by this problem of The Shadow, it will be best to keep Hal Rydler here, lulled with the hope of a future chat with Zovex.

He should not have many opportunities to talk with Martha.

"Soon after our other plans are in operation, young Rydler will leave. Perhaps he will not actually leave. There are ways to dispose of him here. On the contrary, it may be better to actually send him away, to be handled outside."

Cliff nodded. Caglio was counting upon a mob such as Squint's.

"Our basic policy," reminded the professor, "will be to bring my niece to a state of quietude, with all her suspicions gone. Once she believes that Hal Rydler is free from danger, Martha will again be useful."

PROFESSOR CAGLIO was drumming the desk top as he spoke. Cliff could see that the old inventor was a capable analyst. Caglio had covered the situation well. His policy was obviously planned to cover up the future, as well as the present and the past. Yet Cliff could not picture the old man as the actual plotter.

Did Caglio, himself, consult the Oracle?

Was he but the servant of his own invention?

Cliff wondered; and with the thought came new speculation regarding Zovex. The Head had looked mechanical. Cliff had so described it to The Shadow. But there were reasons why it might be real.

Caglio's own actions indicated that The Head must live. The professor's explanations of the Oracle's mechanism had been glib ones. He had bluffed both Cliff and Squint last night; yet, today, Caglio was talking straight. So long as his speech did not concern the secret of the Oracle, Caglio lacked guile.

This made Cliff believe that the old man's actions had been ordained by some master whom Caglio himself served.

By Zovex.

Yet Zovex was not a human being. He was a head!

Even as Cliff pondered, the answer came. Caglio was studying Cliff's countenance. It was a poker face that gave the old man no inkling of Cliff's own thoughts. Caglio knew only that his companion was engaged in speculation. Admiring Cliff's keenness, the old man suddenly became confidential.

"I mentioned a model of an invention," cackled Caglio, leaning forward. His eyes were alight and wide. "My invention! My masterpiece! Heh-heh-heh! Few eyes have seen it. Yours will be privileged.

"My invention"—his tone had become a croak—"will revolutionize industry! It will give me commercial mastery of the world! The ways of mankind shall some day follow my dictates. Why? Because human beings are the slaves of the machine age. The man with the greatest machine will rule.

"Zovex is a brain." Caglio grinned, cunningly, showing his stumpy teeth. "I shall count upon him as my adviser. I shall harness my mechanized controllers to machinery everywhere. Power plants, steamship engines, printing presses—all will become perpetual when controlled by my master device. It shall be the heart of industry!"

A clucked laugh trailed from Caglio's lips. The old man arose behind the desk and wagged a bony forefinger.

"Later, I shall show you the Caglio controller. You are a man who would recognize its potentiality."

Cliff understood at last. Caglio was a victim of the mania so common to inventors. He believed that he had solved the impossible. He had been working on a device to produce perpetual motion.

"For years I have endeavored." Caglio's finger was still wagging. "I have approached the threshold of success. A brain greater than my own has approved my efforts. I have gained encouragement from an infallible source!"

The old man had reference to Zovex. Cliff knew the hold that The Head had gained. Caglio had become the Oracle's tool because of his own urge to complete his impossible invention. Zovex had gone in for crime. Caglio had aided willingly; not because he had a lust for evil, but because nothing, good or bad, could stop the old man's mania for the impossible.

Zovex had humored Caglio. The professor had returned the favor. He owned full fealty to The Head.

How far Caglio would have followed his present tangent, Cliff never learned. Amid the trail of the professor's maddened cackle came an interruption. It was a knock at the door of the study. Caglio recognized it. His manner changed. He clucked an order to enter.

Havelock came into the room. The chauffeur was wearing cap and gloves. He had evidently come back from a trip in the big roadster, for he was carrying a folded newspaper beneath his arm. Havelock's face was serious.

"What is it?" demanded Caglio. "You have brought news, Havelock?"

The chauffeur nodded. He was shifting the newspaper.

"Look at this, professor." He spread the newspaper upon the desk. "It's about Pinky Garson. He was in an auto smash. Coming through New York."

Caglio seized the newspaper. He muttered; then spoke:

"Garson should not have come back to the city."

"Nobody had anything on him," reminded Havelock. "He was just going through on his way South, when he smacked that taxi under the Sixth Avenue 'L.' He must have bounced off and hit a pillar. He's in a hospital. Looks like it was curtains for him."

"He has not recovered consciousness," remarked Caglio, studying the newspaper. "There is a chance, though, that he may."

"That's just it," agreed Caglio. "And

if he don't know where he is, maybe he'll say too much——"

"That can be learned. Go downstairs, Havelock. Await orders there."

Havelock retired. Caglio slapped the newspaper to the desk. He turned to Cliff.

"Go back to the living room," urged the professor. "Engage the others in conversation. Tell Proddock that you admire my invention. Say that I shall let him see it later. That will give me a chance to talk with him."

As Cliff strolled from the room, Caglio followed. Cliff saw the old man press the outer knob. Caglio pointed frontward. Cliff went to the living room. As he entered the door, he glanced sidelong and saw Caglio stepping in the opposite direction, toward the door of the room where he housed his automata. Cliff guessed that Caglio had gone to speak with Zovex.

ONCE inside the living room, Cliff had a mission to perform. He knew that The Shadow had not overheard the conversation with Caglio. The Shadow could not have opened the panel from the spy room, for that would have extinguished the lights. It was Cliff's job to pass word. He had a way to do it. He nodded to Squint Proddock; then strolled to the big Argus mirror. In nonchalant fashion, Cliff began to adjust his necktie.

"The prof has a swell invention, Proddock," remarked Cliff. He avoided the nickname "Squint," because Hal and Martha were present. "It ought to bring a lot of money. All it needs is a promoter."

"What's the invention?" queried Squint. He had caught on to the bluff this time. "Did you see it work?"

"I saw the model."

Cliff paused. His eyes were moving. Left—straight — upward — downward. Letter by letter, Cliff was spelling a message. It was a system that he had learned from The Shadow: Speech through motions of the eyes. Slight head tilts added to the code. Cliff was a slow speller with the system; but he managed his first message:

"*Rydler—is—safe——*"

"You saw the model?" Squint was questioning. "What does it do?"

"You'll see it later." Cliff had brought a comb from his pocket. Using the comb in front of the mirror, he flashed his eye signals:

"*Prof—with—Zovex——*"

A pause. Then:

"*News—in—study——*"

Cliff turned away from the mirror. He pocketed his comb and sat down to talk with Squint. He knew that The Shadow, ever watchful, had seen his message through the silvered glass.

The door of the living room opened immediately afterward. Professor Caglio entered. Smiling benignly, he closed the door. He noted that Marley, the servant, had gone. Caglio addressed the others:

"Dinner will be at seven o'clock. I notice that Marley has gone to prepare the meal."

From behind the Argus mirror, keen eyes had noticed the professor's lips. The Shadow, already cognizant of Cliff's message, could also see that Caglio intended to remain here. The professor was just inside the closed door. Evidently he wanted to keep every one in the living room.

The Shadow stirred within the spy room. He had the right opportunity to enter the study, knowing that Caglio had not returned there after his visit to Zovex. The Shadow opened the panel. Darkness greeted him; but as soon as he had gained the study and closed the panel from that side, the lights came on again.

The newspaper was on the desk. The Shadow eyed the headlines. He saw the news about Pinky Garson. The crook was in a New York hospital. As The Shadow read, he detected a sound. It came from beyond the wall between the study and the automata room.

The Shadow sprang across and listened by a narrow panel. It was from that spot that the noise came most plainly. A scuffling; a slight scrape; then a thump. A *click,* like that of a doorknob.

Swiftly, The Shadow reached the light switch and extinguished the glow in the study. He placed his hand upon the doorknob, intending to open the barrier and peer into the hall. Some one had left the room where Caglio kept the Oracle!

The doorknob would not turn. It was locked from the outside. The Shadow turned on the light and made for the rear of the room. He gained the hidden passage that skirted the living room. Though silent in tread, he was speedy. He arrived at the end of the passage, at the elevator shaft. He heard a rumbling sound. The elevator was descending with a passenger.

The Shadow had arrived too late. Some one, coming from the automata room, had gone along the hall past the closed door of the living room. That person had already descended to join Havelock in the roadster. There was no chance to overtake him and block the departure.

The Shadow returned to the study, via the skirting passage. The lights went out as he entered the spy room. They came on again, after the panel closed. Ensconced behind the Argus mirror, The Shadow viewed the living room. Caglio was still standing just within the door.

Whispering lips chilled the tiny chamber wherein The Shadow stood. The exit of a dweller from the automata room was to The Shadow's liking, even though he had failed to see the one who had departed. Actually, The Shadow had gained an advantage.

Soon he would have a chance that he had purposely postponed: A visit to the room wherein the Oracle dwelt. The Shadow would later form his own conclusions regarding Zovex, The Head that lived!

CHAPTER XV.
AT THE HOSPITAL.

"Too bad about Pinky Garson. He had a clean bill."

Joe Cardona, acting inspector, made the statement, from behind his desk at police headquarters. His words were addressed to listening reporters. One made an objection:

"Thought he was a slick con man, Joe?"

"Pinky was," admitted Cardona, chewing at the stump of a cigar. "You're right on that guess, Burke. But Pinky squared that part of his past."

"Then you're not going up to see him?"

"Why should I? Markham here talked with him just a little while ago. Pinky was conscious for five minutes, wasn't he, Markham?"

Detective Sergeant Markham nodded.

"And what did he have to say?"

"Nothing important, Joe."

Reporters shuffled out, Cardona smiled. He had bluffed Clyde Burke, sharp news hawk of the tabloid *Classic*. Secretly, Burke was one of The Shadow's agents.

Markham started to speak. Joe motioned for silence. He wanted to be sure that the reporters were out of earshot. At last, Cardona nodded.

"Pinky wants to talk to you, Joe," informed Markham. "Says he'll only talk to you alone."

"Got the car out back?"

"Yeah."

"Let's go."

The dashboard clock showed seven when the police car stopped in front of a small hospital near Sixth Avenue. Cardona entered alone. He encountered an interne, showed his badge, and was conducted to a tiny private room.

"We had him moved in from the ward," informed the interne. "It's all right to talk to him; but he won't last long."

CARDONA entered the room. The interne closed the door from the outside. Pinky Garson, head bandaged, opened his eyes and looked up with glassy stare. He recognized the swarthy face that bent above him, in the glow of a bed lamp.

"H'lo, Joe. Guess I'm woozy."

"How's that, Pinky?"

"Can't see nothing but your head."

"You've got a concussion. That's the way it hits you. I had one once."

"I'm done for, Joe."

Cardona made no reply. Pinky reached feebly for a glass of water. Cardona raised the tumbler and pressed it to the dying man's lips.

"You're a square-shooter, Joe," whispered Pinky. "Wisht I'd been the same. I oughta stayed straight."

"Thought you did go straight, Pinky."

"Yeah. I did. But I slipped back. I'll tell you how and why, Joe—if you'll promise to do something for me."

Cardona made no response. He was noncommittal.

"Nothing that'll put you in Dutch, Joe——"

"All right. Let's hear it."

Pinky's glazed eyes saw friendliness in Cardona's gaze. The dying man motioned for another sip of water. Cardona supplied it. Pinky spoke.

"It's this, Joe," he affirmed. "I had two keys on me. The interne's got 'em, I guess. Both are to safe-deposit boxes. In the same bank. You'd have trouble finding the bank and learning the name the boxes are under. I'll tell you both."

He gave Joe the name of a bank in Cleveland, and the name under which the safe-deposit boxes were held.

Cardona scribbled the facts on a pad.

"Listen, Joe." Pinky was pleading. "One box has dough that's mine. Twenty grand, that I'd built up out of good investments. I gotta couple of kids, in Cincinnati. I ditched 'em years ago. The dough's for them, Joe.

"They say crooks have pals. That's the bunk. Every crook's a rat! I'm a rat! I'd double-cross a dying pal! That's the kind of a mug I am. The only decent guys I've ever met was the fellows I done dirt to. Fellows like you, Joe.

"That's why I wanted you to come here I don't want no rat to get the mazuma that I made when I played straight. It's for the kids. If you say they'll get it, I'll die knowing they will."

Pinky paused. His eyes closed. He was awaiting Cardona's reply. Joe's answer came low, but emphatic.

"The money goes to the kids," assured the ace. "Tell me about the other deposit box, Pinky."

Pinky managed a smile.

"This'll throw you, Joe," he said. "Y'know what's in it? Some of them bonds that Threed shoulda got. I was the guy that staged that job, Joe. I turned 'em over to The Head. He kept more'n half o' em; but wanted me to drag some along an' peddle 'em out West.

"If it worked, I was to bring in the dough, and take out some more of 'em. Being a con man once, it looked like a pipe. I took a trip to Buffalo, before I started to peddle. Thought I'd come through New York, go South, then head up to Cleveland. But that don't matter. I'm through. Them bonds is yours, Joe. You'll turn 'em back to Threed."

CARDONA was silent. Pinky opened his eyes.

"I know what you're thinking, Joe," said the dying man. "The dough ought to go to Threed, too. It ought to make up for the rest of them bonds. I know that, Joe; but the kids have got to get

the twenty grand. That's why I'm telling you where the rest of the bonds are put.

"Not just them, but other swag. The gold from the steamship *Arabia;* the fifty grand that was took from Sautelle; the diamonds that was Percy Rydler's— those weren't my jobs, Joe. But the swag all went to the same guy. His name is Professor Caglio. He lives near Littenden, New Jersey."

Pinky reached for Joe's pad. Weakly, he traced lines to indicate a route. He finished with a square that represented Caglio's house. An arrow served to show the entrance.

"Caglio ain't the big-shot, Joe." Pinky's words came with an effort. "The brain is called 'Zovex.' The prof called him that; but we called him 'The Head.' That's what he is, Joe—a head.

"Sounds screwy; but it ain't. Zovex is The Head. He's a konk with a clockwork brain. And The Head is smart. It won't do to barge in there with a squad. Unless you call in G-men. You can do that, if you know the lay. And the only way to get wise is to get there alone and see The Head. Don't trust nobody, Joe. Nobody but yourself."

"How do I get in?" queried Cardona.

"Drive in," replied Pinky. "Alone. Talk to the prof. Ask to see Zovex. Tell The Head you was with Pinky Garson. Tell him I talked because I was through. Say that you're Tony Darelli, from Cleveland. The Head won't know Tony.

"And there won't be nobody there that knows you. The guys with the prof ain't gorillas. They don't know nobody in New York. There was guys like me that worked for The Head; but they all took it on the lam. The Head don't keep 'em around that joint.

"You can swing it, Joe; but I'm telling you, it's a one-man job. You can't take no chances on nobody but yourself. Don't use no outside cover. The Head might get wise. The guys outside might get jittery. The Head will want to use you. Savvy it, Joe?"

"I get it." Cardona nodded, as Pinky sank back and closed his eyes. "I can go in and out as Tony Darelli."

Pinky smiled, and nodded feebly. He did not open his eyes.

Cardona waited a few minutes; then departed. Downstairs, he asked for Pinky's effects and received them. He found the safe-deposit box keys in an envelope. He handed the latter to Markham, when he had joined the detective sergeant.

"Take me to Tom's garage," ordered Cardona. "I'm going to use that old coupe he keeps there."

"Pinky wised you to something?" queried Markham.

"Yeah," returned Cardona. "You'll know about it later. I'm going somewhere alone. You can slide back to headquarters and keep mum."

Lights were gloomy in the downstairs corridor of the secluded hospital. The interne had left the office. On the ledge lay a sheet of paper with a notation referring to Pinky Garson and the dying man's room number.

A strange sound came from the hospital entrance, a dozen minutes after Cardona had gone. It was a thumping succession of footsteps. Into the dim light clumped a horrendous figure. It was the square-formed creature that Hal Rydler had seen that night at his brother Percy's.

The monster was wide and bulky. Limbs and body were thick and rounded. Its arms extended oddly, hanging short from square-rigged shoulders. Heavy, clumsy gloves covered the hands. Above the thick-sweatered body was a down-turned head, its features lost below the visor of a pulled-down cap.

The clumping visitor stopped by the window of the office. He saw the paper that bore Garson's name. With an evil snarl, the fiendish creature thumped

toward the stairs. Upward it went with steady, heavy footsteps. At the top of a flight, it paused.

A nurse had heard the sound and was standing in the hallway. She could not locate the direction from which the thumps had come. The nurse went along the corridor. Peering from the stairway, the clumper saw her departure. He moved forward and reached Pinky Garson's door. He opened the barrier and entered.

Pinky was lying with closed eyes; but his ears sensed the thumps as the figure thudded up beside the bed. An interval followed. Pinky opened his eyes. His half smile faded. His lips gasped. All that Pinky could see before him was a face. He recognized that fiendish, leering visage with its gloating leer, its squatty nose, its bulging bulbous eyes.

"The Head!"

Venomous eyes saw Pinky's consternation. Evil lips phrased grating words that were as nothing human:

"You have already told your story!"

"I—I couldn't help it!" gasped Pinky. "It—it wasn't no squawk. Honest, Zovex! I didn't think you could come here. The Head—always stayed—there in the room——"

"I can be anywhere!" The words were vicious. "You knew that I would find you!"

"I—I wasn't sure. 1 was croaking; I had to send for a pal. Honest, it was a pal I talked to! Tony Darelli, from Cleveland——"

Furious lips twisted as they spat a demonish snarl. Thick gloves gripped Pinky's throat. Half choked, the dying man heard the fierce-mouthed challenge.

"It was *not* Darelli!"

Pinky gurgled. The clutch was relinquished. Panting, Pinky gulped:

"I—I thought it was Darelli. He said he was Tony. But I wasn't sure—until after—after I'd told him to go to you, alone——"

"Then you knew——"

"Yeah. It—it wasn't Tony. It was Joe Cardona. But he's—he's gone out alone——"

Spasmodically, Pinky had uttered the words despite himself. His eyes had never closed since the moment that he had seen the face he dreaded. The past had surged through Pinky's brain. He had quailed, unable to resist the evil might of Zovex.

The Head had come here! That very impossibility had overwhelmed Pinky Garson. He had not wanted to blab regarding Joe Cardona. Pinky had tried to play straight with the ace detective. But he had failed. Zovex had arrived to gain last-moment knowledge.

While the glaring face still loomed above the dying man, Pinky Garson gave an involuntary gulp. His rigid form relaxed as the sound left his lips.

Pinky Garson was dead.

The face of Zovex remained within the focussed glow of the bed lamp. Seconds passed; then gloating lips showed new distortion. Projected eyes glittered in satanic triumph. The face moved upward. Circling in its steady stride, the wide, squatty figure stamped from the dead man's room.

No one was in the upper corridor. The interne had not yet returned when the horrible figure passed the office. The clumping creature reached the street and clumsily shifted itself into a waiting roadster. Havelock was at the wheel. The car rolled away.

Zovex had learned of Pinky Garson's confession. Joe Cardona had started on a mission that would prove a snare soon after The Head returned to find him at the windowless abode. Death would be designed for Joe Cardona.

Only The Shadow might avert it!

CHAPTER XVI.
THE LAST INTERLUDE.

DINNER had begun at Professor Caglio's. The meal had been delayed, probably through some fault of the serv-

ant Marley's. Hence the clock in the living room was chiming half past seven when the expectant diners were called.

The Shadow, watching through the Argus mirror, saw the last of the throng depart. He turned about and opened the panel to the study. He stepped into the silent darkness. Light came on as The Shadow closed the wall.

This was The Shadow's hour of opportunity. He had delayed in order to make sure that Caglio would not return to the study. Knowing that the old professor would be at dinner, The Shadow had time to operate.

His first goal was the narrow panel on the other side of the study. It was there that he had heard the sounds from the automata room. The Shadow knew that there must be a hollow space beyond the narrow panel.

He had not learned that fact upon his previous investigation. That was because he had tapped the broad panels only. All other special panels had been wide ones. This narrow space was inches, only. It could not serve as a way to a regular passage. In view of present circumstances, however, the narrow panel demanded survey.

The upright strip opened under proper pressure. It slid aside. The study lights revealed a space between brick walls. It was a cleft straight through to the next room, with another barrier at the other end. The space was considerably less than six inches in width.

The Shadow could not squeeze his shoulders through it. Nor could he manage to reach the barrier at the other end. He had found a passage to the room that he wanted to reach; but the avenue was useless.

The Shadow closed the panel. He tried the door of the study and found it locked from the outside. He took to the roundabout passage that skirted the living room. He came to the end of the elevator shaft. Cautiously, he opened the final panel.

From the end of the hall, The Shadow could see into the dining room. Professor Caglio was seated at the head of the table, with Martha on his right and Hal on his left. Cliff Marsland was seated next to Martha. Squint Proddock was beside Hal.

Marley entered from the kitchen. The servant was carrying a platter. Martha took a helping; then, the professor. While the old man was engaged, The Shadow edged out into the hall and closed the panel. Neither Caglio nor Marley saw his advent. As for Hal and Squint, their backs were toward the hall.

If Cliff saw, it would not matter. The Shadow was running a risk only so far as Martha was concerned. As it happened, Cliff did not spy The Shadow. But Martha, chancing to look toward the hall, caught a full view of the cloaked figure.

THE SHADOW saw the girl's stare. He had closed the panel. Martha did not know whence he had come. For an instant, burning eyes were focussed from a distance. Then The Shadow had swept noiselessly along the hall.

Martha blurted a cry of surprise. Cliff looked toward the girl and saw the direction of her gaze. He knew that Martha had seen The Shadow. With quick impulse, Cliff scuffed his chair backward and snatched at a glass of water that was near Martha's plate. His action caused the others to look toward him. Martha looked with the others.

"Clumsy of me!" exclaimed Cliff. "You will excuse me, Miss Keswick. I don't blame you for being startled. I almost toppled that glass of water."

The girl delivered a relieved smile. She did not know that Cliff had purposely covered the lapse that she had made. She thought the incident of the glass was a chance one. It gave her time, however, to regain her composure.

Martha knew that this house held secrets. She had seen the Oracle; she had guessed that there was a lurker here whom she had never seen. Hal's experience had added to her belief. Sight of The Shadow had startled her but momentarily. Her conclusion was that the cloaked shape must be identified with Zovex. The girl was glad that she had been able to gain an excuse for her alarm.

IN the hallway, The Shadow had passed the door of the study. He stopped at the door of the automata room and found the knob pressed inward. He turned it. The door opened. The Shadow gained his first entrance into the abode of Zovex.

The Shadow had known that this door would ordinarily be locked from the inside. But since some one had departed from the room, he had inferred that it would be locked from the outside only. In order to be sure of later exit, The Shadow pulled the outside knob outward. Then, in the room itself, he closed the door behind him.

The Shadow noted the mechanical chess player and the doll-like writing figure. He passed beneath the cages with their artificial birds. He saw the boxes of heads upon the shelf. He picked a closed one and opened it. Inside he saw the head he wanted. It was the Oracle.

The Shadow studied the leering face of Zovex. The bulging eyes were glaring, despite their glassiness. The Shadow removed The Head from its box. He studied the surface of the evil, V-lined face. It was not ordinary waxwork; nor was it an embalmed head. The Oracle was made of some peculiar composition that possessed flexibility.

The Shadow opened the back of the head and examined the interior mechanism. He tested various levers, set them; then placed the head upon the square-topped table. The Shadow waited. The lips began to move. They

made no sound. The Shadow had not started the ribbon rollers.

Lips stalled. The Shadow jogged the table. An interval; the lips moved again. They stopped. Eyelids dropped with a slight *click*. The Shadow lifted the head, opened it again and made another inspection. He pressed a catch. The eyes opened.

There were six roller ribbons inside the head. The Shadow counted them; but made no test. He knew that they acted as phonographic records. He saw no reason to make the head speak. He replaced the automaton in its box and put the latter upon the shelf.

The square-topped table interested The Shadow; for it was there that the head had rested, according to Cliff's account. The Shadow removed the top of the table. First, he studied the top itself.

It was formed of nine squares, each about six inches across. These were grooved together to form a solid top. They were held compact by a four-sided border, that added six inches to each edge. Thus the entire top measured about two and one half feet across.

That space was considerably more than the pedestal, which The Shadow estimated to be twenty inches square at the top. The Shadow saw the array of batteries nestled in the pedestal. He removed them. The pedestal narrowed downward on the outside. Viewing its interior, The Shadow saw that the cavity tapered in similar fashion.

The Shadow tested the batteries. They were dead. Caglio's explanation of electromagnetism was sheer bunk.

WITH a whispered laugh, The Shadow replaced the bordered table top. He had learned one fact. He wanted another. He went to the waxwork chess player and opened the door in its chest. He also unclosed the two doors in the supporting oblong box. He saw the array of interior levers; but he needed his flashlight to make a full inspection.

By the glimmer of the little torch, The Shadow studied the machinery. The levers were not thickly placed; for he was able to extend his arm up through the hollow body of the chess player. A glow shone through the door in the figure's chest. The door was merely a light framework, its front stretched with cloth.

The Shadow extinguished the flashlight. He walked about the room, tapping at every panel, broad and narrow. The only one that opened was the panel that connected with the cramped passage into the study. Hence The Shadow had no outlet except by the door of the room.

Finished with the panels, The Shadow went to the safe. It was unlocked. All that The Shadow found inside was a long box that looked like a carrying case; but there was room for other objects, if required. The Shadow opened the carrying case. It was empty. It had plush-lined sections; and all of these were curved, in both top and bottom of the hinge-lidded box.

It was easy to see that the box had contained cylinders of various lengths and widths. If hollow, larger cylinders could have held smaller. This was likely for, beside the box, The Shadow found fiber wedges. With large cylinders inside small ones, these plugs would prevent the interior tubes from rattling.

The Shadow shut the carrying case and closed the safe. A repetition of his low-toned laugh told that his inspection was concluded. The room was as The Shadow had found it. He made his exit into the hall. He closed the door and pressed the outer knob.

Instead of returning toward the front end of the hallway, The Shadow chose the stairway to the second floor. He had seen every one in the dining room, except Selfridge. It was likely that the technician would be in the garage dur-

ing Havelock's absence. The second floor proved clear; and The Shadow chose a room on the living-room side of the house. He found its secret panel and descended by a spiral stairway to the study.

The Shadow crossed the lighted room and stopped at the panel to the spy room. He had accomplished his intended purpose. He had visited the room where Professor Caglio kept the talking head. For the present, The Shadow desired a return to obscurity. He was upon the point of gaining it.

JUST as The Shadow pressed the panel to produce darkness, his ears caught a *click*. It came from the door of the study. It meant that Professor Caglio had returned from dinner. The warning sound was the old man's pull upon the outer knob. Methodically, Caglio was following the sensible procedure of assuring himself an unlocked door when he came to make his later exit.

Had The Shadow paused one instant, Caglio would have discovered darkness when he entered the study. The Shadow's plans would have been crimped. But, to The Shadow, the warning *click* was an immediate spur to quickness. He swung into the spy room and closed the panel behind him. Lights were on again at the moment when Caglio opened the door from the hall.

Behind the Argus mirror, The Shadow saw the diners returning to the living room. Cliff Marsland strolled in front of the mirror and glanced at his reflection in the glass. Cliff's eyes moved, choosing varied directions. The Shadow's agent was passing a brief message to his hidden chief.

All was well for the present. Cliff would be on watch, ready to give word of any important event that he might notice. He was counting upon another trip to the closed room. Cliff expected that he and Squint would soon hold an interview with Zovex.

The Shadow, watching, knew facts that Cliff did not recognize. He doubted that the interview would come as soon as his agent anticipated. For The Shadow had learned new and deeper secrets through his visit to the Oracle's abode. He had solved the riddle of The Head that lived.

Strange events would soon be due. The Shadow was prepared for them, now that the last interlude was ended. The master sleuth had completed plans of action. They might alter, however, should chance compel it.

It was well that The Shadow had made such allowance. Within the next half hour, he was to be faced by complications that even he had not foreseen!

CHAPTER XVII.
THE NEW ALLY.

MARTHA KESWICK seemed very weary, as she seated herself beside the fireplace. The Shadow could see that the girl was drowsy. Several minutes passed; Martha suddenly roused from her stupor. The Shadow saw the girl rise and speak. He read her lips. She was stating that she planned to go upstairs and nap.

Apparently, Martha had decided that no harm would befall Hal Rydler during the evening. Cliff Marsland and Squint Proddock had played their part as guests. Cliff, through his natural courtesy; Squint, by saying little. Though she still held mistrust of her uncle, Martha felt certain there would be no danger to Hal while the others were about.

The girl was intending another all-night vigil. Therefore, she felt the need of sleep in preparation for the later hours.

Shortly after Martha had left, Professor Caglio entered. He noticed that Hal was reading a book. With a slight smile, Caglio spoke to Cliff.

"Perhaps you and Mr. Proddock

would like to see the model of my invention?"

"Certainly," interposed Cliff. "Come along, Proddock."

The three strolled from the room. The Shadow knew that they were bound for the professor's study. He would hear from Cliff later. That assumption was correct; but The Shadow's contact with his agent was to come in a different manner than by eye signals through the Argus mirror.

IN the study, Professor Caglio spoke:

"I have heard from Selfridge. He telephoned up from the garage below. A stranger has arrived. Selfridge is in doubt about him."

"Who is it?" queried Squint. "Any guy I might know?"

"Possibly," replied Caglio. "The newcomer claims to be a friend of Pinky Garson. Selfridge, of course, disclaimed any acquaintance with Garson."

"What moniker did the bird give?"

"He calls himself Tony Darelli. He claims to be from Cleveland."

"Tony Darelli, huh? I've heard of him. He's from Cleveland, all right. Pinky should have knowed him. Ever meet Tony, Cliff?"

Cliff shook his head in response to Squint's question.

"I should like you to·observe him," remarked Caglio. "Both of you can deliver sound opinions. I shall have Selfridge conduct him to the living room, so that I may interview him there."

"Is that where we'll lamp him?" questioned Squint.

"Yes," replied the professor, "but he will not see you. Come. I shall show you an interesting feature of this room. Do not be disturbed when the lights extinguish automatically."

He stepped to the panel on the living-room side. He opened it; the study lights did a quick black-out. The glow

from the Argus mirror greeted Cliff and Squint.

"Step forward," ordered Caglio. "Wait here until I return. Watch through the mirror."

The panel closed. Squint whispered to Cliff.

"Ain't this the hot one!" declaimed the crook. "Say—I'd never have guessed that the mirror was a phony!"

"Stick close to the center," suggested Cliff. "Keep watching for Tony to show up."

Cliff knew that The Shadow was here in the darkness. He added information that he knew his chief would appreciate.

"Pinky must have talked to Tony Darelli," remarked Cliff. "The prof is

wise, though, having us here to look Tony over. Here's the prof coming into the living room. I guess Selfridge is on his way up with Tony."

"Here they are now," put in Squint. "Selfridge is showing the guy in——"

The sentence ended with an oath. Squint followed with a harsh whisper of recognition:

"Joe Cardona!"

Cliff grunted.

"The mug's got crust!" added Squint. "Say—Pinky must have spilled something and then croaked! So he calls himself Darelli, huh? Wait'll we give the lowdown to the prof."

"The prof is introducing him to Rydler," remarked Cliff.

"Yeah," nodded Squint. "And Joe's

The Shadow removed The Head from its box. He studied the surface of the evil face.

wise that this bird is some relation to the guy whose place was cracked. Joe thinks he's getting somewhere."

"Looks like he has."

Cliff's remark was significant. It indicated trouble for the ace detective. Squint gave a chuckle.

"The prof is leaving Selfridge with them," he declared. "He's gone out and he's closed the door. He'll be calling us in a minute."

SOMETHING gripped Cliff's hand in the darkness. Gloved fingers thrust a wad of paper into the agent's fist. A message from The Shadow.

The panel opened a minute later.

There was a whisper from the darkness of the study. Cliff and Squint stepped back into the large room. Squint was talking as the lights came on. The professor heard him from beside the panel.

"It's Joe Cardona!" exclaimed the crook. "Used to be a fly-cop; now he's acting as an inspector. He's the smart guy that's been trying to get wise to our jobs."

Professor Caglio glared. His lips moved, seeking words.

"We gotta smear him," added Squint. "Say—putting him in there with Rydler was a bum guess."

"Perhaps not." Caglio's voice had returned. The old man had calmed. "It may work to our advantage. Remember, Marsland?—I told you this afternoon that I was prepared for such emergency as this."

Cliff nodded.

"If this detective has brought others," clucked Caglio, "we shall handle him politely; and Rydler as well. But if he has come alone——"

"The spot for both of them, huh?"

Caglio nodded slowly, as he heard Squint's interjection.

"Probably," decided the professor. "First, I shall seek the advice of Zovex. I shall visit the Oracle presently——"

A rap at the door. Caglio's eyes gleamed. He gave the summons to enter. Havelock appeared.

"Where's Selfridge?" queried the chauffeur. Did he bring any one up?"

Caglio nodded, wisely.

"A fellow named Cardona?"

Another nod to Havelock's query. The chauffeur grinned.

"Keen work, prof! We figured he'd be here by now. We were looking around when we came in by the drive. There's nobody outside——"

"Go below, Havelock. I shall confer with The Head."

Caglio's cackled statement was emphatic. The professor followed the chauffeur from the room, leaving Cliff and Squint alone by the desk.

"Looks good, Cliff," chuckled Squint. "Some easy work for The Head, before he figures out how to get The Shadow."

"It looks good for us," agreed Cliff, "but it looks sour for Joe Cardona."

"That cluck was due for trouble some day."

"This is the day he's gotten it."

SEATED by the desk, Cliff had opportunity to open the folded paper, without Squint noting it. Cliff read coded lines in bluish ink. He understood their meaning. Brief instructions from The Shadow. The writing faded. It was in a special disappearing ink. Cliff let the paper flutter beneath the desk.

Five minutes passed. The door opened and Professor Caglio entered. The old man's face showed a pleased leer.

"We shall make a test," informed the inventor. "Cardona shall see The Head, along with Rydler. The Head, in turn, will see them. Our purpose will be to lull them. Zovex will learn the extent of their suspicions. Their reactions will determine the measures that will be taken to dispose of them."

"Curtains for both?" queried Squint.

"Death," assured Caglio. "But not until afterward. Unless some unforeseen emergency should arise. In that case, I shall call upon you. Be in readiness."

Chuckling, Caglio left the study. Cliff rubbed his chin; then spoke to Squint.

"I'm going to take another look through that mirror," decided The Shadow's agent. "Stick here, Squint."

Cliff went to the light switch.

"You don't have to turn out the lights," observed Squint. "The prof didn't douse them."

"I don't want to take chances," returned Cliff. "He did something at the panel. I'd better be sure."

"Guess you're right. Any glim would queer that phony mirror."

Cliff turned off the lights. Edging through darkness, he found the panel. He opened it as Caglio had. Light showed from the living room; then ended as Cliff stepped into the space between and shut the panel after him.

Quickly, Cliff whispered the news to The Shadow. He told of the proposed visit to Zovex; of Caglio's verdict; and finally that he and Squint were to stand by.

The Shadow spoke in response. Cliff saw his silhouette against the silvered glass. The Shadow was looking through the Argus mirror. Caglio had not come back to the living room.

"Open the panel!"

Cliff obeyed the whispered order. He stepped into the darkness of the study. He blundered toward the door, to find the light switch. Cliff did not close the panel. He had left that to The Shadow.

A muffled *click* came from the back of the room. Promptly, Cliff turned on the lights. He saw Squint, staring. The crook turned about.

"Funny," remarked Squint. "I thought I heard something at the back of the room; like the light switch was there."

"You can't guess sounds in the dark, Squint."

"You're right. Say—what was doing in the living room?"

"Nothing. Cardona was chinning with Selfridge. Rydler was looking on."

"The prof wasn't there?"

"Not yet."

"Guess he's in with Zovex, then."

Cliff was pleased. Squint had dropped the subject of that muffled *click*. It had been a deliberate signal from The Shadow. The cloaked chief had gone through the study in the darkness. He had taken to the wall passage that offered access to the upper floor. Cliff had abetted the process, stalling with the light switch until The Shadow was clear.

Such had been the purpose of The Shadow's message. He had wanted to gain an exit from the spy room. Cliff's coöperation had aided him. But Cliff had not guessed The Shadow's motive. He would have been astonished, had he seen the sequel.

UPSTAIRS, The Shadow appeared suddenly in the mellow light of the vacant hall. He had come through one of the rooms on the study side of the house.

He moved toward a door, stopped there and tapped softly on the door.

Martha's voice came from within: "Who is it?"

"Important!" The Shadow's response was in a breathless tone that simulated Hal Rydler's. "I must see you at once, Miss Keswick!"

The door opened.

Moonlight showed Martha Keswick, standing within the room. A gasp came from the girl. She could see The Shadow plainly in the light of the hall.

For the second time, Martha was viewing that weird figure. But on this occasion, she was faced squarely by the eyes that burned from beneath the hat brim. One fearful thought gripped the frightened girl.

"Zovex!"

Martha was barely able to phrase the terrible name. The Shadow's whisper came in sibilant return.

"Not Zovex," he declared. "I am a friend! One whom you must trust!"

The words carried a commanding force. Martha nodded.

"Another guest has arrived," pronounced The Shadow. "He is a detective named Cardona. Like Hal Rydler, he stands in danger."

"At this moment?"

"No. The danger will strike later. It can be averted."

"But—but how?"

"By forcing it. The present task is yours. The rest will be mine."

Martha nodded soberly. There was a calming quality in The Shadow's tone. The burning eyes brought confidence. They always did to those who were worthy of a trust. But to men of crime they delivered a fear that nothing could overpower.

"Go to the living room." The Shadow's tone was emphatic. "Speak to Hal Rydler. Tell him to insist upon two points after he has visited Zovex."

Martha nodded her understanding.

"First," enumerated The Shadow, "he

must request another brief interview with The Head. Second, he must ask for a full explanation of the mechanism in the automatic chess player."

"I shall tell him," stated Martha. "He is to insist after he has first talked with Zovex to-night."

"Yes. After he has left the room where Zovex is."

"And then?"

"You will return upstairs. Remain here."

The Shadow had moved backward across the hall. Martha closed the door of her room. She turned to look for the mysterious being in black. The Shadow was gone. He had merged with the darkness of some doorway. Martha looked about in vain. She heard a whispered voice that uttered a single word:

"Proceed!"

Nodding, the girl hastened toward the stairway. As she reached the end of the hall, she caught the tones of a subdued laugh. It came from unseen lips, a whispered note of mirth that brought a shudder through the corridor.

Yet, strangely, the weird mockery did not bring fear to Martha Keswick. Instead, it was an urge; a final inspiration that gave determination to complete the mission. It was a reminder of the promise that the girl had given.

Such was the laugh of The Shadow.

CHAPTER XVIII.
THE DOUBLE GAME.

JOE CARDONA was still talking to Selfridge when Martha Keswick entered the living room. Professor Caglio had not returned. The girl sat down and found opportunity to speak with Hal Rydler. The Shadow had foreseen this situation. He knew that Selfridge would be busy making conversation with Cardona.

Quickly, Martha repeated the instructions. Hal looked puzzled; but his trust in the girl was sufficient. He nodded his agreement. Martha arose and was idling toward the door when Caglio arrived. The professor eyed his niece shrewdly; Martha met his gaze mildly. Caglio suspected nothing.

He paused long enough, however, to see the girl go upstairs. Then he entered the living room and spoke to his two guests.

"Come," suggested Caglio. "We shall visit the Oracle."

Hal and Cardona followed the professor to the room at the end of the hall. Selfridge came along. Marley went by them on his way to the kitchen. The professor opened the door of the end room. Cardona stared about as they entered.

"I hope this will interest you, Mr. Darelli," said Caglio, in a polite cackle. "I do not recall the name of the man whom you mentioned. Who was it again?"

"A fellow named Garson," returned Cardona, gruffly. "He said you'd know him. Pinky Garson."

"He must have jested," decided Caglio. "My patrons do not make themselves known by their nicknames. Mr. Garson must have been a stranger who came here with one of my wealthy clients."

"He said The Head would talk to me."

"Quite true. Here is The Head. But, as I have explained to Mr. Rydler, it is nothing but a mechanical device."

Hal started an objection.

"Last night," he reminded. "You spoke of the theraphim——"

"Ah, yes." Caglio caught himself. He had chosen the wrong story. "I told you the legends of the theraphim and the androides. I spoke of the head of Mirme. I said that the theraphim were supposed to be embalmed heads.

"Heads with gold plates beneath their tongues. But this head has no such device. Perhaps you misunderstood me,

Mr. Rydler. I meant that the head of Zovex simulates those that the ancients knew."

CAGLIO had brought the talking head from the shelf. Cardona and Hal were viewing the evil face through the opened front of the box. Caglio placed the box upon the table; then removed the head itself.

He opened the back of the head and showed the mechanism. He chortled as he closed the hinged section and placed the ugly head in its usual place within the box. Shrewdly, Caglio began an eccentric part. He tapped his forehead; then spoke:

"Some say that I am lacking here. That is not true. I am a dreamer. I have visioned a mechanical brain. That may be why people form strange theories. Some think my own brain is incomplete. Others—superstitious persons, of course—believe that I have actually achieved my dream.

"They believe that Zovex lives. That he thinks. They have attached odd meanings to the words that mechanical lips have uttered. Because of that, I no longer demonstrate the Oracle without explaining the truth about it.

"See? The Head is ready. It will answer questions; but its range is limited. Suppose, Mr. Darelli, that you tell the Oracle who you are. Then listen for its response."

Cardona faced the evil-eyed visage of Zovex.

"I am Tony Darelli," stated Joe. "Tony Darelli, from Cleveland."

Caglio was beside the table, watching The Head. The lips of the image moved. They grated a reply:

"Zovex has heard."

"Ask a question," suggested Caglio. "Hear what The Head replies."

"Tell me what I'm here for," put Cardona.

Again, The Head responded:

"Zovex will answer."

Cardona narrowed his gaze. The answer was an evasion.

"When will Zovex answer?"

Caglio, himself, put the last question. The Head replied:

"To-morrow."

Eyelids clicked shut. Caglio bowed. "That is all," he decided. "Come! Look at the automatic chess player. It is a marvelous curio! Ah! The board is set for checkers. Try your game, Mr. Darelli."

Cardona began the game of checkers. He was usually good at the pastime; but to-night he lapsed. Joe thought the waxwork Turk a poor opponent; moreover, he was constantly forgetting his moves in order to glance toward the head of Zovex.

"Heh!" Caglio's chuckle made Cardona stare at the checkerboard in time to see the automaton negotiate a triple jump. "You are beaten, Mr. Darelli! You made one bad move. That was a mistake."

Caglio motioned toward the door. The visitors filed out with Selfridge. They walked toward the living room, where the professor expressed an invitation.

"MARLEY reports that the sky is clouding," declared the professor. "It will probably storm to-night. Both of you must remain here as my guests. You will sleep better, Mr. Rydler, than you did before. Soon there will be no moonlight to disturb your rest."

"I'd sleep better if I talked to The Head," grumbled Hal, suddenly. "You promised me that opportunity, professor."

"You heard Zovex speak to-night."

"And say the same things that he said before. Only I talked twice to The Head last night. The second time, it gave a better demonstration. It was more like an Oracle."

Caglio was shrewd in his gaze. He saw that Cardona was interested in Hal's statements.

"You may both have another interview," remarked the professor. "But I can promise very little more than you already heard. The device is purely mechanical. You must allow me time to make adjustments."

"All right," agreed Hal. Then, as Caglio turned, "One other thing, professor: a favor that I know you will readily grant. I'd like to know more about the chess player. Its operation amazes me.

"You forgot to show Mr. Darelli the machinery. I think he'd like to see it. He would realize then how complicated it is. I suppose, of course, that the figure can be removed from the big chest? To give a better view of the mechanism?"

Caglio hesitated; then replied:

"I think I can arrange it. I shall adjust the mechanism in the head; then I shall consider the matter of the chess player."

The professor left the group. It was five minutes before he returned to the living room.

"The Head is adjusted," he cackled, "but I shall need your aid, Selfridge, to dismantle the chess player. Let us go to the room."

THEY returned to view the Oracle. Selfridge set to work at once upon the chess player, while Hal faced Zovex and spoke:

"I have a question."

The eyes of Zovex glared. The lips rasped:

"Zovex will answer."

"I should like to know more about the subject that we discussed last night. Where are my brother's jewels?"

Cardona wheeled about when he heard Hal's question.

"Zovex sees no jewels," hissed The Head.

"You saw them last night," retorted Hal. "Why can't you see them again?"

"Zovex has spoken!"

There was finality in the Oracle's tone. Professor Caglio chuckled.

"That is all," he decided. "Look! Selfridge has dismantled the chess player."

The technician had removed the wax-work figure from the oblong box. The chess player was lying on the floor, tilted over. The observers saw that it was hollow. They looked down into the oblong box. Hal put a surprised exclamation.

"The machinery is only at the front!" he ejaculated. "The rest of the box is empty."

"No more mechanism is necessary," explained Caglio.

"Then why such a large box?" asked Hal. "And such a large figure? The player itself contains only a shell of mechanism."

Without knowing it, Hal was making the same discovery as The Shadow; but without a probe of his own. Hal was acting as The Shadow had expected. More began to occur in accordance with The Shadow's hopes. The Shadow had pictured Hal Rydler and Joe Cardona as a competent pair—Hal to produce statements that would bring hunches from Joe. It was Cardona who spoke next.

"Say—that thing trimmed me," grumbled Cardona. "I don't care how it works. I'd like to have another game."

"The automaton is dismantled," reminded Caglio.

"It only took a few minutes to get it apart," remarked Joe. "As I see it, there's only a couple of levers to be hooked and it will work again. How about it, Selfridge?"

The technician was caught wordless. Professor Caglio glared. He suddenly changed policy.

"We shall replace the figure," he decided. "That is your task, Selfridge. Perhaps you will need Marley——"

THE professor stepped over and opened the door to the hallway. He went out to look for Marley; but returned a half minute later to find that Cardona had already aided Selfridge. The automaton was on its pedestal. Selfridge was attaching levers.

Caglio shouldered forward and pushed the technician aside. He reached in through one of the doorways in the box. He tugged at a lever. Something snapped. Caglio cackled angrily. He withdrew his hand, bringing forth a broken rod of metal.

"Bah!" announced the professor. "The automaton will not operate. It will be three days before I can replace this broken part——"

"That you broke yourself!" growled Cardona. "I'm wise to your bluff, professor. I don't know your game; but its phony! You made a slip when you showed us the inside of this thing.

"Why?—because there's too much space there. Plenty of room to hide a man and have him move around——"

"By opening one door after the other!" interjected Hal. "That's it, Darelli!"

"I'm not Darelli," inserted Joe. "I'm from New York police headquarters! My name is Cardona and I know the inside of this racket! You're coming clean, professor——"

Selfridge made a spring for Cardona. The technician was whipping out a revolver. Cardona was quicker. The ace detective already had a grip on his own gun. He jabbed a stubby revolver into Selfridge's ribs and snapped an order to Hal.

"Grab the professor!"

Hal snatched at Caglio's wrist. He wrenched the professor's hand from his pocket. A revolver plopped to the floor. Caglio shouted a cry for aid. Men pounded into the doorway with leveled guns. Cliff and Squint had arrived at the professor's call.

Cardona stood dumfounded, while Hal grunted a hopeless utterance. And

from across the room, the face of Zovex glared triumphant from the box upon the table!

CHAPTER XIX.

THE LAST ORACLE.

"STICK 'em up!"

Squint Proddock barked the words. With Cliff Marsland beside him, the narrow-eyed ruffian was ready to deliver massacre. He wanted his foemen helpless before he started.

Hal's hands raised. Cardona's gun fist slowly drew away from Selfridge's body. Then came a steady order:

"Drop the rod, Squint!"

Cliff Marsland was the speaker. From behind Squint's left shoulder, he jabbed his automatic hard against the crook's ribs. Squint's eyes blinked; his lips snarled.

"Drop it! Quick!"

The revolver thudded the floor. Gunless, Squint lifted his own arms. Cliff was grim, as he spoke to Cardona.

"Keep Selfridge covered, Joe. You, Rydler, watch the professor. I came out here, just for this!"

Cardona was amazed. He had known Cliff Marsland as a character in the bad lands. For the first time, Joe realized that Cliff was on the side of the law. A sudden explanation struck Cardona. The Shadow had been in the earlier game. Cliff must be one of The Shadow's aids.

Cliff grinned at Cardona's surprise. He was sorry that the issue had been forced—for he had long kept the police in ignorance of the parts that he had played in aiding The Shadow. Some day, Cliff had known, his role would have to be found out. Only The Shadow was keen enough to permanently play a hidden part. His agents lacked that ability.

Cliff was glad, though, that Joe was the only representative of the law upon this scene. Joe would keep mum. Cliff could still be useful to The Shadow, in New York.

Then speculation ended.

It came when a rasped tone sounded from across the room. All eyes turned as listeners heard. It was a venomous utterance that only fiendish lips could have voiced. That snarl was the challenge of Zovex!

THERE was a clatter. As men stared, Professor Caglio cackled an echo to The Head's demoniac snarl. The box upon the table was hurtling upward, the table top with it, impelled by the spring of swiftly rising shoulders. Away went the box, to crash upon the floor, bottomless. The table top whirled after it, struck by an upward-swinging forearm.

From the pedestal projected a distorted figure that had bobbed up like a jack-in-the-box. It was a body of skin and bones, a dwarfish, long-limbed shape garbed in tight-fitting jersey. Upon twisted shoulders rested the head of Zovex.

That head was real! Full-sized, it formed the only normal portion of the monstrosity that had sprung from the cramped pedestal. The arms, though scrawny, were as quick as whiplashes. Long limbs sped forward from a side-arm swing. Clawish fists were aiming ready revolvers that Zovex had held within the compact hiding place.

Zovex was a freak who would have attracted thousands to a side show. More than that, he was a murderer, ready to put on a swift performance. His itching fingers were upon the gun triggers. He had taken his opponents unaware; point-blank, he was about to mow down startled men with quick, successive shots.

Hard upon the fiend's snarl came a chilling laugh, that drowned Professor Caglio's intervening chuckle. The peal of mirth sounded from the doorway. Zovex heard. His bulging eyes saw. His snarl repeated, he forgot all others.

He jabbed both guns straight for the doorway.

There stood The Shadow.

This climax was one that he had planned. He had learned the secret ways of Zovex. He shared none of the bewilderment that gripped the others. He had expected this spindly creature to rise from the interior of the pedestal. The Shadow's investigation of this room had given him every clue he wanted.

Zovex had whipped upward with the flashing speed of a cobra. The Shadow, watching from outside the door, had barely matched the fiend's swiftness. Zovex had spied him instantly. As the creature aimed, his vicious eyes were wild in their gleam. His lips spat his harsh-rasped verdict:

"Death!"

WITHIN the doorway The Shadow stood, his left hand extended gloveless. His thumb and second finger were pressed tip to tip. The girasol glimmered from his hand. His right fist was half beneath his cloak, stalled on its way to draw an automatic.

No wonder Zovex had again played the part of an oracle. His one word—"Death!"—seemed a positive prophecy!

Long arms, as thin as tentacles, were coming in to center. The fingers of scrawny hands were on their triggers. Only split-second speed could save The Shadow. It came.

His thumb and finger snapped. Blazed thunder split the cramped atmosphere of the room. From The Shadow's left hand came a vivid flash, with the blinding effect of lightning. A puff of smoke enveloped the black-hued form.

Bulging eyes were dazzled. Scrawny hands faltered. Dazzled by the flash squarely in his path of vision, Zovex was halted. Then he pressed the triggers. His aim was wide. The fiend's revolvers rocketed their bullets to the panels on each side of the door. His centering guns had stopped too soon.

Simultaneously, The Shadow acted. His right hand had whipped from beneath his cloak. With a short wrist-snap, he aimed a .45 and blazed a shot that accompanied the fire of Zovex.

The booming automatic tongued straight to its mark. A bullet withered the evil heart of Zovex. The power behind the speeding slug was terrific. It produced an unexpected result.

Zovex had recoiled with the fire of his own guns. The impact of The Shadow's bullet trebled the jolt. Backward went the livid-faced fiend, carrying the table base with him. The pedestal thudded the floor. Out spilled Zovex, to sprawl like a long-coiled devilfish landed upon a ship's deck.

The Shadow had gained the vital edge in this amazing combat. That flash from his finger tips had stopped The Head's aim.* Hard upon his dazzling stroke, The Shadow had delivered his close-range shot. He stood, triumphant.

SHOTS ripped from the hall. The Shadow wheeled, his left hand drawing a second .45. His new target was the elevator at the front of the corridor. Three men had arrived. Havelock had come up with Marley. They were bringing an unexpected newcomer—Moose Sudling, the murderer who had left Manhattan.

Jemley's killer had picked a bad time to visit The Head. Moose was the first of the trio to taste The Shadow's lead. The arrivals had fired too quickly. Havelock and Marley regretted it, when Moose sprawled between them. Again, The Shadow's guns were tonguing doom.

─────────

*Note: The explosion from the finger tips, produced by the action of two chemicals, is terrific in its power. It is extremely dangerous in use; for an overamount, even though seemingly slight, will produce an explosion with the effect of TNT. The Shadow has used it but seldom; on those occasions, with the strictest care. Properly produced, the explosion is so instantaneous that the operator remains uninjured. Because of the danger from these chemicals, I have never made a copy of the formula; and can answer no requests concerning it.—
Maxwell Grant.

Two bullets had found Moose. A third clipped Havelock's gun arm. The chauffeur dropped to the floor, howling. Marley threw up his hands, delivering his gun with a wild toss.

From inside the room, one man made a frenzied attack. Squint Proddock, snatching up his gun from the floor, was on the aim for The Shadow. Squint had lunged Cliff aside. Before The Shadow's agent could recover, a revolver spoke. It was Joe Cardona's.

Squint toppled to the floor, his gun jouncing from his fist. Cardona had finished the thuggish killer. Selfridge was too slow to make a move. Caglio, breaking away from Hal, found Cliff on hand to cover him. Wildly, the professor backed away; then stared toward the dead form of Zovex.

Sight of the slain monstrosity brought a terrible cackle from the old inventor's lips. Cliff and Hal seized him as he clawed the air and uttered maddened screams. Caglio suddenly collapsed within their grasp and floundered to the floor. He lay there, groaning, muttering.

Selfridge, subdued, spoke to Cardona:

"He counted on The Head. To back him with his impossible invention. We couldn't help it, Marley and I. Havelock was the only bad one among us. Marley and I played along. But we weren't for it."

Marley was coming into the room, aiding Havelock. Cardona ordered Marley and Selfridge to attend to the crippled chauffeur. Joe stepped to the hall, expecting to see The Shadow. The cloaked fighter was gone. He had given an order to Marley; then he had departed. Cardona could hear the rumble of the elevator.

Martha Keswick was standing in the passage from the stairs. The girl stepped forward as Cardona spoke to her. Looking past Joe, Martha saw Hal Rydler stepping soberly into the hall. The girl gave a choke of thankful happiness. Cardona grinned; then went back into the room.

Joe joined Cliff. Together, they stood beside the toppled pedestal. Solemnly, they eyed the dead form of Zovex. Twisted crazily, long arms and legs outspread, the spidery creature looked like nothing human. Its overlarge head was tilted back upon the floor. Glazed eyes stared sightless toward the ceiling.

The lips still wore their twist, fixed in their finish of the fiend's last word. The Oracle had made its last speech. It had phrased a sentence that had been executed:

"Death!"

In oracular manner, Zovex had decreed it. Like all evasive oracles, he had failed to specify upon whom the doom would fall. Zovex had tried to carry out his own verdict, with The Shadow as the victim. Zovex had failed.

The Shadow had completed the decree. He had ended the vile career of Zovex, the monstrous murderer.

The Shadow had placed death where it belonged!

CHAPTER XX.
RIDDLES ARE SOLVED.

HALF an hour later, Joe Cardona and Cliff Marsland stood again in the room where battle had been fought. They had opened the safe beneath the shelf. From its interior, they had brought a medley of objects.

One was the carrying case that The Shadow had found there previously. It was filled with cylinders, large and small, made of light fiber and stacked together. Stuffed in the case were garments—sweater, trousers, shoes, gloves and cap, all of an overlarge size.

With the case they had found the mechanical head. They had observed how closely the composition face resembled the V-furrowed countenance of Zovex. They had discovered a single square of wood, six inches in diameter. It was the center of the table top. With it were the batteries that had once been wedged into the pedestal.

"A great racket," decided Cardona, with a shake of his head. "When the professor flashed the clockwork head, Zovex stayed in the chess player. When the Oracle was to stage a real show, Zovex crawled into the pedestal and shoved his head up through the hinged bottom of the cubical box."

"After he put away the dummy head," nodded Cliff. "Along with the center square of the table top, and the batteries. They stayed in the safe. The pedestal was a cinch for Zovex. That spindly body of his could get into anything."

"Even that passage we found, from this room to the professor's study," explained Joe. "A special exit for Zovex, if he wanted it. No good for anybody else. Nothing wider than a cat could have gone through it. Zovex must have made it just wide enough for his head. His body didn't count. Say—he could have pulled those legs and arms underneath a door! Pretty nearly, anyway."

"These cylinders were the great gag, Joe. With those around his body and on his arms and legs, Zovex must have looked as wide as he was tall."

"Sure! That's what Hal Rydler was telling us. He was fooled when he saw Zovex down at his brother's. He never would have dreamed that anybody like that could get into the chess player, let alone the pedestal."

"Easy enough for Zovex to work the chess player when he was in it. He did it by putting his hand down through the hollow arm and looking through that cloth door at the front. Easy to shift around, too, when the professor opened the doors."

"As easy as the game of being The Head. One thing, though, I can't dope. Zovex was scrawny. How did he look so wide, even with the cylinders?"

Cliff considered. Then he found the answer. He extended his own arms straight out from his body and let his forearms dangle.

"That was the stunt," he explained. "The top half of his arms made the shoulders, to match up with the big cylinders around his body. The forearms, dangling, looked long enough for full arms."

"They would," agreed Joe—"considering that Zovex had arms that were twice too long for his own body."

HAL RYDLER called from the hall. Cliff and Joe went from the room. They saw Hal pointing into the study. Selfridge had opened the professor's safe.

The top half of the vault beyond the panel contained the model of the perpetual motion machine. Beneath it were boxes. Selfridge opened them. Cardona saw the green of bank notes; a mass of printed bonds. One small box showed the sparkle of Percy Rydler's diamonds.

"This one is too heavy to move," stated Selfridge. "It must contain the stolen gold. Everything is here, sir. If——"

"It will go easy with you and Marley," interrupted Cardona, catching the gist of the technician's unworded plea. "How's Havelock? We don't want any trouble from him."

"Marley is guarding him in the living room."

"And the professor?"

Martha Keswick answered. The girl had arrived at the doorway and was standing there with Hal Rydler.

"My uncle has gone to sleep," stated Martha. "But I am afraid——"

"I know," nodded Cardona. "We'll take care of him."

"He will think of nothing but perpetual motion," affirmed Martha. "It was only Zovex who could talk him into other schemes. Ones that were worse

than his mania. But I did not know. I thought that The Head was mechanical —one of his inventions. I suspected that some creature lived here. That was all."

"You were never sure?"

"Never! Otherwise, I would have informed the law. The only secret that I learned was the method of unlocking the doors by pulling the knobs."

The girl paused; then added:

"There are others who will take care of my uncle. It was only at his request that I came to live with him. Once I was here, he would not let me leave."

A BABBLE from the stairway told that Professor Caglio had awakened and was coming to the ground floor. Cardona ordered a departure. They took the cackling old professor with them. Selfridge and Marley brought Havelock. Before arranging the parties in the automobiles, Cardona drew Cliff to a corner, where they had previously carried three bodies. He pointed to the twisted form of Zovex.

"Remember The Strangler of a few years back?" queried Joe. "The one they were after, but never got? He used to go up ivy vines to the second floor. Some people saw him. He was a burglar by trade."

"And a murderer by inclination," added Cliff. "Zovex was The Strangler? Is that your hunch?"

"It fits," affirmed Cardona. "Hal Rydler saw The Head in his room. He felt a clutch at his throat, just before the girl came in to help him. It's another reason why Zovex went around in that clumsy outfit. He didn't want to be spotted as he was."

"He was a deep schemer," nodded Cliff. "Getting facts from dupes; then tipping off crooks like Pinky, Squint and Moose."

"And covering," put in Cardona. "He smeared any tracks that Moose left at Percy Rydler's."

AUTOMOBILES rolled from beneath the windowless building. They skirted the house and headed for the road. They were bound for the town of Littenden, where Cardona could report to local authorities. A drizzle had begun. The cars moved carefully.

As the procession slowed at the outlet to the road, a sound came from the gloom. Cliff Marsland alone knew its source. It was from a parked coupe hidden off the drive—the car that had trailed Squint Proddock when he had brought Marsland to this lair.

The sound was a weird laugh. A tone of finality, from somewhere near the house where horror had held sway. Solemn, it began as a knell. Rising strident, it changed to a peal of eerie triumph.

It told of hidden prowess, that token of The Shadow. It was the mirth of a master who had solved and ended the riddles surrounding Zovex. It was a reminder, that taunt, that The Shadow had fathomed every move. That he had tricked a supercrook to his undoing.

Through Martha's word to Hal, The Shadow had begun the climax. Hal's double request had caused Professor Caglio to confer with Zovex. To lull the prospective victims, The Head had moved from the chess player to the table pedestal. Zovex had placed himself where he could not fire from ambush.

Then had The Shadow counted upon the moves of others. Watching, he had known that The Head would be forced to show his game. In the crisis, Zovex lacked the sure position that he would have had within the chess player. He had been handicapped, hurling away table top and cubical box. Despite his speed, The Head had been too late. The Shadow had tricked, then downed, the murderous fiend.

The chilling laugh was a saga—a full recounting of The Shadow's deeds. Fading amid the patter of the rain, the shuddering echoes faded; but their memory persisted within the minds of those who heard.

The Shadow had won the verdict against crime. His triumph laugh predicted that new tasks would follow. The Shadow's cause would continue, ceaseless.

Justice was the watchword of The Shadow!

THE END.

The
Teeth of the Dragon

Once again the mighty Ying Ko—The Shadow—glides through the perilous mazes of Chinatown, to pull the dripping fangs of death that were the

Teeth of the Dragon

A Complete Book-length Novel from the Private Annals of The Shadow, as told to

Maxwell Grant

CHAPTER I.

SOUTH OF FRISCO.

THE powerful, low-slung roadster was spinning southward along a highway that overhung the Pacific's shore. Brilliant headlights showed the broad stretch of highway fairly pouring beneath the huge-tired wheels.

With all its speed, the motor's tone was rhythmic. The car never slackened as it took the sweeping, well-banked curves. A forceful driver was at the wheel of that surging roadster. His eyes were constantly on the highway ahead. Not once did they wander to look at the speedometer on the dashboard.

The speed that was registered there was one hundred miles an hour. The needle held to that mark as if glued.

Eyes alone were visible within the darkness beneath the roadster's low racing top. Eyes that burned from beneath the brim of a slouch hat. The rest of the driver's face was obscured by the upturned collar of a jet-black cloak. Like his body, his gloved hands were invisible in the gloom.

The Shadow was speeding to a mission where the delay of even half a minute might cost the lives of innocent men.

The big car zoomed past a looming headland. Below, off to the right, lay a stretch of absolute blackness that represented the broad expanse of the Pacific Ocean. Under the clouded night sky, the sea had become a Stygian pool of limitless extent.

Then, from that blackness twinkled lights. A ship was hovering in toward the shore.

The Shadow knew the identity of that vessel. It was the trawler *Tantalus,* its skipper a Captain Malhearn. The ship held a human cargo. It was here to unload Chinese upon the California coast.

There was time to arrive at the beach before the small boats from the *Tantalus* reached it. The *Tantalus* was slated for trouble from the Coast Guard; and that could mean murder of the Chinese cargo, unless some one intervened. The chink-runners had an unpleasant habit of dumping human evidence overboard, when pressed.

They wouldn't work that game tonight, if The Shadow showed up on the deck of the *Tantalus,* out of a small boat coming from the shore.

At the moment when he spied the trawler's lights, the time element was all in The Shadow's favor. Then, in an instant, that situation was reversed.

The Shadow's right foot shot from the accelerator to the brake pedal. With quick jabs, he broke the big car's speed and pumped pressure into the hydraulic brakes. As the roadster sliced down to fifty, The Shadow jammed the brakes hard. The huge automobile swayed and screeched to a stop, only a dozen feet short of a rock barrier that stretched across the road.

WITH a flick, a gloved hand turned off the ignition and extinguished the lights. The door opened; a cloaked form flung itself into darkness.

The Shadow's move was none too soon. Three flashlights glimmered as a trio of huskies pounced from stony hiding places. Guns in their fists, they sprang to the stalled roadster, expecting to overpower its unfortunate occupant.

Oaths were rasped when the thugs found the big car empty. Those mutters, like the flashlights, betrayed the positions of the trio. Before they could rally themselves, the cover-up crew was met by The Shadow's counter-attack.

A thug by the left side of the car was the first to take it. He swung his flashlight, to catch The Shadow's outline in its gleam. The hoodlum saw his foe too late. Looming upon him from beside the car's big hood, The Shadow sledged a long arm for the fellow's head. A heavy automatic sideswiped a capped skull. The thug thudded the concrete road.

A second rowdy had reached the roadster's steering wheel. He heard his pal slump. He aimed blindly into the blackness above the car door. That darkness solidified into a human shape. From it sped a free, gloved hand that throttled the crook's throat with a paralyzing grip. The thug's head went back; his arms dropped. His revolver clanked the handle of the hand brake.

With a side fling, The Shadow

slammed his second foeman flat on the floor of the car. Clearing the way, he did a headlong dive clear over the other door, straight into the glare of the flashlight that bobbed there. The Shadow's surge blotted the light's rays. Flinging aside his .45 as he came, he locked with the last thug before the fellow could aim.

The third struggle was as swift as the others. The Shadow took his adversary off balance; sprawled him to the edge of the highway, where the thug's head took a jolt that left him senseless. The Shadow had settled the entire group, without a single shot to alarm the main gang on the beach below.

KEEPING his flashlight low, The Shadow found a jagged path between high rocks. Going through, he found himself upon a high promontory. Again, the lights of the *Tantalus* twinkled, very close to shore. Lanterns were swinging from the beach. Boats were preparing to put out, to bring the Chinese ashore.

The Shadow had a difficult quarter mile to cover, to reach that crowd on the beach. The only path was a precipitous one, down from this high ground. At that, The Shadow might have reached his goal before the last boat started; but before he could begin his foray, another circumstance intervened.

A long-beamed searchlight cleaved the blackness. It shone from a full mile off shore, and its sweeping path finally settled on the clumsy hulk of the trawler *Tantalus*. A Coast Guard cutter had arrived to pick out the smuggler ship.

The cutter's approach was untimely. It foretold death to the helpless Chinese. Halted on the path, The Shadow could picture those Celestials going overboard in deep water, weighted with chunks of iron. Runners like Malhearn were merciless, when they thought they would be caught with the goods.

The Shadow's race seemed useless, when a strange thing happened. The lights of the trawler came moving inward, straight for the shore!

That meant one thing only; Malhearn was going to beach the *Tantalus;* wreck it in the booming surf. There was but a single reason possible for such sacrifice. The skipper was determined to unload his Chinese cargo intact, despite the risk of capture and the sure loss of the ship.

Others than The Shadow stared at the unusual sight. That gang along the beach could not understand Malhearn's folly. A shell whined from the cutter; it whistled across the trawler's bow and splashed the waves. The *Tantalus* kept moving shoreward.

There was a lull; another warning shot had no effect. During the next interval, the only sounds were the roar of the rolling surf and the pound of the trawler's engines. The cutter began fire in earnest. A shell ripped away the trawler's funnel; another shot shattered the deck near the stern.

The lights of the *Tantalus* quivered. The chunky ship was beached. Firefly gleams from the cutter told that its crew was boarding small boats, to take up the chase ashore.

Near the bottom of the path, The Shadow saw men dragging water-soaked Chinese into the light of the lanterns. One small batch was hustled away, in a direction opposite The Shadow's. They were being taken to trucks, hidden by rocks on the highway, somewhere beyond the barrier that had halted The Shadow.

More Chinese were hauled ashore, but no more groups were started on their way. The cutter's boats had landed. Government men opened fire, above the heads of the men who were in the open. Some made a dash for the road. The rest threw up their arms and surrendered, along with Malhearn and the trawler's crew.

By the rocks beside the road, a dozen men were waiting in ambush, their rifles covering the beach. One of them, serving as temporary leader, snarled to his companions:

"They've grabbed Malhearn and the rest of the shore gang! They've got the chinks, too! They'll be heading here to snatch the bunch that we just ran through to the trucks. Here they come! Let 'em have it."

Rifles crackled from the rocks. There were answering shots from the beach; then the Coast Guardsmen dropped for cover. There were raucous shouts from the crooks in ambush. This time, the advantage was theirs. They had the government men in the open; the crooks intended to give no quarter.

Slaughter was their plan; then the release of Malhearn and the other prisoners, and a recapture of the Chinese. Long-range flashlights beamed through the darkness, to show up the fighters who were flattened along the unprotected beach. Three minutes were all that the dozen snipers needed to wipe out the Coast Guard crew.

As the first rifles rattled, seeking the right range, a pair of automatics spoke from a rocky crevice. Flames tongued straight toward the snipers. Those bursts were from The Shadow's automatics. The cloaked fighter had reached a ledge above and to the right of the ambuscade.

Clustered sharpshooters sprawled. Their pals swung savagely to meet the flank fire. They fired their rifles toward the crevice. The bullets ricocheted without effect. The Shadow's ambush was a perfect one.

His automatics continued their close-range pour. Unwounded thugs did not wait for that volley to finish. They made a break for the road.

That took them to rocks above, away from The Shadow's fire. They were spotted by lights from one of the cutter's boats. Riflemen from the beach began to pick off the fleeing thugs, while others hurried forward to gather in the crooks that The Shadow had wounded.

Shifting back toward his rocky path, The Shadow could see the results. He had accounted for half of the ambushed crooks. The remaining six were dropping one by one, toppling from rocks as rifle shots winged them.

From a final vantage point, The Shadow could see a waiting truck, beyond the range of his automatics. Its motor was roaring, ready for the getaway, when a lone member of the ambush party staggered into the glare of its headlights.

Rocks protected the truck from the Coast Guard fire. The driver lingered long enough to haul the wounded man aboard. Then the truck was off with a roar, carrying its small cargo of Chinese —a mere three or four who had come from the *Tantalus*.

The Shadow reached his roadster. He arrived in time to subdue one of the thugs who had recovered. He bound the hoodlum, along with his stunned pals, and left all three by the rocks, where the Coast Guard could find them. Stepping into the roadster, The Shadow turned the car about and started back toward San Francisco.

A WEIRD laugh sounded from the darkness of the roadster. Its chilling tones blended with the pound of the Pacific's surf. Though luck had interchanged to-night, the final result had been success. The Shadow had thwarted men of crime; he had saved men of the law from doom.

There was no chance to pursue the fleeing truck; for it had started southward from a spot beyond the blocking road barrier. The Shadow was content to let the few surviving crooks have their small success, carrying through a very few of the smuggled Chinese.

Though he had not yet learned it, The Shadow had missed the greatest of to-night's opportunities. The escape of that lone truck and its small cargo was destined to plunge The Shadow into a series of strange and desperate adventures.

CHAPTER II.

A CHINAMAN'S MESSAGE.

ABOARD the fleeing truck, a steady, hard-faced driver was choosing a roundabout way back to San Francisco. The ugly look on his square-jawed face showed that he was contemptuous of pursuit. He knew these roads like nobody else. That was why he had been given the job of handling the truck.

The driver's name was "Lubber" Kreef; and he considered himself an ex-member of Malhearn's trawler crew. Lubber had quit the *Tantalus* because he had never been able to find his sea legs. When Malhearn had given up trawling to run Chinese, he had found Lubber and signed him up as shore man for the outfit. What Lubber had failed to learn about handling a trawler, he had made up for with his knowledge of managing a truck.

Lubber was growling as he drove along. Though loyal to Malhearn, he thought the skipper crazy, because he had beached the *Tantalus*. He was sore, too, because the shore gang hadn't brought all the Chinese to the truck. It would be a long rap for Malhearn and the crew of the *Tantalus*. Lubber didn't care about the shore gang. They were hired hoodlums, who didn't belong with the trawler.

All except the fellow that Lubber had dragged aboard the truck. He was Steve Henney, from the *Tantalus*. Steve had come along to see that the Chinese reached the truck. Recognizing him as an old pal, Lubber had dragged him into the truck.

It didn't seem much use, though. Slumped beside Lubber, Steve looked like he was through. A couple of Coast Guard bullets had clipped him.

"Lubber—Lubber"—Steve stirred to gasp the name—"they—they got me!"

Lubber shot a sidelong glance toward Steve's drawn face.

"You're O. K., Steve," growled the truck driver. "I'll get you to a croaker when we hit Frisco. I'll drop you there before I deliver the chinks. It won't be long, Steve."

"I—I can't last, Lubber."

Steve coughed the words. Lubber didn't doubt the statement. He had figured that Steve would be dead before they reached San Francisco. Lubber thrust out his right hand, to quiet Steve as the fellow writhed in the truck seat. Steve sagged; but his hand came tugging weakly from his pocket.

"Take this, Lubber!" Steve managed to press an envelope into the driver's hand. "A Chinee give it to me —on the boat. It means—means five grand—if you deliver it to the guy it's meant for! The dough's yours—Lubber——"

Steve went limp. Thrusting the envelope in his pocket, Lubber leaned from the wheel to eye his companion. Steve was dead.

"Five grand," muttered Lubber. "Steve meant it, too. Boy, this is a break, now that Malhearn's racket is on the fritz! When I get to Frisco, I'll give that envelope the once-over."

Lubber finished his comment with a nod of thanks to the dead form of Steve Henney. Perhaps Lubber would have omitted the courtesy, had he known the person for whom the message was meant.

Astonishing though it was, that envelope that had passed from one crook to another was addressed to The Shadow!

NEAR San Francisco, Lubber conveniently disposed of Steve's body; but did not look at the envelope. When he reached the city, he drove to a garage, where a crew of mysterious, lurking Chinese took over the Celestials who were in the back of the truck.

Driving away, Lubber headed for another garage and stowed the truck there. Coming out on the street, he took his first glance at the envelope that Steve had handed him.

Lubber's lips phrased an oath.

The only name and address that showed on the envelope were two Chinese characters. As near as Lubber could figure it, they represented some one's name; but that didn't help. Lubber couldn't read Chinese.

There was one place where the riddle could be answered. That was Chinatown. The Oriental district wasn't far from the garage. Soon, Lubber was footing it along steep-pitched streets where yellow faces were in abundance.

Stopping by the brilliantly lighted front of a Chinese theater, Lubber accosted a Celestial who looked like a doorman. He shoved the envelope in front of the fellow's almond eyes, with the query:

"Say, Johnny, tell me who this is for, will you?"

Slanted eyes became beady. The Chinaman showed a frightened look. His lips muttered a name that Lubber could not hear. Sidling away, the Chinaman entered the theater.

There was a Chinese girl in the box office. Lubber flashed the envelope there. The girl's eyes stared as though they were looking right through Lubber. Mechanically, the girl spoke in English:

"Your pardon, sir. I cannot read Chinese."

Lubber had gone half a block before he realized that the girl's words must have been false. What was she doing, working for a Chinese theater, if she couldn't talk the lingo and read Chinese?

At a lighted corner where a pagoda-shaped auction house towered, Lubber stopped a passing Chinese and showed him the envelope, with the hoarse demand that the fellow interpret the characters.

The Chinaman twisted away, while Lubber clung to him. At last, the man mumbled the words:

"Ying Ko—Ying Ko!"

"Who's Ying Ko?" jabbed Lubber. "Where'll I find him?"

The Chinaman didn't answer. They had reached a handy alley. He broke away and darted from sight before Lubber could stop him.

Some other Chinese had seen the episode. They were gathering close to Lubber. To explain the matter, he showed them the envelope. Two or three moved away hurriedly. Another pair made a move as if reaching for knives. Lubber decided to clear that neighborhood.

REACHING another street, Lubber felt nervous. Who was this Ying Ko, that some Chinese didn't want to talk about; whose name was like a threat to others? Had the tougher-looking Mongols passed the word along?

Lubber thought so, for he fancied that he could see passing Chinese stare at him; while others, squatted in shop windows, gazed askance.

Lubber found an alleyway that suited him and cut through to another street. He grunted with relief when he saw no sharp looks from the next Chinese whom he passed. But he kept the envelope in his pocket.

There was a tea shop on this street; in front sat a benign old Chinaman who puffed a long pipe. Lubber stopped there; easing his usual gruff tone, he remarked:

"I've got a message for some Chinaman named Ying Ko. It's in Chinese. But nobody will put me wise about this guy Ying Ko."

The old Chinaman stopped his contented puffing. His mild eyes had a piercing glitter as they studied Lubber. His placid pose returning, the Chinaman said quietly:

"Come into the shop."

Lubber followed the old man inside. There, the Chinaman requested to see the message. Lubber produced the envelope. Studying the Chinese characters, the tea-shop owner questioned:

"Have you shown this to any one?"

"Yeah," replied Lubber. "To a theater doorman; to a girl in the box office——"

Lubber halted. He decided that he had told enough. The old Chinaman evidently believed Lubber, when the crook added:

"They told me it was for Ying Ko. That was all."

"Perhaps," suggested the Chinaman, "they mentioned who Ying Ko might be?"

Lubber shook his head emphatically. The Chinaman looked at the envelope; for a moment, Lubber thought that he intended to open it. With five thousand dollars promised for the safe delivery of the message, Lubber didn't want that. He made a hurried snatch for the envelope. Lubber's sincere eagerness to protect the message impressed the Chinaman.

"You will promise," he said, "to show that message to no one else. Nor will you mention the name of Ying Ko to any one. If so, I shall see that Ying Ko learns of it."

Lubber agreed. The Chinaman asked him for his address. Lubber scrawled it on a piece of paper. Blandly, the old man led him through the rear of the shop to a door that opened on an alleyway. He bowed Lubber out into the darkness.

As soon as Lubber had gone, the old Chinaman went to a telephone and called a number. There was an answer; the tea-shop owner gave his name. To the listener, he stated:

"I have called you, Doctor Tam, because you are a friend to Ying Ko—The Shadow. To-night, I have seen a message addressed to Ying Ko. It is held by one who does not know that Ying Ko is The Shadow. This is his address. . . ."

The address given, the old Chinaman went out to the front of the shop and resumed his chair there. He puffed his pipe as contentedly as if he had totally forgotten Lubber's visit. But behind the old Celestial's placid gaze lay watchfulness. He was making sure that no spies appeared along the street. Seeing none, the Chinaman was pleased.

That tea-shop proprietor was neither a superstitious Oriental who feared mention of the name Ying Ko, nor did he belong to an evil brood of Mongols, who sought to thwart The Shadow. He was a friend of Doctor Roy Tam, a modern Chinese, who stood for progress. Doctor Tam, so a chosen few understood, owed much of his success to The Shadow's aid.

UNFORTUNATELY, the quiet of the tea-shop street was misleading. There was a reason why lurkers did not come there. Lubber Kreef had unwisely poked himself in the wrong direction; he was back on a lighted street where spies persisted.

Though evil-eyed Mongols knew nothing of Lubber's stop at the tea shop, they had his trail again. They knew that he was the bearer of a message to Ying Ko. The rumor passed to other Chinese of a skulking type.

Clawish hands hoisted **The Shadow** from the floor. . . . Chinese began a slow, triumphant march from the room

Heading toward the water front, Lubber soon realized that he was being watched. He was near the outskirts of Chinatown; he saw a big truck halted at a corner. It was pointed in the direction that Lubber wanted.

Lubber hopped aboard without ceremony, and introduced himself to the driver as a fellow truckman.

"Thanks for the lift, buddy," voiced Lubber, when they neared the water front. "I'll drop off here."

Lubber picked a corner near a grog-shop that was frequented chiefly by seamen. He figured that he needed a few stiff drinks, to forget those peering yellow faces that had watched him everywhere.

At a battered corner table in the booze-joint, Lubber was pouring himself a third glass when a big hand thwacked his shoulders. Lubber winced; then grinned as he recognized the man who sat down beside him.

The fellow was "Shiv" Faxon, a racketeer whose business frequently brought him to the docks.

A smooth customer, Shiv. Thin-faced; tight-lipped; with eyes that stared like little beads. His hands were quick, restless, as if they itched for action. They could give it, too. The racketeer was a speedy man with the "shiv," the slang term for a knife. It was his ability with the dirk that had produced his nickname.

Shiv had learned his knife-work in Mexico. Since his sojourn in that country, he rarely carried a gun. But he never lacked a knife. Shiv had a collection of those tools; his hardware included bolos, machetes and stilettos. He always seemed to have the right dirk with him on the required occasion.

"H'lo, Shiv," greeted Lubber. "Wish you'd been with me up in Chinatown. Lot of chinks up there looked like they wanted to jab me with a toad-sticker. You could have scared 'em off me."

"Yeah?" Shiv was curious with his sharp tone. "What was it about, Lubber?"

Lubber produced the envelope; flashed it so that Shiv could glimpse the Chinese characters.

"This come from a chink that was run through to-night," confided Lubber. "Those letters ain't laundry marks. They're the name of the guy that's to get the message. Five grand for me when I deliver it. Only, a lot of chinks were leery when I showed it to them."

Lubber had an idea that five thousand dollars was small change to Shiv. He saw no harm in mentioning the amount; in fact, he thought it would put him higher in Shiv's estimation. Lubber refrained, though, from mentioning the name of Ying Ko. He shrugged his shoulders and pocketed the envelope, when Shiv asked where the envelope was to be delivered.

"The right guy will come for it," assured Lubber.

At a near-by table sat a stooped man, whose face had a yellowish tinge, although he didn't look like a Chinese. His eyes had noticed the large characters on the envelope, when Lubber happened to turn it in his direction. Finishing a drink, the stoopish man arose and sidled into a back room, to reach a telephone.

Ten minutes later, Lubber said good night to Shiv and left the grogshop. From the moment that he reached the street, he was followed.

No ordinary trailers, these. They were the pick of Chinatown's stalkers. They shifted from doorway to doorway; clung to the darkened fronts of piers. They were close behind Lubber when he took a side street and entered the house where he lodged.

There was a short passage beside the house; it ended in a blocking, ten-foot wall. Watching from the tiny blind alley, two lurking Chinese saw the light of a gas jet flicker from a corner window at the rear of the third floor. They had marked Lubber's room. Sidling away, they babbled in low tone to other Chinese.

Three minutes later, there wasn't a single yellow face in sight anywhere along that block. The Chinese trailers had returned to their usual haunts. Their part of the work was finished.

More minutes passed. Beneath the glow of a dingy street lamp came an evasive streak of darkness, that flitted weirdly into view, then faded. It told of a living shape, blended with the blackness of the house fronts.

The Shadow had heard from Doctor Roy Tam. He had come to find the man who held a message for him.

Gliding noiselessly along the front street, The Shadow made positive that there were no lurkers present. He noted the house number; then moved into the blind alley. From there, he saw streaks of light from the edges of Lubber's third-story window, where the crook had drawn the shade.

Lubber was at home, ready to receive his mysterious visitor. Blackness moved toward the front door of the house; The Shadow entered a dim hallway, where he faded from sight as he approached a flight of stairs.

The Shadow had chosen the usual route to Lubber's room, on a mission that seemed simple and direct. Yet, when he crossed that threshold, The Shadow was moving into danger as insidious as any that he had ever encountered.

CHAPTER III.
THE HATCHET MAN.

ALL was placid in Lubber's room at the time when The Shadow had observed the light that fringed the shaded window. But circumstances were due for a sudden shift there—one that came within the few minutes that The Shadow required for his trip up from the street.

There were two windows in Lubber's room. The Shadow had observed the one that opened on the side of the house. The other was in the rear wall. Lubber had drawn the shades of both windows, but he had not locked the sashes. They were battered and rickety, with no catches.

Moreover, Lubber saw no danger from the windows. The side one was three floors above the ground. The rear window was above an eight-foot drop to a porch roof that was on a level with the second story.

The door was locked, with the key in it. Lubber was seated at a corner table, staring at the envelope that bore the mysterious name of Ying Ko. In addition to the table, the room had a few rickety chairs and a battered bedstead. There was also a large, clumsy piece of furniture in the shape of a big wardrobe, that stood against the wall by the rear window.

As Lubber figured it, that bulky wardrobe was useless. It took up what he termed "half the room"; and he had no use for the big drawers with which the wardrobe was provided. Lubber kept all his belongings in a suitcase.

Itchily, Lubber fingered the envelope. He remembered that the Chinese teashop merchant had wanted to open it. Shiv Faxon would have liked to do the same. Lubber was feeling the same impulse; but the thought of five thousand dollars restrained him. There wasn't going to be any squawk from Ying Ko, whoever he might be, when he came to get the message.

Half aloud, Lubber expressed the speech that he expected to deliver for the benefit of some owl-faced Chinaman.

"Five grand, Ying Ko," repeated Lubber, "and it's yours. Take a gander; see for yourself that nobody's looked into it. Don't ask me who it's from. All I know is what it's worth. Take it or leave it!"

DURING his mumble, Lubber failed to hear a sound behind him. There was a flutter from the curtain of the rear window. That shade was too old to give a warning crinkle. What Lubber should have heard was the creak of the rickety sash; but he didn't.

The curtain raised. From beneath it peeked a wicked yellow visage, with an ugliness that outmatched any face that Lubber had seen in Chinatown to-night. Long, spidery arms reached for the floor; clawish hands spread flat, while a twisty body and scrawny legs sidled over the sill.

The grotesque creature that crouched on the floor by the window could scarcely be classed as human. His face showed him to be a Chinaman; but his dwarfish, hunchy body looked like the figure of an undersize orang-outang. His limbs were also apelike.

The ugly visitor had scaled the wall for a meeting with Lubber Kreef. He was clad in darkish, baggy garments, with a big belt around his spidery waist. From that belt, the distorted man drew the most terrible of Chinese weapons: an odd-shaped hatchet. That instrument, so often used in tong assassinations, was the weapon that the crawly visitor intended to use upon Lubber Kreef.

The hatchet man unlimbered. Edging forward, he halted suddenly and stretched against the wall near the window. Lubber had thrust the envelope deep into a pocket. He was rising from the table. Dotty eyes watched him. If Lubber turned toward the rear window, the hatchet man would spring. If not, he would wait.

Lubber unwittingly did just what the assassin wanted. He stretched himself; then decided to sit down again. He opened the table drawer, brought out a grimy pack of playing cards. He began to shuffle the pasteboards for a game of solitaire, while he waited for Ying Ko.

Lubber never dealt a single card.

The riffle of the pack was loud enough, close enough, to prevent Lubber from hearing the hatchet man's approach. With long, creepy stride, the killer came forward; drew back a thin arm and made a straight leap. His hatchet descended with terrific impetus, squarely upon Lubber's skull.

The blow cleaved bone and brain. Lubber's shoulders seemed to telescope, then flounder sideways. He flattened, face-upward, on the floor, his head in a pool of blood.

THE killer thrust his hatchet beneath his belt. Crouching above Lubber's body, he dipped his clawish fingers into the dead man's pockets. He was probing for the envelope; but all the while, his dotlike eyes were fixed elsewhere. They were watching the door, the one place from which the hatchet man thought trouble might come.

The hatchet man's fingers had not reached the envelope, when his eyes saw something. The key in the lock was turning, in so slow a fashion that its motion was barely perceptible. It stopped at intervals; then moved again. Some one in the hallway had pushed clippers through the outside keyhole, to clamp the key itself.

Lubber, had he lived, would certainly have failed to detect that motion, which announced the secret arrival of The Shadow. It took the keen eyes of the hatchet man to spy it.

The spidery assassin grimaced; took in his breath with a low, sucking hiss. He shot a quick gaze about the room, saw the big wardrobe. The hatchet man leered.

Rising from the body of his victim, the killer used his clawlike hands to draw open the middle drawer of the wardrobe. It was loose; it came open with only the slightest scrape. The drawer was empty; the size of a large suitcase, it was just what the hatchet man wanted.

He swung his body over the front of the drawer; doubled himself like a contortionist until he fitted inside. His fingers gripped a brace above the drawer; with a motion of his arms, the hatchet man slid the drawer shut, with himself inside it.

The ruse was a perfect one. The average person, finding Lubber's body, would suppose that a man of brawn had delivered the fatal hatchet stroke. The wardrobe drawer was scarcely large enough to contain a midget. The peculiar, scrawny build of the hatchet man served him as ably in finding cover, as it had in scaling the wall from the porch roof below.

Through a big keyhole in the drawer an evil eye watched the door key complete its turn.

The door edged inward. The watching eye saw The Shadow peer into the room. Then the eye was gone, so that even its glisten could not betray the hatchet man. In place of his eye, the vicious murderer had planted his ear to the keyhole. That ear blocked the light, and could not be seen. But it enabled its crafty owner to gauge, by sound, every move that The Shadow made.

Seeing Lubber's body, The Shadow paused to study the room. His fist gripped a heavy automatic. He was ready for any sudden attack. He saw no space where a normal killer could be hidden. The room was closetless; the gaslight showed vacancy beneath the bed.

There was a rustle from the rear window. The Shadow went there, lifted the shade that a slight breeze had moved. He found the sash raised. Looking below, he saw the roof above the back porch; beyond it, the darkness of a cement courtyard between this house and the row on the next street.

The Shadow had heard a slight, scrapy noise while he was working on the door lock. The opened window seemed to account for it. A departing murderer, squeezing through, could have caused the noise before he dropped to the porch. That conclusion fitted so well, that The Shadow ignored the big wardrobe cabinet as a possible hiding place for the lurking assassin.

WITH all evidence pointing to the killer's departure, The Shadow approached Lubber's body. He recognized that the murder was the work of a Chinese hatchet man. It was obvious that Lubber must have talked to too many people in Chinatown.

Though he no longer expected to find the mysterious envelope on Lubber's person, The Shadow hoped that other articles might produce a clue.

The Shadow began a search through the dead man's pockets.

Within a quarter minute, he made a significant find. Papers in an inside pocket bore the name of Lubber Kreef; they certified that he had belonged to the crew of the trawler *Tantalus*.

The Shadow traced back the connection. The message that Lubber carried must have come from one of the smuggled Chinese aboard the trawler.

The Shadow had left the door of the room unlocked, and slightly open. On that account, he was doing as the hatchet man had done. He was watching the door while he searched Lubber's body. His back to the wardrobe, The Shadow could not see the change that took place there.

The eye was again at the keyhole of the drawer.

The evil killer saw gloved fingers probing Lubber's pockets. The Shadow's hand was coming to the coat pocket that held the vital envelope. Slowly, the wardrobe drawer inched outward.

The hatchet man's present move was noiseless. His weight provided pressure that kept the drawer from creaking, as his hands worked it outward. When the drawer had moved a scant foot forward, its occupant changed his tactics.

Squeezing his thin body upward, the hatchet man raised head and shoulders from the drawer. His right claw gripped the ready hatchet. Up came the weapon from the killer's belt.

The Shadow's back was scarcely four feet from the wardrobe. Stooped, the cloaked searcher's form blotted the rays from the gas jet, to obscure Lubber's body. The Shadow was just within the range that the hatchet man required.

MORE STATIONS!

As we told you in the previous issue, there are more and more radio stations being added to the nationwide hook-up which feature The Shadow on the air! We have two new ones to give you now: Station WCS, Portland, Maine, at 4:00 P. M. every Sunday afternoon; and Station WNBF, Binghampton, New York, at 5:30 P. M. every Sunday afternoon. These in addition to the stations given before; the complete list now appearing at the foot of this page.

By the time this is in print, there will be many more. Because we must prepare our issues far in advance, on account of worldwide circulation, we cannot give you last-minute news here, but your daily paper, and your news dealer, can keep you informed. Watch for posters announcing The Shadow on the air in your locality, or his appearance in your neighborhood theatre in the full length picture, THE SHADOW STRIKES.

On the air, The Shadow is sponsored by Blue Coal; on the screen, The Shadow is produced by Grand National Pictures. Rod La Rocque stars as The Shadow. We want our readers to feel free to give us their comments on both radio and movie. We are doing our best in both, and want to improve each performance according to our readers' suggestions. So come on, tell us what you think!

City	Station	Time	City	Station	Time
Boston, Mass.	WNAC	4:30 P. M.	Baltimore, Md.	WBAL	5:30 P. M.
Hartford, Conn.	WTIC	"	Philadelphia, Pa.	WIP	"
Providence, R. I.	WEAN	"	Buffalo, N. Y.	WKBW	"
Worcester, Mass.	WTAG	"	Detroit, Mich.	CKLW	"
Schenectady, N. Y.	WGY	"	Atlantic City, N. J.	WPG	"
New York, N. Y.	WOR	5:30 P. M.	Syracuse, N. Y.	WSYR	4:00 P. M.
Portland, Me.	WCS	4:00 P. M.	Binghampton, N. Y.	WNBF	5:30 P. M.
	Chicago, Ill.	WGN	4:30 P. M., C. S. T.		

REMEMBER: You can read about The Shadow only in THE SHADOW MAGAZINE.

As he had watched Lubber, so did the hovering killer eye The Shadow. Stretched from the opened drawer, his hand was raised high. He was waiting for the moment best suited for his stroke.

That time would come when The Shadow drew the envelope from Lubber's pocket. Once The Shadow saw the message that bore the name Ying Ko, his attention would be concentrated. The hatchet man leered with relish for the climax would follow.

Death, to Ying Ko, The Shadow!

The killer would see The Shadow's gloved hand, for his higher position enabled him to peer across the cloaked shoulder. Gloved fingers plucked something from Lubber's pocket. They drew the corner of the envelope into view. The claw that held the looming hatchet tightened for its downward sweep.

The Shadow had reached the verge of death. His own action would become the signal that would bring the fatal slash!

CHAPTER IV.

THE MISSING MESSAGE.

THE crinkle of the envelope, the sight of its projecting corner told The Shadow that he had found something that he did not expect. Both touch and sight proved that the envelope's substance was of Chinese texture.

The Shadow knew, without drawing the envelope farther, that it must be the one that bore the name Ying Ko.

That fact told more. Much more.

A hatchet man had slain Lubber Kreef for a single purpose: to gain the message that the truck driver carried. Since the envelope was still in Lubber's pocket, the killer could not have gone.

No chopping killer would be scared away, with his real work undone. Hatchet men were lurkers, who saw their jobs through. The Shadow divined instantly that Lubber's murderer must still be in this room.

Two thoughts flashed simultaneously. One concerned the hiding place—the only spot where the killer could still be. That was in the big wardrobe just behind The Shadow's back.

The Shadow's other consideration was the envelope. It was the cue that the murderer awaited for his next move. The hatchet man was using it as bait for The Shadow.

These instantaneous conclusions came from The Shadow's knowledge of Chinese assassins and the methods they employed. He knew that it would be fatal to draw that envelope farther. Once its inscribed characters appeared in the light, The Shadow would be doomed.

Death would be his lot, also, if he lingered; or tried to spring away. Hatchet men could lash with the whipping speed of a cobra. There was only one way to meet the chopper's strategy. That was to restrain him by offering even better opportunity. As long as the hatchet man saw a chance to improve his stroke, he would wait.

With such tactics, The Shadow must avoid any suspicious move; he needed also to put himself in a position from which he could deliver a counteracting thrust. The Shadow saw the proper measure. He began a bold, deliberate maneuver.

Shifting slightly, he let his hand come from the envelope, to probe to another pocket, as if he had seen something of more consequence than the envelope. That move did not arouse the hatchet man's suspicion, for he knew that The Shadow had not yet seen the characters upon the envelope.

Moreover, The Shadow's change of position seemed advantageous to the killer. Cloaked shoulders were backing closer to the wardrobe drawer. The head beneath the slouch hat had lifted. Instead of a chop for The Shadow's spine, the spidery Chinaman would soon have chance for a skull stroke.

There was something, however, that the killer did not spy; he was too engrossed in watching The Shadow.

THE shift of the cloaked figure had brought The Shadow from the path of the gaslight. No longer was the floor blotted beside Lubber's body.

There, silhouetted upon the pool of blood, The Shadow saw the outline of the hatchet man's big head and long, raised hand. Blocky blackness registered the shape of the hatchet. As effectively as with a mirror, The Shadow could spot the coming move.

Slowly, backward and upward, The Shadow brought his head and shoulders closer to the slayer. His face was toward Lubber's body, but his eyes, hawklike, were watching telltale blackness. The Shadow's own silhouette was creeping toward the killer's outlined profile. The hawkish visage would soon eclipse the shading of the hatchet.

Before that came, The Shadow halted. He gave a sideward sway, then a forward feint, as though he intended to stoop again. The killer above him saw opportunity. The hand drove its hatchet.

Timed to the first waver of the floor blot, The Shadow threw himself straight backward. His straightening body thwacked the open drawer. His arms sped upward in piston fashion.

Down, over The Shadow's shoulder, came the slashing hand-ax. The hatchet man had overswept his mark. Had The Shadow swerved from his purpose and tried to stop the incoming lunge, he would have been too late.

Instead, The Shadow had gripped straight to another objective: the stretching body above him. His hands clutched the scrawny Chinaman beneath the arms; gloved fists flung forward, as the hatchet circled for The Shadow's heart. The Shadow's speed won.

Lurched from the drawer, the killer was whipped through the air, his driving weapon halted short of The Shadow's chest. Coming to his feet, The Shadow had jerked the lurking murderer completely from his hiding place.

Whirled in a headlong somersault, the hatchet man flew clear across Lubber's body and rolled halfway to the door. For the first time, The Shadow actually sighted his grotesque adversary; and in the next few seconds, he witnessed one of the most amazing recoveries that he had ever encountered.

THE hatchet man seemed to turn himself inside out as he struck the floor. By an incredible twist, he changed his landing into a spring, straight back toward The Shadow.

Half across the flattened shape of Lubber, The Shadow had not regained his balance from the hurling swing by which he had catapulted the hatchet man. Unable to reach for an automatic, he could only manage to lunge in under the wild swing of the killer's hatchet. The Chinaman had held his weapon despite the tumble.

The drive of the spidery Chinaman threw The Shadow back to balance. Gripping the killer's body with one arm, The Shadow shoved a cloaked fist for the hand that had the hatchet. He reached as far as the killer's forearm and gained the hold he wanted. For the next two minutes, the struggle was all to The Shadow's advantage.

Hard though the hatchet man lashed, he could not escape the python grip that The Shadow applied. Like deadly coils, The Shadow's arms tightened, drawing the squirming killer into a stronger embrace. The yellow face came before The Shadow's eyes. Dotted eyes were enlarged, bulging from their almond-shaped sockets. Nevertheless, the apish man was still tricky with his twists; any squirm might luckily free him.

The Shadow chose a sure, quick way to settle this enemy.

The grapple had brought them beside the rear window. Bracing one foot against the heavy wardrobe, The Shadow shifted his hold. He gave a terrific, outward lunge, smashing right through the window shade.

Long, twisted legs were hooked about The Shadow's body; he expected them to loosen from the force of that fling. The hatchet man was scheduled for a lone dive to the porch roof below the window.

Instead, the killer jerked his hand sideways, despite The Shadow's grip. As the gloved fist loosened, to give the yellow arm speed through the window, the Chinaman hooked his hatchet to the window frame. The Shadow twisted about, half across the sill. He saw the hatchet chopping toward him. There was only one way to avoid it. The Shadow did a back dive through the window.

He carried the hatchet man with him. They were spinning as they struck the porch roof, and they divided the shock between them. Then they were rolling down the slant—the Chinaman trying madly to make another chop, The Shadow foiling him with new grabs toward the hatchet.

The strugglers reached the roof edge. They locked upon the brink; hovered momentarily in the darkness. Each made a last, desperate grapple; they took the plunge. tightly locked.

That instant on the roof edge marked the real finish of The Shadow's struggle with the hatchet man. In the final display of strategy, The Shadow outguessed his foeman.

What the killer sought—and managed to get—was a high, free-arm position from which he could drive a sure hatchet stroke when they landed in the courtyard. What The Shadow acquired was a momentary foothold that would retard his body slightly, as the plunge began.

Headlong the two figures drove to the cement, the hatchet man first. The Shadow had transformed the fall into a dive; there wasn't time for the grapplers to flatten, before they hit. They were diving at an angle when they struck; and the Chinaman's oversize skull took the impact.

His body acted like a shock-absorber. Coiling beneath The Shadow's weight, the killer crumpled from the fists that gripped him. Shoulder-first, The Shadow thumped the paving. His slouch hat squashed as his head took a side blow.

The cloaked fighter rolled over and lay motionless beside the doubled form of his spidery opponent.

WINDOWS opened. Roomers on the second floor stared into the darkness. They had heard the thump on the roof; they looked for signs of the scufflers. Hearing nothing more, they forgot their curiosity. Some looked upward; but they could not see the tattered remnants of the window shade that hung in Lubber's window.

Minutes lapsed. The Shadow stirred. Slowly, he came to his feet and sagged against the wall. His head began to clear as he rested in the darkness. He found his tiny flashlight; flicked it on the mass of bone and flesh that lay near him.

The hatchet man was dead. His skull was bashed; the twist of his head showed that his neck was broken also. The Shadow searched the killer's clothing and found an important object.

It was a long, spikish tooth, that the hatchet man carried in a pocket of his blouse. An inch in diameter at the base, it tapered three inches to a sharp point. The tooth was too fantastic to be real; inspection showed The Shadow that it was made of some composition material.

The Shadow's low-toned laugh was sibilant in the darkness.

He knew what this token represented. It was supposedly a dragon's tooth, symbol of the Jeho Fan, once a powerful organization in China.

Bound by secret vows, members of the Jeho Fan called themselves Teeth of the Dragon. The leaders of the order used it to their own advantage. The rank and file were superstitious Mongols who actually believed that the tokens they carried were teeth of some ancient dragon.

Long defunct, the Jeho Fan had recently been re-vived in China; and The Shadow had learned that it had also become active in San Francisco. Doctor Tam had reported rumors concerning the Jeho Fan; but hadn't been able to acquire o n e o f t h e tooth-tokens that its members carried.

The Shadow had gained a dragon's tooth himself, as fitting trophy of the battle he had waged against the hatchet man who served as an assassin for the Jeho Fan. The Shadow kept the token. It could prove useful later.

No longer groggy, The Shadow tried to calculate how long he had lain sense-less. The precise interval was difficult to estimate. The Shadow decided that it did not matter.

When he passed between houses on the rear row and came to the front street, he detected no sign of lurkers. It seemed definite that other members of the Jeho Fan had not yet learned of their hatchet man's failure.

Moreover, The Shadow doubted that they would send a crew of their shock troops to this vicinity. The minions of the Jeho Fan belonged in Chinatown; if they ventured far from the limits of that quarter, they would not stay long. Their strength depended upon secrecy. They needed to remain where they could lose themselves among other Chinese.

KNOWING that limitation of the Jeho Fan, The Shadow took the old route that he had used to reach Lubber's room, confident that he would encounter no more opposition when he found the en-velope.

The room was exactly as The Shadow had left it. The half-opened wardrobe drawer, the ripped window shade were the only testimonies to the battle that had been waged.

Neither signified a visit by The Shadow. The opened drawer appeared purely accidental; the torn shade indicated only that Lubber's murderer h a d made a hurried exit. The body was lying as it had been when The Shadow had first viewed it.

Stooping to Lubber's pocket, The Shadow felt for the envelopes. His fingers found nothing. Though no new lurker was within the room, the message addressed to Ying Ko was gone!

Alone in the room of death, The Shadow uttered a sinister, whispered laugh. The loss of that message might hinder his plans; but it did not mean defeat. Instead, it gave The Shadow new urge to follow the dangerous trail of intrigue that he had begun to-night.

Curiously, the theft of the Chinese message was destined to bring The Shadow an advantage which even he could not foresee!

CHAPTER V.

THE SHADOW VISITS.

THE capture of the trawler *Tantalus* made big news in the morning dailies; but the evening newspapers spread new sensation through San Francisco, when they told of later finds. Lubber's body was discovered after daybreak; the dead hatchet man was found in the lower courtyard.

Theories were as hazy as the typical San Francisco fog. It was either a spite murder, because the *Tantalus* had failed to deliver its full cargo; or Lubber had been chopped down because he might have known the name of certain Chinese connected with the smuggling ring.

Whatever the case, Lubber was dead; and the hatchet man—according to the newspapers—had lost his hold coming down from the window; hence his plunge to the cement. That statement amused The Shadow, when he read it. The hatchet man had certainly lost his hold, but it had taken plenty of persuasion to make him do so.

Late in the afternoon, The Shadow entered the twentieth-floor offices of a large marine-insurance company. Attired in street clothes, he tendered a card that bore the name "Lamont Cranston." When he asked to see Mr. Richard Vayne, he was conducted to a reception room.

A girl was seated in the reception room; her desk bore the name-plate: "MISS RELDON." She was Vayne's secretary; and she acted as receptionist. It would have been difficult to picture any young woman better suited to the double job.

Miss Reldon had a distinct charm of feature and expression; her smile was the sort that would place any visitor at ease. With that graciousness, she also possessed a brisk business manner that contrasted with her social air.

That marked her as unusual. Her appearance, too, provided contrast. The girl had the light complexion of a blonde; but her large, clear eyes were definitely brown. Her thin eyebrows were light in color; the fluff of her hair made it seem light-brown against the sunlight. The Shadow noted, though, that it was darker when viewed from another angle.

The girl sensed the piercing effect of Cranston's eyes. In her turn, she studied the visitor, while she pressed a switch to connect her telephone with Vayne's.

Despite a calm expression, a leisurely manner, Cranston impressed the girl as a most remarkable visitor. His immobile face was masklike. His hawkish features suited his keen eyes. Strange eyes, that subdued when others met them. Yet, with a quick, intuitive glance —the sort that Miss Reldon could give —it was possible to detect a sparkle in Cranston's gaze.

RICHARD VAYNE was standing behind his desk when the girl ushered Cranston into a sumptuous inner office. Tall, with thin gray hair and birdlike eyes, Vayne had the square chin and firm hand-clasp of a man who liked action.

He bowed Cranston to a chair; then noted that Miss Reldon had gone to a filing cabinet in the corner. Impatiently, Vayne asked:

"What do you wish, Myra?"

"The Transpacific policies," replied the girl. "The messenger will be here for them."

"Ah, yes. I had forgotten. Very well, Myra. You will not disturb us."

Turning to Cranston, Vayne smiled as he remarked:

"This is our first meeting, Mr. Cranston, although we have held some correspondence. I knew that you would be in San Francisco to-day. I am greatly pleased that you dropped in to see me."

"I came to express my thanks," Cranston's tone was even. "You did me a real favor, arranging my passage aboard the China Clipper."

"You leave for China to-morrow," nodded Vayne. "I wish you a delightful flight. When you return, I shall be pleased if I can be of any other service. Perhaps"—Vayne's smile broadened—"there is something that I can do for you to-day."

"There is," was Cranston's calm announcement. "I am here to request that you cancel my passage on the China Clipper."

Vayne sat back in his chair. He

tried to smile, as though he thought the request a jest. Noting at last that Cranston was serious, Vayne clasped his hands and looked puzzled.

"I can cancel it," he assured, "quite readily, Mr. Cranston. But, really, I— well, I just don't understand."

"Perhaps," observed Cranston, "you have learned the reason why I intended to go to China?"

Vayne nodded.

"It is quite obvious," he admitted. "The Chinese government wants to raise one hundred million dollars, immediately. Ten million, to pay the ransom of General Cho Tsing, who was kidnaped and carried to the interior of China. The rest, to provide a national defense, which the abductors demand as part of the deal.

"The Chinese government prefers to float the loan through private individuals. Large interest payments will be met, with the best of security. You, Mr. Cranston"—Vayne's smile was wise— "are not the only American millionaire who is China-bound, to be on the ground floor. But wait"—Vayne's smile ended —"you say that you are not going to China."

FOR a moment, the glow of The Shadow's eyes was visible. Their burn seemed to bring light to the restrained features of Cranston. The words that came from Cranston's straight lips offset that flash; for they were in the usual deliberate tone that The Shadow used with this rôle.

"There is no need for a trip to China," emphasized the visitor. "The ransom of Cho Tsing will prove unnecessary. Therefore, no loan will be required!"

Vayne's face looked doubtful. He shook his head as though he had heard other opinions regarding Chinese affairs, and believed them unreliable. Cranston's gaze remained steady, adding emphasis to the words. Vayne was impressed despite himself.

"You seem convinced, Mr. Cranston," he declared. "Very well. I shall arrange to cancel your reservation. Do you have the ticket?"

Cranston produced it. Vayne spoke to Myra Reldon. The girl came from the filing cabinet. She took the ticket mechanically; her eyes were fixed upon Cranston.

Some hidden thought was passing through the girl's mind. She, too, had heard the emphasis of Cranston's statement. She was unable to fully hide her interest. But by the time that Cranston's eyes met hers, Myra had regained her usual expression.

As the girl went out into the other office, Vayne leaned across the desk.

"Mr. Cranston," he said, slowly, "I shall not ask the source of your information. Instead, I give you this warning. Do not mention your opinion to any other person. I trust that you have not spoken to any one, previous to this meeting."

"Only to a few."

"Even one may be too many," warned Vayne, "if it should be the wrong one. Look; did you read this?"

Vayne picked up the morning newspaper. He tapped the paragraphs that referred to the capture of the *Tantalus.* Cranston nodded; then commented:

"The smuggling of Chinese is a common occurrence. It can have nothing to do with political disturbances in China."

Vayne shook his head.

"Those poor fellows came from China," he reminded. "Ignorant coolies, staking their life earnings to reach America. Some one in China sold them the idea. Moreover, that is but one aspect of the case. Huge quantities of opium have been reaching California. Matters to-day are more critical than they have been in years!"

FROM his desk, Vayne procured a batch of credentials, that he passed across to Cranston. They announced that Richard Vayne was invested with the authority of the United States government, to conduct special inquiries into shipping affairs.

"For months," explained Vayne, "I have been working on these cases. This is confidential, Mr. Cranston; strictly confidential. I have investigated dozens of boats like the *Tantalus,* and have found them clear of suspicion.

"Then, like that!" Vayne snapped his fingers—"a ship in good repute proves to be a bad one. Whatever I do or plan, the word gets there ahead of me. We have searched for leaks, but have found none."

Vayne arose from his desk. He conducted Cranston to the window. Below, to the north, he pointed out the sprawling buildings of Chinatown, dwarfed against the background of Telegraph Hill. To the east, he indicated the long stretch of the massive bridge that led across the bay to Oakland.

"I live over there," stated Vayne, "although I spend some nights at an apartment here in San Francisco. I never go near Chinatown. Nevertheless"—he drilled his words with wags of his forefinger—"the Chinese are watching me!

"They will spy upon you also, Mr. Cranston, if they suspect that you have pried into their affairs. There is a fine, invisible line"—Vayne drew his finger up and down—"and to cross it means disaster. Remember that, Mr. Cranston.

"Meanwhile"—Vayne extended his hand for a parting shake—"you must not visit here again. You are another man who apparently knows too much. Since we belong to the same clan, it would be unwise for us to be seen together."

VAYNE ushered Cranston to the outer office. Myra Reldon was busy at her desk; she looked up to see the tall visitor walking toward the outer door, alone.

"Mr. Cranston!" called the girl. Then, as Cranston turned: "You will pardon me—but I should really like you to tell me at what time you are dining with Mr. Vayne; and where. He has a habit of forgetting the hour and the place, when he makes such engagements."

Cranston's lips smiled slightly, as he spoke: "I am not dining with Mr. Vayne."

Myra looked puzzled.

"But he has no other engagement." The girl referred to an appointment book; then laughed: "I understand. You were the one who had a dinner date. You had to refuse Mr. Vayne's invitation."

"I have no engagement," remarked Cranston. "Nor did Mr. Vayne extend an invitation."

Myra's business manner ended. Her tone became a charming one; her words as subtle as they were honeyed. With it, the girl feigned anxiety; almost distress.

"Mr. Vayne is so forgetful!" she expressed. "Really, I *know* that he intended to dine with you. I should remind him; but he is so sensitive about such matters. On the contrary, he would never forgive himself, if he realized that no one entertained you during your stay in San Francisco. If I could only tell him——"

"That I did have an engagement this evening?" supplied Cranston.

"Yes," returned Myra. "But I would have to be honest about it. Whom do you know in San Francisco?"

"No one, except Mr. Vayne——"

"And, of course, myself." Myra smiled winningly. "Don't forget, Mr. Cranston, that you met me before you met Mr. Vayne."

Cranston's smile matched Myra's. They laughed together. The next suggestion was Cranston's.

"If I knew the right place to dine," he remarked. "Somewhere more secluded than a stodgy hotel——"

"There is one," inserted Myra. "The Yangtse Restaurant. A Chinese place, but not in Chinatown. One might define it as on the outskirts. Look, Mr. Cranston."

The girl drew a diagram on a sheet of paper. She indicated the intersection of two streets; the building that housed the Chinese restaurant. She marked a side entrance; a staircase.

"You go up these," explained Myra. "Then to the left. You find a row of private dining rooms, all decorated differently. The fourth room on the left, Room D, is the nicest. And *real* Chinese food. Since you *aren't* going to China, you should at least dine at the Yangtse."

Cranston was noting the diagram as he asked:

"At what time shall I meet you there, Miss Reldon?"

"But—but——" Myra's stammer was a clever pretense. "Really, Mr. Cranston, I didn't mean——"

"You can mention that I dined with a friend."

"Of course. No, no! I mean——"

Myra's eyes met Cranston's. Their gaze held. With a slow, beautiful smile, the girl spoke softly:

"Half past eight."

MYRA'S smile vanished as soon as Cranston passed through the outer door. Her lips tightened; her whole expression was completely changed. Quickly, the girl approached the door to the inner office.

She listened intently, to make sure that Vayne had not overheard her conversation with Cranston. Her face showed a much less pleasant smile than the one that The Shadow had last seen.

Whether or not that smile betokened it, the future was established. When The Shadow kept his engagement with Myra Reldon, he would step into danger far greater than last night's menace.

CHAPTER VI.

CROOKS CONFER.

THE matter of the stolen message to Ying Ko was unknown to the newspapers; and The Shadow had not discussed it with Richard Vayne. That subject was a live one, however, elsewhere in San Francisco.

Two men were seated in a garish apartment. One was Shiv Faxon, the water-front racketeer. Shiv's companion, who lived at this apartment, was another expert in the racket line. He was "Brig" Lenbold, an opportunist who gave "protection" to a batch of second-rate night clubs that disliked trouble of the sort that Brig could produce.

"So you found this on Lubber." Brig spoke gruffly, as he toyed with the Ying Ko envelope. "And he said it was worth five grand. Well, we'll look into it."

"I must have got there pretty soon after the hatchet man croaked Lubber," informed Shiv, with a squint of his beady eyes. "I didn't stick there long."

"Don't blame you."

Brig's growl was a contrast to Shiv's sharp tone. Their appearance, too, was different. Shiv was slender and wiry; his tight lips and quick eyes gave the impression that he was guarding himself whenever he spoke.

Brig was husky; broad-shouldered and big-fisted. He talked bluffly; when he said too much, his eyes glared from the round sockets of his flattish face, as if warning listeners to forget what they had heard.

Shiv knew Brig's tendency. The tight-lipped fellow rapped a reminder.

"Lubber got into a jam, showing that envelope to too many chinks. We don't want to do the same, Brig."

"Don't get jittery," rumbled Brig. "There's only one bird that's going to see it. He'll read it for us. Or else! He's due here any minute." Brig looked through the window, to note the gathering dusk. "And he's coming here, thinking it's about something different."

"Who is he?"

"Dow Yoang. A Chinee that wants to open a new hop-joint. He thinks I can fix it for him."

It was not long before Dow Yoang arrived. He looked like the keeper of an opium den. The Chinaman was rat-faced, with slanting forehead. He studied Shiv suspiciously; then decided that Brig's companion was of the proper ilk.

In an ugly, croaking tone, Dow Yoang began to hint about the hop-joint. Brig interrupted.

"Something else, first," he rasped. "Take a squint at this envelope, Dow Yoang. Who's it for?"

There was a grimace of Dow Loang's tawny features. The Chinaman looked fearful, hunted, as though suspecting a trap. A stare from Brig to Shiv re-assured him. In company of such no-torious crooks, the hop-den owner could speak.

"It is for Ying Ko."

Brig rubbed his chin. He knew plenty of Chinese big-shots by name, but he had never heard of Ying Ko. Nor had Shiv. Dow Yoang explained.

"To you Americans," croaked the Chinaman, "Ying Ko is known as The Shadow!"

THAT was a bombshell. Brig reached for the envelope; but Shiv snatched it first, as if reminding that it was his present property. Ripping open the en-velope, Shiv unfolded a rice-paper note. It was written in Chinese. Shiv handed it to Brig.

"Read it for us," growled Brig, giv-ing the note to Dow Yoang. "Give us the low-down."

The Chinaman hesitated, as his eyes scanned the characters. His delay was a mistake. Brig thrust his big face close to the Chinaman's.

"No stalling, Dow Yoang!" Brig's

tone meant business. "If you try any phony stuff, we'll put the heat on you! What's more"—the next threat was potent—"I know a couple of Chinese guys who don't like you, Dow Yoang. I'll get one of them up here to read that letter, after you get through. If the two of you don't check——"

"I will read it," babbled Dow Yoang. "It is wise that only one should know. But you must speak to no one!"

"O. K.," agreed Brig. "It stays be-tween me and Shiv."

Carefully, Dow Yoang ran a long-nailed forefinger from character to char-acter, translating the letter in explana-tory fashion.

"It is to Ying Ko, The Shadow," de-clared the Chinaman. "It says that the man who writes it is helpless. He is held by enemies who call themselves"— Dow Yoang twisted his lips; then caught a glare from Brig—"who call them-selves the Jeho Fan. He wants Ying Ko to aid him."

Dow Yoang started to fold the letter, with the placid statement:

"That is all."

Brig's big hand clamped the China-man's wrist. It was Brig who pointed to characters that looked like a signa-ture.

"What do those mean?" he demanded. "Aren't they the name of the guy that wrote the letter?"

Dow Yoang stared as though he had not previously noticed the signature. With a reluctant nod, he admitted:

"Yes. The name is Cho Tsing."

Dow Yoang might have slipped that past Brig Lenbold. The husky racketeer was trying to connect Cho Tsing with Chinatown. Shiv Faxon's quick thoughts went farther than San Fran-cisco. Shiv became excited.

"Cho Tsing!" he exclaimed. "He's that chink general that was snatched! A bunch of bandits took him to some mountains, off in China. They want twenty million bucks to let him go."

"Twenty million, Mex," corrected Brig. "That's ten million in our money."

"Plenty of dough either way."

"Only, what does it mean to us?"

Shiv's tight lips spread. His beady eyes became very wise. Dow Yoang shifted nervously. He knew the guess that was in Shiv's mind.

"That letter," Shiv told Brig, "was given to a guy on the *Tantalus*. It means that Cho Tsing isn't in China. It tells why old Cap Malhearn was crazy enough to ditch his trawler. There was one chink that he had to put ashore. That was Cho Tsing!"

BRIG thwacked his big left palm with his huge right fist.

"That tells it!" he boomed. "The guys that snatched Cho Tsing couldn't swing the deal in China. That's why they smuggled him over here. What a set-up! They can't be grabbed for staging a snatch that wasn't done in this country!

"They've paid Malhearn plenty to take the rap, on a smuggling charge. He's keeping mum, so he won't get himself in worse. The guys that are holding Cho Tsing can claim they thought he was just another Chinaman, if it comes to a pinch. Say, Dow Yoang"— Brig swung suddenly—"what was the name of that outfit?"

Dow Yoang hesitated; then replied:

"The Jeho Fan."

"Never heard of 'em," rapped Brig. "Spill what you know."

Dow Yoang became evasive. No one knew much about the Jeho Fan. The order was supposed to exist in China only. If members were in San Francisco, they must have come here recently, without any one's knowledge.

Brig didn't like the Chinaman's obvious stall.

"Talk fast, Dow Yoang!"

The grated tone meant business. Dow Yoang weakened.

"It is possible," he admitted, "yes, very possible, that the Jeho Fan is active in San Francisco. The members call themselves the Teeth of the Dragon."

"Yeah?" Brig was interested. "And who's the big-shot?"

"No one knows." Dow Yoang was earnest. "He is the Tao Fan. Tao means leader."

"And where would the Tao Fan be keeping Cho Tsing?"

That question hit home. It was plain, from his wince, that Dow Yoang knew the answer. The grimace ended; in its place, a cunning gleam lighted the eyes of Dow Yoang.

"There is one man," declared Dow Yoang, "who is neutral in all Chinese affairs. He is Li Sheng, the merchant. The hospitality of Li Sheng is unbounded. His home would be the proper place to receive so honored a guest as the General Cho Tsing."

The racketeers had heard of Li Sheng. The merchant's residence was situated within a half block of solid, squatty houses in Chinatown. It was an oasis of elegance, secluded amid the ugliest of slums. There was an arched passage, with big gates at its inner end, that afforded the only entrance to the home of Li Sheng.

"So we've got to get to Li Sheng," grated Brig. "How do we manage that, Dow Yoang?"

Shiv guessed suddenly that the question was the very one that Dow Yoang wanted.

"It is very easy," informed Dow Yoang. "All are welcome through the portals of Li Sheng. Go there, and crave admittance. You will be well received."

"And after that?" put in Shiv.

Dow Yoang shrugged.

"Perhaps you will learn much from your visit," he remarked. "Perhaps not. At least, you will make the acquaintance of Li Sheng. There is nothing to be lost."

Brig started to say something. Shiv intervened.

"That makes sense," he interjected. "Let's go there, Brig. We can't lose."

Dow Yoang looked pleased. Shiv coolly drew a cigarette from his pocket; as he was lighting it, he spoke a single word, as if addressing it to the air:

"Ixnay."

Dow Yoang didn't understand hog latin. He missed the inference of that "nix" that Brig caught. What came next was up to Brig. Shiv had hopes. They increased, as Brig began to talk very openly.

"We're going into the snatch racket ourselves," declared Brig. "This is a natural; we can't pass it up. We'll snatch Cho Tsing from Li Sheng and put him in bad with the Jeho Fan. That bunch can't squawk to the Feds. We'll send Li Sheng a note, calling for a fifty-fifty split. We'll get our divvy when they're ready to collect from the Chinese government."

Brig stepped to the door; he placed his hand on the knob, while he beckoned to Dow Yoang. As the Chinaman approached, Brig promised:

"Five hundred grand for you, Dow Yoang. Half a million bucks, American money! Just for reading that letter, and keeping mum. Maybe there'll be more, if we can use you."

Brig was nodding as he spoke. The motion of his head was meant for Shiv. The wiry racketeer stepped up behind Dow Yoang, laid his left hand on the Chinaman's right shoulder. Dow Yoang turned, in the direction that Shiv wanted.

Shiv's right hand whipped upward from beneath his coat. The long, driving thrust came too quickly for Dow Yoang to even see the glimmer from Shiv's fist. A tapering, thin-bladed knife burrowed to the Chinaman's heart.

Shiv was searching the victim's body before the last writhe ended. Just as Dow Yoang stiffened in death, Shiv found the object that he wanted. He held it up for Brig's inspection. It was identical with the whitish spike that The Shadow had taken from the hatchet man.

"A dragon's tooth," declared Shiv. "Like I figured it, Dow Yoang was with the Jeho Fan."

"Sure," agreed Brig. "But they won't know he was up here. We'll get rid of this"—he nudged toward the body— "and then figure out how we'll handle Li Sheng."

"Only we won't go to see Li Sheng," added Shiv. "It's a bet that his joint is being cased by the Jeho Fan. That's why Dow Yoang wanted to steer us there."

"I'm thinking of a way to get to Li Sheng," announced Brig. "There are guys that can tell us what his place is like inside. That's all we'll need to know."

Brig spoke with solid assurance. Shiv didn't ask the details. He reached down to pluck up the letter to Ying Ko. Dow Yoang had dropped it; he had been handing it to Brig when Shiv's interruption came.

"One thing else this letter tells us, Brig," chuckled Shiv. "The Shadow is out of the picture. He don't even know that Cho Tsing is in Frisco!"

Shiv Faxon would have been astonished, and Brig Lenbold likewise, had they guessed how much The Shadow did know. Like these racketeers, The Shadow was concerned with the fate of General Cho Tsing. These crooks would meet The Shadow later, unless circumstances intervened in their behalf.

At that, the odds favored the crooks. Unlike the racketeers, The Shadow was ready to begin his action by a meeting with massed members of the Jeho Fan.

That boded ill for The Shadow.

CHAPTER VII.

HORDES OF THE FANS.

At half past seven, Myra Reldon was in the living room of a small apartment, when a key turned in the lock. Another girl entered; her face was pale, her eyes troubled. She was Helen Toriss, who shared the apartment with Myra.

"I've just come from dinner," informed Helen, "and I'm sure that there are Chinese watching this house!"

"Probably," answered Myra. "They spy on Mr. Vayne. I am his secretary, so it is natural that they would watch me also."

"But," Helen gasped, "what are we to do about it?"

"Nothing," replied Myra, "unless they try to enter. Then call the police."

Calmly, Myra arose, with the remark that she must turn off the water in the bathtub. She added that she had a date at half past eight.

"What about the Chinese?" expostulated Helen.

"They won't be close," assured Myra. "I'll go down the fire tower, like I have before. They won't see me. Just the same, though——"

Myra paused; then requested:

"Please call the Yangtse Restaurant, Helen. Tell them that if I am not there by half past eight, I won't be able to come at all. Just in case any one inquires."

Myra went through her bedroom, to the connecting bathroom. She locked the door that led into Helen's room. When he finished her bath, Myra donned an oversized Turkish bathrobe and stepped into a pair of slippers. Coming through the bedroom, she peered into the living room, Helen had forgotten the menace of the Chinese and was reading a magazine.

Myra closed the bedroom door and locked it, with care. She went to a bed in the corner and grasped a strap that hung from the end of the box spring. A large, secret drawer slid into view.

That drawer was filled with garments quite different from Myra's clothes, that lay upon a chair. It also contained a flat make-up kit and a large jar of cold cream. The make-up box was all that Myra wanted, for the present.

The girl carried the kit to a dressing table. She slid her arms from the sleeves of the bathrobe. Lifting her arms, she wrapped the robe tightly about her body, above the level of her elbows. Tying the sleeves together, Myra seated herself in front of the dressing table.

The mirror showed her light-hued face; her shapely shoulders and slender arms, smooth and white like ivory. That reflection told that Myra would have been extraordinarily attractive in an evening gown, thanks to the beauty of her skin.

Yet the girl's first move was to obliterate that whiteness.

From the make-up kit, Myra took a sponge and a bottle of yellowish fluid. Unsparingly, she daubed the thick liquid on her hands and wrists; swept the sponge up to her shoulders. Her face, her throat were next; using a hand mirror, the girl dyed the back of her neck.

She tapered the color downward from her neck and shoulders, until the yellow lessened and blended with the whiteness. Above the bathrobe, Myra's face, neck and arms all possessed an even yellow tone.

Still she would have looked well in an evening gown, but her complexion belonged to a Chinese beauty.

Perfect though the dye was, cold cream would remove it swiftly. Later, Myra could regain her whiteness as swiftly as she had assumed that yellow surface.

Next came the facial make-up.

Myra removed fluffs of false hair. Her

real hair was darker brown. It seemed almost black when Myra combed it straight and pressed it thickly. From above her forehead, she combed short locks downward. Ordinarily hidden, they became a short-clipped bang, dyed jet-black.

With make-up pencil, Myra matched her eyebrows to the bangs. She rouged her face cleverly, to give it a high-cheeked effect. Artful work with a lipstick made her mouth appear more pursed.

For a finish, Myra used two tiny strips of transparent mending tape. She moistened them; applied one to the outer corner of each eye. Carefully, she drew the strips outward, pressed them against her skin, creasing the bits of tape with her finger nails.

Flesh covered the drawn strips, rendering them invisible. Myra's eyes were totally changed. From a roundish shape, they had gained a cunning, almond slant. They looked black, between the tightened eyelids. With mascara, Myra blackened her lashes.

The face that peered from the mirror bore no resemblance to Myra Reldon's. It was the visage of a Chinese beauty— exotic, alluring, but with an expression that bore cruel malice.

Kicking off her slippers, Myra listened as she unwrapped the bathrobe. There was no sound from Helen. Quickly, Myra glided over to the bed and began to don the Chinese garb.

She dressed rapidly, for all the garments were in perfect arrangement. When she was dressed, she replaced the make-up kit in the secret drawer; then hung her own clothes in the closet.

Black crêpe slippers; black silk skirt. Above, an embroidered jacket with high, military collar, close about the neck. Long bell-sleeves, black like the body of the jacket, showed embroidered cuffs that matched the wide strips of the jacket front.

Myra slipped a large jade ring upon one finger; she raised her hand to display it, as she posed in front of a full-length mirror. Her lips wreathed a bitter smile, like the one she had shown when alone in the office.

That smile suited the Chinese girl that she saw in the mirror. That singsong damsel looked smaller than Myra Reldon. The black was responsible.

STEALTHILY, the Oriental figure approached the door; listened, then spoke in the voice of Myra Reldon, calling Helen Toriss. The other girl answered, through the door:

"What is it, Myra?"

"I am going out." The tone was odd, from those Chinese lips. "Just walk down the hall, as far as the elevator, to make sure that no one is watching from there."

Helen complied. She had furnished this precaution in the past. As soon as the outer door closed, Myra turned her own key and stepped from the bedroom. Crouching, she hurried through the kitchenette and unlocked a door to the fire tower. She was descending in darkness, before Helen returned to the apartment.

No Chinese were near the back of the secluded apartment house. Spying eyes could not see the girl's slinky figure, as she came from the fire tower. But it would not be long before she would encounter a prowler. Myra knew that from past experience. Occasionally, on these excursions, she met a challenge.

To-night, watchers were more prevalent than usual. That was why Helen had noticed them.

Skirting the courtyard in back of an adjoining apartment house, Myra heard some one in the darkness. Her hands were close to her embroidered jacket. She stretched one arm, to feel a brick wall. Instantly, a clawlike fist plucked her wrist.

The girl's other hand pressed a flashlight. It showed her upraised hand,

Myra tilted the flashlight to show her disguised face. The same rays revealed the leering visage of a Chinaman.

"Ming Dwan!" The accoster spoke the name in a tone of respect. Then, in babbled Chinese: "We are keeping good guard, most honored one."

Myra replied in the same language;

Skirting the courtyard, Ming Dwan heard some one in the darkness. Instantly, a claw-like fist plucked her wrist.

with its yellow dye, gripped by fingers of the same hue. Her hand was fisted; she unclenched it. From her palm glistened the white shape of a dragon's tooth.

The gripping hand loosened, when eyes sighted the token of the Jeho Fan.

her singsong tone carried harsh authority.

"Make sure that the girl does not attempt to leave her abode," she ordered. "If any one must enter, send word to me. I, Ming Dwan, am ready. Later, I shall return here."

The Chinaman mumbled his obedience. Extinguishing the flashlight, Myra continued to the street. She took a course that led to Chinatown—a fact that explained why she had suggested that Cranston meet her at the Yangtse Restaurant.

THAT café, on the fringe of Chinatown, was one place where the girl could appear either as Myra Reldon or Ming Dwan.

Her possession of the dragon's tooth; the command that she held over those watchers, told that Ming Dwan belonged to the inner circle of the Jeho Fan. The rank and file carried the same tokens; but they took orders. They did not give them, as Ming Dwan had.

The minions of the Jeho Fan believed Ming Dwan to be a genuine Chinese. No traitor could ever blab that she was actually the American girl, Myra Reldon. That chance was spiked by the policy that the Jeho Fan maintained; their constant watching of Myra's apartment house.

Thus did the girl cover her secret work.

Richard Vayne believed that his secretary was entirely loyal to the cause that he had sworn to uphold, that of uncovering the Chinese smuggling ring. Myra had told him that Chinese had watched her apartment. Vayne had checked that fact to his own satisfaction.

Therein lay Myra's cleverness. She had concealed her true identity even from members of the inner circle; it was she, Ming Dwan, who had insisted upon the vigil at the apartment house.

Myra wanted the Jeho Fan to keep actual watch upon her actions, so that her alibi would be a real one. In that way, she had completely outwitted Vayne.

Whenever Myra forwarded information to the Tao Fan, insidious leader of the Chinese group, she saw that it took a roundabout course. That was not difficult. Ming Dwan belonged in Chinatown, where, as the only woman member of the Jeho Fan, she could penetrate anywhere, unsuspected.

The Tao Fan had paved the opportunity that enabled the girl to play her double part. He wanted Ming Dwan to appear only at night; to keep her abode a secret. She was a mystery to the inner circle of the Jeho Fan; the Tao liked it all the better when she became something of a mystery to him, as well.

Pride in her own secret methods could have produced the pursed-lip smile that Ming Dwan displayed, when she reached the streets of Chinatown this night. Soon she would meet more members of the Jeho Fan. After that, she would reach the Yangtse Restaurant.

The arrival of Ming Dwan would have much effect upon the future plans of the gentleman who called himself Lamont Cranston.

There would be a surprise for The Shadow, when Ming Dwan kept the date that Myra Reldon had made.

CHAPTER VIII.
MING DWAN'S GUILE.

IN his suite at a fashionable San Francisco hotel, Lamont Cranston was donning tuxedo for his dinner date with Myra Reldon. He adjusted his black bow tie in front of a mirror. As he did, he kept a watchful eye upon the reflection of the room.

Two spots were of particular importance: the door to the hallway, which had a transom above it; a half-opened window that gave onto a courtyard.

The Shadow had made sure that those were the only two directions from which danger could come.

Since his coat and vest were still in the closet, Cranston stepped away from the mirror, picking up a watch and chain that lay upon the bureau. He pushed a chair aside; its scrape told that he was changing his position in the room.

That sound could have been heard beyond either the transom or the window.

Stepping in the opposite direction, Cranston approached the closet. He was glancing at his watch, noting the time as quarter past eight. The watch was an old-fashioned type, with hinged front.

The polished gold interior of that watch front made a perfect mirror as Cranston's hand turned it.

Keen eyes caught the reflection of the window, still blank. As the watch turned, eyes spied the transom. A face disappeared from the transom. Some spy had bobbed up in the hallway, to note Cranston's actions.

The fellow was gone, confident that Cranston would be busy for the next few minutes looking for his coat and vest. That was why Cranston halted. Swinging the closet door almost open, he stepped beyond it. Against the wall, he could not be seen from either the transom or the window.

A sighing hiss reached The Shadow's ears. He could not have detected it had he been inside the closet. The sound must have been uttered from some hallway window, for it came faintly through the courtyard.

Yellow face and hand came over the sill of Cranston's window. A limber Chinaman swung to the carpet. His right hand, following his body, had a grip upon a hatchet. This new assassin looked as vicious as the one that The Shadow had finished the night before.

Though the newcomer lacked the hideous, spidery proportions of his dead associate, the long stalk that he took across the room was proof that he was swifter and more powerful.

As he reached the opened closet door, the hatchet man swerved; he poised for a powerful forward spring, expecting to sight Cranston's white-shirted form.

The Shadow heard the suckish intake of the killer's breath; knew that the leap was due. With a hard, one-arm snap, The Shadow slammed the door.

The whizzing barrier smashed against the hatchet man before he could dive from its path. With sideward sprawl, the invader cracked against a radiator in the corner, losing his hatchet when it clanged the metal.

Cranston's long form followed the door's sweep. His arms pinned beneath him, his throat pressed by choking fingers, the hatchet man was staring at the hawkish face of his tall captor.

Soon, the hatchet man lay bound and gagged in the closet, where the inside spy could release him later. Cranston's bags were on their way downstairs, to be checked by the porter. Smoothing his tuxedo coat, Cranston entered the elevator.

THE departing guest carried one small piece of luggage with him from the hotel. It was a pliable briefcase; when empty, it could be rolled and folded into a very compact space.

Entering a taxi, Cranston gave an address not far from the Yangtse Restaurant. Before the cab reached its destination, a wadded bill thumped the driver's knee. He noticed it, because it was weighted with coins inside. Stopping, the taxi man picked up the money. He looked into the back seat; turned on the light.

His passenger was gone.

The Shadow had donned black garments from the briefcase. Leaving the cab while it was halting, he had closed the door before the driver could observe it.

Along darkened, steep-pitched streets, The Shadow had become a swiftly gliding wraith. He was taking a short route to the Yangtse Restaurant, to make up for the minutes that he had lost at the hotel.

The Jeho Fan had staged a crafty preliminary thrust, to lull The Shadow.

The Tao had gained an exact description of Lamont Cranston. Whether or not the Tao identified Cranston with

The Shadow, he had certainly learned that Cranston was not the sort to be side-tracked by one unpleasant episode.

The Tao Fan had sent the hatchet man to Cranston's hotel, believing that any outcome would be advantageous. If the hatchet man had slain Cranston, it would have suited the plans of the Jeho Fan. The killer's failure also accomplished something.

It gave Cranston reason to suppose that the Jeho Fan was not informed of his date with Myra Reldon.

Perhaps The Shadow had been deceived by that bit of trickery. True, since discarding the guise of Cranston, he was traveling with utmost stealth. That, however, was The Shadow's usual policy when venturing on dangerous ground.

The Yangtse Restaurant was a place of good reputation; but it was close to Chinatown, the headquarters of the Jeho Fan. The hatchet man in the hotel room had come from the Chinese district. That was sufficient reason for The Shadow to be elusive, even on the outskirts of Chinatown.

In New York's underworld, The Shadow had the reputation of moving unseen, to arrive suddenly in the midst of startled foemen. Ying Ko was credited with the same ability in San Francisco's Chinatown.

THE side street by the Yangtse seemed deserted. The Shadow entered a blackened doorway; found the stairs with silence, amid utter darkness. Lights should have been gleaming from the hallway above. There was none. The gloom was well-suited for a secret entry, either by Lamont Cranston or The Shadow. That, however, gave it a greater menace.

The Shadow suspected lurkers all along the route. As he paused on the stairs, he could almost hear the breathing of hidden men. If such were here, one misstep could mean death. The same was true when The Shadow reached the second-floor hall.

Any lurking Chinese were disappointed, without realizing it. Guiding by the wall, The Shadow picked out doorways with the touch of his gloved fingers. He arrived at Room D without a betraying sound. He tried the knob in clickless fashion. There was no noise when he opened the door inward.

By the feel alone, The Shadow could tell that the door rubbed a thick carpet, the sort that would block out light when he closed it. Shutting the door as noiselessly as he had opened it, The Shadow felt along the wall and found a light switch.

He did not press it. Instead, he edged away until he encountered another object, which he identified as a wheeled serving table. Reaching out, The Shadow discovered something that he expected: a threefold screen that hid the table.

The wheels could squeak, despite precaution. That was one reason why The Shadow slid the screen instead. He had another reason; he wanted the screen closer to the light switch.

Reaching to full arm's length, The Shadow fingered the switch and stroked it downward. With the motion, he wheeled away; the rapid spin carried him behind the screen. Though light came instantly, the quickest eye could not have spotted that sudden face of a black-cloaked form.

The glare showed a dining room, decorated with Chinese murals. At the far side of the room, curtains intervened between the paintings. Peering through the crack of the screen, The Shadow saw the heavy drapes stir.

Eyes peered; the curtains opened. Each delivered a pair of squatty Mongols, who swept the hanging aside as if by signal. They blinked; their pockish faces looked puzzled. Each of the four held a revolver; but none knew where to aim. Their natural target was the light switch, where some one should have been. No one was there.

These gun-toting tools of the Jeho Fan lacked the cunning of the hatchet men. A crafty killer might have suspected the ornamental screen as The Shadow's hiding place; but the gun squad stared blankly.

The lights were on; some one must have been at the switch. There was no hiding place near by. The best guess that the Mongols could make was that some one had reached through the door, to get at the switch. Gabbling among themselves, they began to steal in that direction.

A chilling laugh halted them.

Where the mirth came from was a mystery. It crept with quivering, whispered echoes from the walls of the room itself. The Mongols were rooted. The lips of one muttered the dread name:

"Ying Ko!"

WITH a sharp clack, the screen was swept aside. The noise made the gun squad turn. There, flanking them, was Ying Ko, himself!

The Shadow had used one hand to sweep aside the screen; the other fist waggled a .45 automatic in a slow arc that covered the four Chinese.

The Shadow's lips voiced a low command in the language that the Mongols knew. One move from any member of the squad would mean instant death to all. Such words, coming from Ying Ko, were to be believed.

The Shadow let his foemen hold their guns. He knew that a Chinese gunner invariably kept an empty chamber under the hammer. Any of the four who tried attack would need two trigger tugs before he could dispatch a bullet. That would be fatal, under present circumstances.

The Chinese knew that The Shadow could wither them. They stared sullenly, wondering what he would do next. They saw Ying Ko sidestep toward the door. A quick tug of the knob—a crouching Chinaman took a sprawl in from the hall. Another tried to leap away. The Shadow caught him with a forearm bend and hauled the second snooper to the floor.

All the while, he covered the original four. Before the newly tricked pair could aim from the floor, The Shadow's free hand opened before their eyes. In the gloved palm lay the dragon's tooth that The Shadow had taken from the hatchet man.

The pair lowered their guns; The Shadow's open hand went from sight beneath his cloak. It whipped into view again, this time with an automatic. A brace of big guns unlimbered, The Shadow held six Chinese helpless.

There was only one course open. The Shadow intended a false move toward the hall. Then quick shots, to quell the trapped Chinese when they began their fire. Clipping a few of them would scatter the rest. Then The Shadow could drive for the stairs.

Squarely in the center of the doorway, The Shadow was ready for the action, when he caught a sound from the gloomy hall. It was not the creep of more gun-bearing Mongols; instead, The Shadow recognized the soft *click* of a woman's footfalls.

He gestured his automatics toward the men in the room; as they cowered, The Shadow leaned back into the hall and flashed a glimpse toward the stairs.

In that quick glance, he saw the girl who was known to the Chinese as Ming Dwan.

The girl's arms were folded lightly, each palm resting flat just above the other wrist. Her smile was solemn; the look in her slanted eyes was awed, yet friendly.

The voice of Ming Dwan spoke words in quaint-toned English. Her speech was low, reassuring; pitched so that it could not reach the Chinese in the inner room.

The voice of Ming Dwan spoke words in quaint-toned English. Where a crew of Mongol gunners had failed to influence the formidable Ying Ko, this mystery girl of Chinatown was smoothly gaining the result she wanted. The Shadow's prowess was melting beneath the guile of Ming Dwan.

The Shadow listened. Ming Dwan stopped short enough so that she could not be seen from the room. The promise that she gave was aid, that could prove timely to The Shadow. Her utterances were persuasive; they impressed The Shadow.

Where a crew of Mongol gunners had failed to influence the formidable Ying Ko, this mystery girl of Chinatown was smoothly gaining the result she wanted. Still covering the armed men, The Shadow could only listen. No longer did he see the girl's almond eyes.

Those eyes alone betrayed the fact that the girl did not intend to keep the promise that she spoke. The trust that the dulcet voice inspired was to produce

a consequence quite different from the result that The Shadow anticipated.

The Shadow's prowess was melting beneath the guile of Ming Dwan.

CHAPTER IX.
THE LAIR OF THE FAN.

THE first words that Ming Dwan breathed seemed proof that the Chinese girl had brought a message from a friend.

"Some one was to meet you here," informed Ming Dwan, softly. "Some one who could not come. She was in danger. I, Ming Dwan, have come in her place."

A pause. The Shadow seemed impressed by the reference to Myra Reldon.

"There are enemies below," continued Ming Dwan. "Many enemies. You, Ying Ko, can conquer them; but only by surprise. That cannot be if there is trouble here.

"You must trust in me." The tone was earnest. "I, Ming Dwan, can command the ones that you hold helpless. I shall tell them that Ying Ko is to depart."

Silent, Ming Dwan watched for a sign of reply. She saw The Shadow's head incline. The nod brought a curled smile to Ming Dwan's lips. Her opportunity was established.

Ming Dwan stepped close. Her elbow pressed The Shadow's. The nudge was gentle; her spoken word was a command, persuasive and final.

"Move forward. I, Ming Dwan, must pass."

Even the girl's whisper seemed laden with a fragrant perfume, that surrounded her exotic presence. One hand moved slightly, to touch The Shadow's cloaked arm. Lulled by that mild pressure, The Shadow obeyed Ming Dwan's wish.

Two straight steps forward brought the cloaked fighter almost upon the cowering Chinese. Huddled, those foemen were loosening their fingers, anxious to drop their guns before Ying Ko showed his full wrath. It was sight of Ming Dwan that stayed them.

Squinty eyes could scarcely believe it when they saw the girl step calmly in beside The Shadow.

Ming Dwan's smile ended. At The Shadow's elbow, she gave her first sign of hesitation. Ming Dwan had expected to see the gun squad helpless—but never so beaten as they appeared. She pursed her lips tightly, wondering if her secret scheme could work. Then came a stir among the men who hunched before The Shadow's guns.

Ming Dwan, herself, had given them courage.

Conflict of thoughts deluged the brains behind those yellow faces. The bold-ness of Ming Dwan made them realize that The Shadow was human. But when the girl spoke, their return of savagery made them rebel.

In Chinese, Ming Dwan told them to drop their guns.

They hesitated. The Shadow backed the order with a gesture of his automatics. Revolvers fell from sullen hands. Glares were directed at Ming Dwan. The Mongols suspected that she had betrayed them.

The jade ring glittered from Ming Dwan's left fist. The sparkle disappeared as the girl turned her knuckles toward the huddled men and opened her fingers. She displayed the token of the Jeho Fan.

"By this dragon's tooth," spoke Ming Dwan, firmly, "I promise death to any one who disobeys! Not one hand must move until my words command!"

Glares ended. Mongols remembered that Ming Dwan held full authority from the Tao Fan, their merciless leader. Like whipped curs, they mumbled their willingness to obey Ming Dwan.

They heard the whispered laugh of The Shadow and it irked them. But, as that tone ended, they saw the hard smile that came with the glitter of Ming Dwan's eyes.

"Remember. No one is to move——"

As she gave those words, Ming Dwan whipped her right hand from her left arm. A tiny revolver glittered; its muzzle jabbed cold against The Shadow's neck, below his ear. In English, the girl hissed:

"The same order applies to you, Ying Ko!"

CROUCHING Mongols showed their fangish, yellowed teeth in ugly joy. Ming Dwan had shown her mettle. One press of her tapered forefinger would mean death to Ying Ko. The Shadow's big guns were useless. Instant doom would come with his first attempt at slaughter.

Sneaky hands were creeping, crablike,

for dropped revolvers, when Ming Dwan stopped them. Her command was harsh. It held the Mongols motionless.

"Ying Ko will drop his guns," the girl told them. "When I speak the word, you will capture him alive. He is to be the prisoner of the Jeho Fan; the gift of Ming Dwan, to our great Tao!"

Exuberance seized the Mongols. They knew that Ying Ko had heard the girl's decision. They saw her press the gun muzzle deeper. They heard the fierce hiss from Ming Dwan's lips, giving The Shadow his choice of present death, or the privilege of being hailed before the Tao Fan.

Gloved hands opened. Big automatics thudded the floor. Ming Dwan beckoned to the eager squad. The attackers sprang upon The Shadow, smothering his cloaked form to the floor. While Ming Dwan watched, they bound and gagged their prisoner.

They were snarling gleefully, those Mongols, promising Ying Ko an unhappy future. Quick death from a revolver was better far than the fate that the Tao would declare. Ying Ko was a fool, as he would learn.

Ming Dwan ordered silence. The Shadow's hat had tilted back; she saw the face of Cranston staring up from the floor. Despite his predicament, The Shadow met Ming Dwan with burning eyes, that appraised her as keenly as they had studied Myra Reldon.

The girl's lips contorted into a downward smile. She was confident that even The Shadow could not penetrate the perfect disguise that she wore.

Grasping clawish hands hoisted The Shadow from the floor. Like pallbearers, the Chinese began their slow, triumphant march from the room. Ming Dwan followed; she passed them in the hall. The first to reach the stairs, she gave a spoken signal to hidden men below.

Lights appeared. A dozen waiting Chinese chattered their evil delight when Ming Dwan pointed to The Shadow, as he was borne down the stairs.

"Ming Dwan is clever. She has tricked Ying Ko——"

"We are children of fortune, since Ming Dwan came to guide us——"

"Only our Tao is greater than Ming Dwan——"

Ming Dwan silenced those appreciations. Her face showed triumph; and well it might. She had told that lower squad to remain downstairs, while she went to learn what had happened above. They had reluctantly obeyed her command.

They knew, at last, that Ming Dwan was more capable than an entire horde of battling Chinese.

THERE was a rear route from the Yangtse Restaurant, and that was the course that the procession followed. A truck was waiting in a steep, narrow street. Outwardly, it looked like a vehicle due for the junkyard; but when Chinese lowered the back, the interior proved otherwise.

The inside of the truck was metallined. Bolted to the center of the floor was a square cage of huge iron bars, so crisscrossed that a hand could not be thrust through. The Shadow saw it by the glare of flashlights and recognized it as a Chinese torture cage.

The contrivance was designed to make its occupant as uncomfortable as possible. Within it, a prisoner could neither stand, lie down, nor seat himself. Bad enough under ordinary conditions, it was to prove worse for The Shadow; for his captors did not unbind him. Instead, they doubled his body with vicious pressure and shoved him into the cage. They slid the door downward and bolted it.

Four Chinese boarded the truck and squatted at the corners of the cage. A hanging electric lantern showed The Shadow, twisted grotesquely within the painful cell.

His head tilted sideways, The Shadow saw Ming Dwan look into the back of the truck, to make sure that the guards were at their posts.

Ming Dwan's stare was merciless; foreboding.

The Shadow knew the rules that governed societies such as the Jeho Fan. Torture was their favorite sport; and

the choice of ordeals rested with those who made the capture.

There was no doubt that Ming Dwan would provide unique measures for The Shadow's future entertainment. Those would come after the Tao gave the command for death. Even the brutal strokes of a hatchet man would be soothing, compared to the torture devices that would be at Ming Dwan's disposal.

The back of the truck clamped shut. The journey that followed was a constant reminder of the punishment that the Jeho Fan could give to prisoners. The driver took a twisty course. Perhaps he was making sure that the truck was not followed, but it seemed that he was making the tortuous turns for The Shadow's benefit.

The grades of those San Francisco streets rolled The Shadow forward and backward; every swing of the truck hurled him against the side of the cage. The swinging lantern was rocking like a pendulum, its rays sending long, changing silhouettes across the floor.

Steadying themselves by gripping the corners of the cage, the Chinese guards bared their teeth in smiles of relish, as they watched The Shadow's form go through its pretzel twists. Every time his face bashed the bars, they nodded to each other, chattering like apes.

When a hard jolt cracked The Shadow's head against the cage door, the watchers grimaced their disappointment, to see his face slump forward to his knees. With Ying Ko senseless, the fun was ended.

The stopping of the truck partially revived The Shadow. His eyes opened weakly as he heard the clank of the lifting door. He shook his head to toss away the blood that trickled from a gash above his forehead.

Guards hauled him from the cage; his limbs pained, as they were stretched from their cramped position. The Shadow felt his hat fall from his head; a pair of grimy yellow hands plucked it from the ground and jammed it down over The Shadow's eyes.

There were a few breaths of fresh air; then four carriers took their battered prisoner through a street door, into a blackened passage. They came to a stony, square-shaped room with a single light. A door opened to another passage; The Shadow whiffed the scent of opium smoke.

He was passed to another group of bearers. Down stony steps, through a narrow corridor where water trickled. More darkness; finally, a hard thump as his captors dropped him on a slab in the corner of a pitch-black room. There was the tramp of departing footsteps; a long, monotonous wait.

At last, the *click* of a secret door. New hands found The Shadow in the darkness; lifted him for another journey down a flight of Stygian steps. Though wearied, The Shadow could hear the babble of these carriers; he knew that he had reached the end of his trip.

The Shadow's new custodians were members of the inner circle. Soon, the prisoner would face the chosen few who ruled the Jeho Fan. In a burrowed lair, beneath the streets of Chinatown, the mighty Tao would pronounce the doom of Ying Ko.

CHAPTER X.

THE BLADE OF DEATH.

THE underground headquarters of the Jeho Fan was the most grotesque meeting place that The Shadow had ever seen. Secreted among forgotten catacombs of Chinatown, its location was untraceable. Confident that the stronghold would ever be secure, the Jeho Fan had spent a fortune in its embellishment.

The result was a garish, hideous medley that resembled an opium smoker's nightmare.

The square room was illuminated by a sickly, greenish glow. In that olive-tinged light, The Shadow saw monstrous faces peering down from every corner. They were huge statues, each of a Chinese joss, that stood as ten-foot guardians over the meetings of the Jeho Fan. Carried on the shoulders of four men, The Shadow stared into the faces of those looming idols.

The odd light was hurtful when The Shadow stared upward, for it glared from a ceiling dome. The Shadow closed his eyes; he felt himself lowered to the stone floor. There, he lay silent, while hands used knives to slash his bonds. Slowly, The Shadow came to a half-seated position. He opened his eyes.

Looking about, the cloaked prisoner viewed the entire room. He saw two brass doors at the end of the room from which he had arrived; between them, a low platform. At the other end of the meeting place was a huge box that looked like a tea chest.

From that floor, more statues were visible, set between the giant images that stood in the corners. Some were figures of Chinese devils, slightly larger than lifesize. Others were dwarfish idols, squatted upon taborets.

On the walls were tapestries, with woven dragons of silver and gold. Their coils were twisted as in combat; and each dragon face showed a yawning mouth, with long, sharp teeth.

The dragons evidently symbolized the Jeho Fan. The huge joss figures would be logical in any Chinese meeting place. But The Shadow could not understand the purpose of the devil images; nor why there were so many. What perplexed him more was the absence of the Jeho Fan. Even the carriers who had brought him here were gone.

Hazily, The Shadow was recovering from his daze. Objects began to take clear shape in the unnatural green light. A few moments more, The Shadow would have made a discovery of his own accord. A boomed voice made that unnecessary.

The tone came from the platform.

As The Shadow looked in that direction, the devils came to life.

They were the inner circle of the Jeho Fan, garbed in grotesque costumes; each wearing a leering head. Such costumes were used in Chinese ceremonies; but they looked different than any that The Shadow had previously seen. The green light was responsible. It absorbed the colors; gave the costumes the dull tint of old bronze.

The echoing tone had come from the central figure on the platform. He stepped forward; others spread apart to reveal an ornate throne, which two of the group carried forward.

Another monstrous member clanged a huge gong that sent long reverberations through the room. The sound dwindled, step by step; when its last faint clangor sounded, the members were in their places.

The central figure was seated on the throne. He was the Tao of the Jeho Fan.

Two of the demons stepped from the side walls. They clamped hands upon The Shadow's shoulders, hauled him to his feet. Their hands were covered with heavy gauntlets, spiked with metal that dug through the prisoner's cloak. With a forward sweep, the pair sprawled The Shadow at the feet of the Tao Fan.

The leader delivered an ugly, basso laugh. It brought a response from the devil-members. Their harsh mirth was loudened within the domed room, giving it a demoniac fury. The chorus ended. The dozen members of the inner circle awaited the word of their leader.

"You are Ying Ko." The Tao spoke in low-pitched, choppy English. "You are an enemy to the Jeho Fan. Unless you can give reason why you should live, you must die!"

The Tao waited. Slowly rising, The Shadow looked into the white orbs of false eyes that bulged from the devil-mask. He could see the glitter of evil eyes within. His answer was a sinister laugh; the square walls plucked it. The mirth became an amplified peal that shivered the thick atmosphere.

By contrast, the concerted glee of the Jeho Fan was pitiful. The Shadow's challenge told that he understood the acoustic properties of these walls, where any small sound could be magnified. The Shadow was treating the assemblage of demons like a masquerade.

Just how that impressed the Tao, could not be discerned. The oversize head that covered his own enabled him to keep his facial expressions to himself. When he spoke, however, his clipped tone was as harsh as before. The voice issued an insidious pronouncement from the big-fanged mouth of the demon's head.

"You choose to die," declared the Tao. "Remember, Ying Ko, there is such a thing as choice of death."

The Shadow's manner was indifferent. The Tao raised his claw-shaped gauntlets, clapped his hands together. Two of the Jeho Fan stepped from the dais. Pointing to The Shadow, the Tao ordered:

"Let Ying Ko see!"

THEY took The Shadow to the far end of the room. One of the demonish members opened the great chest; laid the lid against the wall. He pointed for The Shadow to peer downward. As he did, The Shadow heard a steady, rhythmic whir.

The chest was the sham covering of a tube that extended down into the wall at an angle of forty-five degrees. The tube was a large, smooth-lined pipe, some four feet in diameter. At the end of fifteen feet, it was blocked by a glittering obstruction that disappeared just as The Shadow saw it.

The tube went farther beyond, merging into darkness. The Shadow watched; a second later, the glitter reappeared.

The edge of a gigantic cleaver slith-

Two of the demons stepped from the side walls. They clamped hands upon The Shadow's shoulders, hauled him to his feet.

ered across the tube. The Shadow's own reflection was mirrored from it, remaining constant upon the moving blade. In fact, the massive slicer did not seem to be moving at all, until its back edge came into view. Then it was gone again, only to complete the circuit a second later.

Half a minute passed, while The Shadow stared as if fascinated by the constant reappearance of the blade. The purpose of the device was obvious. It was used to deliver death—a doom that could never be escaped by any one thrust within that tube.

The Shadow could picture the varied experiences of past victims, all of which had ended in the same result.

Sliding body, released from the mouth of the tube, would be no more than halfway through when the slicer chopped. Its speed was timed accordingly. That would happen if the person arrived after the rear of the steel had just passed.

If a skidding body arrived when the tube was blocked, the force of its slide would be halted. Once the blade passed, no one could cling to the slippery interior of the tube. The slide would begin again. As surely as a sucking whirlpool, the victim would go to doom. If he tried to scramble through, it would be no use.

With the momentum of a slide once lost, sufficient speed could not be regained to avoid the inevitable blade.

The masked members of the Jeho Fan produced a dummy figure, of human size. This would show the fearless Ying Ko how the big blade worked. The dummy was weighted; they let slide, while the silvery surface was in view. It neared the fatal spot just as the blade went by.

For an instant, the dummy's slide was unimpeded; then the massive knife swung through to cleave it squarely at the waist. The lower half was gone; the rest remained.

When the blade cleared, the rest of the dummy figure sped down into the pit.

A handclap from the Tao; the sound was hollow in that room. Masked men brought The Shadow back to the evil chief.

"You have seen, Ying Ko," pronounced the Tao. "I tell you that our other tortures are such that you will shriek your preference for the blade of death. Then, it will be too late."

The Shadow showed no alarm. The Tao became more specific.

"You received a letter from the General Cho Tsing," he announced. "Tell us the import of that letter. I shall then promise you swift death."

A figure stepped suddenly to the dais; huge-gloved hands lifted to whip off the demon's head. The member who interrupted the Tao Fan was Ming Dwan. The greenish light, catching the yellow dye, gave an olive hue to the disguised features of Myra Reldon.

The girl's teeth were gritted. In that glow, Ming Dwan's face was more demonish than the mask that had covered it.

"The prisoner is mine, Tao!" spoke Ming Dwan, in Chinese. "I demand the right to name a torture. Your promise cannot hold!"

The Tao stood motionless; then from the depths of his mask came the announcement:

"My promise was unwise; but it was given. If Ying Ko speaks, he will die without torture."

Ming Dwan faced The Shadow. Her eyes caught the greenish light; they gleamed catlike between their drawn lids. Furious, the girl seemed ready to strike down the prisoner if he denied her the right to have him tortured.

The Shadow did not speak. Ming Dwan leered toward the Tao, awaiting his decision. The masked leader gave the nod that the girl awaited. Ming Dwan eyed The Shadow, like a cat above its prey. Suddenly, her expression changed. She spoke in a low tone to the Tao.

"You are right, Ming Dwan," acknowledged the leader. "Ying Ko must be made to speak. Therefore, you have chosen well. We shall consign him to the Dragon Cell.

"That cell, Ying Ko"—the Tao's

false eyes were upon The Shadow— "is where men lose their reason, when they breathe the gas we call the Dragon's Breath. Hours will pass; perhaps a day, or more; at last, your tongue will begin its babble.

"All that you know will be spoken. There is no escape from the Dragon's Cell. Outside it, there will be one constant listener: Ming Dwan. Afterward, she will choose a further torture."

The Tao clapped his hands, appointing followers to carry away The Shadow. His eyes turned toward the men he chose. Four devil-masked captors closed in upon The Shadow.

The Shadow's right hand went beneath his cloak, where there no longer was a gun. It came out bare, its tattered glove fallen from it. At last, the iron nerve of The Shadow seemed broken. He sagged weakly.

A muffled laugh sounded within the Tao's mask. The lips of Ming Dwan were scornful.

They did not know how swiftly The Shadow's thoughts were running. Whatever the Dragon Cell might be, captivity there would mean lost time. The one chance for the break was here. That was why The Shadow had thrust his hand from view.

His fingers had not sought a gun. Instead, they had found a tiny pocket—no more than an opened seam—within his cloak. From that crevice, The Shadow had gained a pinch of powdery substance between his thumb and second finger.

The powder needed moisture. The Shadow ran his doubled hand to his forehead. His forefinger dipped into the blood that still oozed slowly from the gash. The forefinger joined the others. The whole move of The Shadow's hand looked as he intended it. He had apparently reached to press a painful wound.

Captors swung The Shadow to his feet. They were dragging him away,

while the Tao and Ming Dwan watched as scorners. Then, from a pitiful, sagging slight, The Shadow became a power. His whole body whipped to action.

His right forearm sliced upward; cracked the chin of a big false head and sent it flying, to reveal a wizened, baldish Chinaman instead. Twisting from the grip of those on the left, he drove his left hand in a hard punch toward the other captor on the right.

The Shadow's fist smashed the papier-mâché devil's head and found a human jaw beneath it. The head rolled free when its owner fell. Another yellow face looked dusky in the greenish light. Before a single hand could rise to stop him, The Shadow was springing for an inner corner of the room, toward the huge metal joss that towered there.

Members of the Jeho Fan were whipping off their gauntlets; false heads went plopping to the floor. No longer did these murderous Chinese worry about hiding their identities. They had guns; they wanted to use them, with The Shadow as their target.

Using his left hand only, The Shadow was clambering up the statue. He was clinging to its shoulder as he turned. He saw the eager, vicious faces just beneath him. Revolvers were snapping those first empty chambers, as the unmasked Chinese aimed.

Beyond, on the platform, stood the Tao. Arms folded, he still wore his devil-mask. Beside him was Ming Dwan. Both saw the amazing climax that came when The Shadow, leaning forward, thrust his right hand toward the faces below.

The Shadow snapped his fingers. A flash of light, a puff of smoke; with them came a startling explosion, that was thunderlike within the close-walled room.

The stroke came with the blinding speed of lightning. The Chinese dropped away, their arms before their eyes. Amid the echoes of the surprise blast came the laugh of The Shadow.

The Tao pulled a revolver, to aid his dumbstruck subordinates. He had no time to throw off his mask, or jerk away a gauntlet. Those adornments handicapped him. He was too late to halt The Shadow's next move.

With a powerful kick, The Shadow was toppling the big joss outward from the wall. It was slowly overbalancing, at an angle toward the false chest that occupied the end wall. The Shadow did not wait for the massive image to crash. His eyes were toward the tube; they saw the glitter of the circling death blade.

The Shadow's arms shot forward, downward. The dive that he took brought a gasp of amazement even from Ming Dwan, as she saw the cloaked form straighten like an arrow.

Eight feet through the air, from the figure of the tumbling joss; at a perfect angle, The Shadow's whole form disappeared, squarely within the slippery tube that offered a sure route to doom.

The Shadow was giving the blade of death a test that had never occurred to the members of the Jeho Fan.

CHAPTER XI.

DEATH IN THE DEPTHS.

THE instant that his elbows grazed the inside of the tube, The Shadow doubled them. His chin tilted upward, his hands beneath it, as he whizzed toward the silvery blade. The Shadow had staked life and escape upon this one calculation.

The blade was timed to slice bodies that were released from the top of the tube. By his long, hard dive, The Shadow had gained double the speed for which the blade was timed. But he could not keep his hands ahead of him. If they struck the blade before it passed, his fast slide would be slowed.

The Shadow's face seemed sure to hit the surface. The Shadow's own reflection was shooting up to meet him. Then it was wiped away, as the back of the blade went by. The Shadow doubled his legs as he whirled across the inchwide crevice that marked the cleaver's path.

That last move was vital. Even with his speed, The Shadow could not have passed the danger point completely, had he been fully stretched. Just as his knees were across the crack, the edge of the blade sliced in from the side of the tube.

All that the knife garnered was the fringe of The Shadow's cloak, which followed his doubled legs. The blade was cheated of that small trophy, for The Shadow's zooming slide whipped the cloak hem from the knife-edge.

Then the closing metal surface obliterated the last of the greenish light. The Shadow was plunging headlong to the end of a darkened trail.

UP in the meeting room, the staccato barks of a revolver had accompanied The Shadow's slide. They were the shots fired by the Tao. His bullets flattened against the front of the false chest. As he fired the second shot, the Tao voiced a bellowed warning. The shout, like his bullets, was useless.

The great joss had reached the limit of its balance. Its two-ton weight crashed down upon the members of the Jeho Fan. Their arms away from their eyes, they were starting to look for The Shadow, when they saw the Juggernaut descend. Their incoherent screams told that they thought the joss had come to life.

Even that mighty statue seemed leagued with Ying Ko! The startled men beneath it had thought that the joss —not The Shadow—had hurled the blinding thunderbolt.

As a dozen frantic Chinese scrambled in every direction, the statue landed in their midst. It literally mashed a swath across the inner circle of the Jeho Fan. Three of the dozen were killed outright; two more were half crushed by the joss. Only their bodies and shoulders could be seen.

The Tao had no regard for cripples. Springing from the platform, he silenced the two writhing men with bullets through their heads. Though the deed was actually merciful, that was not the Tao's thought. He wanted nothing to retard the pursuit of The Shadow.

Though he leaped to the tube and stared downward, the Tao knew before he looked that The Shadow's speed had whizzed him past the blade. The Tao saw the cleaver's bulk slide past, its surface clear, without a streak of blood.

Huddled, the gowned members of the Jeho Fan were against the side walls of the meeting room, fearful that some other joss would drive down upon them with avenging thunder.

The Tao rallied them, when he yanked open a brass door and pointed to a downward flight of steps. Ming Dwan was the first of the followers who joined the Tao's rush.

BELOW, The Shadow was breaking his speed as he reached the bottom of the lower tube. His hands struck a bamboo matting that covered a stone floor. With the skill of a tumbler, The Shadow somersaulted across the floor and landed with a thump.

A door opened in the darkness. A hand found a light. In the glow that came, The Shadow saw a big, dull-eyed Mongol, who had come expecting to find a truncated body on the floor. The guard recognized the figure of Ying Ko. He reached for a knife.

The Shadow launched forward, upward, from hands and knees; his head hit the guard's chest like a battering-ram. As he bowled the Mongol to the floor, The Shadow snagged the knife with a sideward grab. Springing

through the doorway, The Shadow reached a dank, unlighted passage. He bolted the door behind him, to imprison the big guard.

As The Shadow started to grope along the pitch-black passage, a sudden glare came from the far end. The Tao had arrived. He was directing a spotlight from a room that opened into the dismal corridor.

The leader of the Jeho Fan was beyond the light. His devil-mask was off his shoulders; he was holding it beneath his left arm. His right hand, no longer encumbered by a gauntlet, drew a revolver to take steady aim along the brilliant passage.

All that was invisible from The Shadow's position, for the Tao stood in absolute darkness behind the floodlight. The menace, though, was clear. The Shadow met it.

With a sudden turn, The Shadow drove straight along the passage, in the direction of the light. The glow showed a gigantic shadow on the wall behind him; as cloaked arms spread, that shade had the appearance of a mammoth bat, with wings outstretched.

Five long, swift strides, as the Tao fired. Tricked by the grotesque illusion on the wall, the Tao aimed too high. His bullet sizzed above The Shadow's head.

With the report, The Shadow's lunge ended. From his flinging hand scaled the captured knife, hurled for a spot above the brilliant light, where his keen eyes had marked the faint stab of the Tao's gun.

End over end, its whirl a dazzle in the spotlight, that knife was winging for the Tao Fan. Its spin rendered its flight deceptive and dangerous. If it struck point first, it would pinion the Tao. If the handle hit him, the result would be the same. The knife would take another turnover, to bury itself in its human target.

The Shadow had practiced that end-over-end hurl often. It was a sure system with a borrowed knife.

LUCK saved the Tao. The spotlight's rim was oversize; something that The Shadow had not been able to observe. The spinning knife glanced the metal above the glare. Like a stone skimming from water, it took a long bound over the Tao's shoulder, to clatter on a stone floor beyond.

The Tao made a belated dive. Flattened, he lost his chance to aim again from darkness. He managed to snarl a fierce order in Chinese, calling upon those who followed him to finish The Shadow.

From the darkness past the spotlight sprang Ming Dwan.

Coming into the path of light, the girl covered The Shadow with the same toy-like gun that she had used at the Yangtse Restaurant. Ming Dwan had heard the knife's clatter. She knew that The Shadow was weaponless. Instead of wasting long-range shots, she was moving close to her cloaked quarry.

Nearly forty feet intervened—and The Shadow had no retreat. The rear of the passage was blind. The room from which The Shadow had come was another dead end.

Ming Dwan's smirk challenged The Shadow to come closer, seeking a chance to grapple. But the steadiness of her shapely tapered forefinger told that she could pump the revolver trigger without hesitation.

The Shadow crept forward. He was crouched, his course a weaving one. Ming Dwan shifted, keeping the revolver muzzle constantly upon The Shadow. She could see the burn of The Shadow's eyes. He could not spy the glitter of hers, for her back was to the light.

Nevertheless, The Shadow could tell from the girl's actions that Ming Dwan was not deceived by any move he made.

A duel appeared impending; The Shadow, barehanded, against a girl sharpshooter who possessed uncommon speed and skill. While it impended, The Shadow had one benefit. His crouch, his weaving tactics, kept Ming Dwan always in his path.

Behind the spotlight, others of the Jeho Fan had joined the Tao. Revolvers ready, they were watching that huge blackness that spread from the end walls, marking The Shadow's closer approach to Ming Dwan.

They were confident that the girl would fire in time to halt The Shadow. If she failed, it would be their turn to deliver doom. No matter how speedily The Shadow grappled, he could never wrest away the girl's gun before the inner circle surged.

If he expected that he could use Ming Dwan as a shield, The Shadow was far wrong. Among the Jeho Fan, the life of one meant nothing, where the benefit of all was concerned. Those who made mistakes were apt to pay for them.

Ming Dwan understood that rule. If clutched by any foeman, she would be the first to shriek for slaughter; calling for her own death to insure the obliteration of the enemy.

But Ming Dwan did not intend to let The Shadow reach her.

Only five paces separated them. The Shadow could see the tightness of the girl's hand. It was a warning as significant as the clatter of a rattlesnake. The Shadow could not venture a half foot closer. If he retreated, Ming Dwan would fire.

THE SHADOW stood motionless. How long Ming Dwan might allow that was a question, for she had the range she needed.

The trap was hopeless as it stood. Yet The Shadow sensed that there might be some unexpected way by which to escape this dilemma. His eyes roved swiftly, seeking an answer.

To left and right of Ming Dwan lay blackened walls, for she was close to the spotlight, and its widening beam had not reached the full extent at the spot where she stood. Just past the fringe of light to the left, The Shadow detected the background of the wall; but his glance to the right showed deeper darkness.

Only The Shadow's keen eyes could have told that the deep gloom marked the outlet of a side passage.

The Shadow made a quick twist to the left, bringing himself into the view of those who stood behind Ming Dwan. As he feinted, he thrust his right hand beneath his cloak.

The Tao saw the move; his snarled voice gave warning to Ming Dwan. The Tao thought that The Shadow was reaching for another pinch of that powdered compound that boomed like dynamite when he snapped his fingers.

Ming Dwan saw. She acted as The Shadow expected. The girl made a quick step backward, raised her left sleeve to her eyes and jabbed her gun in The Shadow's direction. One second later, she was tugging the revolver trigger, stabbing blind shots toward the wall.

The Shadow was no longer there. With Ming Dwan's fire came a shuddering, outlandish laugh, that quivered from every wall. The Shadow had wheeled to the center of the corridor. He took a long lope, at an angle to the right, past Ming Dwan. Blinking at sight of nothingness, the girl spun about.

She threw her back against the wall on her right, as she saw The Shadow blend with the void across the corridor. The guns of the Jeho Fan were blasting, too late to halt The Shadow's surprise dive into the right-angle passage. Only Ming Dwan was in position to deliver direct fire after The Shadow. The girl emptied her revolver into the darkness.

Surging forward, the others of the Jeho Fan had reached Ming Dwan, when they heard The Shadow's laugh resound

from darkness. The redoubtable Ying Ko had turned a corner in his new passage, away from Ming Dwan's fire.

The Tao clicked off the spotlight. Electric torches gleamed instead, from the fists of the Chinese who formed the vengeful council of the Jeho Fan. Armed pursuers sprang into the side passage.

Ming Dwan, hastily reloading her revolver in the darkness, was joined by the Tao. They, too, took up pursuit.

THE chase led through a maze of passages, which were puzzling even to the members of the Jeho Fan. Only the Tao's constant shouts directed them. At intervals, pursuers sighted The Shadow and fired useless shots. Ying Ko was elusive in this labyrinth.

At one turn, The Shadow came face to face with a foeman. The fellow shouted as he aimed; The Shadow was upon him before he could fire. A few seconds later, the Chinaman lay slugged by his own gun.

The Shadow gained a flashlight with the weapon. Pausing only to fire at pursuers who poked their faces from a corner, The Shadow was off again.

He came to a door where a huge guard stood on duty. This underground watcher had a revolver; he aimed it for The Shadow's light. The Shadow beat him to the shot. Above the guard's slumped body, he unbolted the door and took a stairway to a higher level, just as pursuers began to fire from the rear.

New passages brought The Shadow to a big brass door with ornamental facing. The Shadow could find no catch to open it. He rapped a summons on the door with his gun handle, thinking that the signal would be heard by some one on the other side.

It was; but the guard was foxy.

The floor moved beneath The Shadow's feet. Only his quick clutch of the door saved him, as a trap dropped. The revolver went through the hole; The

Shadow needed both hands to claw the facing of the door.

As his toes dug in, he heard the gun splash, far below. There was the sound of seething water.

That chasm was an underground inlet from the bay. Victims who reached its depths would remain forgotten, their bodies washed by the subterranean current that sighed like an imprisoned monster, seeking its way back to the sea.

Like a beetle clinging to the brassy door surface, The Shadow was helpless. Soon, his grip would slip and he would drop. Unless the members of the Jeho Fan arrived before then, to shoot him from his slippery perch.

The guard beyond the door did not pull the lever to bring the trapdoor up in place.

That was explained when the brass door slid part way open, carrying The Shadow with it. A yellow face poked through the opening, to stare downward with a demoniac leer. The trap-puller hoped to catch a glimpse of the victim that he had consigned to the swirling depths.

Instead, the fellow received the clamp of a hand upon his neck. The Shadow's grab was timely. It saved him from the drop, for his hold on the door had almost yielded. Before the guard could shake off the clutch, The Shadow's other hand was in action.

The Chinaman was brawny. Instinctively, he was trying to haul himself back into the passage beyond the door, to escape a fall through the trap. The Shadow relaxed, to aid the guard's effort; but tightened when the Chinaman tried to shake him loose.

Wedged in the doorway, The Shadow braced. His feet pressed the frame, his shoulders drove the door full open. With a twist, he was away from the guard's grasp. But the big man pounced upon him. They grappled in a square space, at the foot of a darkened stairway.

The Chinaman's fingers plucked The Shadow's cloak. Wrenching away, The Shadow whipped the garment over the fellow's head, with smothering folds. As the Chinaman clawed the cloak downward, quick fingers reached his throat. Their numbing pressure paralyzed the guard's whole body, even to the yellowed fingers that tried to pluck a knife.

THERE was a shrill call from the passage that The Shadow had left. Turning, The Shadow saw Ming Dwan beckoning to others of the Jeho Fan. As the girl turned away, The Shadow took a long, quick chance.

He twisted the big guard toward the open door; shoved the fellow to his knees. Releasing the guard's throat, The Shadow whipped off his slouch hat and clamped it on his enemy's swaying head.

The Chinaman's eyes lost their staring bulge. Coughing as he gripped his tortured neck, he stared at The Shadow, in the tuxedoed guise of Cranston, making a quick dash up the stairs. Forgetful of the cloak and hat, the guard reached for his knife. He started to rise.

A barrage boomed from the corridor that fronted the open door. Three of the Jeho Fan had joined Ming Dwan. They were firing at the back of a cloaked figure that they took for The Shadow.

The black-cloaked form swayed backward; took a twisting side-pitch down into the open hole below the trapdoor.

The Tao arrived to see the plunge. Ming Dwan and the others heard his hollow chuckle. They turned to see their leader, his mask again upon his head, his arms folded, like a Chinese image of fate.

Ming Dwan babbled that she had seen a struggle; that the guard must have pitched through the trap, for The Shadow was alone when the others had joined her. Ming Dwan was apologetic over the loss of the guard.

"What is one servant?" voiced the Tao. "It is good that Ying Ko should have company. His spirit might be lonely, in that pit where his corpse will wash forever!"

The Tao, like his chosen followers, was satisfied that they had seen the last of The Shadow.

CHAPTER XII.

ALONG THE WATER FRONT.

THE next afternoon, a telegram was delivered to Richard Vayne. Myra Reldon received it and took it into the inner office. At his desk, Vayne opened the message. The gray-haired man smiled as he read the telegram.

"From Cranston," he said to Myra. "He is on his way back East. He flew to Denver this morning, from Los Angeles."

"Which means," added Myra, "that he must have gone to Los Angeles last night."

Vayne nodded.

"I had hoped to hear from Cranston," he remarked. "I was worried about him, and thought that it would be unwise for me to be with him last night. I think you understand, Myra. The Chinese are——"

"I know," interposed Myra. "Some of them were watching my apartment house, last night. So I stayed at home."

Vayne strummed the desk. His worriment remained; but his concern was for Myra, now that Cranston was out of San Francisco.

"I have many friends," Vayne told the girl, "and servants, at my home in Oakland. I am safe, wherever I go. I can afford to ignore any Chinese spies. But you lack safety, Myra."

"I can depend upon the police," assured Myra. "Don't worry, Mr. Vayne. I'll look out for myself."

Vayne was doubtful; but Myra's de-

termination made argument useless. Vayne gave her the telegram to file. As she walked from the inner office, her back was turned toward Vayne. The girl could safely smile in the fashion of Ming Dwan.

She said nothing to Vayne about her date with Cranston. As for the telegram, Myra kept silent on that matter, also. She knew that the Tao had been responsible for the telegram. When Cranston's disappearance became a nationwide mystery, police would believe that the millionaire had vanished elsewhere than in San Francisco.

EVENING brought brilliance to the bizarre streets of Chinatown. Thousands of peaceful Chinese were abroad; but among them were camouflaged members of the Jeho Fan. Ming Dwan was one.

There were streaks of darkness in the Chinese quarter: alleyways between the lighted streets. Into one of those alleys stepped a tall American, whose face, though hawkish, bore little resemblance to Cranston's. The American carried a package that looked like a purchase from one of the Chinese bazaars.

Paper crinkled in the alleyway; silence followed. The narrow street was empty.

In a near-by building was an office that contained a solitary Chinaman. He was garbed in American clothes. In the glow of a desk lamp, he was opening letters addressed to Doctor Roy Tam.

Blackness gathered beyond the lamp. There was a momentary *swish*. Tam looked up; he saw The Shadow, garbed in a new outfit of black.

"I expected you, Ying Ko," announced Tam, "despite the rumor that the Jeho Fan had slain you."

"Let them believe me dead," returned The Shadow, his whisper sinister. "I have learned much regarding the Jeho Fan. One fact will astonish you. The Tao does not have the letter from Cho Tsing."

Tam was puzzled. He was positive that the missing message must have reached the Tao Fan. He would not have believed the statement, had it come from any one other than The Shadow.

"Since the letter is elsewhere," came the whisper, "perhaps you can suggest the name of the person who holds it."

Doctor Tam shook his head.

"All matters in Chinatown," he stated, "are known to the Jeho Fan. The Teeth of the Dragon bite everywhere. Even here, Ying Ko, although those fangs are wary, because I am well protected. No one in Chinatown could hold that letter without the knowledge of the Jeho Fan."

Tam's opinion was emphatic. The Shadow considered its possibilities. The Tao had believed that The Shadow held the message, and probably still believed it. That, however, did not alter the situation.

The spies of the Jeho Fan were everywhere, as Tam said. In their methodical way, they had probably pried into the affairs of many Chinese, to make sure, by elimination, that only The Shadow could have gained the general's letter.

There was only one answer. The Shadow spoke it.

"Lubber Kreef knew no Chinamen," The Shadow told Tam. "The fact that he talked to persons at random is proof of it. We can assume that Lubber spoke to others."

The statement was sufficient. The Shadow stepped toward the door. Doctor Tam knew that he was about to fare forth to conduct investigations elsewhere. Even though he was sure that Cho Tsing was in San Francisco, The Shadow did not intend to let the mystery of the letter go unsolved.

Such details could bring dangerous cross-currents into any campaign.

Before departure, The Shadow added one reminder.

"New facts will be useful," he told Tam. "Anything concerning Li Sheng, the merchant whose name you mentioned. Also, any new word direct from China."

The Shadow merged with darkness. Doctor Tam heard the soft close of the office door.

LATER, a cab rolled toward the outskirts of Chinatown, passing the almost-forgotten street where the residence of Li Sheng was located. That cab seemed empty; but from its interior, keen eyes saw the arched entryway that led to the merchant's hemmed-in mansion.

There were Chinese along the street who could be termed lurkers, although all seemed to have business there. Perhaps they were members of the Jeho Fan, watching the way to Li Sheng's. For the present, The Shadow was leaving such research to Doctor Tam.

The cab was out of Chinatown. It swung past an old, abandoned storehouse that could be classed as a dividing line; it stretched a short block inward, toward Li Sheng's house. It belonged to Chinatown, that building.

The Shadow recognized it as a storage building that had once held goods for the Chinese bazaars. Their business had outgrown it. The building was condemned.

When it was torn down, another chunk would be lopped from the Chinese quarter, bringing the border to the narrow, darkish street behind the hidden home of Li Sheng.

The cab neared the water front. An ungloved hand paid the driver. A shrouded figure alighted; lost its shape beneath the overhanging gloom of steamship piers. The Shadow did not emerge from that darkness.

Instead, came a limber, stoopish ruffian, his scarred face marked by its high-bridged, ugly nose. He was wearing khaki pants; a gray-striped jersey. An old checkered cap was tipped over one of his eyes. He looked like a roustabout who had failed to get a seaman's berth aboard a tramp steamer.

This product of the water front soon showed up in one of the toughest dives in the dock district. There, he was regarded as just another wharf rat, until he produced a wad of grimy bank notes so thick that he couldn't get his fist halfway around it.

When he gruffly ordered drinks for every one in the place, the stranger promptly gained the attention of the greedy-eyed riffraff that were present.

His name was Moggler, he told them, and he was in from Shanghai. That was where he had gathered his wad; how he had gained the money was another matter. The most important detail was that Moggler intended to blow the bank roll; and his listeners had a chance to get their share.

"Whatta I hear when I get ashore?" demanded Moggler, his eyes darting from face to face. "I'll tell you. Them heathens is come down from Chinatown to chop a matey of yours. And whatta you done about it? Nawthing!"

With that reference to the murder of Lubber Kreef, Moggle brandished his money close to the faces that surrounded him.

"That ain't the way it would go in Shanghai," he added contemptuously. "We'd go where the Chinese is—an' there's millions of 'em—to let 'em know how we was feelin'; an' there'd be profit in it. Like this!"

His final reference concerned the money. Thrusting the roll in his pocket, Moggler nodded wisely as he surveyed the group. They caught the idea quickly enough. He wanted to head a looting expedition through Chinatown.

There were grumbles; objections. Frisco wasn't Shanghai. The Chinese kept their wealth in vaults. Besides, San Francisco had a police force; something, perhaps, that Moggler didn't know. Avenging Lubber's death was a good idea. But the profit wasn't a sure thing.

Big-nosed Moggler had an answer for that objection. He pounded his pocket with his tight fist.

"There's plenty there," he told them. "Enough for two hundred dollars' bounty to each man as goes along, pay in advance! Only there's gotta be enough of us. Get me thirty recruits by midnight."

Moggler considered the matter settled. Some of the shifty listeners decided to go through with it. Their job was to spread the news along the water front. They started out on that task, leaving Moggler in the grogshop that formed his temporary headquarters.

While he waited, The Shadow was confident that his ruse would bring results. He knew that Lubber must have talked to some one after leaving Chinatown, on the night of his death. The contact must have occurred somewhere along the water front. The person who heard Lubber's story was the one who had later found the Cho Tsing letter.

That same person would be interested in anything that concerned Lubber and Chinatown.

It wasn't an hour before Shiv Faxon arrived near the dive where recruits were signing up to join the expedition. Entering a side door, Shiv reached a back room and found the proprietor there. Shiv rapped a command:

"Show me this lug Moggler!"

The proprietor opened a convenient door; Shiv peered through and took a survey. He noted that only a few ratty recruits were with the stranger.

Shiv departed. He met with a dozen husky dock-wallopers. His instructions were brisk:

"Gang the guy! You'll find him down at the Rat Hole."

SHIV followed along to witness the result. He was in the back room when his crew of huskies entered and singled out

Moggler. When a couple of dock-wallopers announced that they had business, Moggler's recruits began to slink away.

Two seconds later, the action started, but not the sort that the peering Shiv expected.

A husky grabbed Moggler's shoulder. The limber roustabout twisted away; snatched up a table with one hand. As fists hooked toward him, he handled that table like a baseball bat. Moggler bludgeoned one walloper to the floor; came back with a back slash that felled another.

Huskies grabbed up tables of their own. Some yanked blackjacks; others pulled guns. Their weapons didn't help. Moggler was among them, flaying the table with his right hand; warding blows with his left arm. From the mêlée, he singled out the men with revolvers and slashed them to the floor.

The wallopers who had tables couldn't swing them with Moggler's speed. Those who gripped blackjacks couldn't get close enough to tap the fighter from Shanghai.

The wharf rats rallied to Moggler's support. The proprietor doused the lights, to save the dock-wallopers from complete rout. The fracas continued, until the arrival of police interrupted it.

Patrol wagons clanged along the water front. The law took over. From the side door, Shiv saw battered hoodlums dragged aboard the black Marias.

Moggler wasn't among them. When the police had gone, Shiv stared amazed, when the limber roustabout came strolling around the corner. The fellow looked along the street, as if seeking a new headquarters.

Shiv came from his doorway, gripping a knife handle. His first thought was to get close to Moggler and sink a dirk in the victor's back. Shiv dropped that idea as he sneaked forward. A better idea occurred to him.

It was lucky that he changed his plan. Before he was within range of Moggler,

the tall fighter bounced about. Seeing Shiv, he shot a clamping fist to the racketeer's right wrist.

Shiv chuckled as he showed a weaponless hand. He had played the right hunch.

"Save it, bozo," gruffed the racketeer. "I'm all for you! They say you're the guy that wants to get even with the chinks that croaked Lubber Kreef?"

Moggler nodded.

"I'll show you how," promised Shiv. "A better way than the one you figured. I got a partner in the proposition; we can use you. Only one thing—no rough stuff until the right time. Savvy?"

"It suits me," growled Moggler. "I'd just as soon save my bank roll, after seein' how yellow them guys was. The ones I hired."

"Wharf rats," snorted Shiv. "Stick with me and I'll steer you into a *real* outfit. You're death on the chinks; all right, we'll give you a chance to knock off plenty. And double that roll of yours, as part of the bargain."

The deal was made. The grimy lights of a steep street showed Shiv and Moggler heading away from the water front.

The Shadow was on his way to meet Brig Lenbold.

CHAPTER XIII.
WITHIN THE CORDON.

Two quiet days had passed; a period so lulling that it promised a smash of future events. Richard Vayne had heard no more from Lamont Cranston, and had practically forgotten the millionaire who had met him only during a single day's stay in San Francisco.

That fact pleased Myra Reldon; and the girl had another cause for elation. Whatever the plans of the Tao Fan, they were due to crystallize very shortly. The Tao had passed word through Chinatown that all members of the Jeho Fan were to remain strictly under cover until the next day.

That enabled Myra to discard her disguise of Ming Dwan. She was confident that when she again assumed her Chinese character, she would be assigned to the most important task that Ming Dwan had ever undertaken in the service of the Jeho Fan.

From the opposite camp, Doctor Tam had reported very little, when The Shadow made cloaked visits to Tam's office. Tam had gained some information regarding Li Sheng, the merchant, with a good description of the wealthy

Moggler handled the table like a baseball bat. From the mêlée, he singled out the men with revolvers and slashed them to the floor.

Chinaman's home. He expected more; also a confidential report from China.

Meanwhile, The Shadow had progressed as Moggler; only to encounter a lull in the affairs of Brig Lenbold and Shiv Faxon.

Brig was pleased with Shiv's report of Moggler's prowess. The racketeers had been looking for fighters of that sort. They needed shock troops for some enterprise involving Chinatown, and Brig supported Shiv's statement that Moggler would have plenty of opportunity to take a whack at some Chinese.

In proof, they took their new henchman to their secret headquarters. The trip proved their point; and it told the supposed Moggler much more than either Brig or Shiv suspected.

The place was the abandoned Chinese warehouse, a block away from the mansion of Li Sheng.

The Shadow had noticed no activity at the warehouse the time that he had passed it. That was explained by the fact that everything was taking place inside the walls. Patrolling toughs kept under cover in the warehouse. Moggler was placed on patrol duty, with orders not to poke his big nose outside.

He had his suitcase there, with them; like other rowdies, he was quartered in a room on the ground floor.

There was a stairway that went below. Only Brig and Shiv went beyond it, although they had men working in the cellar, who were never seen by the ground-floor guards. A lookout was posted at the bottom of the cellar steps. He had orders to let no one through.

On this particular night, Brig rapped for entry at a side door of the warehouse. The guard who admitted him was Moggler. Sharp eyes watched Brig's face, as long fingers turned a wick to increase the glow of a lantern. Light was all right, once the door was tight shut.

Brig was pleased about something. He spoke cryptically to Moggler.

"There won't be long to wait," informed Brig. "Maybe to-night will be the time, Moggler. I'm going downstairs. When Shiv comes along, tell him I'm there."

Brig went below. As his footsteps faded, Moggler's stooped form left the range of light. There was a slight *swish* in the hazy darkness; when he returned, the guard was Moggler no longer.

The Shadow had resumed his cloak and hat. His gloved fingers adjusted the lantern to only a tiny glow.

Moving silently through the darkness, The Shadow reached the stairway to the cellar. This wasn't the first time that he had explored that far. He had even reached the bottom of the steps, unknown to the lower guard. That was as far as he had penetrated. Wisely, The Shadow had waited until positive that crooks intended action.

Nearing the bottom of the steps, The Shadow saw a hanging lantern that threw a small circle of glow. There was a sweatered figure seated beyond; The Shadow recognized a rough face. The lower guard was a beefy fellow named "Butch." The Shadow, as Moggler, had heard his name mentioned.

There was a stir on the steps. Butch growled:

"Who's that?"

"It's Shiv." The Shadow voiced a sharp imitation of the racketeer's tone. "Say, Butch, did Brig go through?"

"Yeah. He's waiting for you. Didn't Moggler tell you?"

"No." The faked tone was anxious. "Nobody's up there. You'd better go up, Butch, and find out what's wrong!"

Butch started upward. He was on the second step when massed darkness launched upon him. Hurled from balance, the beefy guard was easy prey for The Shadow. Within a few minutes,

Butch lay bound and gagged, staring from a corner.

The Shadow lowered the lantern's wick. The circle of light was lessened. Butch's trussed form was out of sight against the wall.

Moving farther into the cellar, The Shadow saw the glow of lights from a far corner. As he approached, he observed Brig, stooped in conference with members of the cellar crew.

The glow came from the floor. It fitted with what The Shadow had expected to find. As he drew closer, The Shadow saw Brig rise. The bulky racketeer was coming in his direction.

This time, The Shadow used different tactics. He spoke, in the sharp tone that resembled Shiv's; but his voice carried a warning note. Brig halted.

"What's up, Shiv?"

"It's that guy Moggler," returned The Shadow. "He's quit!"

"What for?" demanded Brig. "He didn't squawk to me, when I came by."

"Maybe not. But he was coming down to find you. Butch stopped him; chased him upstairs again. He wasn't there when I came through. When Butch gave me the low-down, I told him to go out and hunt up Moggler."

Brig didn't like the news. He figured that Moggler's desertion could make trouble, and said so. As Shiv, The Shadow argued the opposite. If Moggler couldn't keep in line, it was better to be rid of him.

"Anyway," snapped The Shadow, from the darkness, "what if Moggler does start a brawl with some chinks? Maybe that'll help us, Brig, the way things stand."

"I guess it will," agreed Brig. "It's all set, Shiv. Like we thought it would be. Half past ten will be the dead line."

Brig wanted Shiv to follow him to the corner. Shiv's excuse was that he ought to make sure that Butch had started outside. Brig heard him promise to return as soon as he had checked that detail.

Returning to the stairway, The Shadow heard steps coming down. He edged past the light; gave a boomed tone:

"That you, Shiv?"

Shiv took the voice for Brig's. From the steps, he wanted to know why the outside door was unguarded.

"It's that guy Moggler," Shiv heard Brig's tone inform. "He quit. I chased Butch out to look for him."

"You don't think Moggler's starting something on his own——"

"What if he is? Maybe it will help us. Moggler don't know what our racket is. Everything's set, Shiv. Half past ten will be the dead line."

Shiv voiced his approval. He heard a suggestion in Brig's tone:

"Take a gander outside, Shiv. If everything's cool, roust out some guy to take over Moggler's lookout. Then come down; only don't say too much. We don't want to worry the crew."

Shiv went up the stairs. Quickly, The Shadow sprang to the corner and hoisted Butch over his shoulders. He carried the husky like a dummy figure. The Shadow was on the steps before Shiv's footfalls had faded above.

At the top, The Shadow waited, resting Butch's trussed weight against a stack of boxes. He heard Shiv return to appoint another lookout. With long strides, The Shadow carried Butch to the outer portal. He shoved the door open; he was in the alleyway, with the door swinging shut behind him, when distant paces told that Shiv was coming with the new guard.

It wasn't long before Shiv joined Brig in the cellar. Each thought he had talked to the other previously; their brief comments furnished no inkling of The Shadow's double hoax.

Shiv simply said that he had put another guard on duty, to replace Moggler.

That suited Brig. After that, their talk concerned events that were due at half past ten.

Meanwhile, a shrouded form was blending through the darkness of Chinatown, burdened by a prisoner's weight. It wasn't far to Tam's; and The Shadow knew a route that offered alleys and passages, all the way. His arrival at Tam's lacked its usual silence, but it produced a startled reaction from the businesslike Chinese.

As the door opened, Tam saw a big figure loom from darkness and settle sideways to the floor. It was the bound form of Butch. The prisoner rolled helplessly into the light. The Shadow stepped in view. He propped Butch against the wall; removed the gag and untied the prisoner's arms.

Butch didn't like his surroundings. He knew that Brig and Shiv had been plotting against certain Chinese; and he figured that Doctor Tam was one of them. Being brought here by The Shadow was another ominous feature of Butch's capture. Butch blinked, worried, when he heard The Shadow talk to Tam in Chinese.

After that, The Shadow let Tam be the spokesman. In precisely worded English, Tam promised Butch freedom, at a later hour, if the prisoner would comply with certain terms. They were simple enough: a telephone call to a number that connected with a special extension to the warehouse.

Butch made the call under The Shadow's surveillance. He worded it exactly as Tam dictated, even though he didn't understand what it was all about. Butch had found Moggler, brawling with some Chinese outside the old Mukden Theater, in the portion of Chinatown most remote from the warehouse. Butch had pitched into the fray.

Cops had ended it. Both Moggler and Butch were pinched. Butch knew a guy who could spring them, without dragging Brig or Shiv into it. But the racketeers would be short two men until to-morrow.

Butch sold his story well. He heard Shiv say "O. K." across the wire, adding that it would be all right with Brig.

When Butch hung up, Doctor Tam nodded solemnly, to indicate that the prisoner had fulfilled his part. Tam pressed a buzzer. Some Chinese servants entered and carried away the prisoner to a place where he could cool until Tam released him.

That done, Tam seated himself at the desk and began to spread report sheets for The Shadow. Doctor Tam had gathered facts that he knew would be useful to The Shadow; but he did not regard them as highly valuable. In fact, Tam thought this conference would be a mere routine.

In that, Tam was mistaken. The Shadow had already garnered details of his own, that he was to fit with those provided by Doctor Tam. To-night, The Shadow stood on the threshold of new adventure—a bold, daring course that he alone could risk.

The Shadow was planning a thrust to rescue General Cho Tsing; if that stroke succeeded, disaster would await the Jeho Fan.

CHAPTER XIV.
THE HOUSE OF LI SHENG.

UPON the desk, Tam spread diagrams that formed a ground floor plan of Li Sheng's mansion. They showed a large room in the center, with many small apartments surrounding it. There were passages, too, all shown in careful detail.

It had been easy, Tam explained, to gain a simple description of the hidden house. Various persons—Americans, as well as Chinese—had been guests at the merchant's home. All knew about the square, high-domed room in the center.

It was furnished in lavish style, that

room, with a fountain playing into a shallow pool. In that rounded basin, Li Sheng kept brands of Oriental fish that could not be duplicated in any American aquarium.

Li Sheng lived on the ground floor; only servants occupied the upper stories. Tam's finger pointed to a suite of rooms at the back of the ground floor. They were reached by steps leading up from the central reception room.

"The guest quarters," explained Tam. "It is there that Cho Tsing will be found —if the general is living there, as we suppose."

The Shadow studied the diagrams. He spoke his appreciation of Tam's careful work. It had been difficult for the Chinaman to piece these many details. There was more, however, to come.

"Li Sheng is wary," declared Tam. "He pretends that all guests are welcome; but they are not. There are certain ways by which they may be conducted to his reception room; and along those passages, strange accidents may happen.

"Never anything that Li Sheng could foresee; not, at least, so one could prove. He regrets accidents, does Li Sheng. Nevertheless, they occur. He has many servants, also, who obey even the slight uplift of his finger. Within his own abode, Li Sheng has rights."

Doctor Tam referred again to those rights, when he analyzed the probable position of Cho Tsing.

"If Cho Tsing has entered the house of Li Sheng," announced Tam, gravely, "he was welcomed there as a guest. As such, he will have remained. For it is as dangerous to leave the hospitality of Li Sheng as it is to reach his presence, unless Li Sheng is disposed to permit.

"Should persons come to pay the ransom of Cho Tsing, they would find other guests awaiting them—members of the Jeho Fan. They would know, of course, that Li Sheng had received return for

his services; but proof would be impossible to gain.

"Therefore, the position of Li Sheng is secure. He has always kept it such; and always shall. Li Sheng is a law unto himself; but he keeps within the laws of others, also."

From Tam's declaration, Li Sheng could be regarded as neither friend nor foe, unless something could be proven against him. That, in Tam's opinion would be a titanic task, even for The Shadow.

THE SHADOW changed the subject with the question:

"What news has come from China?"

"Doubtful news," replied Tam, seriously. "Two members of the Nanking government are coming to America by clipper plane, and will arrive to-morrow. Report says that they are coming to raise funds for the ransom of Cho Tsing; but, perhaps——"

"Their mission is to pay for the release of Cho Tsing."

The Shadow's pronouncement came as an undisputed verdict. Doctor Tam saw the logic. Representatives of the Chinese government would not have to leave China to negotiate a loan. They could do so if they chose; and they were using that fact as a smoke screen. But behind the scenes lay the answer that The Shadow understood.

Tam could picture coming consequences.

Chinese emissaries would visit the neutral domain of Li Sheng. They would leave there, taking Cho Tsing with them. He would return, disguised, to China; later, a fictionized story of his release would be made public.

The world would never know that Cho Tsing had been brought to America. The coffers of the Jeho Fan would be ten million dollars richer, less whatever amount Li Sheng might demand for intermediary services.

The greatest ransom in history would

be completed by to-morrow night. With new wealth in its possession, the Jeho Fan could expand its size, to become the most formidable of evil organizations. The power of the Tao would be limitless.

One being, alone, could block that outcome.

That being was The Shadow.

Yet, to win the victory, The Shadow would have to accomplish the incredible. He must enter the house of Li Sheng and release the captive Cho Tsing. He would be treading on preserves where a single false step would mean death.

Li Sheng, foxy, ever evasive, could twist the facts to prove himself right. The Shadow, if he fell into the toils, would be branded as the malefactor.

Dangerous though the task was, The Shadow intended to undertake it this very night; for this would be the last opportunity, before the Chinese officials recognized the Jeho Fan.

Tam knew The Shadow's determination. Despite the ruin that it might bring him, the sincere Chinaman offered his full coöperation.

"I can assemble trusted men," declared Tam. "They will battle those of the Jeho Fan who wait outside Li Sheng's gates."

"Such conflict would be useless," objected The Shadow. "By the time the way would clear, Li Sheng would be warned."

"Then you intend to fare alone?"

"Yes. Through the lines of the Jeho Fan."

"And my men——"

"They will be needed," interposed The Shadow. "But for a different purpose. One block from the house of Li Sheng is an abandoned warehouse. Your men will surround that building."

Tam was perplexed. He had not yet heard of The Shadow's complete discoveries concerning the racketeers who were trying to muscle in on the Jeho Fan's game.

The Shadow's arrival with Butch as burden had partially explained that situation; but Tam had not guessed the location of the headquarters that Butch had telephoned.

The Shadow gave the details. Tam listened, his face a curious study. Slowly, he grasped the full significance of The Shadow's plan. The Shadow told the part that he intended to accomplish; then explained the exact extent of Tam's required coöperation. Tam smiled gravely when The Shadow had finished.

"Many deeds must be accomplished," declared Tam. "Some seem impossible; others offer no difficulty. You, Ying Ko, have reserved the impossible tasks for yourself; the possible are to be mine.

"That, Ying Ko, may mean success. When Ying Ko undertakes the impossible, it becomes the possible. You are wise as well as bold. You may depend upon my men to perform the part that you require of them. It will be your task to deal with Li Sheng; mine, to be ready afterward."

It was nearly nine o'clock when a solitary figure arrived on the street that fronted the archway to Li Sheng's forgotten mansion. A gliding shape of blackness, that form was not seen by the skulking watchers of the Jeho Fan. They had noted every previous passer but they did not see The Shadow.

Between two buildings lay the arched passage that led to Li Sheng's. It formed a tunneled route, that ended in dull bronze gates, where visitors rang for entry. The passage was lighted; and watching eyes were concentrated upon it.

If an unwanted visitor approached those gates, the Jeho Fan was ready to intervene. Within a dozen seconds, the passage could become a death trap. The Shadow knew that choice of that route would be a play into the hands of the Jeho Fan.

The only course was to enter the courtyard by one of the buildings that surrounded it. That was difficult, for every doorway had a hidden watcher. For The Shadow, there remained one alternative.

Keeping to darkness, he found a stretch of blackened wall. Rough, crumbling stone felt the grip of The Shadow's probing fingers.

Upward, a blackened figure made its precarious climb. The Shadow's fingers found useful crevices. He remembered them, and gained toe-holds with his soft-tipped shoes.

Three squatty stories brought The Shadow to the ledge that fronted the roof. Flattened, to avoid the glow of Chinatown's lights, he rolled across the parapet.

It was dark, all along the roof. Crouching as he proceeded, The Shadow reached the rear edge. He looked down into a square-shaped courtyard, that was sunk below the street level. The buildings that surrounded it were mounted on windowless foundations that made a veritable wall.

There were stone steps that led up to the rear of the big gates. By observing those, The Shadow checked the exact position of the archway.

Facing into the courtyard, occupying a space of equal size, was the house of Li Sheng. It was a stone house, three stories high, that looked like a relic of old San Francisco. Some previous owner had preserved that mansion, while other buildings were erected around it. That must have been years ago; for the girdling structures were old ones.

How long Li Sheng had owned the forgotten mansion, was a question; but the crafty merchant had made a good choice of residence.

A complete silence gripped the courtyard. Even from the parapet, that hush was apparent. The roar of San Francisco's traffic, the jumbled sounds of Chinatown were totally obliterated from this isolated spot.

The roof of the mansion was solid.

The windows of the upper floors were barred. Those on the ground floor were equipped with tight-closed metal shutters. The Shadow decided, however, that entry would be possible if he once reached the mansion's roof. He could swing from it, and work on a barred third-story window.

To gain the roof, The Shadow had to move along the parapet and turn a corner. He had just begun that course when creeping footsteps halted him. The Jeho Fan had guards up here. One was making his rounds.

Stretched against the parapet, The Shadow waited for the Chinaman to pass.

The guard turned his flashlight in The Shadow's direction. He was holding the torch low; its beam did not reach the arm that stretched across The Shadow's face, holding the upturned cloak collar. Seeing nothing but blackness, the guard turned away. He stumbled against the corner of a chimney.

The dropped flashlight took an unlucky bounce almost to The Shadow's feet. As he regained it, the Chinaman happened to tilt it upward. The chance angle of the light flickered a hawkish silhouette along the parapet.

The watcher started an amazed shout: "Ying Ko!"

The cry was no more than a gargle, for gloved hands had the Celestial's throat, while a rasped whisper called for silence. The goggle-eyed guard regretted his shout; but he was too late to recall it. Other flashlights bobbed.

The roof was alive with lurking cohorts of the Jeho Fan.

The Shadow flung his prisoner against the chimney. As the Chinaman flattened, The Shadow went across the back parapet. Others saw his head and shoulders drop from sight. Yellow faces peered from the roof edge, their slanted eyes seeking one more glimpse of The Shadow.

The darkness of that rear wall was a perfect cover for the cloaked adventurer. The Shadow was descending recklessly, digging for any hold that offered. The rear wall was badly crumbled. That helped.

Flashlights did not spot The Shadow until one Chinaman leaned far over the edge above. As he saw a cloaked bulk at the second-floor level, the fellow yelled and jerked a knife from his belt.

The Shadow's right hand clawed the stony wall. His left poked an automatic upward; pulled the trigger just as the Chinaman slung the knife from above.

The bullet clipped the man on the roof. Overbalanced, he was toppling as his knife whizzed past The Shadow. That member of the Jeho Fan was doomed. He came hurtling from the roof, wailing as he sped past The Shadow. There was a crash from the courtyard.

Other fighters were leaning over the edge. The Shadow sprayed bullets along the line. One foeman sagged, hanging crazily from the parapet. Two more went rolling back to the roof. Others dived away. They were easy targets against the glowing sky.

The Shadow made a quick shift downward. From directly above the arch, he dropped to the stone steps. Turning, he sprang down into the deep courtyard. He saw the cover that he wanted. It was the deep recess of Li Sheng's front door.

SPINNING as he dashed, The Shadow blasted bullets to the roof to drive back any aiming sharpshooters. He reached the doorway; its overhanging eaves gave shelter. The guards on the roof no longer mattered. Trouble was due from another direction.

The alarm had spread from the roof. Vassals of the Jeho Fan were in the arched passage, clanging at the metal gates.

Those barriers were locked; but massed strength overcame them. His guns reloaded, The Shadow waited. He was ready to snipe that horde when it poured through. If he clipped them fast, they would tumble down the steps. Thinning the ranks would break the attack, and enable him to charge through.

The Shadow was not worried over the outcome of such battle. His one regret was his loss of an opportunity to enter Li Sheng's mansion.

A gate swung clear. Yellow faces peered above the steps. His back braced against Li Sheng's big front door, The Shadow aimed both automatics, ready to deliver a double dose of lead. His fingers were beginning their smooth squeeze. Only the totally unexpected could have halted The Shadow's opening volley of leaden slugs.

The unexpected came. With a sudden jerk, Li Sheng's big door swung inward, so suddenly that The Shadow went with it. He was too late to hook the door frame with a gun hand. The bash of his automatic against the side of the doorway, only added a twist to the tumble that The Shadow took.

The door slammed shut as The Shadow sprawled. The closing of the big barrier cut off the raucous shouts of those Chinese who were pouring into the path of The Shadow's fire. The turn of events had saved a squad of reckless fighters for further service with the Jeho Fan.

As for The Shadow, only the future could tell what his case would be. In a twinkling, he had gained the chief thing that he wanted: entrance into the house of Li Sheng. But the surprising manner of his entry foreboded ill.

Doom awaited those who were unwary within the walls where Li Sheng ruled; and The Shadow's forced arrival there had been anything but clever. In the duel of wits that was to come, Li Sheng had gained the first advantage.

CHAPTER XV.

TRAP FOR TRAP.

DESPITE his twisting tumble, The Shadow came up with an aiming gun. He was crouched on one knee, his left hand resting its automatic on the floor, while his right fist gripped a leveled weapon. Had there been sudden opposition, The Shadow could have met it. But there was no cause for battle.

A robed Chinaman was calmly bolting the big door. He turned about, to show a pair of outspread hands. His face was bland, suiting his Oriental garb.

Solemn, owlish as he gazed through big-rimmed spectacles, the Celestial bowed.

"You are welcome, Ying Ko," he said mildly, in English. "All who reach the portals of Li Sheng are welcome as his guests. I shall conduct you to my master, the merchant Li Sheng."

A muffled tumult was fading outside the huge front door. Some one from above had shouted at the entering mob. The hordes of the Jeho Fan were retiring from the premises of Li Sheng.

The Shadow placed his automatics in holsters deep beneath his cloak. He turned to the bland Chinaman who was to be his guide. The Celestial stepped to the rear of the entry and stopped before a brass door.

"This will interest you, Ying Ko," he announced. "A press of this concealed knob—the door rises. But watch!"

The Chinaman paused, pointing. Three seconds passed. The door dropped with a terrific *clang*.

"Li Sheng designed that to keep out enemies," explained the guide. He pressed the knob and waved for The Shadow to go through, as the door rose. "But of course, Ying Ko"—mildly, the Chinaman plucked The Shadow's cloak sleeve—"you are no enemy——"

The Shadow's interruption was a whipping twist that carried him through the doorway. He was on the threshold at the instant when the guide so gently distracted his attention. The Shadow's quick move was timely.

The door crashed as he whisked away, missing The Shadow's shoulders by a scant inch. That brass barrier weighed a half ton. Its drop would have been death to any one beneath it.

The Shadow waited in a short hallway. The door came smoothly upward; the bespectacled guide strolled through and the door clashed shut behind him.

"Very, very sorry," apologized the owlish guide. "It was forgetful of me to speak while you were passing beneath the door."

THE first of Li Sheng's "accidents" had failed with The Shadow. The guide seemed unperturbed. Calmly, he conducted The Shadow through a side passage that ended in another doorway.

There was no trick about that barrier. The guide opened it in ordinary fashion. They stepped into a square-walled room.

The walls were lined with woven drapes that depicted scenes from the ancient Ming dynasty.

"Very beautiful," announced the guide, referring to the Chinese art. "The story begins here"—he pointed to a cloth picture in the corner—"and follows along the wall. But we must not linger, Ying Ko"—the guide paused, his eyes fixed on The Shadow—"because Li Sheng expects us."

The mild tone perfectly disguised the warning that it carried. The guide had timed his final words to the instant when he knew that The Shadow's attention was centered on the woven picture.

Even to The Shadow, that wall scene had a compelling fascination that made him linger. No eye could escape it. The study of one detail led to notice of another.

Though The Shadow paused, the guide's words echoed in his mind. He sensed, also, that the Chinaman had stepped away. Turning, The Shadow saw the robed man waiting at another doorway. Even then, the trap would not have been apparent, except for the fact that the guide had gone to the top of a short flight of steps.

With quick strides, The Shadow crossed the room. He was at the steps when a dizziness seized him. The whole room whirled; the pictures made a fantastic jumble. For the first time, The Shadow sensed a thick aroma; the atmosphere of some overpowering drug, that was odorless until it took effect.

Swaying, The Shadow felt that the next pace he took would bring him to disaster. The floor was motionless; but to his eyes, it seemed to revolve.

With an effort, The Shadow closed his eyes and stumbled forward. He was dizzy; but the steps were solid. The Shadow managed to reach the top.

In the air of the higher passage, he steadied. He opened his eyes, saw the bowing guide.

The Chinaman was quite indifferent to the fact that The Shadow had escaped the second trap. He merely remarked that some visitors found the Ming room so delightful that they remained there.

The subtlety of Li Sheng's traps lay in the way they varied; also in the false ones that were introduced.

As they descended a flight of short steps, The Shadow twisted aside as a huge vase came tumbling from a shelf above the stairway, to crash in many fragments. The guide was very sorry about that, also, particularly because Li Sheng would be disturbed when he learned that he had lost a priceless piece of crockery.

In the room at the bottom of the steps, the guide motioned to a potted bush of magnificent roses, remarking that they were scentless. When The Shadow accepted the statement without test, the Chinaman smelled the roses himself, proving that they hid no soporific drug.

THE guide opened the door and pointed to a narrow passage.

"Let me go first," he remarked. "Do not follow until I have reached the far end. Moreover, there is a word that you must remember: 'Penang.' A password."

Half turned, the guide repeated the word as he entered the passage:

"Penang."

The Shadow watched. The passage was gloomy; halfway along, the floor slid open when the guide had passed. It remained in that condition until the robed man reached the far end. When he halted, the floor slid shut. The Chinaman beckoned to The Shadow.

Walking through the passage, The Shadow crossed the trap. It slid wide behind him. Simultaneously, a paneled door clicked in the wall. A huge Mongol sprang out to bar The Shadow's path. The challenger's hand drove a terrific lunge.

Twisting sideways on the very edge of the floor opening, The Shadow came in past the Mongol's sweep. As they locked, The Shadow went to one knee; hoisted upward and backward. The jujutsu trick lurched the Mongol headlong into the space that had been intended for The Shadow.

The guide came back along the passage. He and The Shadow peered below. The muscular Mongol was crawling to his feet beside the wall of an eight-foot pit. He had profited by the added impetus that The Shadow had given to his lunge.

The center of the pit was a bed of upright spikes; an ordinary shove would have impaled the victim upon them.

"The guard is not badly hurt," observed the bland guide. "That will please Li Sheng. It was too bad"—he turned to The Shadow—"that you forgot to state the password, as I did. The guard expected it."

The guide had not mentioned that the word "Penang" applied specifically to this passage. The Shadow, though, had understood it. He had deliberately let the guide's ruse reach its climax, in order to view another of Ling Sheng's accidental traps.

The Shadow expected one more snare; for they were nearing Li Sheng's reception room.

"WE have reached the triple doors," declared the guide, stopping before a solid copper barrier. "We must pass each one singly. I shall show you the combination."

He turned a dial while The Shadow watched. As he finished, the guide tipped his little finger slightly and pressed an ornament beside the dial. The movement was almost too trivial to notice. The guide went through when the door swung inward.

The Shadow duplicated the combination, as soon as the door had clanged shut. He did not forget the important touch to the ornament. He heard a tiny *click,* telling that the added press was part of the combination. The door swung ahead. The Shadow joined the guide.

For the first time, the Celestial was dour. The second door had the same system as the first. When they had passed it, The Shadow stepped ahead of the guide, to open the third door. The guide intervened.

"This leads to the reception room," he told The Shadow. "I must go first, to announce you to Li Sheng."

The Shadow's fingers were at the dial. As he drew his hand away, he applied the finger touch to the ornament. The guide did not notice it. The Shadow stepped back to watch the result. When the guide worked the combination, he unwittingly gave the secret spring one press too many.

Instead of swinging ahead, the door reversed. The wall opened automatically, at right angles, and the door carried the astonished Chinaman with it. There was a *clang* as the smug Celestial was locked in a tiny, metal-walled cell.

The final door was open. The Shadow saw a large, vaulted room, where a spraying fountain played beneath the soft tints of changing lights. He heard a melodious chuckle, indicating that Li Sheng had seen the reversed sweep of the last door. The merchant evidently supposed that The Shadow had been tricked by the last of his traps.

The Shadow stepped across the threshold. He saw Li Sheng, seated in a teakwood reclining chair, beyond the fountain. The merchant was smallish; his long, wizened face seemed colorless, above the rich crimson of his gold-embroidered robe.

Li Sheng's cackled mirth ceased when he saw The Shadow. It was surprise, more than fear, that gripped him. Then, with a quick move, Li Sheng gave his hands two short claps.

Four gowned servants bobbed into view, two from each side of the room. All had revolvers, that they swung toward The Shadow. They halted their guns half-drawn. The Shadow's fists had produced a pair of automatics. The big muzzles were trained at angles. Li Sheng's men were covered.

TRAP for trap, The Shadow had balked Li Sheng's moves. Here, in the heart of the merchant's stronghold, he still held the advantage. Wisely, though, The Shadow refrained from using it. He knew that Li Sheng possessed reserve forces that could be summoned.

Boldly, The Shadow had proven that he could master each menace that arrived. Li Sheng was wise as well as shrewd. He had not unleashed his power to the limit; but neither had The Shadow. The old Chinaman accepted the situation, in wily fashion.

Li Sheng spoke to the servants. Slowly, they put their guns away. The Shadow thrust his automatics beneath his cloak. Li Sheng rose from his chair, delivered a profound bow.

"Welcome, Ying Ko," he said. "My pitiful home is exalted by the presence of so honored a guest."

Though the merchant's words were solemn, the corners of his lips retained an upward twist, that gave The Shadow a recollection of the old man's high-pitched laugh.

Li Sheng had accepted The Shadow's arrival. But it was plain that he would present new obstacles to stay The Shadow's departure.

CHAPTER XVI.

LI SHENG OBJECTS.

THE domed reception room was a fantasy of Oriental splendor. Located in the center of the mansion, it was windowless. The soft, many-hued lights came from an indirect system. The side walls had square niches, set at intervals; those contained huge vases, all of rare Chinese pattern.

The tinkle of the fountain gave the room a lulling tone. The fountain, itself, was in the shape of a three-foot dragon, made entirely of silver. The coiled monster had its head tilted upward; from its open mouth sprayed the jets of water that fell into the shimmering pool surrounding the fountain's base.

The pool contained Li Sheng's rare fish. They were curious creatures, that rested lazily in the water, as though they liked to pose. Their colors formed ever-changing blends, thanks to the variations of the light that struck the water.

While The Shadow surveyed the room, Li Sheng extended a scrawny hand toward another teakwood chair. The Shadow noted the invitation to be seated. Calmly, he removed his hat and cloak.

A servant came to take the garments, but The Shadow motioned him aside. He flattened the cloak over the arm of the chair; laid the slouch hat upon it.

The Shadow was wearing the guise of Cranston. He had changed his features and donned his tuxedo, before leaving Doctor Tam's.

The tiny, glittering eyes of Li Sheng watched the hawk-faced visitor. Whatever Li Sheng's opinions, he did not betray them.

It was a certainty that Li Sheng knew of The Shadow's adventures with the Jeho Fan, and therefore had believed that The Shadow was dead. His first guess to the contrary had come when battle started in the courtyard. Watchers from Li Sheng's windows must have seen The Shadow cross the court and reported to the merchant.

By admitting The Shadow and welcoming him as a guest, Li Sheng had shown his great cunning. He had foreseen trouble for the Jeho Fan's attacking horde. He had preferred to handle Ying Ko, himself.

There was a splash from the fountain pool. The Shadow looked in that direction. He saw fish leaping wildly, away from the attack of finny foemen. The attacking fish were small, but hideous. Their gobbling mouths displayed tiny, vicious teeth.

"They are the dragon fish," remarked Li Sheng, in gloating tone. "They disturb the others, and drive them into hiding places. Often, the dragon fish overtake their victims and kill them.

"There is one fish"—Li Sheng craned his head toward the pool—"who avoids the dragon fish, by staying constantly away from danger. He must be hiding among the rocks, as usual, for I cannot see him.

"Besides, he is jet-black, that fish. Therefore, he is wise to hide himself in darkness. I have named him Ying Ko."

The symbolism of the dragon was represented by the silver fountain; also by the fighting fish in Li Sheng's pool. The Shadow noted a golden dragon woven into the crimson of the merchant's robe.

Those symbols, however, could not be taken as proof that Li Sheng was the hidden leader of the Jeho Fan. The dragon was the ancient standard of old China. Li Sheng's love of the departed past could be sufficient reason for the dragon tokens.

Subtly, Li Sheng broached the vital subject.

"I SHALL speak freely, Ying Ko," croaked the old merchant. "There is no need to ignore the purpose of your visit. I have as my guest a person who calls himself the General Cho Tsing. A few nights ago, he came to my door, craving admittance.

"Cho Tsing, it seems, was threatened by a secret group called the Jeho Fan, so I persuaded him to remain here, in safety. To-morrow night, I expect representatives of the Jeho Fan; also emissaries from the Chinese government.

"Both shall enjoy my hospitality, while they settle the troublesome details that concern Cho Tsing. Those details, I understand, involve a matter of ten million American dollars."

Sadly, Li Sheng shook his head, as he added:

"It is unfortunate that men should dispute over so trifling a sum."

The merchant arose. Smiling, he extended his thin hand toward broad steps at the rear of the reception room.

"Perhaps, Ying Ko, you would like to talk with Cho Tsing?"

The Shadow accepted the invitation. As he arose from his chair, he placed his cloak and hat over his arm. Servants watched the tall form of Cranston ascend the short flight of steps beside the stooped figure of Li Sheng.

A curious clock spoke the hour, with the discordant clangor of Chinese chimes. It was ten o'clock.

Straight across the hall in back of the reception room was a wide, deep-set doorway, guarded by two powerful Mongols, who stood like statues. Each held a long, curved sword crosswise in front of his body.

As Cranston and Li Sheng passed between the silent sentinels, the merchant remarked dryly:

"I stationed these guards, to keep unwelcome visitors from the apartment of Cho Tsing. Such an honored guest must be protected."

The "protection" reminded The Shadow of Li Sheng's "accidents." It could work two ways. There would be trouble for any one who tried to enter the guest apartment without Li Sheng's permission. There would be disaster, also, for any one who tried to leave the guest chambers.

That applied definitely to General Cho Tsing.

Li Sheng rapped at the door. It opened; two servants admitted Li Sheng and Cranston. The Shadow knew at once that these servants were Chinese who had been smuggled through with Cho Tsing.

Li Sheng inquired for the general. A voice spoke from beyond a curtained doorway; the tone was distinguished in its accent, but weary. It called for the visitors to enter. A servant pulled the curtain aside. Li Sheng bowed for Cranston to cross the threshold.

A figure was reclining in a large, canopied bed. By the glow of a table lamp, The Shadow recognized the face of Cho Tsing, propped against the pillows.

Brilliance came to large eyes as they saw Cranston. Cho Tsing's iron jaw tightened. Rising from the pillows, the general thrust out a hand in greeting.

Cranston seated himself beside the bed. Li Sheng remained in the doorway, to watch the conference between the two old friends.

"I AM ill," spoke Cho Tsing. "My journey from China was a tedious one. My quarters were not quite so pleasant as the ones that Li Sheng has provided."

The Shadow knew that Cho Tsing was faking illness, and doing it well. His firm handclasp, unnoticed by Li Sheng, had been the give-away. The purpose of the general's ruse was plain.

At some time, Cho Tsing hoped, there would be a chance for a break from this luxurious prison. He believed that by pretending to be weak and ill, his chances would be better when the time came. So far, he had gained nothing by his pretense.

Whether or not Li Sheng had guessed Cho Tsing's hope, the merchant constantly kept two swordsmen on guard duty outside the general's apartment.

The Shadow spoke to Cho Tsing. His voice was that of Cranston, talking in Chinese, with pauses between each sentence. Those intervals were natural; for Cranston seemed to be thinking in English; translating his ideas to Chinese before he voiced them.

Though Cranston's face was turned so Li Sheng could not see it, the merchant suspected nothing. He did not hear what Cho Tsing heard.

During each pause, Cranston's lips moved; a low whisper escaped them. Between sentences of ordinary conversation, The Shadow was giving suggestions to Cho Tsing. There was a way whereby the general's imprisonment might end to-night. The Shadow expected him to be ready.

The short chat ended. Cranston rejoined Li Sheng. Together, they passed between the sentinels. The Shadow observed the lights in the hallway. Unlike the reception room, the glow in the hall came from ordinary sockets set in the ceiling.

There were three such lights; the central one was directly in front of Cho Tsing's apartment.

The low doorway to the reception room cut off the soft light from that direction. That was something that could prove of value to The Shadow.

WHEN they reached the reception room, Li Sheng was more than courteous. He apologized for the fact that Cho Tsing was ill; he assured Cranston that the sea voyage had been responsible. Since his arrival here, Cho Tsing had enjoyed real hospitality.

"You will learn that for yourself, Ying Ko," concluded Li Sheng, "since you are to be my guest for a while to come."

Cranston's expression showed open doubt of the statement. Li Sheng added reasons.

"You will remain," he asserted, "until after the Chinese delegates have completed their business with the Jeho Fan. When Cho Tsing has left here, I shall open the way for your departure.

"Of course"—Li Sheng added the statement archly—"the Jeho Fan may not be pleased with my decision. But I can assure you, Ying Ko, that they will accept my advice.

"Whatever their Tao says, is law, with the Jeho Fan. I am quite sure that the Tao Fan will give them any order that originates from myself."

Slow minutes followed Li Sheng's utterance. Cranston seemed to be considering the merchant's verdict. At last, the tall guest arose from his chair. Methodically, Cranston reached for his black cloak. He slid it over his shoulders.

Gloves were next. When Cranston had drawn them on his hands, he picked up his slouch hat. As he pressed the brim down upon his forehead, his face was lost from sight. Hidden lips whispered a sinister laugh that did not please Li Sheng.

The Shadow turned toward the outer door. Li Sheng sprang sprily from his chair. He leaped past The Shadow; spread his long-sleeved arms to block the way.

"You shall remain, Ying Ko!"

Four servants were in sight again; but The Shadow's hands whipped from his cloak, bringing the holstered guns from beneath his tuxedo jacket. He held the servants covered.

The big Chinese clock was chiming the half hour. Amid that clangor, Li Sheng stepped aside, as if acknowledging defeat. Suddenly, the merchant sprang beyond the silver fountain. Shielded by the squatty metal dragon, his position was safe. He was ready to let his servitors battle The Shadow.

Li Sheng screeched a command. There were sounds, like the clash of cymbals, from the side walls of the room. Huge vases split, their fronts swinging wide. Squatted in the niches were a dozen more Chinese, six to each wall.

Their revolvers were leveled. All they awaited was the snap of Li Sheng's fingers. That given, they would riddle The Shadow with their bullets.

THOUGH the odds were sixteen to one against him, The Shadow still moved slowly forward. Li Sheng croaked an unheeded warning. Then came the finger snap.

The Shadow whisked about. While guns were sounding their preliminary *click*, The Shadow headed for the steps that led to Cho Tsing's apartment.

The unexpected twist startled the Chinese. So did the shots that The Shadow fired as he whirled. The Shadow picked no targets; his purpose was to throw temporary confusion into the Chinese ranks.

Li Sheng's warriors leaped for the floor, dropping low. Their guns were talking, though, before The Shadow reached the steps.

Timely jabs from the automatics gave The Shadow a moment's respite. An instant later, the reports were lost amid a mighty blast that far outthundered The Shadow's guns. The whole floor rocked, sprawling the aiming Chinese before they could clip The Shadow.

With that explosion, the center of Li Sheng's reception room hoisted. The silver statue split into fragments. The

fish pool vanished in a geyser of spreading water. Amid the cascade went the shimmering shapes of the merchant's rare fish.

From the quaking floor, The Shadow reached the steps, to look back on the havoc. Jets of water were shooting upward from broken pipes. Instead of the shallow basin, there gaped a widespread hole. As puffs of smoke blew clear, heads and hands came through the opening.

Tough fists gripped revolvers, below ugly faces. The zero hour had struck. Brig Lenbold and Shiv Faxon were making their thrust to wrest Cho Tsing from Li Sheng's possession. Their sappers had followed underground passages, to make a final burrow beneath the center of Li Sheng's home.

Blowing their way up from below, the crooks had come to battle it out with Li Sheng's servants. Timing his own moves to that scheduled invasion, The Shadow was ready to attempt his lone rescue of Cho Tsing.

CHAPTER XVII.

CLOAKED FLIGHT.

BATTLE was raging in Li Sheng's reception room—a wild, swift fray, with hand-to-hand tactics taking preference. Brig and Shiv were coming through, with a dozen followers. The Chinese were coming in from circled formation, hoping to beat them back. Gun hands were slugging as fast as fingers could tug triggers.

The Shadow's business took him elsewhere. He was at the top of the steps, driving for the big guards who stood outside of Cho Tsing's apartment. As The Shadow sidestepped, one of the Mongols slashed with his curved sword.

Driving in beneath the blade, The Shadow met the sword at the hilt with an upsweep of an automatic. The slash flung wide, away from The Shadow's head. There was a back-swing of The

Shadow's arm. A gun-weighted fist clipped the Mongol's chin. The swordsman sagged; his weapon dropped from his hand.

The Shadow could waste no bullets. They would be needed later. He twisted away from the second guard. Shoving his guns beneath his cloak, The Shadow made a quick grab for the sword that was on the floor. He came up, spinning, in time to parry a hard stroke from his remaining opponent.

A taunting laugh punctuated the strange duel that followed. The Shadow handled the clumsy Mongol in whirlwind fashion. Every flash of the blade was followed by a thrust that drove The Shadow's foeman farther along the hall.

The guard had a two-handed grip on his sword's hilt, hoping to wield it in broad-ax fashion. He never had the chance.

While the muffled staccato of revolvers told that battle continued in the wrecked reception room, The Shadow slipped past his adversary and turned about. He was driving the Mongol back toward Cho Tsing's apartment.

Past the foeman were the three lights that glowed from the ceiling. They explained the purpose of The Shadow's odd tactics.

A sword thrust; The Shadow's hand whipped back and swung the curved blade with an overhand stroke. The Mongol leaped back without need. The stroke was not intended for him. Thanks to the length of the sword, The Shadow reached the first light in the row and smashed it with his sword's point.

New thrusts drove the clumsy Mongol farther. Another quick slash; The Shadow clipped the second light from the high ceiling. He drove his adversary past the third. This time, the Mongol thought he knew the game.

As The Shadow swung for the light, the big guard came hacking with a long, two-armed sweep, using his sword like a sledge hammer. That clumsy slash was telegraphed the moment it began.

The Shadow twisted his swing. It came downward; then into a side-armed whip. The flat of the blade lashed the Mongol's neck, just below his ear. He jolted; the lines of his tawny face froze in an ugly grimace, as the guard kilted sideways.

Before the guard's body had time to thump the floor, The Shadow thrust his own sword upward and shattered the glass of the last incandescent. The hall was darkened, save for the faint glow that came from below the stairs.

GUNSHOTS were less frequent. One side had gained the advantage. The Shadow had lost valued time. He sprang to the door of Cho Tsing's apartment. It was open; the lights of the apartment were out, in accordance with The Shadow's instructions. Cho Tsing was on the threshold.

Shouts sounded from the reception room. The cries were in Chinese. Li Sheng's cohorts had repelled the invaders. They were coming to fight The Shadow. The clatter of their footsteps pounded from the stairs. Seeing darkness, the Chinese halted, babbling for lights.

As flashlights glimmered, The Shadow's automatics spat from the darkness. Chinese dodged and flattened; the path was cleared. Li Sheng, standing below the steps, heard the shout of General Cho Tsing:

"Go, Ying Ko! Lead the way! I follow!"

Down from the darkened stairs surged the cloaked figure. The Shadow's guns were emptied; Li Sheng was treated to a display of swordsmanship. Wheeling through the scattered Chinese, the cloaked fighter lashed across the floor, to reach the pit that invaders had blasted.

That spot was vacated. Brig and Shiv were crippled prisoners; the rest of their attacking crew were wounded or dead. They were counting on the arrival of reserves. Meanwhile, they saw the ruse designed by The Shadow. The hole through which invaders entered was being turned into an exit.

Li Sheng saw a gloved hand beckoning back toward the stairway. But Cho Tsing wasn't following The Shadow. Li Sheng cackled gleefully. All had gone well with The Shadow's plans until this final moment; but it had changed, to give Li Sheng his opportunity. The Shadow was speedy; Cho Tsing was slow. Fate was kind to Li Sheng.

Half a dozen quick-witted Chinese rallied like clockwork to Li Sheng's howled command. Three of them dashed for the stairs, to cut off Cho Tsing. The others drove for The Shadow. Skidding on the slippery, fish-strewn floor, they tried for close-range aim.

The cloaked swordsman was at the pit. He saw the menacing guns. He made a quick drop through the opening. Bullets chopped stone fragments from the fringe. Not a shot reached the human target.

Li Sheng fumed at The Shadow's escape. He hesitated; then padded up the steps, to see what had happened to Cho Tsing. The lights in the general's apartment were on again.

Cho Tsing's two faithful servants were shoving their protesting master headlong into the curtained bedroom. They had good reason for such action. Li Sheng's servants were at the outer door, covering them with revolvers.

One big swordsman was rising from the floor. Li Sheng ordered him to watch Cho Tsing's door. New servants had arrived. Li Sheng added them as reserve guards. Taking his three fighters with him, he led a new dash down to the reception room. There, three waiting Chinese were pleased when they saw their chief's intention.

Li Sheng was taking up the pursuit of The Shadow.

DOWN through the pit, the seven found a passage. It led them to another burrow; after a second turn, they saw their cloaked quarry straight ahead of them.

Powerful flashlights illuminated the outline of The Shadow. Almost instantly, there was a blaze of light from the opposite direction.

This passage was wide. At the far end of it, Li Sheng could discern four rough-clad, waiting men. They were the reserve force that Brig and Shiv expected. The situation was sweet for Li Sheng. The Shadow was trapped between two forces.

Li Sheng croaked an order. Let the others fire first. They could have the privilege of finishing Ying Ko, before he reached them with his sword, the only weapon that he still could use. While those invaders were gloating over The Shadow's death, Li Sheng and his men could repulse them.

The plan was crafty; but new intervention ruined it.

The shots that sounded from the far end of the passage were not directed toward the approaching figure in black. They came from beyond the corner. Bullets sprawled the thugs who awaited The Shadow. Yellow faces poked in sight above the sagging hoodlums. The arrivals were Doctor Tam's loyal Chinese.

Li Sheng's opportunity was lost. He saw Tam's men spread, to let The Shadow through their cordon. A gloved hand flung away its sword, to receive a revolver. Li Sheng's henchmen quailed. Tam's men were opening fire along the passage; soon, Ying Ko would be shooting with them!

The trap didn't suit Li Sheng. He had the wrong end of it. He didn't wait for his followers to desert him. He shouted for retreat; joined the scramble back to safety. Bullets pinged the wall where they had been. Fearful that The Shadow would overtake them, the merchant and his men scurried upward into their own premises.

Theirs was a mad flight; so rapid that they did not linger long enough to hear The Shadow's laugh. Once in the reception room, Li Sheng ordered his men to fill the pit with chunks of stone. They did it in a hurry, much to Li Sheng's satisfaction. There was plenty of débris; enough to block The Shadow and his new allies.

No attack came. Evidently, The Shadow could foresee its fallacy. Brig Lenbold and Shiv Faxon had fared badly with their invasion. Li Sheng was better prepared to meet a new thrust.

From somewhere, distant from the house, there was a muffled explosion that satisfied Li Sheng. Tam's men had closed the underground passage, back at the warehouse end.

In the darkness of that abandoned building, Tam's followers were making their departure, proud that they had served Ying Ko.

Outside the warehouse, they saw The Shadow meet Doctor Tam. The two rode away in an automobile, while the remaining Chinese spread and departed on foot. They felt that they had won a victory.

Li Sheng's opinion was the opposite. Secure in his own citadel, the merchant ordered his workers to begin methodical repairs. The triumph was his, for he had thwarted The Shadow's rescue of Cho Tsing.

After giving instructions for the confinement of Brig Lenbold and Shiv Faxon, Li Sheng went to Cho Tsing's apartment.

Both swordsmen were on duty, motionless at their posts. When Li Sheng rapped, the door was opened by Cho Tsing's fearful servants. Li Sheng smiled blandly when he saw their shakiness. Dryly, he commended their faithfulness to Cho Tsing.

Li Sheng could be generous when he had won a victory. Had he felt himself defeated, Cho Tsing's servants would have had good reason to quake.

"Your master sleeps?"

Li Sheng put the query mildly. The answer came from the bedroom, in the weary voice of Cho Tsing:

"Not yet, Li Sheng. You may enter."

Drawing aside the curtain, Li Sheng saw a head rise from its pillow. Cho Tsing's anxious question was the one that Li Sheng expected.

"What of Ying Ko?" was the query. "Did he make a safe escape?"

"Ying Ko escaped," assured Li Sheng. "But his mission remains unfulfilled. He can find no way to enter here again. To-morrow night, Cho Tsing, your visit here will be ended. At that time"—the merchant's cackle was expectant—"your ransom will be paid to the Jeho Fan."

Leaving Cho Tsing silent in the darkness of his bedroom, Li Sheng returned to his damaged deception room. Calmly, he seated himself in his teakwood chair and surveyed the destruction. Li Sheng's reaction was a slight shrug of his shoulders.

His ruined silver fountain, his lost collection of rare fish were trifles to Li Sheng. He had accomplished enough to recompense him. He had thwarted The Shadow's purpose; he, Li Sheng, had actually driven the formidable Ying Ko to hurried flight.

The Jeho Fan had learned that The Shadow still lived. Precaution would be taken to prevent his interference outside. That accomplished, Li Sheng would give one absolute guarantee. When the ransom meeting once began, The Shadow would not enter this mansion to interrupt it.

Li Sheng's confidence was justified. There were circumstances that made it impossible for The Shadow to enter the merchant's portals. To-night, The

Shadow had reached high-water mark in his effort to thwart the Jeho Fan.

The Shadow had come here knowing that flight would mean failure; the end of his struggle against the Jeho Fan. He had staked everything on one bold stroke. His whole cause depended upon it.

Crime, it seemed, would at last prevail despite The Shadow.

CHAPTER XVIII.
TEN MILLION DOLLARS.

THERE was news, the next day, of a riot in Chinatown, near the home of Li Sheng. Malefactors had scattered; the police had found a dead Chinaman in the courtyard. They had made inquiry at the merchant's house, to be politely informed that all was well there.

No facts leaked regarding the blast in Li Sheng's reception room, and the subsequent turmoil at the old warehouse. Those episodes had been confined within muffling walls.

To Myra Reldon, the news was significant. She knew that the shock troops of the Jeho Fan had watched the home of Li Sheng. The turmoil outside that house meant that some one had tried to penetrate to the merchant's domain. There was only one person bold enough to make that attempt.

The Shadow.

The cloaked fighter's return worried Myra. She wondered how the Jeho Fan would handle it. There was no way that she could learn until to-night, when she resumed the guise of Ming Dwan. The inner circle was scheduled to meet soon after dusk.

The question that Myra asked herself was whether or not she would reach the meeting.

As Myra Reldon, she was known to The Shadow. It was she who had suggested that Cranston meet her at the Yangtse Restaurant. As Ming Dwan, the girl had told The Shadow that she knew of the appointment. Though she was positive that The Shadow did not recognize her double identity, he could certainly suspect an acquaintanceship between Myra and Ming Dwan.

If was true that The Shadow had been at large for several days, since his escape from the Jeho Fan, and had not sought out Myra during that interval. But that was explained by the fact that the mysterious avenger was hard upon another trail.

If blocked in his foray against Li Sheng, The Shadow might return to the beginning of his quest. If so, Myra could expect a visit from the cloaked foeman of the Jeho Fan. Myra didn't like the thought.

She had worked long to gain her present status with the Jeho Fan; at present, she rated next to the Tao himself. To-night, of all nights, was the time when Ming Dwan must meet with the inner circle.

Yet, if The Shadow decided that Myra was important, he could easily eliminate her from the proceedings.

As she sat at her desk, the girl's face showed an expression that would have suited Ming Dwan. If she had suspected that last night's trouble was due, she could easily have transferred her Chinese garb to some place other than her apartment. Once she had reached the office, that step was too late.

Myra would have to trust to chance that The Shadow would not interfere with her part in the schemes of the Jeho Fan.

As five o'clock approached, Myra was faced with other difficulties. They began when Vayne summoned her into his office. The gray-haired man was studying a sheaf of reports.

"New mystery from the water front," Vayne told Myra. "A pair of notorious racketeers have disappeared. One of them—Shiv Faxon—controlled a group of rowdies who made trouble there a few nights ago. The other—Brig Lenbold—took protection money from cheap night clubs. It appears, though, that the two worked hand in glove.

"The police think that they have 'lammed,' to use the slang expression. But there is no reason why they should have fled from San Francisco. Both were so well established, that they had nothing to fear from the law."

Vayne sorted the papers; shook his head.

"I wonder," he mused, "if that pair had Chinatown connections? There was trouble in the Chinese district last night. I think, Myra, that I shall call a conference to-night, to discuss these matters with the proper authorities. Call up Mr. Jocelyn and arrange the appointment. You will go with me, Myra, to take notes."

Myra was chewing her lips when she reached her own desk. Jocelyn was an assistant to the Federal district attorney. Vayne had conferred with him previously; and Myra had been there. That was one night when she hadn't become Ming Dwan.

It hadn't mattered on that occasion. But it would ruin everything to-night.

Myra decided to fake some reason why Jocelyn couldn't meet with Vayne. Things broke well when she telephoned the D. A.; he wasn't in his office. He had gone away that afternoon, and his return was not expected.

Myra gave that news to Vayne, concealing the elation that she felt. Jocelyn's absence was something that Vayne could check for himself, if he wanted.

Promptly at five o'clock, Myra left the office. She knew that there was a chance that Jocelyn would learn of Vayne's call; if so, he would telephone back. Myra didn't want to be around, if such a call came in.

She reached the apartment, to find Helen Toriss there. Soon afterward, the telephone bell began to ring. Myra told her friend not to answer it. The call was probably from Vayne, to say that he had contacted Jocelyn and would need Myra after all.

He could do without her, or postpone his conference with the assistant D. A., whichever he chose. To-morrow, Myra would alibi that she had been out to dinner when the call came.

Chinese watchers were absent to-night. They were needed in Chinatown, to cover the assemblage of the inner circle.

Ordinarily, that would have pleased Myra, for it showed how well she had preserved her dual identity, even from the Jeho Fan. To-night, though, she would have preferred the Chinese cordon, as a protective ring against a visit from The Shadow.

MYRA was nervous as she sat before her mirror, streaking her shoulders with washable yellow dye. She saw a motion of the window shade, reflected in the mirror. She bobbed from the chair and grabbed the revolver that was with the Chinese costume.

As she stood there, aiming with one hand while she clutched the girdling bathrobe with the other, she was neither Myra Reldon nor Ming Dwan. Her features were American; their color Chinese. Below her shoulders was the revealing line where yellow ended and white began.

If The Shadow had reached that window, he had certainly learned the girl's game.

The shade stirred again. Myra decided that it was moved by a fluttering breeze, through the half-opened window. She returned to her dressing table and completed her make-up. She dressed in the Chinese clothes and smiled as Ming Dwan.

Her false countenance gave her a return of nerve. Stepping to the door, the girl used Myra's voice. She asked Helen to post an important letter that was on the living-room table.

As soon as she heard the outer door close, Myra slipped through the living room and went out through the back darkness.

Though she had the dragon's tooth in her hand, Ming Dwan had no need to display that token. Chinese were absent from the gloom behind the apartment building. Nevertheless, Ming Dwan's course was more cautious than ever. At any moment, the girl expected a gloved hand to *swish* from darkness and clamp her shoulder.

What she would do if The Shadow trapped her, was a pressing problem to Ming Dwan. She could be persuasive when it came to explanations; but she doubted that The Shadow would accept them. He had gone through a grueling ordeal, the last time he listened to Ming Dwan.

It seemed ages to the girl before she reached the streets of Chinatown. Once there, she breathed easily as she joined the shuffling crowds. All nervousness had left the features of Ming Dwan. Her expression was tinged with the contemptuous smile that pleased the members of the Jeho Fan.

At a given spot, Ming Dwan saw a lounging Chinaman. She showed the dragon's tooth. He displayed the same token; motioned the girl to the doorway of a curio shop. Once inside, Ming Dwan was admitted to a basement, where another servant of the Jeho Fan steered her to an underground passage.

There were many ways to the underground headquarters. Old routes vanished after they had once been used. As usual, Ming Dwan traveled a new path to-night.

She reached an anteroom; but did not bother to don a mask that she saw there. The others could use them if they chose; but Ming Dwan considered a mask unnecessary. As the only woman in the inner circle, her identity was known. Moreover, Ming Dwan's own face was a clever mask in itself.

THE Tao was on his throne. He spoke in pleased tone, through the lips of his devil-mask.

"You have foreseen my choice, Ming Dwan," announced the Tao. "One of us must go, undisguised, to speak with the delegates from China. Others"—he waved his hand toward the masked group —"have too much at stake, to let themselves be known. They hold important places in the usual affairs of Chinatown.

"You shall leave San Francisco after you have completed to-night's mission. You shall be rewarded, both for your effort and the inconvenience that will follow. These two"—he delegated a pair of members—"will accompany you. But they shall remain masked."

The Tao placed a small silver box in Ming Dwan's hands. Rising from his throne, he strode from the meeting room. Others of the depleted inner circle went along, to receive the Tao's own instructions.

When Ming Dwan opened the silver box, the only men present were the two that the Tao had appointed to accompany her.

In the box, Ming Dwan found instructions, with a complicated diagram that showed a chain of underground passages, with pitfalls along the route. She destroyed the paper after memorizing its details. With the two men following, Ming Dwan started from the meeting room.

She used a flashlight to pick the path through darkened passages. At times, they came to lighted corridors. They met brawny Mongols who barred the way with snarls and revolvers, to step aside when Ming Dwan gave the proper countersigns.

Along the route, Ming Dwan noted that connecting corridors had been chiseled through the rock, to reach other underground avenues. It was fully twenty minutes before the trio arrived at a cellar where a few guards were on duty.

One of that group solemnly conducted the arrivals up a flight of stairs to a small room that had one other exit. The door was opened; Ming Dwan and her masked companions stepped into a courtyard.

The newly fashioned route had brought them through one of the old buildings in the block surrounding Li Sheng's mansion. They were in the space that fronted the merchant's house. Ming Dwan could see the backs of the metal gates that the Jeho Fan had stormed. Those barriers were mounted on new huge hinges, stronger than before.

Ming Dwan knocked for admittance at Li Sheng's front door. She knew that eyes were peering from windows above; that gun muzzles were poked through gratings that served as loopholes. If any unwanted visitor approached tonight, death would welcome him.

Li Sheng was ready for The Shadow.

The bland, bespectacled doorman admitted the visitors. He conducted them by a direct route to Li Sheng's reception room, avoiding all the pitfalls that The Shadow had encountered.

Li Sheng was standing in welcome. To-night, his reception room boasted no tinkling fountain, with its pool of dragon fish. Instead, the center of the room formed a platform, surfaced with slabs of stone. There was a table placed there; two gloomy-faced Chinese were seated at it.

Ming Dwan recognized their faces. They had been pictured in the morning newspapers. They were the delegates from China, who had come to America for the supposed purpose of raising funds.

Between them lay a large, brass-bound box. As Ming Dwan and her associates approached, one of the Chinese delegates unlocked the box lid and raised it.

There, stacked in compact bundles, were piles of United States currency, big figures showing from the crisp green paper. Openly, the men from China were acknowledging the power of the Jeho Fan. They were ready to pay the full ransom for the delivery of General Cho Tsing.

Ten million dollars awaited the grasp of Ming Dwan's slender hands; and the ominous figure of The Shadow was not present to prevent it!

CHAPTER XIX.

HALTED RANSOM.

The Chinese delegates showed perplexity when they saw Ming Dwan. One turned to Li Sheng, with the question:

"Is this woman the Tao of the Jeho Fan?"

Li Sheng shook his head.

"I have never met the Tao face to face," he declared. "I know only that he has chosen this woman—Ming Dwan —to act in his behalf."

Looks were exchanged by the two delegates. They could see a reason for Ming Dwan's appointment. If Li Sheng were the Tao Fan, he could not receive the ransom money personally and still be present as a neutral.

Li Sheng saw the looks. His smile was bland, inviting the delegates to seek all the proof they wanted. They could never establish the theory that Li Sheng and the Tao Fan were one.

"I am honored," croaked Li Sheng, "to be of service to all. I have shown hospitality to the man who calls himself Cho Tsing. I am master of this house; and I pledge myself to fairness. I have been careful to admit only those who have a right here.

"Once the ransom is paid, I shall insure the safe departure of each faction. You, Ming Dwan, shall carry the ten million dollars to your Tao. Cho Tsing shall go with the friends who have ransomed him. But before payment is made"—Li Sheng raised a long finger—"we must make sure that my guest is actually Cho Tsing."

There was no doubt in Li Sheng's tone. The merchant knew well enough that he had received the kidnaped general within these portals. But it was Li Sheng's wary way to maintain pretense throughout. That would protect his position afterward.

Clapping his hands, the old merchant spoke to waiting servants:

"Summon the one who called himself Cho Tsing!"

Soon, a procession came from the stairway at the rear of the reception room. First, one of Li Sheng's sword-bearers. Then the figure of Cho Tsing, garbed in a long, drab robe; a skullcap on his bowed head. The prisoner's steps were draggy. His servants were supporting him on either side. Behind them came the second Mongol guard.

The Chinese delegates lowered their own gaze. They knew the misery that this could mean to Cho Tsing. It would mean the end of the general's long career; a voluntary retirement through self-accepted disgrace. China would lose a valued military organizer, noted for his ability to bring peace between warring factions.

The ransom, once paid, would be a reward for Cho Tsing's past services; not for his future efforts.

There was no pity on the face of Ming Dwan. Her curled smile showed a hard disdain, that pleased the lieutenants who were with her. Their eyes glittered through the bulging fronts of the devil-masks.

Li Sheng registered no feeling whatever. He waited until Cho Tsing had slumped into a chair at the end of the table. In his croaked tone, Li Sheng repeated his reminder:

"If this man should not be Cho Tsing, there will be no ransom. He will be free to depart——"

A strange laugh riveted Li Sheng, along with the others. The figure of Cho Tsing straightened. A shake of the head sent the skullcap to the floor. Quick hands threw back the robe; discarded it with one sweeping motion.

The personage who stood before the amazed onlooker was an American, clad in tuxedo. His hawkish countenance was that of Lamont Cranston. The challenging laugh from his fixed lips announced the identity that lay beneath his guise.

The Shadow had replaced Cho Tsing!

Li Sheng's eyes blinked as the riddle unfolded itself within his brain. The Shadow had expected last night's thrust by Brig Lenbold and Shiv Faxon and had prepared a ruse to follow it. He had foreseen that Li Sheng's chief effort would be to prevent the escape of Cho Tsing. Therefore, The Shadow had prepared a way out for the captive general.

In the darkness outside the guest apartment The Shadow had covered Cho Tsing with cloak and hat. The Shadow had fired the last shots from his automatics, to clear the way. Cho Tsing had shouted for The Shadow to lead.

But the figure that had dashed down the steps, swinging a big sword, had not been The Shadow. That cloaked form was Cho Tsing, wearing the garb that The Shadow had given him!

As his guest for the past twenty-odd hours, Li Sheng had been keeping the formidable Ying Ko. All the while, the crafty merchant had been taking every possible measure to prevent The Shadow from again entering his door.

All this was a blank to the Chinese delegates. They simply arose and locked the box that contained the ransom money. While one tucked the box under his arm, the other pointed to Cranston.

"This is not Cho Tsing," said the delegate. "We have no cause to remain,

Li Sheng. Let your servants conduct us to the door."

Ming Dwan let her slanted eyes shift from Cranston, to watch Li Sheng's reaction. Would the merchant act as the intermediary that he was supposed to be; or would he reveal himself as the Tao, here ahead of his own representatives, receiving them in another guise?

Li Sheng retained his neutral manner.

"You may go," he told the delegates, as he waved his thin hand toward the doorway. Then, facing Cranston, he added, blandly: "You also, Ying Ko. I have no cause to insist upon your presence, since Cho Tsing is no longer here."

Was Li Sheng's statement a sincere one??

Or was the merchant shrewdly planning a trick?

The Shadow watched for the answer. Li Sheng nodded to the bespectacled guide. Whichever door the man opened, Li Sheng's purpose would be known. There were several doors; one of them offered a direct route to the courtyard. The Shadow knew that door from the plans that Doctor Tam had shown him.

The direct door was the one that the servant approached.

There was a sparkle from the eyes of Ming Dwan. Her pursed lips tightened. That was the door through which she and her companions had come. She knew that Li Cheng was fulfilling his promise to the Chinese delegates; that he had bowed to The Shadow, also.

Ming Dwan's companions likewise saw the situation.

Before the girl could utter a word, the two masked men started a protest to Li Sheng. Their gestures carried threat; but the merchant merely smiled. He snapped his fingers; four servants closed around the masked paid and forced them from the table.

Solemnly, Li Sheng bowed to Cranston, indicating that The Shadow could accompany the men with the ten million, to serve as their protector.

The Chinaman with the spectacles was opening the door. Some one gave it a thrust from the other side. A booming voice hurled challenge from the threshold. In the doorway stood the masked figure of the Tao Fan!

THE leader of the Jeho Fan had come without announcement. Behind him, grouped in a supporting cluster, were the other masked members of the inner circle. As the Tao stepped toward Li Sheng, the rest formed a compact rank in back of him.

Li Sheng met the challenge. He snapped an order to his servants. Only two responded; they were the Mongol swordsmen. Threateningly, they approached the Tao. A laugh of hate came from his devil-mask. The Tao gave a hard clap with his gauntlets.

Li Sheng's four servants trained their guns on the merchant. The vases cracked open along the walls, to reveal rows of aiming marksmen. But those Chinese servitors were not looking to Li Sheng for orders. They were taking their instructions from the Tao.

Despite his shrewdness; his willingness to deal with the Jeho Fan, Li Sheng was a man who kept the promises he gave. That was why the Jeho Fan had used him as an intermediary; but it also explained the present surprise.

The Tao had secretly bought out the bulk of Li Sheng's bodyguard. Only the bespectacled guide and the two swordsmen remained loyal to their master. The rest belonged to the Jeho Fan.

While others stood stupefied by new circumstances, The Shadow acted. He had foreseen trouble from the moment that Li Sheng admitted defeat. As the big vases opened wide, The Shadow's guns whipped into view. As Cranston, he lacked the formidable appearance of

Ying Ko; but that did not mar his speed in battle.

Roaring their accompaniment to The Shadow's weird, sardonic laugh, big automatics tongued their messages toward the walls. Chinese sharpshooters toppled before they could fire. Li Sheng's treacherous servants were as helpless as the racked targets in a shooting gallery, as The Shadow pumped his alternating fire, turning his head with every trigger tug.

The Shadow's action brought prompt response from men who became his allies. Li Sheng usually let others do his fighting; but he discarded that policy. Producing a gun, the merchant aimed for the four traitors who stood near the table. Cho Tsing's servants were armed; The Shadow had seen to that. They followed Li Sheng's lead.

So did the Chinese delegates. They had brought guns to protect their ten million dollars. A terrific fray began about the table, while The Shadow was still popping enemies from their niches.

The big Mongol swordsmen were slashing at the masked members of the Jeho Fan. Those huge curved swords were terrible weapons against fighters less speedy than The Shadow. The fight throughout the reception room was an equal one, when The Shadow finished with the Chinese in the niches.

Then came the break that predicted disaster for The Shadow. Li Sheng saw it; but was helpless to intervene, for he was grappling with one of the masked men who had accompanied Ming Dwan.

Turning to face across the table, The Shadow looked squarely into a gun muzzle aimed by the Tao Fan. That masked leader had left the battle near the doorway, to gain a close-range shot at the figure of Cranston. Occupied with his own target work, The Shadow had paid no attention to the Tao.

It was too late, thought Li Sheng, to save the life of Ying Ko, to whom the merchant had promised safe departure.

Li Sheng did not see Ming Dwan.

The girl had dropped from sight, the moment that the battle began. Crouched beside the table, she was clutching her small revolver. Her Chinese make-up gave her face a tigerish look; all the while, her eyes had kept their slanted gaze upon the conspicuous figure of the Tao Fan.

Ming Dawn saw the glitter of the Tao's eyes, through the big orbs in his devil-mask. She spied the aimed revolver in the gauntleted hand that fronted the Tao's brilliant dragon robe. She heard the hard hiss of venomous triumph that issued from the Tao's lips.

It was a moment that Ming Dwan had expected. She knew that the Tao had gained his chance to drill The Shadow, before the latter could prepare to meet the attack.

Ming Dwan fired; her target was the Tao!

The bullet jolted the devil-faced leader of the Jeho Fan. His trigger finger paused, struck by a pang that reached it from his shoulder. His aim wavered; but he tightened, despite another bullet that came from Ming Dwan's gun.

The Tao delivered a single shot; his bullet, coming from a shifted gun, went whistling wide of Cranston's shoulder. The Shadow's automatic answered, drowning the third report that crackled from Ming Dwan's revolver.

The murderous Tao slumped straight downward; his hands flopped the table edge, to sprawl him backward.

Ming Dwan came up beside the table, gazing toward Cranston. The look that he gave amazed her. It seemed to strip away the false features of Ming Dwan, to view the girl as Myra Reldon.

The girl realized that The Shadow had depended upon her action. That was why he had so coolly concentrated on the traitors who lined the walls. The Shadow had known that Myra would aid him in this crisis, shooting down any one who aimed in his direction.

The one foe that The Shadow had expected was the Tao Fan. That enemy had come; and Myra had not failed. The Shadow's laugh was a whispered tone. It told all that he had expected; and more. Instinctively, the girl looked beyond the table.

Myra's eyes were frozen with amazement. The gasp from her lips was her own, not Ming Dwan's. For the first time, she saw the Tao Fan unmasked in the light. The devil's head had rolled from above his shoulders, to display a face that Myra had seen before.

A face that could be recognized, despite the evil gloat that had registered upon it, to remain fixed by sudden death. The Tao Fan was Richard Vayne.

CHAPTER XX.
SHARED TRIUMPH.

BATTLE ended with the death of Vayne. Members of the Jeho Fan saw their dead leader, unmasked like themselves; for they had lost their devil-faces in the fray. Li Sheng saw faces that he recognized, those of men who claimed repute in Chinatown.

Their eyes were squinty, when they saw Vayne's face. For the first time, they learned that their Tao was an American. Suddenly, their own plight struck them. They were prisoners of Cranston, and he was Ying Ko, The Shadow!

Most of the survivors were too crippled to make trouble. A few, however, started frantically to resume the fight. They were near the doorway; one broke through as Li Sheng's Mongols used the long swords to block the others.

To Li Sheng, the escape of one prisoner meant nothing. It was The Shadow who foresaw what the consequence could be. Leaving the prisoners under Li

Sheng's control, The Shadow sprang in pursuit of the one who had escaped.

Myra heard his quick command to follow. She hurried after the striding form of Cranston.

The fleeing member of the Jeho Fan reached the courtyard ahead of them. He had a purpose that gave him speed. The Tao was dead; the others of the inner circle likewise dead or captured. If that one survivor could rally the lurking hordes of the Jeho Fan, he would become the new Tao of a reorganized society.

From the center of the courtyard, the fellow gave a shout. Out from the doorway of the other house came slinky fighters of the Jeho Fan. Ropes swung from rooftops. More men came scrambling downward, like assembling apes.

The Shadow was at Li Sheng's front door. He was calmly reloading his automatics. He was taking advantage of this lull before new battle.

Myra, too, saw a chance to use those moments. As she stopped beside Cranston, the girl placed a whistle to her lips, gave a shrill blast that carried beyond the closed metal gates.

That was not the only signal. The Shadow delivered one—a strident laugh that carried to the housetops. Foemen heard it; they came bounding from all directions, hoping to wrest victory from Ying Ko. The Shadow greeted them with long-range fire. He spilled a foe with every bullet; but still they surged onward.

Shoving Myra behind him, The Shadow used the doorway as cover against flanking fire. He withered those who tried to aim from the open. There was no need to reserve extra cartridges. The Shadow had allies close at hand.

They bobbed up along the edges of the house roofs: Chinese provided by Doctor Tam. During the day, they had made stealthy entry into empty houses, lurking there unknown to the Jeho Fan. They had been watching the roofs, ready to appear there when The Shadow called.

By holding his signal, The Shadow had brought enemies down to the courtyard. Tam's men had no opposition above. From the parapets, they fired down upon The Shadow's enemies, scattering them to cover.

There came an answer to Myra's signal. Shots beyond the big gates; a pause, then an explosion that broke the barrier and tumbled chunks of stone from the archway. In half a minute, a squad was pouring through the gap.

THE SHADOW recognized the leader of that group. He was Vic Marquette, a government man, bringing a squad of Feds. The remnants of the Jeho Fan were scurrying for their ratholes. Myra sprang past The Shadow, shouted to Vic and pointed the way.

The Feds poured in pursuit. Myra saw them overtake the fleeing Chinese, down in the secret passage. Prisoners were hauled up into the courtyard. Among them came that last member of the inner circle, who had fancied himself the new Tao of the Jeho Fan.

Looking across the courtyard, Myra saw Cranston ascending the steps to the broken gates. She called; but he kept out through the archway. Myra hurried after him; when she reached the street, she caught another glimpse.

Cranston was standing beside a halted automobile. Two courteous Chinese were holding a cloak and hat. As Cranston donned those garments, he became The Shadow. He stepped into the car; the Chinese joined him. The big car purred away while Myra stared.

WHEN Myra returned to Li Sheng's she found Vic Marquette in charge. A darkish, mustached individual, Vic usually had a gloomy air about him; but tonight he was elated. He introduced Myra to the Chinese delegates, remarking:

"This is Miss Reldon. One of our undercover agents."

The Chinese were amazed to learn that Myra was an American. Marquette explained further.

"Myra lived a long while in China," he explained. "That's why we put her on the job in Frisco. We couldn't figure where the leaks were coming from in all this smuggling business. So Myra handled a double job. She was Vayne's secretary in the daytime, and Ming Dwan in the evenings. It was as Ming Dwan that she wangled her way into the Jeho Fan."

Vic's tone commended Myra; but the girl was rueful.

"I never suspected Vayne," she declared. "He must have found out that the government put me on the job. I suspected persons at the office, one after another; but every trail proved false."

"Vayne was smart," agreed Marquette. "We'll probably find his office wired, so he could hear everything you said."

Myra nodded. She knew, at last, how the Jeho Fan had learned of her date with Cranston.

"Only there was one thing Vayne didn't guess," added Marquette. "He never linked you as Ming Dwan. So that made it even, Myra."

Marquette talked to the visiting Chinese. He learned that they had heard from Cho Tsing before their trip to Li Sheng's. The general had ordered them to go through with the ransom business, in order to trap the Jeho Fan.

As for Li Sheng, they had no charges to prefer against him. The merchant admitted himself as intermediary; but declared that his fear of the Jeho Fan had been partly responsible for his deed. He had, as yet, received no payment from the Jeho Fan.

Therefore, his support of The Shadow and the Chinese delegates was accepted as proof that Li Sheng belonged on the side of justice. Marquette ordered the removal of all prisoners, including those who had been captured the night before.

AT the doorway, Myra questioned Marquette.

"Tell me, Vic," she asked, "did The Shadow know who I was when he first met me?"

"Probably," replied Vic. "That guy can find out anything."

"Then that was why he suspected Vayne!" exclaimed the girl. "He only talked to the two of us."

Vic nodded.

"I had to meet him as Ming Dwan," reviewed Myra. "But the Jeho Fan had traced him to the Yangtse Restaurant before I arrived there. I tried to help, by taking him to the Tao. I knew that I could rescue him from the Dragon's Cell, when he was placed there.

"Instead, The Shadow aided me. He wanted me to hold my standing with the Jeho Fan. That's why he dived past the revolving blade. I helped him later, though, when I said that The Shadow had thrown the guard into the water pit. I saw what actually happened.

"Only, I never thought I could explain it to The Shadow. I didn't want to meet him, after that. I didn't understand matters until to-night. But The Shadow did; and depended upon me."

Marquette was ready to convoy the ten million dollars to a bank vault. He asked Myra if she wanted to come along. The girl shook her head.

"I'm going back to the apartment," said Myra, "to get rid of these Chinese trappings. Helen will probably faint when she sees me. At last, I can tell her why the Jeho Fan watched the apartment."

There was one more question that occurred to Myra. She began to ask it as they reached the street.

"You said once, Vic, that you had met The Shadow, but didn't know who he was. If The Shadow is Lamont Cranston——"

"He isn't," interjected Marquette. "Nobody knows who he is. He goes places as Cranston, that's all. But don't worry about it, Myra. You won't be seeing him again."

ELSEWHERE, The Shadow was seated with two Chinese: Doctor Roy Tam and General Cho Tsing. His cloak and hat lay on Tam's desk. Garbed in the immaculate style of Cranston, The Shadow was describing the events at Li Sheng's.

The Shadow made a statement that would have amazed Myra Reldon.

"Once before," he remarked, "I met the masked Tao. It began when I recognized Ming Dwan as Myra Reldon, at the Yangtse Restaurant. She thought that I needed her aid to escape. Instead, I had already chosen an easy way to leave that place.

"I was pleased when she offered assistance. It meant that I would be carried to the headquarters of the Jeho Fan. That promised opportunity to destroy the organization from within. I hoped to deal with the Tao then. After that, Cho Tsing, your release would have been a natural consequence.

"Unfortunately" — Cranston's tone showed recollection of that ordeal— "there are snares so deep that they offer no opportunity except escape. That trap was one. I was forced to postpone my settlement with the Tao."

Another postponed meeting came to The Shadow's mind. His smile was Cranston's, as he reached for the telephone.

At her apartment, Myra had lost no time in shedding her Ming Dwan garb. She was at her dressing table, removing the adhesive strips beside her eyelids. He eyes were their rounded shape once more.

Helen watched in astonishment, while the yellow dye disappeared as Myra applied great gobs of cold cream to her face, her arms and shoulders.

The telephone bell tingled; Helen answered the call.

"For you, Myra," she informed.

Myra's slippered feet showed no hurry as she came out to the living room. It was probably Vic Marquette, calling to remind her that he would want a full report. But when she spoke into the telephone, a puzzled expression showed upon the face that was once more Myra's own.

"I am late?" she asked. "Late? For dinner? . . . Why, come to think of it, I haven't had dinner to-night, at all! I'm hours late. . . . What's that? You say I am days late? . . ."

Myra's perplexity faded suddenly. She recognized the voice; something else, that the speaker mentioned. Helen saw a smile as Myra said:

"At the Yangtse Restaurant. . . . Yes, I can make it in half an hour, Mr. Cranston. This time, you can depend upon me. . . ."

Myra's hand was motionless, still holding the receiver. That was why she heard the whispered sound that came from it—an audible, fading tone of mirth, an echo that seemed to nullify all menace of the past.

That tone was the laugh of The Shadow.

THE END.

THE END

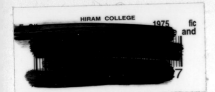